Jessika's

Dilemma

By

Cederick Stewart

Jessika's Dilemma

Copyright © 2017 by Cederick Stewart

All rights reserved.

Published by:

NyreePress Literary Group

Fort Worth, TX 76161

1-800-972-3864

www.nyreepress.com

Interior Design:

Cederick Stewart

ISBN print: 978-1-945304-56-9

Categories: Christian Fiction

Library of Congress Control Number: Pending

Categories: Fiction/Christian Living

Printed in the United States of America

Dedication

This book is dedicated to anyone who had to overcome personal battles with abuse. Your strength lies within you and I hope you find help, relief and strength in God.

Jessika's
Dilemma

Alpha

"Sam, are you okay?

Jessika barely whispered the question to her son Samuel, as she quietly closes his room door ever so slowly behind her because she didn't want to make any noise at all. She locked the door, braced herself against it and waited until he shook his head acknowledging that he was okay before she let out a deep breath and released the tears she had been holding in. The look of shock on his face was tearing her up on the inside but she was just as shocked as he was. What has taken place tonight, was going to be something that neither one of them will ever forget. The physicality of tonight's events was something she has always tried to shield him from. She never wanted Samuel to see the brutality of this abusive relationship but now he has witnessed more than what she ever wanted him to see. The only thing that took her mind off her last thought was the warmth of her blood running down her face. She took her hand and gingerly ran it along the left side of her face. Five minutes ago, she had been body slammed on a glass coffee table and her face took the brunt of it. She felt the glass cut her face and she wanted to know how bad the cut was because her conscience needed to know. It was on her face and that was a body part she always made sure she shielded from the abuse. After all, she has made a good living off her face. Jessika has been modeling since middle school. The agency she was with found her at a basketball game she was playing in. They loved her beautiful dark toffee colored skin with its flawless glow. How she was so graceful on the court maneuvered her to the runways she had the pleasure of being a part of. She wasn't modeling overseas but she was one of the main models her agency used here in Houston to showcase material that had the potential to be seen overseas on the grand stage. Her pictures could be seen on all the stock photo websites and she was somewhat famous as she is recognized when she is out and about but all of that meant nothing now if she couldn't get out of this situation she is in. The cut on her face is going to be a game changer as she can see her career being cut short and that has so much irony that it hurts her deeply. She knew she could hide all the bruises on the rest of her body but the face was too visible. The pain was intense as her face throbbed. She turned around and looked at the mirror that was on the door she was leaning on, held her breath and braced herself for what she was going to see. All she could see was blood streaming down her face like a red veil. Jessika gasped as she has a rush of thoughts run through her mind and everyone had to do with her never modeling again and wasting the talent that she was blessed to have. Her eyes began to tear up because she felt like this was the worst thing that could possibly happen to her. She knew the sight of blood would make her sick so why should this moment be any different. She has had a low tolerance for the sight of blood as far back as she can remember. Jessika believed it was the very first time she saw her own. Just like this time, it was because she didn't adhere to the dinner schedule. She knew that now wasn't the time to get sick because they were hiding in Samuel's room for a reason. The rest of the house was nearly destroyed. The kitchen was torn to pieces with broken dishes everywhere. Some were smashed in a fit of rage and some were thrown at her. She blocked most of the dishes that were thrown at her but she could only brace herself from being pushed around the kitchen like a rag doll. The living room was a disaster with the television, tables, lamps, pictures destroyed or used as weapons against Jessika. The walls had holes in them and all the work that was put into decorating this house, over the years, was destroyed in less than an hour. Now here she was hiding in Samuel's room but in all reality, Jessika has been literally hiding her whole marriage. Hiding her pain and suffering from all who cared about her. Hiding her fear and despair from those that could help. Hiding her disappointment of her marriage in her silence. It has gotten her to where she is hiding from the reality of her abusive marriage with Raymond and thinking about her cut on her face had given her the chance to forget about him. But, how could she? He was the reason for what was taking place now and over the past seventeen years. Raymond was very controlling and everything had to go his way. Things had to start on time or it was going to be big trouble. Jessika thought it was stress or maybe he was having a hard time adjusting to the fact he had gotten a seventeen-year-old pregnant. Then realizing she could no longer go to school because of the severe sickness she endured being pregnant. With the coaxing of her parents, Jessika dropped out of high school and they got married but she would eventually lose the baby due to a miscarriage in the third trimester. It was because of the miscarriage Raymond began to become a monster. He felt like Jessika didn't do all she should have and that she was the reason behind the miscarriage. He watched her give her all when it came to modeling and photo shoots but he didn't see the same effort put into her pregnancy. So, Raymond made up a schedule for her to adhere to pregnant or not. He felt like she dedicated too much of her time to her career and not on the marriage. He watched her work long hours and sometimes traveled for weeks on end but he felt like she was not making enough time for him. Raymond decided that the schedule would balance things in his favor. He wanted equal time for her career and for their marriage. He resented her career and the freedom it afforded her. Not only was the schedule used to control her but he felt like he had to break her will. In his eyes, she was too strong willed as she took control of her career and didn't need him for anything. He had to break her down systematically over time so he would say mean and spiteful things to her to make her feel like no one would love her and if she spoke up for herself he would be even more verbally abusive. He degraded her by reminding her of the fact she never graduated and if it wasn't for her looks that she would be nothing. He would humiliate her about her skin color because she was dark skinned and he was much lighter than her. He would complain about what assets she didn't have physically and laugh at how she wasn't shaped like other black girls. Jessika had always been thin framed and that was what helped her become such a viable model. He talked about her body so much that she wished she had larger breasts or a bigger backside like most black women do. He would go at her harder if a lady of another race was around and she was shapelier than Jessika was. He would say and use whatever he could to break her down to tears and very seldom would he build her back up. There were a few occasions where he would act like he was going to hit her but he would stop himself so she thought she could handle the verbal abuse if it never got physical. Jessika, felt he wouldn't physically hit her but she was mistaken. She didn't want an abusive marriage so to please Raymond she was willing to do whatever it takes. So, she agreed to cut back on her career to make him happy. The only way that was going to happen was for her to be more of a housewife than a career oriented wife. She took it in stride and tried to focus herself on doing just that. She made sure the house was always clean and she got up every morning and made him breakfast making sure that she never made the same breakfast twice in a week. For lunch she would make sure she never repeated a meal twice in a month. Raymond also wanted dinner ready when he got home and it had to be exactly as the schedule he made. Even though he never came home at the same time or called to tell her for that matter, never the less, it had to be hot and ready to go. It went on for seven years and all the while Raymond kept on pressuring her to get pregnant again. He would tell her she was less than a woman because she couldn't have children. So, they would try to get pregnant and every month he would be upset with her if her cycle came. He would call her all kinds of names and the physical abuse began during this period because he felt like she wasn't doing enough to get pregnant so she needed some motivation. Jessika knew the stress of her marriage would probably cause a miscarriage so she quietly prayed to not get pregnant because she felt like she would be worse off having another miscarriage than not getting pregnant again. By the grace of God, she got pregnant and Raymond stopped the physical abuse but if he felt like she got out of order the verbal abuse would be a reminder of his true feelings towards her. During this time, Jessika was reading her bible more and more and she read the story of Samuel and she felt like there were so many similarities to her life and Hannah's so she wanted to do what Hannah did. She prayed to the Lord that if she carried the child to full term, she would give the child over to God. So, she asked Raymond could she name the baby Samuel and he agreed because he felt the name sounded powerful. Jessika knew he knew nothing of the biblical meaning behind it because he never went to church because he said his Sundays are for football and football only. Jessika thought once she had Samuel that his anger would subside. Raymond told her he always wanted a boy and so she thought it would calm him down. Jessika vowed to be the best mom but the only thing she became was the best target for his anger and it came without warning, and sometimes without any reason. It started out being swift but over the years, on occasion, it would become a long drawn out session. Sometimes it lasted hours accompanied by hospital visits. Every abuse was memorable and unforgettable for Jessika. She tried her best to adhere to his wishes and rules. Even when they were too outrageous and degrading, she knew anything was better than being hit. At least she could hide her mental beating. She would try her best to hide them from her family, friends and most importantly, from her son Samuel. Samuel grew up during her getting physically abused and he recognized it and became real protective of her. It was the only real comfort and strength she had in her life. The only person that was worried about if she was happy or not, and now he is ten but he was very mature in her eyes. He knew his father was hitting her on occasion. He has known for years, ever since the night he saw Jessika lying on her stomach and his father had his knee in her back as he held her down. Samuel stood there watching and listening to her useless screams and without warning Raymond punched her once in the head, stood up and walked off like nothing happened. Jessika didn't know if the pain from the hit was worse or seeing her son cry because he felt her pain. She felt more helpless than

she already was because she couldn't even comfort him.
Isn't that what parents are for? To help and comfort their
kids in their time of need. She knew he would be scarred
because of this. How could a kid get over watching his
mother being punched by his father? Being treated so
harshly and to be made to seem helpless. To be helpless as
a child is scary, but seeing your mom just as helpless can
take away a child's sense of safety.

Suddenly Samuel began to shake Jessika to snap her
out of her last thought. Samuel eyes were real big and he
had a frightened look on his face. Jessika felt she knew why
he felt that way because on the other side of the door she
could hear Raymond's footsteps. The way Raymond
dragged his feet when he walked was scarier than Jessika
could ever imagine. It was a bad habit he had that irked
Jessika to no end but now it helped her hear him coming
and that gave her a second of relief. Her heart began to
beat real fast because the only thing stopping him from
coming in the room was a four-inch door. Raymond began
to turn the knob, back and forth, to open the door. Once he
realized it was lock he began to turn the knob even harder
and when that didn't work he began to kick the door. At
that point, Jessika and Samuel backed up to the farthest
point of the room because they both felt like the door was
not going to stop Raymond from coming inside. Jessika
knew that she had to get Samuel out of the room because
she would stand up to Raymond to protect him. She turns
around and quickly goes to the window and opens it up.

"Samuel, climb out the window and go over to
Janice's house to get help."

"I don't want to leave you momma." Samuel says as he starts to cry. Jessika wished she could go with him but she felt like Raymond would just keep on coming if she didn't stand her ground and let Samuel go for help.

"Go Sam. I love you." Jessika says as she pushed Samuel towards to the window. She literally pushed him out of it because she was so scared for the both of them.

"I love you too momma." Samuel says as he takes off running towards Janice's house. Jessika watched Samuel run off and she was relieved for once this whole night. All the while Jessika was helping Samuel climb through the window, Raymond was still working on trying to knock the door down. After a few more well-placed kicks, the door began to start cracking and Jessika was waiting for what may come her way. Then after one last powerful kick the door knob drops to the ground and Raymond pushes the door and it slowly creaked open and Jessika was frightened when her eyes met Raymond's. He sees Jessika standing by the window and his facial expression showed his anger he had for her. Raymond slowly walks over towards her as he wipes the sweat off his forehead with one of the handkerchiefs from a set she brought him. Imagine her seeing him use it to help him at that moment, caused her to feel nauseated.

"I have told you so many times to stick to the schedule. What is so hard about that you sorry black piece of trash?" Raymond says as he stands in front of Jessika so they could be face to face.

Jessika couldn't do anything. She felt so powerless. Raymond stood 6 feet, 3 inches, and weighed 230lbs. That was one of the things that attracted Jessika to him was the fact that she felt he could protect her. Little did she know that she would need protection from him. Her parents were the ones that got them together. They were very much old school and her parent's parents fixed them up so they felt it worked well for them that it could work for her too. Her mom tried to better that by thinking that Jessika should be with an older man because he would know how to take care of her and treat her right. Jessika's dad worked at a design company and a few months before he retired he became friends with Raymond who also worked there. Jessika's father liked his desire and the things that he was looking for in a woman. He told Jessika's mom about Raymond, her mom met him and she fell for him immediately. After all he is tall, light skinned, rugged looking with his salt and pepper stubble on his face, and very muscular. Jessika saw him and she was willing to be with him. She didn't really like him at first but after a few months dating he grew on her. He was charming, sweet, caring and real responsible. Jessika thought it would be neat to start her family early so she could enjoy being with them later. All her classmates thought it was cool to be with an older man. Jessika, wish she would have done what she really wanted to do. It was a cool idea to be with an older man but it didn't sit well with her. Doubt and caution was always there about their relationship. If he was such a good man then why was he by himself? Why couldn't he find someone his own age? These were the questions that popped up in her mind at that time but her immaturity gave way to her thinking and she went along with her parent's plan. There was no bigger cause of her regret than that choice.

"I told you that on Thursday's we eat chicken. Oh no, you had to make burgers and fries. You are so stupid and I know your parents wished they would have aborted you." Raymond says as he punches Jessika in her stomach and watches her double over in pain. Jessika lost her breath and her heart started pounding because she momentarily couldn't breathe. She tried to inhale air but it wasn't happening. She figured that if she was going to die that it might as well be now. Just then, Raymond slams his open hand on her back and the force of it starts a change reaction that causes her to catch her breath. Jessika drops to her knees and she quickly begins to take in deep breaths. The pain from the slap was worse than the pain from the punch to her stomach. Raymond then grabs her by her hair again and stands her up. Then he grabs her by her face and she could feel the cut on her face stretching. He looks her in the eyes and Jessika could not believe anyone's eyes could be that piercing. She remembers the first time she looked in his eyes and there was compassion in them but now there is only a blank stare and that scares her. Raymond begins to smirk and he pushes Jessika clean across the room. Jessika stumbled into the wall and knocked down all the pictures and plaques that were hanging up. She tried to get up before he came over to her but she couldn't. She knew that her mind was telling her she was a defeated person and her body listened. She gave the command to move but her body wouldn't obey. Physically she was helpless and mentally she was near hopelessness.

"Why would you not do what the schedule said? I made it for a reason. Do you hear me, I said why?" Raymond says as he walks up to Jessika.

"I did it because Sam made the honor roll and he received the plaque from the mayor for saving his son from choking in the cafeteria." That was all Jessika could get out before Raymond pushed her head against the wall and started rubbing her head against it. He did it repeatedly until her scalp started to burn. She just hoped that he didn't cause her to lose any hair.

"Who cares about that? Does Samuel pay the bills? Does he break his neck for his family every day? NO! He just lives off what I give him. He is not the head of this house." Raymond said, as he looked Jessika in the eyes like he was going to kill her.

"Why are you so evil? What have I truly done to warrant you beating me like this? You are letting the devil control you. What man would beat his wife?" As soon as that rolled off her tongue she regretted it. Jessika hardly spoke up for herself. Now she has just done that and she knew that would set him off even more. Raymond jerked his head back and gave her a look of total confusion. A look that was basically saying, "I know you didn't". Raymond grabbed her up by her head and tossed her clear across the room and she landed on Samuel's Lego city that he has been working on for over five years. All that hard work and effort was destroyed by the weight of Jessika. She landed with a thud and when her back landed on the Legos, a sharp pain went through her back and she begin to feel back spasms. The spasms were quick and relentless as the pain caused her eyes to tear up. She knew she had to stand up to defend herself. She wasn't going to lie here and let him get on top of her because she didn't have the strength to get him off her. She closed her eyes and focused pass the pain in her back and tried to roll over so she could get her legs under her. She succeeded in getting one foot on the ground under her when she felt a hard, pointy object hit her in the back and she fell back down on her stomach as the back spasms crippled her. The pain she felt in her back was unbearable and she could not straighten up.

"Get up black monkey. Get up right now!" Raymond says as he walks over to Jessika and stands over her.

"Ok." Jessika says as she tries to get up but the pain from her back, stomach and face was getting the best of her. She wanted to get up and run out the room but she couldn't muster the strength to take a deep breath without having pain shoot through her whole body.

"Now, you GED having dumb piece of trash." Raymond says as he jerks her up by her arm and turns her around so she can face him. Jessika felt a sharp pain in her shoulder that went down to her elbow.

"Pick up that precious plaque." Raymond says as he points to the plaque that he threw at her back. It was the plaque Samuel got from the mayor. Jessika hung it up in the living room and Raymond brought it with him into Samuel's room for no other reason than to use it on Jessika. That only added insult to injury because that was part of the reason for tonight's abuse.

"I can't." Jessika says as she attempts to bend over to get it. She wanted to appease him and hope that this whole episode would finally be over.

"Oh, yes you can." Raymond says as he pushes Jessika down and her face slams on her knee. If Raymond weren't holding her down, she would have fell backwards on her back.

"Hurry up, you dark skinned retard. You are lucky that I married you because you aren't crap. No one will ever love someone as ugly and bony as you. You are shaped like a little boy and I am surprised you were able to have a child but that is all you will ever be good for. You are too skinny to be lady like and too ugly to be considered a woman." Raymond says as he pushes down on her back, momentarily causing her to lose her breath. Just like the first time, she panicked because losing your breath is a scary feeling. Jessika could taste the blood from her nose, when it slammed on her knee, running into her mouth. Jessika closed her eyes and reached for the plaque until she grabbed it in her hand. Raymond jerked her up and snatched the plaque out of her hand.

"See stupid, here is your precious plaque that you love so much. It is funny because I do more for you than this stupid plaque but you honored this more than me. That right there just shows how much you respect me. I am your husband and the head of the household. I am the only boss in this house. I make the rules and decisions around here and nothing changes without me changing it. No special occasion is considered special until I say so. Samuel receiving this plaque is cool but it doesn't override the schedule. As a matter of fact, this cheap plaque isn't even worth getting excited over." Raymond says as he looks at the plaque then at Jessika and she knew what he was going to do next. Jessika watches him raise up the plaque and before he brought it down to strike her head; she closed her eyes and welcomed unconsciousness. The plaque came down with a thud and Jessika fell back onto the pile of Legos. It felt like she was lying on a bed of needles. She felt sharp pains on just about every inch of her back. Jessika just laid there going in and out of consciousness. She peeked out of one eye just to see what Raymond was doing and the sight almost made her jump up with fear. He was holding the plaque with two hands over his head. He was staring at her stomach and she could only imagine what he was going to do next. Jessika was in too much pain to move or do anything in her defense. Jessika was helpless and the only thing that went through her mind was the prayer she made up to make her pain go away. Every time the abuse was taking place, Jessika said this prayer because she knew God hears it and he will answer it. So, Jessika closes her eyes and start whispering: "God protect me from the pain and misery. All of this will only last a short time and your love is forever. Help me now as I am losing my faith because my prayers have not been answered. Give me the strength to endure. Amen."

Jessika opened her eyes because she was waiting on the impact and she saw Raymond staring at her with an evil look in his eyes.

"What? You are praying for this to stop? You think God wants to help a slut like you? I can't believe that you think God can help you right now. I am in total control of...." Was all Raymond could get out as he fell on top of Jessika.

"Get off me." Jessika says as the weight of Raymond on her was making her back hurt even worse. She tries to push him off her but she is too weak.

"Raymond. Get up. What are you doing?" Jessika says as she realizes that Raymond is not moving at all. She can feel his chest going in and out so she knows he is alive. She doesn't know why he fell so suddenly. The first thing that went through her mind was God gave him a heart attack as he finally answered her prayers and for the moment she felt good.

"Mom. Mom are you alright?"

"Sam. Is that you?" Jessika says as she tries to look past Raymond's limp body. She totally forgot that Samuel ran to get help.

"Mom, let me help you. We need to hurry up before he gets up." Samuel says as he grabs Raymond by his shirt and pulls him off Jessika.

"Thank you, Sam. I just knew he was going to kill me."

"I wouldn't let him do that to you. I ran as fast as I could to Janice's house and she called 911. Then I ran to the backyard and got my baseball bat and I knocked him out." Samuel says as he shows Jessika his bat.

"Sam, I love you so much. Thanks for being so smart." Jessika says as she tries to hug Samuel but she was in too much pain. Her head, hands, knees, and back was throbbing. It felt like a moving vehicle hit her. She didn't know which part of her body was bringing her the most pain. She looks down at herself and she sees that her shirt is covered with blood. "Ok baby, we need to get out of here."

"Mom, why does Dad beat you?" Samuel asks as tears form in his eyes and he just stares at her. Jessika can still remember the first-time Samuel asked her that question. On the last minute of a 35-minute beating, Samuel heard Jessika being beaten and he came in to plead with his dad to stop, Raymond just looked at him and told him to go back to bed. Samuel refused to go until Raymond stopped so Raymond walks up to Samuel and orders him to his room. Raymond follows him and when Samuel entered his room, Raymond locks Samuel in the room. Samuel starts to beat on the door, begging and pleading for Raymond to let him out. Raymond starts to walk back towards Jessika when suddenly, she hears a loud crash. Raymond turns around and runs back to Samuel's room. He unlocks the door and runs into the room. Jessika ran to help protect Samuel from whatever Raymond had his mind set on doing. She runs in the room to see Raymond looking out the window and Samuel sitting on his bed with a baseball bat in his hand. Samuel had thrown his television and Xbox360 out the window. The same one his dad just brought him for his birthday two days earlier. Raymond turns around and motions towards Samuel. Samuel immediately raises up his bat and looks Raymond dead in his face.

"Samuel. Put that bat down. You are now on punishment. You don't know how much all those things costs and you ruined it. Now give me that bat."

"NO!"

"Samuel, I paid too much money for that stuff so you will pay for that one way or another."

"All you care about is money. I don't care about those things. I care about mom."

"You right. All I care about is money. Money and being in control is everything to me. Your mom means nothing to me and since you destroyed something that I care a lot for then I guess it is time for me to make things even." Raymond says as he walks up to Jessika and before she could cover up, he punches her in the chest and she flies into the wall with a thud.

Raymond watches Jessika lying there, clutching her chest. He looks back at Samuel, sitting on his bed. "Even

Steven." Raymond says as he starts to laugh and walks out the room. Samuel runs up to Jessika and starts to yell.

"I HATE YOU. I WISH YOU WERE NO LONGER MY DADDY. YOU HEAR ME? I HATE YOU AND I WILL NEVER FORGET THIS, NOT FOR AS LONG AS I LIVE." Samuel says, as the anger he has for his dad seems to be seeping out of him. It was the first-time Samuel stood up to his dad. Even though Raymond never hit Samuel, he knew how to get to him without physical pain. He knew bringing harm to Jessika would bring out the pain he couldn't inflict with his fists. Jessika never could figure out why Raymond would beat her and no matter what Samuel did; he never even put his hands on him. It seems that Raymond just hates her for some unknown reason and that hurts her the most because she hasn't done anything to Raymond to make him have such strong feelings against her.

"Jessika, Samuel?"

"Janice, is that you?" Jessika says as a feeling of relief came upon her. She knew that since Janice was here, she had an ally to help her get away. Janice has always been there for Jessika but now she was needed more than ever. Janice Sledge was Jessika's neighbor and she has been Jessika's friend since the first day Jessika and Raymond moved into the neighborhood. Every time something went down, Jessika would go to Janice with a lie about what happened to her. Jessika felt her lies were pulling one over on Janice but at times she couldn't even hide what happened. Janice has always tried to get Jessika to admit that she was being abused but Jessika was too embarrassed to admit it even though she couldn't hide it. Janice was the type of friend that would do anything for someone regardless of the consequences. Jessika and Janice had grown close in the years that they have been neighbors. Janice has worked a few of the photo shoots that Jessika was a part of and Jessika loved sharing her career with Janice.

"Oh, no Jessika." Janice says as she runs up, puts her hands to her mouth as she sees Jessika's face covered in blood. "No Jessika. Look at you. Your face is cut up, girl. You don't deserve this." Janice says as she starts to cry. Janice knew that Jessika was being abused but she never seen it so soon after it happened. Jessika made sure that no one seen any marks or bruises until they were almost healed. She never wanted anyone to know the seriousness of them.

"Girl, how do you put up with this?"

"Where am I going to go, Janice? My Mom and Dad are too old to do anything and they feel that this is their fault because they were the ones to introduce us. They told me married folks handle their own problems. What happens in the home stays in the home. You don't put your problems out in the open for all to see."

"I am sorry Jessika but your parents are crazy. How could someone let this happen to their own daughter? You are their flesh and blood." Janice says as she wipes the tears off of her face and finally gets the strength to come closer to her.

"Well, come to find out my dad has been doing the same to my mom for years. He doesn't beat hear as bad but she gets her fair share of them." Jessika says as she thinks about the first time her mom told her that and that floored her. She didn't think her dad had it in him to do something so low down as hit her mom. Jessika couldn't even look at her dad the same and her conversations with him became less frequent.

"She should understand how you feel. Besides she should make sure that you don't go through the same thing she does. What is wrong with her?" Janice says as she tries to wrap her head around what Jessika just told her.

"My mom is old and she figures her life will be over soon so she doesn't worry about it too much. My dad's health has taken a turn for the worst so he isn't able to beat her anymore. She figures that if she can outlast it then so can I."

"You are not going to outlast it. You are going to die." Janice says bringing her point home.

"Mom he is moving again." Samuel says as he jumps up. Jessika was too scared to move and Janice stood up and started to back away.

"Come on mom, let's go." Samuel says as he grabs Jessika by her arms and starts to pull her up to her feet. "Mom. You are covered in blood." Samuel says as he lets go of her hands and begins to wipe his hands on his pants legs.

"I am sorry Samuel, but you can't worry about that now. We have got to get your mom out of here." Janice says as she walks back towards Jessika.

"Yes ma'am." Samuel says as he grabs Jessika's arm again.

"On three we pick her up, ok Sam?"

"Yes ma'am."

"One. You need to get a grip with both hands." Janice says to Samuel. "I thought we understood that we have to move past the fact she has blood on her. Stop acting like that Sam. I know you are better than that." Janice says to Samuel to let him know that this was not the time.

"Two." Janice says as she tightens her grip on Jessika's arm.

"OUCH!" Jessika yells as pain shoots through her arm.

"You are going to have to suck it up, Jessika. You put yourself in this predicament so you have no choice." Janice says as Jessika shakes her head in agreement. Jessika knew that Janice was right. Janice had no patience for people who complained about a situation that they got their self in. She felt that if you are willing to be part of a situation then you better be willing to get out of it.

"Ok, three." Janice says as her and Samuel start to pick Jessika up simultaneously.

Jessika fought the pain from them trying to pick her up because everything was hurting and she was feeling very sick to her stomach. She was waiting on the sound of the police sirens but at this moment she couldn't hear anything but the beating of her heart. Jessika tried to get her legs to obey her mind but they wouldn't move. The pain was too much for her and she felt like sitting back down.

"Jessika let's go." Janice says as she grabs Jessika from behind and pushes her up. Jessika struggles to her feet. She hadn't experienced so much pain before.

"Come on Jessika. You must help yourself because I can't carry you." Janice says as she grunts. Jessika was only 120 pounds and stood 5' 9" tall. She was petite by most standards but when the body doesn't want to move that makes it dead weight. Janice for all purposes was the same size as Jessika. They have been mistaken for sisters with their black hair, brown eyes, and petite frames. They had similar facial features and the real difference between them was that Janice was two years older than Jessika. Jessika knew she had to dig deep. She had no time to feel sorry for herself because she knew she had to get away.

"Oww! That hurts so bad." Jessika says as she starts to walk. She was bleeding and in constant pain every time she moved any part of her body.

"There you go girl, just keep walking. Once we make it outside, my car is pulled up to the front door. I wonder what is taking the police so long, they should have been here by now."

Jessika was starting to get a feeling of relief. It has been seventeen long years of beatings and abuse. She never had anyone help her except Samuel and he could only do so much. Now she wished she had asked for help sooner. Here she is ten feet from the car and she knew that once she gets outside, she would have taken her first step of getting away from Raymond.

"Open the door Samuel." Janice says as she balances Jessika against the car. Jessika was happy to not be moving because she felt more pain moving than when she was still. Suddenly Jessika started to black out. Janice notices her head fall forward and she knew she had to do something.

"Hurry up Samuel and open the door." Janice says impatiently.

"Yes ma'am." Samuel says as he grabs the door handle and opens the car door.

"Thank you. You get in the back and I will put your mom in the front."

"Ok Miss Janice, I will." Samuel says as he puts his seat belt on.

Janice sits Jessika down in the front seat and puts her seat belt on her. Janice then closes the door, runs around the car, and gets in on the driver's side.

"Jessika wake up. You can't go to sleep. Samuel look in that gym bag on the floor and get a towel out of there. There should be a bottle water in there also. Wet the towel and hand it to your mom." Janice says as she starts the car. "Better yet, wipe your mom's face off with the towel and talk to her. I am taking us straight to the hospital."

"Look at me, Momma." Samuel says as he raises the towel and starts to wipe Jessika's face. The pain from Samuel wiping her face made her snap out of her temporary sleep.

"Not so hard Sam because that hurts." Jessika says as she turns her face towards the window.

"Sorry Momma. Some of the blood has dried and it is caked on." Samuel says as he starts to wipe more gently.

Jessika looks toward the house and she sees the front door is still open. She knew she could not see

Raymond because he was in Samuel's room which is down a hallway. That gives her a sign of relief.

"Let's go Janice." Jessika says as she gets a weird feeling suddenly.

"Ok. Oh man."

"What's wrong Miss Janice?" Samuel asks as he tightens up his seatbelt.

"I can't find my cellphone. Shoot, that's right. I left it in my house."

"No time to get it now. Let's just get to the hospital." Jessika says as she glances back at the house and she sees no signs of Raymond at all.

"Ok, let's go." Janice says as she puts the car in drive and begins to steer the car off the lawn and on the street. "As luck would have it, I need to get some gas. I am almost on empty." Janice says as the low fuel light comes on. Janice had a terrible habit of riding on fumes and her bad habit has put them in a predicament.

"Aww man. What are we going to do now? How are we going to make it to the hospital?" Samuel asked as fear was profound in his tone.

"Don't you worry Samuel; we should have plenty of gas to get us there. If not, then we might have to stop at a gas station to get some gas." Janice says as she starts driving.

Jessika wasn't paying any attention to their conversation because she knew a greater danger was still in the house. She was focusing on the house because she was just waiting on Raymond to come running out looking for her. She can picture him doing something as extreme as running and jumping on the hood. As if on cue, she notices the garage door rising and at that moment, a nauseating feeling came over Jessika. She was frozen with fear and she wanted to say something but she couldn't. A teardrop falls on her check.

"Jessika, you can stop looking back now. Once we get to the hospital everything will be ok. We can call the cops again and you can tell them the whole story. I am not going to let this happen and we not say something. You are saying something tonight, regardless if you want to or not. Hey, why are you crying?" Janice asks as she looks over at Jessika.

Jessika couldn't answer her. She just looked Janice right in her eyes.

"Here he comes." Samuel says as he starts to push Janice to get her attention.

Janice glances up in the rear-view mirror and she sees Raymond's SUV pulling out the driveway and he pulled out so fast that he ran over their mailbox and jumped the curb in his haste to catch them.

"Crap. I hope we have enough gas to make it to the hospital." Janice says as she rechecks her fuel level on her car's display.

"Isn't this car faster than that SUV? This is car is much smaller and sporty." Samuel says, as he makes sure his seat belt is tight for the third time.

"Samuel, this is a Dodge Neon. You could walk faster than this." Janice says as she picks up speed.

Jessika just sat there, heart pounding, as she looks at the passenger side mirror. She notices Raymond slowly catching up to them and she knew it was too good to be true. She should have known that he was not going to let her get away that easy. All the years of abuse, he never once threatened her, if she decided to leave him. He never had too because Jessika never tried to leave. Not once in seventeen years and she had many chances but she never took them. For whatever reason, she stayed. Now that she has tried, she got the answer she was wondering. Raymond was not going to let it be easy. Jessika watched headlights from Raymond's SUV get closer and closer until it was right behind them. Suddenly Raymond's SUV slams into the back of the Dodge Neon. The force from the hit jerked everyone forward. Janice almost slammed her head on the steering wheel. Jessika head jerked forward and the belt pulled against her throat momentarily choking her. Samuel's neck snapped forward but he was pretty   much protected because he had on two seatbelts. The car skidded somewhat out of control until Janice tightened up her grip. Jessika immediately looked in her passenger side mirror again and she saw the SUV gaining on them.

"Please Janice, go faster." Jessika says as her she begins to get dizzy. She has lost a lot of blood and the sudden jerk of the car is only making her head hurt worse.

"I am trying. Once we get on the entrance to the freeway, we should be able to get help from someone else or we might even see a policeman." Janice says as she keeps on looking in the rearview mirror.

Jessika knew that the freeway was their only chance of getting away. She knew that if they stayed on the road they are currently on, it would eventually turn into a dirt road. They lived in a neighborhood that was growing. They finally have an HOA that is putting their money to use so what use to be a large field the children would play on, it is now being developed for more homes to be built. So, they have paved much of the street but there was plenty more to go as the rest of the street was a dirt road. Down the dirt road was nothing but piles of wood and uncut grass. This road extended for about half a mile and people would usually walk their pets down this road because of the wide-open space. That usually took place in the daytime but it is 10:15pm and it is pitch dark down that road. There are no streetlights or anything to illuminate the road. Jessika knew that was the last road they needed to travel on.

"Janice, he is gaining on us." Jessika says, as the lights in the mirror grow larger and larger.

"Come on car." Janice says as she puts the pedal to the floor.

"Momma, here he comes." Samuel says as he ducks down in the seat. Raymond's SUV slams into the car again. Just like before the car skidded forward. Jessika looks over at Janice and she sees the fear in her face and the tears that are falling down her cheeks. Jessika cannot help but wonder what is going on in her mind. What she is thinking? Is she second-guessing helping her? Just watching her sitting there holding on to the steering wheel for dear life, crying, makes Jessika feel sad because Janice is putting her life on the line for her. Janice could have called the police and stayed home but she chose to help. Jessika knew that Janice would die trying to help her and that is why she never asked for her help. I guess Jessika wasn't ready to face what she is facing now.

"God let us make it to this freeway. The entrance ramp is only a few yards ahead. Please God let us make it." Janice says as she glances at the rearview mirror.

Jessika turns around and she sees Samuel crying. His hands are covering his face but she can hear him crying. The mere sight of him doing that makes her cry. He was all she had that was good in her life. She never wanted him to experience something like this. That was one of the reasons why she was glad that all the abuse was towards her and not him. She knew that she would have died a long time ago if she had to protect him. She would not let anything happen to Samuel.

"Come on car, the entrance is right there." Janice says as she pumps the gas pedal. Suddenly, the car starts to slow down.

"What's wrong Janice?" Jessika says as she looks at Janice who now had a look of a person that realizes all hope is gone.

"We are out of gas." Janice says as she glances at Jessika.

"NO!" Jessika screams as the SUV slams into the car again. She braced herself just in time as the car jerked forward and the momentum carried them right pass the entrance to the freeway. Janice wasn't so lucky because she was looking at Jessika at the time and her head slammed on the steering wheel and she laid slumped over it. Samuel just let out a big scream as the back-window shatters and sends glass over him. As the car rolls forward, Raymond, probably sensing something is wrong, starts to bump the car forward and then starts pushing the car with his SUV.

"STOP IT RAYMOND!" Jessika screams as the car is being pushed down the dirt road. Jessika knew the only thing she could do was grab the steering wheel and try to keep them on the road. She had to first get Janice off the steering wheel, so she grabs her by the shoulder and pulls her back with all her might. Her shoulder was hurting so bad that the effort and the pain caused her to start crying even more. She eventually gets her laid back on her seat. Jessika grabs the steering wheel and she tries to keep them going straight. She did notice that they were going slower and slower. All the momentum was coming from Raymond's SUV and she felt he knew that. It never occurred to Jessika that since the back window was shattered, Raymond could see right through the car. Jessika struggled with the steering wheel due to where she was sitting and because of the road, which seem to have more and more potholes the further they went. Jessika wanted to check on Samuel to make sure he was all right. It was hard for her to talk and concentrate on controlling the car. Jessika then decides she was going to take a quick look back just to see how he was doing. Jessika turns to see Samuel looking right at her crying, but from the looks of it he was okay.

Jessika then quickly glances out the shattered back window and she faintly makes eye contact with Raymond. The look on his face sent chills through her. Raymond blows his horn at the fact that Jessika was turned around. The horn startles Jessika, her left arm slips off the steering wheel, and the car immediately turns left. Raymond gives the car a final bump and the car rolls to a stop in some knee-high grass. Raymond immediately stops a few feet pass the car. Jessika quickly turns around and looks towards Raymond's SUV. Her heart was pounding because she was waiting for him to push open the truck's door, get out, and walk over to the car and finish what he had started.

"Janice. Janice, are you alright?" Jessika says as she pushes on Janice with her left hand as she continues to look towards Raymond's SUV. Janice didn't move nor did she make a sound. Jessika begins to shake her harder just to make sure she gave full effort. Still, Janice laid there unconscious.

"Sam, are you okay?" Jessika says as she stretches her hand in between the driver's side and passenger seat. She felt Samuel's arm as she made her way to his hand. Once she grabbed it she squeezed it tightly.

"Yes ma'am. I'm okay."

"Oh, thank God." Jessika says, as she never takes her eyes off Raymond's SUV. She was comforted knowing that Samuel was holding her hand and that he was not hurt. She felt a new sense of strength and courage. Jessika was just waiting on some type of movement or something from Raymond, so she could plan her next move. Raymond just sat in his truck not moving. Jessika couldn't see him because of the way he parked the SUV. Jessika begins to wonder if maybe he is also hurt or knocked out cold. That thought quickly became a dream because as if on cue he floors the gas pedal and the SUV takes off in a cloud of dust. Jessika begins to get scared because Raymond was capable of anything because he just didn't care. Jessika watches as the dust lingers towards the car. She was momentarily unable to see and she was very afraid. She knows that Raymond is willing to do anything to bring harm to her. Jessika just sat there listening to her heartbeat until the dust finally starts to clear. She quickly begins to try to focus on finding the SUV. She knew that the vehicle wasn't moving because she didn't hear anything but crickets. She starts to panic because she could not see or hear him. That was one of her worst fears was the not knowing. About twenty yards away, Raymond turns on his high beams. Jessika thought she had swallowed her heart because she felt it beating all the way in her throat. Samuel finally sits up and he sees the high beams in the distance.

"What is daddy going to do?" Samuel says momentarily breaking Jessika out of her trance.

"I don't know Sam but we need to get out of this vehicle." Jessika says as she finally takes off her seatbelt.

"Where are we going to go?" Samuel says as he begins to look out the window. His eyes showed his fear.

"I don't know, but anything is better than being trapped in Janice's car." Jessika says as she pictures being stuck inside of a small car and Raymond trying to get in. They would be sitting ducks in here and that was something she didn't want to happen.

"Do you mean that we have to get out of the car?" Samuel says with a worried look on his face. His little eyes looked like a deer trapped in some headlights.

"Yes Sam. We can't risk him ramming the car with his SUV. We would be crushed for sure."

"Well, it is dark out there and I am scared." Samuel says as tears start flowing down his face.

"Look Sam. I need you to be strong. We don't need to be scared." Jessika says as her heart beats harder at the fact that Samuel is just as frightened as she is. "We need to look around in here for something we could use. I don't care if it is a pen, mace, flashlight, or something. Anything we can take with us just in case."

"Yes ma'am." Samuel says as he begins to look around in the back seat.

Jessika opens the glove compartment and finds a flashlight.

"Have you found anything Sam?"

"No ma'am. There is nothing back here." Samuel says as he wipes his face with his hands.

"I have found a flashlight so at least that will guide us where ever we go."

"Oh, you did. Good."

Jessika was feeling better because at least they could see if they needed to make an escape. Going out into the darkness was one thing she really feared. Not only could they not see Raymond but also, she had no clue on what was out there. Jessika knew she needed room to run or hide if she had to. She would worry about everything else later. She did know that if she got out of the car, she risked having to face Raymond again. She had to find the strength to get away or die trying. As Jessika is looking out the window, she can hear Samuel crying. She continues to look out the window because she didn't want to start crying also. Not only is she scared but she feels bad that she has put Samuel in this predicament. She has always tried to separate her abuse from Samuel, but tonight she has no choice. She just wants to make sure that no matter what happens tonight, that it is all directed to her and not him. Even if she must die trying and that was something she was willing to do. First, she must get Samuel to calm down and to help him get over being so scared.

"Stop crying Sam, please."

"I am trying Momma."

"What's that bible verse we learned for courage?"

"It is, *"Fear not, for I am with you; be not dismayed, for I am your God. I will strengthen you, yes, I will help you, I will uphold you with my righteous hand. Isaiah 41:10"*

"That's it Sam. So how do you feel knowing that God is with us, always?"

"I feel better but still scared. I know God is with us."

"Just like always Sam, just like always. Ok, do you see that stack of wood flats over there? Let's make that our base until we can work out our next move." Jessika says as she points to a barely visible pile of wood flats that are about six feet tall.

"Ok." Samuel says as he gets out of his seatbelts.

"Here you hold the flashlight and guide us there." Jessika says as she hands Samuel the flashlight.

"Yes, it works." Samuel says to show his excitement for the flashlight working.

Jessika takes another look at the high beams from Raymond's SUV to make sure they had not gotten any closer. Jessika then looks at Janice and she pushes her to see if she was awake.

"Give me that water bottle on the floor." Jessika says as she points to the water bottle Samuel opened earlier. She begins to pour it on Janice's face as she begins to shake her again. Janice began to wake up slowly.

"Oh thank God you woke up." Jessika says as she begins to rub Janice's shoulder as she sits up.

"Oh I am still in the car, I had a dream I was in heaven." Janice says as she tries to crack a joke. Jessika was just happy that she didn't have to attempt to carry Janice. Jessika knew that in her current condition she could not carry her. Even if she weren't so beat up she still wouldn't have the strength to carry Janice.

"Unfortunately, you are not in heaven yet. We are still trapped in your car. See Raymond is parked right over there." Jessika says as she points to where Raymond's SUV was parked with its lights shining in the distance. Janice's eyes got big as the scenario has truly become real again as she is fully coherent now.

"I have a plan Janice. We will make a run for it. Sam and I will run in this direction and you go back towards your home. You are in way better shape than I am to make it. Hopefully the police will be there and you can lead them here."

"No, I am not leaving you and Samuel. No way." Janice says shaking her head in disagreement to Jessika's plan.

"You have to Janice. If we don't split up, we will all be doomed. He is after me not you so you go and get help. Please do that for us." Jessika pleads with Janice.

"That is not a good plan at all but I will run as fast as I can to get help. You run as fast as you can to hide from him. Don't stop running no matter what." Janice says to Jessika as Jessika shakes her head in agreement. "I will come back for you I promise."

"I love you Miss Janice." Samuels says as Jessika felt her heart drop when he said that.

"I love you too Samuel. I need for you to be strong for your mother and help her okay?" Janice says as she kisses Samuel on the forehead.

"Yes ma'am I will."

"I love you Jessika." Janice says as she gives Jessika a hug. Jessika wanted Janice to stay with her because she gathered confidence from her being around but she understood that this isn't Janice's fight and Jessika knows that she will feel bad if something more terrible happened to Janice. So letting her go get help was the best thing for both of them.

"I love you too."

"We are all going to make it through this, don't neither of you worry." Janice says as she grabs Jessika's and Samuel's hand.

"Ok Sam. I am going to open this door and we are going to run for it. We are going to go in that direction and Janice is going in that direction." Jessika says she points things out for Samuel.

"Yes ma'am."

"Ok, one."

Jessika says as she grabs the door handle.

"Two."

Jessika says as she looks in the direction of the high beams and grabs the seat lever so she can move the seat forward to let Samuel out.

"Three."

Jessika says as she pulls the handle and pushes the door open. She is greeted with a warm air that had a smell of burnt wood. She steps out of the car, keeping one eye on the high beams as she pulls the lever up so the seat can come forward. She grabs Samuel's arm and pulls him out.

"Go Janice, hurry." Jessika says as Janice takes off like she was shot out of a cannon. Jessika wanted her to make it to safety so help can find her and Samuel.

"Go Sam." Jessika says as she pushes him so they can begin to run. A soon as she takes a step, she is immediately reminded of tonight's activities as her back and head cries out in pain after a few steps. She begins to get disoriented and is starting to have a hard time running in a straight line. To make matters worse she steps in pothole after pothole, which is keeping her off balance.

"Come on Momma." Samuel calls back to her. Jessika knew he was having the same problem she was and that was seeing each other. Jessika just kept on running in the direction that the wood flats were. She couldn't see Samuel but she could see the flashlight moving back and forth as if someone was running. Jessika was hoping to run a little bit faster than what she was doing but the pain was too much. She was struggling to make it and if Raymond knew that, he would feed off it. Jessika started to wonder where he was. She hasn't heard his SUV moving or anything. She was starting to think that maybe he was truly hurt and he was sitting in his truck trying to recover. Jessika takes a quick look behind her just to make sure that Raymond's SUV was still there, and she sees a flashlight in the distance moving towards them. She knew it was Raymond and she knew that he wasn't finished with her. She looks forward gauging the distance to the wood flats, then she glances back again, and she sees the flashlight getting closer and closer.

"Come on Momma. Daddy is coming." Samuel says as he climbs on top of the wood flats.

Jessika's heart was pounding so hard that she could no longer hear her footsteps. Every step sent pain through her body. Just trying to stay focused on the wood flats took all her energy.

"Momma follow the light." Samuel says as he shines the flashlight in Jessika's face.

"Sam, stop it, I can't see with that light in my face." Jessika says as she holds her hands out in front of her to shield her from the light.

"COME ON MOMMA." Samuel yells.

Jessika slowed down because she could not see. The flashlight shined right in her face and it was going to be a few seconds before she would be able to see again. Jessika knew that when she saw Raymond's flashlight behind her he was a good distance. She hoped he was so far that it gave her time to recover. As she stood there she listened for his footsteps and she could hear them getting closer and closer. She knew she had to run now.

"MOMMA, COME ON!" Samuel screams.

"Ok Sam." Jessika says as she begins to run. She wished she hadn't stopped because the pain was worse. She felt her muscles tightening up making it that much harder to run. "Shine the light in front of me so I can see."

"OK, BUT HURRY." Samuel screamed to encourage Jessika to run faster.

Jessika could see the wood flats getting closer and closer. She knew that once she made it to them, she would still have a battle to get on top of them. She had little strength left and she was in intense pain.

"Come on Jessika, don't you give up." Jessika says to herself as she felt her body betraying her. She was slowing down and she wasn't giving her body the command to. She could see that she was a few feet from the wood flats. A few feet wasn't a lot of ground to cover but it seem to be a great distance because her body didn't seem to want to make it. Jessika knew she had been through a lot and she was really surprised she had the strength to make it this far. Then the worst thing that could happen to her happened, her body just shut down and she fell inches from the flats.

"MOMMA, NO." Samuel screams as he watches Jessika fall to the ground.

Jessika knew she had to dig deep now. Her body didn't want to go any further. Her mind felt like it could but at this moment, the body won the battle.

"God please give me the strength to make it. I am begging you to do this one thing." Jessika pleads as she knew it would be an act of God if she could get up and climb up that stack of wood to safety.

"COME ON MOMMA BECAUSE HE IS RIGHT BEHIND YOU!" Samuel screams.

Jessika knew she must get to her feet if she would have any chance to defend herself. Jessika starts by getting her arms under her like she was in push-up position and starts to push herself up. Her arms began to shake from the weight. Her head started to throb and the cut on her face began to bleed again from her straining. She had picked herself up enough to be able to bring her right leg up. She manages to get to one knee and she took a peep behind her to see the flashlight yards behind her.

"I got you now stupid and I am going to kill you." Raymond says as he closes the gap to Jessika.

"Oh no." Jessika says as she tries to stand up.

"Come on Momma. You can do it." Samuel says as he reaches his hand to her.

Jessika almost gets to her feet when she not only hears the footsteps but she can feel them hitting the ground, which meant he was real close. The fear from that causes her to lose all strength, she falls to the ground, and as if her body knows the routine, she curls up in the fetal position and covers her head.

"Momma no." Samuel says as he watches Raymond run towards her until he is standing over her.

"Now you know you are going to get it now." Raymond says as he drops his knee into Jessika's side. All her breath left her and she cries out in pain. That blow seemed to take all Jessika had left. She could no longer muster any strength to do anything on her behalf. She was weak, tired, and hurting all over. She was waiting on the one blow to end it all.

"STOP IT!" Samuel screams.

Raymond ignores him as he picks up Jessika by her hair and stands her up. Jessika was defeated and she couldn't even pick her arms up to defend herself. She was battered and her spirit was gone. She no longer wanted to run, hide or get away. She wanted it to end right here. She wanted him to kill her so she would suffer no more.

"Stand up you useless piece of trash. I am going to snap your neck and leave you here for the animals to eat." Raymond says as he tries to get Jessika to stand on her own.

Jessika tries to get her footing but there were two large rocks below her so she steps to the left of them. Raymond then puts his flashlight flat on its back, on the ground so it would illuminate on them. He had the huge flashlight that Jessika brought him for his birthday a few years ago. It would light up the area like a lantern if you put it on its back. So now she could see him and she notices that he doesn't even have a scratch on him. Jessika now realizes that he played possum so she would get out of the vehicle. He knew she was safer in the car than out in the open. It finally hits Jessika that even if she had made it to the wood flats she would not be any safer from him because he could still get to her. Jessika knew all of that didn't matter anymore. He has her now and she can't even defend herself. Raymond grabs Jessika by her shoulders and forcibly turns her around as he puts his arm around her neck below her chin. He begins to tighten his arm on her throat and Jessika began to cry because she was too helpless to stop him from choking her. To think that her life was about to end like this and in this moment Jessika felt like a failure and for that she wanted to die.

"LEAVE MY MOMMA ALONE!"

Jessika hears as she sees Samuel jump off the flats onto Raymond's back. Raymond lets go of Jessika and reaches to grab Samuel. Samuel starts to hit his dad on the top of his head with the flashlight from Janice's car. Raymond tries to grab him but Samuel had a choke hold on him with one arm and was beating him with the other. Raymond eventually grabs the arm that Samuel has the flashlight in as they turn in circles. Suddenly Raymond cries out in pain as he turns and Jessika sees that Samuel has bitten Raymond in the face and he still has a grip on him with his teeth. Jessika watches as Raymond starts to hit Samuel to make him stop biting him. Samuel lets go of Raymond's face with his mouth and then Raymond grabs Samuel by the back of the head and flips him over him. Samuel legs swing forward, it catches Jessika on the shoulder, and she falls. She hears Samuel land with a thud. Jessika looks towards Samuel because she was expecting him to get up and go at it again but he just laid there. Jessika then looks harder and she sees that Samuel has landed on one of the big rocks that she sidestepped earlier and he was bleeding from the head and was unconscious.

"See what you made me do Samuel. You deserved that." Raymond says as he stands over Samuel. He showed no concern for Samuel.

"Ok black monkey I am going to finish you. This is where it ends." Raymond says as he takes a step towards Jessika.

"STOP RIGHT THERE. GET YOUR HANDS UP!"

"Who is that? Is that you Janice?"

"THIS IS THE HOUSTON POLICE DEPARTMENT. TURN AROUND AND PUT YOUR HANDS ON TOP OF YOU HEAD. DO IT NOW!"

Jessika turned to see who it was. She could not make out who it was but she knew it was a female. It sounded like Janice but she had no way to tell because the lantern was shining up in her face and she could not see in the direction the voice was coming from.

"Janice when I am through with her, you are next." Raymond says as he tries to squint to see who the female voice was.

"THIS IS YOUR LAST WARNING. IF YOU TAKE ONE MORE STEP, I WILL BE FORCED TO SHOOT."

"Janice, I will be forced to break you off if you don't leave me alone." Raymond says as he runs towards the voice.

Suddenly Jessika hears, *"POW, POW,"* and it was louder than any firecracker she had ever heard. She wasn't used to guns but she knew that was what the sound was. She sees Raymond stumble back into the wood flats and he clutches his chest and stomach. She sees blood flow between his fingers and she slowly starts to faint. Jessika sees a shadow figure step over her and before she closes her eyes, she glances at Samuel and she loses consciousness.

Jessika's

Dilemma

Chapter 2

"The aftermath"

"Jessika. Jessika."

"Yeah." Jessika whispers as she slowly opens her eyes. She tries to move but she felt her back spasms return and every time she tried to breathe in, pains shoots through her body. Her head was throbbing, nose was tender, mouth was dry, she felt a large bandage on her face, her shoulder was sore, she felt bandages on her knees and hands, plus there was an extra pillow that her back was resting on. "Ouch. My body hurts."

"After what you have been through, it should."

Jessika was trying to focus on the person standing in front of her but she couldn't tell who it was.

"Jessika it's me, Sonya."

Sonya Johnson was a nurse that worked at the hospital and she has taken a personal crusade upon herself to help Jessika. She has been working on Jessika since the first time she came to the hospital in need of medical attention. She has been actively trying to get Jessika to do something about her situation before it became too late. Sonya was a middle aged, African-American woman with salt and pepper hair. She doesn't look a day over thirty five but she was in her sixty's. She was all of 4' 8" and 150 lbs. She was one of the most caring person Jessika had ever met. Sonya went out of her way for Jessika and would do anything for her.

"What? Oh, hey girl." Jessika says as she squints to get her eyes to adjust to the voice talking to her.

"Once again, you are in my hospital. You have been worked over pretty good."

"I know Sonya." Jessika says as a culmination of years of abuse hit her like a ton of bricks and she began to cry.

"Girl I have told you many times to do what is right for yourself but you wouldn't listen. You could have been killed. Your face is cut up and I pray the doctors did their best job on your face. You and Samuel both could have died last night.

"Wait. Where is Sam?" Jessika says as she tries to sit up but pain shot through her body. So, she gently placed herself back down on the pillow. She finally focuses on her room and she notices that she is hooked up to an IV. She has all kinds of wires connected to her and to an assortment of machines. She looks around and notices that all the lights were off except the TV mounted across the room, high on the wall.

"Relax, Jessika. He is in the children's wing."

"Is he ok?"

"We are working on him."

"What do you mean?"

"Just that. We are working on him."

"What does that mean? Sonya, please tell me how he is doing." Jessika says as she is fearing the worst.

"I am only telling you this because I love you. I have always taken care of you when you come in here beat up. I love Samuel like a son also, so I am telling you this not to scare or worry you, but to keep you informed."

"All you are doing is scaring me. I need to know." Jessika says as fear has over taken her and the pain she feels means nothing compared to the fear.

"He is in a coma."

"What?" Jessika says as she covers up her face. "Oh no. Please tell me that isn't true." Jessika says as she begins to cry. She could not believe that Samuel, the one person she would die for, was in a coma. He was the one thing that brought total joy to her life when she was feeling down. She loved him more than life and now she was at the point to where she could lose him. She could not deal with the fact that Raymond did this. Jessika knew that she could have done something a long time ago. She could have walked out and things would be different now but since she wasn't strong enough to leave, she is paying a serious price.

"My poor baby. I am so sorry."

"We know that you didn't want this to happen, so don't even begin to feel sorry about anything. What's done is done so now you need to focus on getting healed so you can be by his side. He will need that from you."

"You mean I can't see him now?" Jessika says as she wipes her face.

"You couldn't stand up on your own right now. You need to rest. You have lost a lot of blood and your body is weak."

"I need to see him now. My baby needs me."

"Your baby is in Jesus's hands right now. That is the safest place to be. We need to pray about this. We have tried all we can and now you must trust in the Lord to bring him through this."

Jessika just lowered her head. She was so embarrassed that Samuel was in the hospital yet alone in a coma. She felt that she didn't do enough to protect him and truth be told, she didn't. She didn't do nearly enough to protect him. She knows now that she would have rather died than to let him end up being in the position he is in now but she must face up to what she has done, or better yet, what she didn't do.

"You are right Sonya.

"I know it is tough on you Jessika. It is hard to see the good when so much bad has happened to you. God knows the reason why you are going through all of this. His sole purpose is not to see you suffer. Good will come out of all of this, you wait and see. God is working it out."

"I hear you Sonya. I didn't pray nearly enough nor did I put it all in God's hands either. I kept on trying to avoid what I needed to do for so long. I was just content with the fact that if Raymond wasn't beating Samuel, then I could deal with it but now that he has hurt Samuel, things have changed. I will make sure that he will pay for this. He is not going to get away with this. Wait, I saw him get shot. Please tell me he is he dead."

"Nope. He will recover in a few weeks."

Those were the words; Jessika did not want to hear. She can remember clearly Raymond being shot and the look on his face of total disbelief. The look of fear in his eyes and the shock of being shot made her feel glad but when she looked at Samuel it all went away. Samuel, who looked so peaceful, but Jessika knew that he was seriously hurt. Now he is faced with the possibility of death or some sort of long-term damage from this. Samuel tried to save her, which makes Jessika feel worse because she never tried to save herself. Now that Raymond is still alive, it brings back the fear of knowing that he could try to kill her again.

"How do I know that he won't try to kill me while I am sleep?"

"Don't you worry, he is on a different floor and besides he has a police officer outside his room."

"What happens once he is well enough to go home?"

"Oh, he isn't going home. I do know that the cops are monitoring his recovery so as soon as he is well enough they are taking him away."

"They are going to keep him for how long?"

"I don't know these things. I just know that you need rest. Let's pray and then you can go back to sleep."

"Ok." Jessika says as Sonya grabs her hands and they bowed their heads.

"God, we lift up Jessika and Samuel to you right now. They are going through a crisis right now that doesn't look good. The outcome is bleak but we know through your mighty hands, all can be corrected. We just ask for you to take over the situation. We also pray that Jessika gives up the problem of her abusive husband to you so that you can work on him. We lastly lift Samuel to you and we pray that you give him the strength of a full recovery so they can be reunited as a family. We say this prayer in Jesus name, Amen."

"Amen." Jessika says as she feels guilt creeping up in her spirit.

"Do you need anything before I leave? My shift is almost up but I will be back in the morning."

"Yes, can you give me some strong pain medicine?"

"That is what this line right here is for. Take this and click this when the pain comes back. It will release pain killers in your system but it won't let you have too much so don't get carried away."

"I won't. I just need enough to go to sleep."

"Here is some water."

"Thank you, Sonya."

"No problem."

"Sonya can you check on my baby for me and see if he is alright."

"I will."

"Um can you call me before you leave his room? I want to at least hear him breathing."

"OK. I will call you in a few minutes. Oh yeah, here is the remote for the TV and if there is anything else you need call on Nurse Nancy. She will be working the night shift."

"Ok thanks." Jessika says as she watches Sonya leave the room. Once the door closes, Jessika eyes begin to swell with tears. They are tears of joy from being alive, tears of sadness from Samuel's current state, and tears of fear knowing that Raymond is still alive. Everything she has always feared has happened. She was constantly worried that one day she would end up staying in the hospital for an extended period. The thought of that sends chills down her back. This is far worse than that thought. Now Samuel is in a coma and there is no guarantee that he will recover. That thought makes her cry even harder because she couldn't live with the fact that Samuel could possibly be brain dead or just have brain damage from this ordeal. The fact that her non-actions and Raymond's actions caused all this to happen to Samuel is degrading. How could she not think that the abuse would escalate to someone being seriously hurt or dead? Over the years, it hasn't been getting lighter. The abuse has always gotten tougher to take and now Jessika doesn't see how she could have let it get this far. She looks around the room and it makes her feel worse. She knew that being admitted in a hospital was the ultimate sign that she was being abused. Jessika didn't like the fact that so many people knew it and they would look at her and shake their head. Over the years Jessika felt so helpless and being beaten like this makes her want to die. This beating is one that will leave plenty of reminders. The scar on her face alone will take plenty of getting used to because it will always remind her of what took place. Jessika knows that everyone she knows will ask her all kinds of questions and she better be ready to answer them because she can no longer hide by avoiding people. She will have to make the call to her agency and explain this to them as well. They will be shocked when they see the scar on her face. Jessika can only imagine the look of concern her boss will have. Small blemishes that other models have are frowned on but there has never been a model that has had to deal with such a dramatic cut on her face and now Jessika isn't sure if her career can continue. She will have to face the fact that her story will follow her wherever she goes and for the rest of her life she will deal with the fact that she is an abused wife. Jessika never wanted to say it or believe it. Even though there was no way to deny it, she found a way to pretend that she was one step from being it. If there was such a thing, she knows that the next step must be death. She has endured the same pain and sufferings that she has read about in books or newspaper articles. Jessika stopped reading them when things started to become reality. She cannot remember exactly when things turned for the worst but all she knows is it was a continued pattern that only seemed to get more painful. It seemed the worst thing she did was accept what was taking place. She took the blame and suffered more than she should have because she felt at fault. The only fault she had was that she put up with it for seventeen years. Jessika knew this whole incident could have been avoided if she said something a long time ago. The first hospital visit would have been a good time to do it. The twenty fifth hospital visit would have also been a great time. Instead, Jessika chose number thirty-six to be the one where she says enough is enough. This is by far the worst one but it will forever change her life, no matter what the outcome is. Samuel is in limbo and that is her fault.

Ring

Ring, Ring

Jessika quickly wipes her face and clears her throat.

"Hello."

"Hey it's me, Sonya. I am going to pull the phone towards him, Ok."

"Ok." Jessika says as she already tries to fight the tears that are reforming in her eyes. She knew that the sound of his breathing would not make things any easier but it would let her know that he was still alive. As she hears the phone getting closer to him, she pretends she is in the room listening to him. Jessika can tell that Sonya put the phone close to him because she can tell that the receiver is not being moved. Jessika can faintly hear him breathing and she wishes she were there to hold him, caress him, and rock him to sleep.

"Oh, Sam I am so sorry. Momma loves you so much and I regret what I have done to you." Jessika says as she cries uncontrollably. She couldn't even control it. Jessika hears the receiver moving and then Sonya gets on the phone.

"I have got to go home and get some rest, so you do the same. I will see you in the morning."

"Ok, thank you Sonya."

"No problem. Goodnight."

Jessika puts the phone down and curls up in a ball. The pain from her head and heart was intense. Jessika reaches for the cord that controlled the pain medicine but she pushes it away. She wanted to feel all the pain she could stand. It is nothing compared to the pain she will feel if Samuel dies or is permanently damaged.

"God how could I do this to my son? Why wouldn't I just leave?" Jessika asks as she starts to taste her tears as they roll to her mouth.

"God punish me instead. I would rather go through the pain and suffering from brain damage or even death. Please don't punish my Samuel because he is all I have left. Please God punish me instead. I am begging you. Please God." Jessika says as she sits up and reaches out towards the ceiling.

"You know all the pain and suffering I have endured over the past seventeen years. He was all that I had to pull me through the tough times. He was always there for me and all I truly had." Jessika says as she lies back down. She closes her eyes as pictures of Samuel bounce in her head. She can picture his school pictures, soccer pictures, and his birthday pictures. She just wants to go to his room and be there when he comes out of the coma. She wants to be well enough so she can sleep by his side as he recovers. Just by her thinking happy thoughts, she calmed down and she could relax and let sleep take its course. She turns off the television and takes a deep breath, blows it out, and lets her body go limp. The only sound she could hear was the heart-monitoring machine and she let the beeping of that soothe her to sleep.

Beep

Beep

Beep

Jessika is tired and worn out. Between fatigue and the medicine, Jessika was ready to go to sleep.

Beep

Beep

Jessika feels the last teardrop fall off her face and unto her pillow.

Beep

Beep

"Hey mom, look what I got."

Jessika smiles as she falls into a deep sleep and dreams about Samuel.

"What do you have Sam?"

"The mayor gave me this plaque today." Samuel says, barely able to control his excitement as he runs around the room with the plague, waving it over his head.

"What did he give you that for?" Jessika asks as she tries to get Samuel to calm down.

"I am going to tell you if you give me a chance." Samuel says in one of his usual smart aleck ways. Jessika loved that he joked with her because it brought the needed joy and laughter to her life.

"Ok."

"Anyway, they made an announcement over the PA that we had a special guest. So, everyone got excited and they walked us to the auditorium. The whole school was there and everything. The Principal walks on stage and says; "Can you guess who our special guest is?" Everyone starts to yell out all kinds of people, some were yelling Barney, Power Puff Girls, Stephon Curry, Gordon Ramsey, Houston Texans Football team."

"What did you yell?" Jessika asks even though she knew the answer.

"Denzel Washington"

"I should have known."

"He is my favorite actor of all times. He is too cool."

"He is handsome though. If only." Jessika says as she pretends to be thinking about her being with him.

"Dream on Momma."

"Ok so finish your story."

"Anyway, that went on for about two minutes so then the Principal quiets everyone down. He says; "The special guest is the Mayor." He said it like everyone was going to get excited."

"No one did?"

"Mom come on. The Mayor, you even complain about him."

"That is a whole different story."

"Anyway, when he said; 'The Mayor.' Everyone started to boo him. They were saying, 'Boo who cares.' It was so funny to see the look on the Principal's face."

"Sam that was not nice."

"Hey, I am a kid, what do you expect?" Samuel says as he starts to laugh.

"I expect you to respect grown folks, which is what I have taught you."

Jessika's says giving Samuel a stern look.

"I did. I didn't boo him, I just laughed at the fact the other kids did. Besides if you could see how big his head is. Man, I mean from where I was sitting he looked like a lollipop. It looked like his head was big and round and his body was skinny like a stick. Some of the older kids call him, "Mr. Rucka the walking sucka.""

"Sam? I am not going to let you disrespect him like that. Besides his name is Mr. Rucker not Mr. Rucka and I know you can pronounce words better than that."

"I say it like that because it is funnier that way."

"So."

"You don't think it is funny?" Samuel asks as if he knows that Jessika is lying.

"No. I don't think it's funny." Jessika says as she turns her head so Samuel won't see her laugh.

"If it isn't then why are you sitting there trying to hold your laugh in?"

"Sam move on and finish telling me the story." Jessika says as she gives in and laughs.

"The Principal got mad and he made everyone be quiet. The Mayor walks on the stage and the Principal and teachers start to clap while all of us kids just sat there."

"That is not nice."

"I know. So, the Mayor gets on the microphone and calls my name."

"See and you were disrespectful to him."

"All the kids were looking at me like I was in trouble or something. I tried to take my time walking down the aisle because I was scared. I finally make it to the stage and he hands me a plaque and says; "I am giving Samuel Cotta this plaque for showing bravery in saving my son's life." All the kids start clapping for me. They clapped for a long time."

"How did that make you feel?" Jessika asks proudly because she was so happy for him.

"It made me feel good. Like a super hero or something."

"My Sam. You are too awesome."

"Thank you."

"We need to make room on the wall in the living room for this. We need to put it somewhere where everyone will see it."

"I know something better than that, we need to celebrate by having hamburgers and fries."

"Let me check the schedule first."

"Mom." Samuel says to show his disappointment. Jessika walked to the refrigerator where Raymond put the eating schedule for the month. He would detail each day's meal plan and Jessika had to adhere to it.

"I am sorry Sam but the schedule says chicken and mashed potatoes."

"I know what the stupid schedule says." Sam says as he feels dejected by the fact that he can't have hamburgers and fries to celebrate his accomplishment.

"Sam, you watch your mouth."

"That man always gets his way. He always picks what we eat and where we go."

"That man, who is also your father, works hard to provide and the least we can do is give him what he wants to eat."

"What happens if we don't give him what he wants to eat?" Samuel asks just to see what Jessika would say. He knew what happened the last time that she didn't go by the schedule.

"Let's not go there. Go to your room and finish your homework. I will call you when dinner is ready."

"Yes ma'am." Samuel says, continually showing his disappointment. "Oh yeah, I made the honor roll."

"That is so good Sam." Jessika says as she gives him a hug but Samuel politely brushed her off.

"Yeah it is." Samuel says in a low voice as he walks off towards his room.

Jessika watches Samuel walk out of the kitchen and she feels sorry that she can't do what she wants for him. She picks up the plaque and she smiles as she sees his name on it. It brings her joy to see her son doing positive things and affecting others in a way that they show him love. Jessika knew that was her vision of what she wanted her son to be and Samuel was all that and more. He was everything to her and she couldn't ask for a better son. Jessika grabs a dry towel and wipes the plaque off, and goes to the living room to hang the plaque. She stops by the desk near the front door and pulls out a hammer and nail. She then makes her way towards the living room and walks to the wall she had designated as Samuel's accomplishments.

"Let's see. Which one of these should I take down?" Jessika says as she looks over all the different awards and certificates. Samuel has been very busy collecting different things. Jessika feels that none is more special than this plaque. She decides to keep all of them up but hang the plaque in the middle of them. That way the others will only accent the plaque.

"I am so proud of you Sam." Jessika says as she hangs the plaque on the wall. She knows that if she could, she would have a spotlight shining on the plague as well. "My baby isn't going to leave me room for anything else."

Jessika walks back into the kitchen and sees Sam standing there in the doorway.

"Sam, what are you doing? You are supposed to be doing your homework." Jessika asked as she was surprised to see him standing there.

"I am going to finish my homework. I just decided to write you a poem." Samuel says as he follows Jessika into the kitchen. He then hands Jessika a sheet of paper. Jessika looks at the paper and she starts to smile. She quietly reads it to herself.

Momma Angel

Jessika just closes her eyes and just thinks about how that poem has touched home. Her dream as a mother was to have a child that would appreciate her for what she was worth. This poem has done that for her and then some.

"Oh Sam. This is the most beautiful poem I have ever read, or received. Thank you so much Baby." Jessika says as she walks up to Samuel and gives him a hug and a big kiss on the cheek.

"Anything for you Momma. I mean Momma Angel."

"Ok Sam, I will make burgers and fries for dinner tonight."

"Yes Mom. Thank you. This is a good night. I knew this was my best day I have ever had. I made the honor roll, I got a plaque from the Mayor, my momma likes her poem, and I get burgers and fries for dinner. Yes." Samuel says as he runs around the kitchen jumping and shouting.

"Sam calm down. Go upstairs and finish your homework."

"With pleasure, Mom." Samuel says as he runs out the kitchen.

"Sam, you are so crazy." Jessika says as she turns and walks towards the refrigerator. "Finish all your homework or I will change my mind." Jessika says as she opens the freezer to get out the ground meat. Jessika was so caught up in emotions that she forgot about Raymond's schedule.

"I am sure even Raymond will understand that this is a special occasion." Jessika says as she puts the packet of hamburger meat in the sink and turns the water on it so it can defrost. She then goes back to the refrigerator and grabs the potatoes and puts them in the other sink. She gets the potato peeler out of the drawer and starts to peel the potatoes so she can cut them up and fry them. She looks out the window above the sink and she sees her neighbors across the street coming home from the grocery store. They are talking and helping each other bring the groceries in the house. They seem so peaceful with no fussing and no one complaining, they are just doing what needs to be done. Jessika wished her household were like that but Raymond makes it so hard at times with his demands. He must be in control and that is it and no one can have any part of the control.

"Tonight, we are having burgers and fries and that is it." Jessika says as if she is answering the question from Raymond. "What? I don't care what the schedule says, it is burgers tonight." Jessika giggles at how she is saying things like she really means it. "Oh, you don't like burgers and fries; well take your butt to Fry-that-Bird chicken shack. Get a special because it is on me." Jessika says as she pretends to throw money at Raymond. Jessika is laughing so hard that tears start to come out of her eyes. When she finished laughing, she realizes that she will have to face him and he will question her about this. Any other time she has changed the schedule, it resulted in her being beaten. No reason was good enough so Jessika hopes that this reason is a good one. Jessika decides that she needs to rehearse out loud what she wants to say.

"Hey Raymond, I didn't make chicken tonight because your wonderful son made the honor roll. He also received a plaque from the mayor, and you know you voted for him so that should be something to think about. He also wrote a beautiful poem about me. That's right me and not you. What do you think about that?" Jessika says as she starts laughing. "Girl you are funny." Jessika says as she puts the meat in the microwave so it can defrost faster. She then finishes cutting the potatoes and puts them in a deep fryer. She takes the meat, seasons it, and makes five patties out of it and puts them on the grill and prepares the table for dinner. She grabs the same dinnerware that Raymond likes to eat dinner with. Raymond made Jessika buy three different type of dinnerware to use at all three meals. He was big on having things his way. She had to lay out a knife, spoon, and fork regardless of if they were going to use them. She had to have two napkins, one for the lap and one to lay the silverware on. The drinks had to be on the right-hand side, totally regardless of the fact Jessika and Samuel were left-handed. Jessika knew the repercussions of not having the table set up. It cost her a night in the hospital the last time it wasn't done correctly. Jessika then checks her fries and flips the burgers over.

"Momma, turn the fan on. You are smoking up the whole house."

"Yes sir." Jessika says as she turns the fan on over the stove.

"It smells good too. Remember I want mine burnt."

"I know. You only tell me every time I cook you a burger. What did I tell you about my memory?" Jessika asks as she knows what Samuel is going to say.

"You have a memory like a lost dog."

"Exactly."

"Too bad you are still lost." Samuel says as he bursts out laughing.

"Hey you. Watch yourself." Jessika says as she tries to hide her giggles.

"You left yourself open for that."

"I bet you have been waiting to say that for a long time." Jessika says as she shakes her head at Samuel.

"Ever since I first thought of it, I have been holding it in."

"How about you make some Kool-Aid for us to drink."

"Yes. I am going to mix red, green, and purple Kool-Aid together. Do you know what that makes?"

"No, what?"

"Red, green, and purple Kool-Aid."

"Not funny comedian, stick to writing poems."

"Don't hate, just congratulate."

"That is so played out. Why don't you think of something else?"

"Don't hate, just assimilate."

"Use a word you understand." Jessika says as she knows that he just said a word that rhymes.

"Don't hate, just wait."

"Oh boy, please stop already."

"Where is the bag of sugar at mom?" Samuels asks as he looks in the container that the sugar is normally kept in.

"In the cabinet but don't put the whole bag in there. I want to be able to go to sleep tonight."

"How about I put 95% of the bag in there?"

"Don't play."

"Ok, 75%."

"Look, I don't want diabetes nor do I want to go into a sugar coma."

"Ok, ok. You are going to love this Kool-Aid. I am going to stir it with my hand and everything." Samuel says as he rolls up his sleeves to emphasize his joke.

"You stir it with your hand and you will be the only person drinking it."

"Ok, more for me then. I better not catch you drinking any once you realize how good it tastes."

"Hey, hurry up so we can be ready for your daddy who should be home at any minute."

"You had to ruin the mood, you are a mood killer." Samuel says as he shakes his head.

"Whatever."

Samuel measures his sugar so it would be the right sweetness and adds it to the water. He takes a large wooden spoon and stirs it. Once it was stirred to his liking, he gets a small spoon and tastes it. His eyes got big and he gave Jessika the thumbs up, letting her know he likes the Kool-Aid.

"Ok the burgers and fries are ready. Let's get them prepped so they can be eaten, doctor." Jessika says in her best nurse impersonation.

"Nurse call out the tools." Samuel says as he loves to play this game with Jessika.

"Ok, we have mustard!"

"Check."

"We have ketchup!"

"Check."

"We have mayo!"

"Hey nurse, that is the wrong procedure. This is burgers not chicken sandwiches."

"Sorry Doctor. Will you forgive me?"

"Only if I can have a sundae for dessert."

"We will see."

Ring

"I got it." Samuel says as runs out of the kitchen to answer the phone.

Ring

Jessika finishes drying off the fries and puts all the food and condiments on the table.

"That was dad and he said he wouldn't be home for another twenty minutes so he said we could start without him."

"Are you sure he said that?" Jessika asks because Samuel knows better than to play when it comes to his father.

"Yes ma'am. I wouldn't lie about that. I know how he is."

"Ok then. Let's eat." Jessika says as she is happy to be able to enjoy this meal with Samuel. If Raymond was here, there would be an awkward silence. He didn't approve of most conversations at the table so they had to wait until he brought a topic up.

"Good because I want it to be just me and you." Samuel says as he sits down and the table and looks over the food.

"That will make it special. Just me and my Sam eating burgers and fries which is a meal fit for a king."

"Hey, can we eat like they do in the movies?"

"What do you mean?" Jessika asks not understanding Sam's question.

"Let's get candles like they have in the movies."

"Oh, you mean a candle light dinner. You want to have one with your Mom? Are you sure you don't want your first one to be with your girlfriend?" Jessika asks knowing what Samuel reaction would be.

"Don't make me throw up. Girls are too much trouble."

"Sam, are you trying to say that your mom is too much trouble?"

"Not you mom but those Chicken heads."

"Chicken who?"

"Chicken heads. You know girls."

"Sam, I don't want you calling girls that. I have taught you better than that."

"Everyone calls them that." Samuel says trying to plead his case.

"So, what if they called their moms hood rats, would you call me that?"

"Of course." Samuel says as he bursts out laughing to show Jessika he was playing.

"Boy Sam, I wish you would call me a chicken head or a hood rat. We would definitely fight."

"If I did that and we were to fight. If I asked you to meet me outside to fight and if I don't show up in five minutes, would you start without me?"

"Sam, you think I am that dumb?"

"You told me to never ask a question that I didn't want to know the answer to so I wouldn't ask that question of I was you."

"Smarty pants. You are lucky you are cute so just pour me some of that syrup that you call Kool-Aid."

"Sure, no problem, do you want them on the rocks?"

"What do you know about that?"

"I got that from that movie you told me not to watch."

"I believe you too. Hey, put that burger down and bless our food."

"Yes ma'am." Samuel says as he says the prayer with a mouth full of food. Jessika watches him and she smiles. She then watches him take another bite of his burger.

"How is your burger?" Jessika asks expecting to hear how much Sam liked it.

"I have had better." Samuel says as he tries not to laugh.

"Oh yeah, well it is the last one I will make you."

"Yeah right."

"I am serious."

"Oh, hi Serious. My name is Samuel, glad to meet you." Samuel says as he holds out his hand to Jessika.

"Sam, you are a knucklehead." Jessika says as she takes a bite of her burger and it was so good. She was enjoying it because just like Samuel mentioned earlier, they haven't had burgers in a while.

"The burger is good but the fries taste funny."

"What do you mean? It must be the grease. Does it taste like fish?"

"No, it tastes like potatoes."

"You are getting on my nerves." Jessika says as she rolls her eyes at Samuel.

"Oh, then I better sit over here then." Samuel says as he gets up and moves to the chair next to him. "Next time could you tell me where you put your nerves so I won't get on them?"

"You are on a roll tonight. I wish your daddy was here to see your act."

"Not me."

"Sam. Thinking like that won't make the situation any easier."

"I don't want it to be easier, I don't want to even be a part of it." Samuel says as he begins to eat some of his fries. Jessika hated to hear that but it was her thought as well.

"I understand. We would be happier if things changed."

"A lot happier. This dinner we are having right now is special to me."

"I feel the same way Sam, I really do." Jessika knew that if she had any courage she would make it a reality but deep down inside she was scared to try to do anything like leaving.

"I wish he would be late every day." Samuel says as he stuffs his mouth with his last piece of burger. Jessika nods her head in agreement.

"Sam, take your time before you choke on that burger."

"Mom, hurry up so we can race drinking our Kool-Aid. You know; taking it to the head."

"I am thinking about taking Netflix off your television. You know too much."

"Knowing and doing is two different things."

"Whatever Smarty pants."

"Come on mom. Finish it."

"Ok." Jessika says as she stuffs her mouth with her last bit of burger.

"Oh, that is real classy Mom." Samuel says as Jessika shows the chewed-up burger in her mouth.

"Come on then. The loser has to clean up the kitchen." Jessika says as she grabs her glass.

"Cool. I hope you like dishpan hands." Samuel says as he begins to smile.

"We'll see. Hey, make sure the cups have the same amount in them." Jessika says as she watches Samuel pour more Kool-Aid in their glasses. He set the glasses next to each other and gave it the sight test.

"Ready?" Samuel asks as he raises his cup.

"I was born ready." Jessika says as she raises her cup too. "One, two, three GO!" Jessika says as they start to guzzle their Kool-Aid. It was hard for her to keep a straight face because Samuel had Kool-Aid coming out his mouth while he was trying to keep up with Jessika.

"How did you do that?" Samuel asks, as he is amazed at how fast Jessika finishes her drink.

"I have always let you win." Jessika says as she wipes her mouth. "Get those hands ready, because it's busting suds time, Loser."

"Remember like you tell me. Don't rub it in." Samuel says as he has a hint of disappointment in his tone.

"Not only are you a loser but a sore loser." Jessika says as she makes an "L" with her fingers and raises it to her forehead.

"Hey no name-calling, remember?" Samuel says as his smile quickly turns into a look of fear and he is frozen in place. Jessika looks at Samuel and then she realizes that he is looking at the kitchen door. Jessika knew instantly what was wrong because now she was also scared. She was having so much fun that she forgot that she would have to explain to Raymond why she changed the schedule.

"JESSIKA!"

Jessika jumps up out of her sleep and immediately looks towards the hospital door. Her eyes focus and she realizes that no one is there. She lies back down and checks the clock. She has been asleep three hours. She knew she needed more rest so she can be well enough to go see Samuel. So, she reaches for the pain cord and presses it so the painkillers could take effect. She felt a funny sensation in her arm as the painkillers start to work its way through her system. Before she knew it, she was dozing back to sleep again. The only motivational factor to sleep was being well enough to be with Samuel. She was willing to risk having a nightmare about Raymond again in the process. She knew that thinking about him brought her mental pain but she can handle that if the physical pain goes away. It seemed to be a fair trade to Jessika.

Jessika's

Dilemma

Chapter 3

"The Heartache"

"Jessika, these headshots right here are my favorite. Your beautiful skin is glowing on these so I will use these on the website." Sara says as she points to one of the pictures her and Jessika were looking at.

"I really like that one." Jessika says as she notices how great her pictures look.

"We are going to do a total upgrade on our website and I would be crazy to not use you as the first model they see."

"Wow, Sara you are too kind."

"Flawless Jess. You are a natural. We have a new client that wants you to model her new line of clothing and I agreed that you would be perfect."

"What? I am so honored Sara." Jessika says as she looks over the photos that Sara picked out. It was from her last photo shoot a month ago.

"Jessika, you are our top model and I will do all I can to promote you because it is a win-win situation for both of us."

"Thank you. I appreciate all the work you give me"

"I would give you more if you only had the time. I know that your husband and son are important to you so I will never overstep my boundaries but you could stand to make double or even triple the amount of money you make now if I could have you full time like you were a few years ago."

Jessika hated to hear that. Modeling is her life but Raymond makes it so hard on her. All his rules and overbearing jealousy that he has for Jessika makes it hard for her to do what makes her happy. He wasn't happy that she began to make more money than him and once she began to work more, he was upset that she wasn't home as often as he felt she should.

"I want to work like I did a few years ago but with my son only being a year-old right now, I don't want him in a daycare so I will stay at home with him until he goes to school. Then I will be able to get back into the swing of things." Jessika says as she avoids making eye contact with Sara because she lied with a straight face. She didn't work like she once did because of her husband. He has stymied her growth in her profession for years now. Jessika began an ascent to where she was being noticed in New York and a few agencies reached out to her to see if she could be a fill in just in case they needed a model. The thought that she could one day be on a world stage modeling has been her dream since she first started modeling but her dream seemed so far away because of her controlling husband.

"I do want you to know that this client right here will give you a chance to make a ton of money but she also wants to take you with her on the road as she travels promoting her clothing line. She has so many rich and famous clients that it will give you a chance to make a bigger name for yourself and give my modeling agency the respect it deserves. Think about this chance of a lifetime and what will come of this." Sara says as she looks at Jessika and Jessika knows that look. She has seen it in many board meetings and it is a look of confidence. When Sara spoke, and acted the way she is acting now it means that this is a sure thing and you can take it to the bank. Jessika loved the sales pitch and she so desperately wanted to travel and see the world. She has never left Houston and she was dying inside because of that fact. If this was her big break she wanted to make the most of it besides she could use some time away from Raymond but there was no way she was going to leave Samuel behind.

"Sara, that sounds so good and that is something I could only dream off but I can't leave Sam and travel."

"I told the client you would say that and that's why they said you can bring him with you. Look Jessika, they fell in love with your pictures and I assured them that you would be a wonderful asset to her team of models. So, think about making six figures or more and traveling for no more than five months out of the year. Six figures in five months is a great deal."

"You are right Sara that is life changing money right there. Do you mind if I make a phone call to my husband and talk it over with him?"

"Sure, no problem. I will keep my fingers crossed." Sara says as she crosses her fingers and smiled. Jessika knew in her heart that it will take more than crossed fingers for her to get the okay, it will take an act of God. Jessika knew she had to ask because she wasn't going to let this opportunity pass her by without trying. The only thing that felt funny about this situation is that she feels like a child asking their parent to go on a field trip. It doesn't feel like she is bringing up a chance to make more money and enhance her career to her spouse who would jump at the opportunity to have a successful wife but no she must beg him to let her be who she wants to be. Jessika walks to her office and closes the door. She walks to the window that gives her a great view of downtown Houston. Her heart is beating fast and her nervousness is making her feel nauseous. She takes a few deep breaths and calls Raymond on her cellphone. As the phone is ringing, Jessika begins to pray that Raymond would let her do this one thing. She hasn't asked for much in their marriage because she knew he would say no. She couldn't hang out with friends, take time for herself or do anything without him knowing. He decided what is best for her and that is the way it has been for years. As soon as the phone stopped ringing and Jessika could tell he accepted the call, she began to sweat and feel light headed because she was afraid to ask him what she needed to.

"What do you want?" Raymond snapped at her and Jessika wished she never called him at all.

"Hey Baby, how are you doing?" Jessika asks trying to sound as normal as possible. Even though he treated her like dirt she still spoke to him in a loving manner even though it crushed her inside to do it.

"Look stupid, I said what do you want? Why does it matter how I am doing?"

Jessika took the phone away from her ear as she fought back tears. She longed to hear him say one thing good to her and not always talk to her with an attitude. No matter how hard she tries to be nice he kills it with evilness.

"Baby I was trying to see how your day was going and to ask you a question." Jessika says without letting Raymond know she was getting emotional.

"Well, retard I don't have time for questions. I am at work and you are bothering me. Didn't I tell you never to call me unless it's an emergency?" Raymond asked in an aggressive tone that let Jessika know that she made a big mistake calling him.

"Yes, you did but I just wanted to run something by you to see what you think."

"You knew that but you did what you wanted to do. You are going to pay dearly for not doing what I tell you to do. You are not to change my rules because of how you feel."

"Baby I wasn't trying to change your rules. I have received some good news and I just wanted to know how you feel about it. I promise you I would never try to change your rules. You know that." Jessika says to reassure Raymond of his authority over her.

"You say that yet you are going against my rules as we speak. I got news for you. When you get home, make my dinner and take your ugly looking self into our bedroom and sit there until I get home."

"Okay baby." Jessika says as her tears run down her face. The degrading way he treats her hurts her more than the physical beatings.

"You better be in the bedroom because I will call and check and the house phone better ring once. If it rings more than once you will get a worse beating than the one I am going to give you anyway.

"Okay." Jessika says as she shakes her head wishing things wasn't this way.

"Okay what?" Raymond asked as his voice got sterner.

"Okay Baby."

"Now that you understand that, what was the reason why you called me?" Raymond asks to let Jessika know that she was getting on his nerves.

"Well." Jessika says and pauses because she was terrified to ask him. The excitement she had for the news was now gone.

"Well what? You are wasting my time stalling. This is one of the reasons I hate you so much. All you do is waste my time with stupid stuff. I have so much more important things to do that to sit here and talk to you."

"Baby I was offered a contract with a clothing line."

"NO!"

"I will make six figures or more."

"NO!"

"I will only have to travel for about five months out of the year."

"NO!"

"I can even bring Sam with me so that will be no burden on you."

"NO! Didn't you hear me the first time? You just had to keep on asking me."

"I wanted to at least let you hear the full news."

"Look here idiot, I heard plenty when you first opened your stupid mouth. No, you can't accept that contract."

"Baby that will help us so much." Jessika pleads for him to change his mind. She was going to use this contract to have freedom from him.

"Okay I tell you what you can do. You go in there and tell that slut Sara that you are not accepting that contract.

"Baby no." Jessika says as her heart felt like it stopped beating. She wanted that contract more than anything else.

"You heard me you, ugly jungle dog. That white woman is pimping you and you are too dumb to realize that. Look at you the black coon, thinking that they think your ugly butt is a model. You are dark as crap, skinny as a toothpick and dumb as a rock. They want to parade you around in a circus. Look at the black toothpick. That is why you joined that white modeling agency because you have no shape at all. You would get laughed right out the door at a black one because you have no butt, no breasts and you are shaped like an eleven-year-old boy. You the blackest model they have and they parade you around so they can say they have at least one black model. You better do all your modeling during the day because at night, they wouldn't be able to see you. So, Aunt Jemima, go tell Sara that you don't want that contract and get your butt home. I give you twenty minutes to be home so with traffic you will cut it close but that home phone better ring once or I will come home and beat you, you ugly retarded ape. So, take your coal black butt in there and say what you have to say." Raymond says as he hangs up the phone. Jessika sat there for a second stunned but she knew she couldn't sit there long because she needed to get home fast to avoid an extra beating. So, she walks out her office and let the tears flow because she was tired of trying to hold them in. She was hurt, disrespected and upset. As soon as she made it to Sara's office, she tried all she could to not breakdown crying because she needed to be home soon.

"Okay Jess, tell me you have good news?" Sara asked as Jessika made it to her office door. Sara's smile went away as soon as she seen Jessika's face. Jessika couldn't say a word so she shook her head no. "Are you okay Jess?"

"I have to go." Jessika says as she turns and walks away. She didn't give Sara a chance to stall her because she needed to go home as fast as she possibly can.

"I hate him." Jessika says as she stops thinking about that moment that took place nine years ago. She has had plenty of time to reflect as she sits here looking out her hospital window. She has been anxiously waiting on Sonya to come and get her so she can visit Samuel. She had been pacing all morning waiting for this moment to be with Samuel again. Her anger over what has taken place over the years was seeping up in her spirit as she was thinking about that day. That moment felt like so many others as the same kind of degrading comments were almost as common as breathing for her. Jessika wished she had never met Raymond at all.

"Hello Jessika." Sonya says as she walks into the room. She had an even larger smile on her face than usual.

"Why are you smiling so much Sonya?" Jessika asks as Sonya walks into her hospital room.

"One, God is good and two, I have good news." Sonya says as she walks over to Jessika and gives her a big hug.

"Sam is out of his coma?" Jessika asks as her heart starts to beat fast at the prospect of that being true.

"I wish I could tell you that." Sonya says as she shakes her head no.

"What is the good news then?" Jessika couldn't think of anything that was better than that now.

"I don't think you are ready for it."

"Come on Sonya." Jessika was getting annoyed with Sonya since she wouldn't just come out and say what she was going to say.

"I will tell you in a few but I can tell you this news, Jessika the doctor said to give him thirty minutes and then you can go in and see Samuel."

"Alright, that is what I am talking about. It has been a long four days waiting to get well."

"You did what you had to do and that was get rest. We all know once you get in his room you are not going to want to leave."

"Oh, I already have a plan."

"I figured that, so I left extra blankets and pillows in there for you."

"Thank you so much Sonya, you are heaven sent." Jessika says as she gives Sonya a hug. She thought it was so sweet of Sonya to ensure she had everything she needed.

Sonya has been there for her giving her updates on Samuel as well as spending time with him when she was done with her shift.

"I think heaven bound is better." Sonya says as she gives Jessika a wink.

"You have helped me so much through the years and I never really told you how much I truly appreciate you. I can't even count the times I have been here and you are always willing to help me. That means so much to me."

"It is my pleasure and my duty as a Christian. Ever since the first time you came in here broke down from being abused, I promised myself that I would help you overcome. You are at the point now where you must decide if you will do what it takes to not only get past this, but to move forward."

"I know I have God and you by my side, so I don't see how I can't draw strength from that."

"Praise be to God. That is exactly what I am talking about. God is working things out for you. He is shaking up your life because you have never heeded to what he wants from you. Now you are faced with a circumstance that you need to call on God for all the necessary skills to succeed."

"That is so true Sonya. These past four days, I have found a new love for Christ and strength that I didn't know I had. I hate that it took something so drastic to make me realize that."

"Don't look at it as a bad thing. This whole situation will play itself out and you will see the true plan of God."

"You are right."

"Believe me Jessika, God is working."

"I am glad he is because I need him more than ever."

"While we are talking about God working, I am going to tell you something that you might not want to hear, but it is good news." Sonya says as she sits down on the sofa by the window and motions for Jessika to join her. Jessika was feeling funny about what Sonya wanted to tell her but she sat next to her anyway.

"I am not sure what to make of that statement. What is it?" Jessika asks because she was curious but she didn't know what Sonya was going to say.

"It is not about Sam, it is about Raymond." As soon as Sonya said that, Jessika's nervous smile went away and it was replaced with a look of disgust.

"Nothing short of him being dead will be good news." Jessika says with a tone that showed she meant every word. All these years of putting up with abuse after abuse, Jessika was ready for it to be over and mentally she was ready.

"Come on Jessika. One of the first things you must realize about God's plan is that it is just that; his plan. He is working on things we don't understand or don't see."

"So, what is it then? What could be so great about Raymond that I would want to know?"

"Well, I went by to tell Raymond about Samuel's condition and you know how much he likes me."

"A lot. A whole lot." Jessika says laughing. Raymond hated the sight of Sonya. Every time Sonya would call the house he would huff and puff about how she wanted to pray with him. He did not like church at all and he did not like the fact that people tried to get him to go.

"Right, well I was expecting him to yell at me and tell me to get out like he always does. Instead, he notices me peeking my head in and he actually invites me in."

"What." Jessika says with a confused look on her face.

"I know. So, I walk in and I say I have news about Samuel and he immediately breaks down and starts crying."

"No way. I don't believe you. There is no way that man cried. He didn't cry when his mother had a heart attack and died alone in her apartment. She was the only family that he spent time with."

"I am telling you Jessika that man broke down in tears but let me finish."

"Alright but this story is already unbelievable." Jessika says as she feels she really could care less about Raymond but she knew that Sonya was intent on telling her anyway.

"Like I said he breaks down and starts to cry and I mean real tears were streaming down his face. He starts to blame himself and he went on to say how sorry he was for doing what he did."

"Uh-uh Sonya. I can't believe that at all. That is not the Raymond that I know. Are you sure you were in the right room? Are you sure he is not taking in too much pain killers?"

"Nope he is being monitored just like everyone else that is using them."

"There has to be a reason he is being nice. It must be the fact that he is going to jail. You know how he is Sonya. He hates any and everything that has control over him. That is why every time he came to see his mom when she was at the hospital; he would cause a scene because he wanted to do things his way. How about that time he got his appendix taken out and he acted a fool the whole time? I am not buying into what he is doing."

"Jessika look at you. Can you not see God at work?"

"I don't mean any disrespect but that man has no concept of God. I think anything short of evil possessing him, would change him."

"So, you are telling me that God cannot fix even Raymond?"

"I am not saying that, it is just hard to believe that a few days in the hospital would change him from pure evil to a saint."

"You know what most Christians problems are; their faith. We don't give God credit for things; we immediately try to find other motives for people changing their lives. For all we know, Raymond is ready to change."

"He could be setting you and me up so that he can finish the job. He just wants the hospital to let their guard down and then he will take full advantage of the situation. He has done it the past with my parents, some of our neighbors and at his job."

"Jessika, thinking like that is what is hindering you from fully receiving God's blessing."

"I can't help it Sonya. That man has beat me for seventeen years." Jessika says as she starts crying. "I have been beaten and humiliated time after time. I can't remember going a whole week without receiving some type of physical or mental abuse. That man has made my life hell and I never once received a kind word from him. Not once has he ever thanked me for doing something. He has never hugged or kissed me unless he wanted to be intimate. He never treated me like his wife or even an adult for that matter. It was always him telling me what to do and how to do it. I couldn't do anything I wanted or needed to do. I was constantly under his control."

"I am sorry Jessika." Sonya says as she gives Jessika a hug. Jessika needed a hug but she didn't want to receive the information on Raymond. She was perfectly happy with the old Raymond being hurt in the hospital waiting to be taken to jail.

"I have suffered so much Sonya, because of him. I have never seen a good day from him or any emotion other than anger or lust. Never love and I needed that more than anything. Thank God for Samuel because he gave me love but it still wasn't the kind of love I needed."

"I understand what you feel, Jessika. It is all right to feel that way. I just don't want you to overlook what God is doing, that's all."

"I won't. I just will have to see it to believe it."

"What are you waiting on? Let's go now."

"No way. I am not going to go now. I am not ready for that." Jessika says as she starts to backtrack on her words.

"When will you be ready?" Sonya asks calling Jessika on her bluff.

"After I see Sam, then I will go see him."

"Stop that Jessika. You know that once you see Samuel you are not going to leave him to go see Raymond. We won't be able to pry you from Samuel's room."

"I just don't want to. There I said it. I really don't care about that man."

"Well guess what? I am not taking no for an answer. You don't have to speak to him, I just want you to peek in on him."

"I don't know Sonya. Can you at least see if it is time for me to go see Sam?"

"Let me check and see." Sonya says as she gets on her two-way radio and asks for the doctor in charge of Samuel's care.

"Yes Dr. Page, this is Nurse Sonya. I am checking to see how long before Samuel's mother can visit him." Sonya asks as Jessika moves closer to her so she can hear his response. "Ok, twenty minutes. Thank you, doctor."

Jessika immediately looked away. She didn't want to hear that but she knew she had no way around it now. Sonya was going to make her go even if she had to force her.

"Well." Sonya says as she smiles as if to say, you have no excuse.

"Ok, let's go." Jessika says in a way to show she really didn't want to do it.

"Open your heart to what God is doing Jessika."

"I will try."

"That is all I am asking." Sonya says as she walks towards the door to Jessika's room and motions with her head for Jessika to get up and follow her. Jessika stands up and slowly starts to walk towards Sonya.

"It isn't going to hurt you to see God's work in progress."

"I know." Jessika says as she knows that she must swallow her pride and go see what Sonya is making a big deal about.

Jessika walks up to Sonya, starts to smile, and enters the hallway. Jessika is sort of nervous because this is her first time out of her room since she was admitted four days ago. As Jessika is walking the hallway, she feels awkward because as she passes by people, they are taking prolonged glances at her. She then realizes that she has this huge bandage on her face from the cut. She would rather them stare at the bandage than at the over one hundred stitches in her face. Good thing for her is that they are going to dissolve soon. She is healing up nicely and the cut is long but it wasn't as deep as she thought so the scar will be there but not as pronounced.

"Good afternoon Ms. Cotta. How are you feeling today?"

"I feel good Nurse Nancy. Thanks for asking."

"My pleasure. Good afternoon to you too, Sonya"

"Good afternoon and God bless you Nancy. Thanks for understanding."

"No problem Sonya."

"That was sweet of her to let you take over caring for me." Jessika says as she walks gingerly down the hall.

"She knows how much you mean to me." Sonya says as she grabs Jessika's arm to help guide her. Jessika was still sore and by the amount of pain she has felt, she could have sworn that she was hit by a car.

"Well I am thankful and it goes without saying."

"The elevators are over here." Sonya says as she redirects Jessika. They get on the elevator and they ride down to the 2nd floor.

"I am so nervous." Jessika says as she fights the urge to throw up. She was starting to have a nervous sweat and she wanted to back out of this plan Sonya has.

"I am here so don't you worry." Sonya says as she grabs Jessika's hand.

"What if he sees me?"

"Hold on then." Sonya says as she once again gets on her two-way radio and calls for the nurse in charge of Raymond's care. "Oh, he is in counseling with the doctor, ok thanks." Sonya says as she starts smiling.

"What?"

"He won't even know you are there. His doctor is talking to him, and they usually stand near the window so the patient will be looking away from the door. You will be fine."

"If you say so Sonya, I better not see him looking at me." Jessika says as she imagines walking to Raymond's room and he notices her and rushes at her to finish what he started four days ago.

Jessika can't believe she let Sonya talk her into doing this. After all he has done to her in her life; she wants to see him suffering way more than she wants to see him being content. Jessika doesn't know what she will gain out of seeing him. How will this bless her in any way? In her mind, it won't and that is why she does not want any part of this little reunion of sorts. Changed or not, the fact is he is still Raymond and that makes it hard to accept.

"Alright his room is the 3rd door on the left. Are you ready?"

"Yeah, ready to throw up."

"You are funny, Jessika. I got you and don't you worry. Just remember God is in control."

Jessika can feel her heart picking up pace with every step. She was sure that she was going to have a heart attack. She knew she wasn't over the fact that a few days ago, he tried to kill her. That scares her more than anything because that showed her what he is capable of. Jessika figured that once she got to his room and looked in he would feel her standing there and look at her and wink an evil wink. A wink that was basically saying, "I am just waiting patiently until I can finish what I started."

"Alright. Go ahead and look for yourself." Sonya says as they make it to Raymond's hospital room.

"Make sure he isn't looking first." Jessika says as she pushes Sonya towards the door. She was very skeptical because the last few times they came to the hospital, he acted a fool the whole time. Jessika was so embarrassed that she checked herself out early just so they could leave. He complained every hour on the hour as he tried to fix the situation the way he wanted it to be to where even the hospital gave in to a few of his demands.

"Ok, I will." Sonya says as she looks in the room.

"Well?"

"He isn't even looking this way."

"Ok." Jessika says as she lets Sonya step out of the way and she leans over just enough, so she can see Raymond. Immediately her heart starts to race even more. Ninety-six hours ago he was trying to kill her. She hasn't even laid eyes on him since then and she was starting to get that same scary feeling she had before he was shot. Jessika looks at him and she too noticed something that she had never seen before. Jessika looks harder and then at Sonya.

"I told you he was different." Sonya says grinning.

"I can't believe this. He isn't acting a fool and carrying on. He is just sitting there and he is listening and being attentive. He must be on anti-depressants."

"Jessika, I told you he wasn't so stop taking the glory from God." Sonya says in a scolding way. Jessika knew she deserved it. She could not believe that Raymond was sitting there calm. He was smiling and she hasn't seen that since before they got married. He was being courteous and looking the doctor and nurse in the eye.

"I need to hear what they are talking about. There must be something in that conversation that is helping him calm down."

"Alright, but you will miss a blessing by trying to find a reason to prove it wrong."

"Sonya, you have to understand that I haven't seen him this way since we first met. That was seventeen years ago and that man is whom I made myself love. This man here, I have nothing but hate and discontent for. Of course, I am going to second guess it."

"Alright. Hold on." Sonya says as she presses a button to make the two-way radio vibrate. It gets the nurse's attention in the room who looks towards us. Sonya points to the lady's two-way radio and mouths out that she wants to hear what Raymond is saying. The nurse could make out what she was saying, she looks back towards Raymond, and she press the button on the two-way radio so we could hear what was being said.

"Ok, so I can start moving around tomorrow and if all goes well you won't have to remove the second bullet from me?"

"Yes Mr. Cotta. You will have some pain but the meds they are giving you should help you with that. Other than that, it will take about a week or two before we put you back on solid foods and then you will be discharged."

"Thank you doctor and you too nurse. I do appreciate all you have done for me the past four days."

"You are welcome. Just get some rest." The doctor says as he walks out of the room. Sonya and Jessika turned and faced the other way so the doctor wouldn't know they were listening. Once he gets down the hall, they resumed listening.

"Mr. Cotta is there anything else you are going to need?"

"Yes ma'am. I do need some more ice water so I can relax and read my bible."

Jessika mouth dropped wide open. She could not believe what she has just heard. Not only did he say; "yes ma'am," to the nurse but he said that he was going to read his bible. In seventeen years he never once picked up a bible. He hardly knew anything about the bible or how to even pray. He would try his best to not let her go to church. He hated to hear anything about God and went out of his way to make it known.

"I can't believe it."

"I told you. That is a changed man. Not only that but a man that God has worked on."

"It has only been four days and he is in here. Wait until he gets out, then he will change back."

"What is wrong with you Jessika? Are you afraid that he has changed?"

"There is nothing wrong with me except I am in denial about this whole change of heart."

"It can happen."

"Not to him and not that easy. He is up to something. I know he is."

"Jessika, you are getting on my nerves now. People always knock someone when they change for the Lord."

"Sonya, we don't know if he has changed or gave his life to Christ."

"You are right but I will find out and bring you the news."

"Good and when you do is when I will choose to believe or not."

"Alright."

PAGING NURSE SONYA

PAGING NURSE SONYA

"Let me see what this is about." Sonya says as she walks to the nearest nurse's station. Jessika watches her walk off and she continues to peek at Raymond. She watches him take the bible from a backpack and he smiles and immediately opens the bible up. The nurse walks out of the room and smiles at Jessika and then heads towards the nurse's station. Jessika looks back at Raymond and she watches as he starts to read from the bible. Jessika mouth drops open. She is in total shock behind his behavior. She knows that something is going on with him but she is not sure.

"Jessika."

Jessika turns and she sees Sonya motioning for her to come over to her.

"The doctor said you can see Samuel now."

"Good. Let's go." Jessika says as her heart starts beating fast. She was so excited that she finally gets to go see Samuel that she started to jog to the elevator.

"Slow down." Sonya says as she runs from behind the nurse's station.

"I am sorry. I just want to see my baby so bad. I can't wait to kiss him."

"I know you do."

"I am going to camp out in his room."

"Like I told you before, I have you everything you need in there."

"Everything except my clothes and toiletries and Janice is bringing those things. Oh man. I forgot that she was on her way. She is probably waiting in my room."

"We can go by there before we go to Samuel's room."

"Good."

"It would help if you push the elevator button. Staring at the doors won't make them open up."

"I am sorry Sonya. I am just not thinking right now."

"God bless you girl."

Jessika steps in the elevator and before it closes she thinks back to Raymond and how he has seemed to have made a change. How calm he was and how he was exactly the way he was when they first met. She hadn't seen that part of him in a long time. It was as if that part of him was trapped inside the abusive part and it took him being shot to reverse the personalities.

"Sonya, that was weird."

"What?"

"Seeing Raymond like that. It is like he has a twin. I married the good one but the evil one kidnapped him and I was stuck with the wrong one."

"Sometimes it is like night and day when you change your life. That is how drastic the change will be."

"What if he has changed and that other part died when he got shot?" Jessika asks hoping Sonya could give her answer that would make her situation easier.

"You should be asking yourself that question, not me. What would you do if that is indeed true?"

"I don't know and I am not even going to worry about it. I have got to think about Sam and that is all I am going to focus on. I have to make sure he comes out of his coma and then lives a normal life, even if I have to die trying."

"Just don't forget that in a few days you will have to think about it. He is going to jail and you must talk to him."

"What are you talking about? I don't have anything to say to that man."

"Jessika, you have to talk to him."

"Why Sonya? I don't owe him anything. That man tried to kill me, for crying out loud. You act like I owe him something."

"If Raymond has turned that corner and is finally saved then you owe it to him to forgive him."

"Now Sonya, you are asking for too much. There is no way I can forgive him for all he has done."

"You must because that is the only way you will get past this."

"Oh, excuse me." Jessika says to someone trying to get on the elevator as she gets out of it. "I don't think I can forgive him."

"Have you tried?"

"Sonya, I haven't even thought about it."

"You need to."

"You are asking me to do too much right now."

"Jessika."

"Sonya, I am going to think about Sam and Sam only. I am not going to even go there with Raymond until Sam is well. I don't care if years pass by before I speak to him. It will serve him right."

"Jessika, being ugly is not going to make your situation any better."

"It will feel good, though. I can live with that."

"How can you live with the fact that it is not right?"

"Sonya."

"Jessika, I am going to drop it for now."

"Good."

Jessika knows that this is a problem that is not going to go away. Sonya is not going to be brushed off that easy. She will make sure that Jessika faces Raymond. She will not be able to leave this hospital until she does.

"Sonya, I will do what I have to do. I just need to be about Samuel right now."

"I understand." Sonya says dejected.

"Thank you, Sonya. Say Nurse Nancy, I was expecting a visitor. Has she arrived yet?" Jessika asks.

"Yes Mrs. Cotta. She is in your room now."

"Thank you." Jessika says as she walks towards her room. She looks back, she sees Sonya talking to Nurse Nancy, and she starts to feel bad about their last conversation. Jessika knows that Sonya means well and she has since the first time they met. Sonya has always been right about situations and Jessika knows she doesn't always follow her advice and has paid for it dearly in some cases. Jessika really cannot afford to avoid talking about it.

"Janice?"

"Oh, there you are girl." Janice says as she walks up to Jessika and gives her a hug. "How do you feel?"

"I feel so good today. My soreness is starting to go away and my stitches are going to start dissolving soon so all is well." Jessika says as she is so happy to see Janice.

After what took place four days ago, Jessika is happy that Janice was alright but her car needs a little work. "How you do feel Janice?"

"I am good. I just left my doctor and I am fine. Once these headaches go away then I will be better."

"That is so good to hear. Thank you again for everything. I know I told you already but I feel I can't say it enough. Without you, I might not be here so I owe you big time." Jessika says as she meant every word. Janice has gone above and beyond for Jessika so she will forever be indebted to her.

"Don't mention it. We are family so that is what family does. When I arrived, and saw you wasn't in here, I thought you were already in Samuel's room."

"I haven't been there yet. The doctor needed more time to finish running his tests."

"So, where were you?"

"Promise me that you won't get mad?" Jessika says as she braces herself for Janice's anger.

"You went to go see that fool?" Janice asks as she shakes her head and immediately begins to frown.

"I did but it was Sonya's idea." Jessika answers sounding like a kid blaming her sibling.

"Why would she want you to go see him for? I don't understand."

"Janice, you are not going to believe this but Sonya thinks he got saved."

"Ha-ha, you are right. I don't believe that. I don't think someone that evil could change. That man might be the devil himself."

"I have seen him and there is something different about him."

"If I got shot twice I would change too or if I knew I was going to jail I would be on my best behavior as well. So, what was so different about him?" Janice asks because she was curious to what could be different about Raymond.

"He was just like when I first met him. He was just peaceful and courteous."

"That man is faking. He is acting that way so the judge will have leniency on him. The minute he gets a light sentence, he will do his time and be back on the street harassing you."

"Girl I don't care right now. I just want to go and be with Sam. Let's go girl."

"Ok and here are the things you wanted. I tried to get everything you said but I had a hard time finding some of the things so I stopped by the store and purchased them."

"Thanks. I do appreciate that."

"No problem."

"You want to come with me to see Sam, or do you have to be somewhere?"

"I have time, let's go."

"Let's go meet up with Sonya and she will take us." Jessika says as she grabs one of the bags from Janice and they walk back into the hallway. Jessika was glad to finally be out of her hospital room. No more IV's and no more nurse visits. No more being told to do this and do that. I guess you can say after seventeen years of being told what to do has taken a toll on her and she has a low tolerance for it now.

"You ready?" Sonya says as she meets them halfway down the hall.

"Most definitely." Jessika says as she envisions being in Samuel's room.

"Hey Janice, how are you doing?"

"I am good Sonya and you."

"I am blessed."

Jessika walks ahead of Janice and Sonya because she wants to hurry up and get to Samuel's room. She is longing to be by his side. It has been four and a half days since she seen him and she misses him.

"Come on slow pokes."

"Yes momma." Janice says as she starts to laugh. Sonya just smiles and shakes her head.

"What floor Sonya?"

"Fifth. Jessika, will you calm down."

"I can't help it."

Jessika wanted to just take the stairs and just leave them behind. She wished she didn't ask them to be there. She knew she wanted to go into Samuel's room and lock herself up in there and be alone with him. As the door of the elevator opens up, Jessika notices families sitting in the waiting area. There are people crying and some are just sitting there staring at the wall or the television. Blank expressions on the majority of the people and Jessika could relate to them. Having a child in the hospital is one thing but having your child in intensive care is another thing. No parent wants to see their child hurt or even have a little scratch on them. To have a child in a coma can tear a parent up on the inside. Of course the only thing worse is death but a coma is somewhat of a slow death to the ones that don't recover. Jessika refuses to believe that Samuel will not come out of his coma. She is not even going to think negative. She is going to have faith that God will get him through this and then they can get on with their life together.

"This way Jessika." Sonya says as she grabs Jessika's hand.

"This is so sad to see all these families up here." Janice says as she shakes her head.

"It can break your heart to hear what happened to some of these kids. Many are just accidents but some, well you know the rest." Sonya says as if she knows speaking any further would incriminate Jessika.

Jessika knew her point and she didn't feel like it was directed towards her. Jessika knows she is at fault for what happened to Samuel and she is ok with the blame that comes with it.

"I can only imagine." Janice says as she catches up.

Walking down the hall and looking through some of the open doors, tugs at Jessika's emotions. Seeing children hooked up to machines and surrounded by adults and other children. So many helpless victims to abuse, accidents, or disease is saddening. People don't really realize how fragile children are. Kids are normally going to get hurt and parents can live with that. It is when the parents actions hurt kids is when it goes from okay to something that is very hard to live with.

"Alright Jessika we are here. Do you want to go in first and call us when you are ready or what do you want to do?" Sonya asked

Jessika was glad she asked her that question, because deep down inside she wanted to be alone with Samuel. She didn't want to be interrupted or anything, all she wanted was quiet time with her son.

"Why don't you two go in first and I will wait."

"That is fine. Come on Janice."

"Ok." Janice says as she walks in behind Sonya.

Jessika watched them go inside Samuel's room and before the door closed she felt they were in there too long. She didn't think about the fact that she would be standing only feet from Samuel and she could not see him.

"Be strong Jessika. It won't be long." Jessika says as she tries to get her mind off of Samuel. Jessika looks down the hallway on both sides. She walks in place, then circles, then she walks five steps, turns around, and walks six steps in the other direction and she repeats it and adds on more steps each time. Then she starts to count the floor tiles as she walks because she was just trying to do whatever she could to pass the time. She starts to shadow box and she was all into it. She was pretending to fight Raymond and the thought of that made her punch harder and faster until she was working up a sweat. One of the hospital nurse's walks up on Jessika and Jessika quickly stops and tries to pretend like she was swatting a fly.

"I hope you were winning." The nurse says to let Jessika know she wasn't fooled at all.

Jessika just smiled and once the nurse turned her back, she pretended to box the nurse as she was walking away.

"You don't want any of this." Jessika says to the nurse as she turns the corner.

Jessika then looks back towards Samuel's room door and she was waiting on it to swing open. It seemed like they had been in there a long time but it has only been three minutes. Jessika wanted to knock on the door and tell them to come on out.

"Ok Jessika." Sonya says as she walks out of the room. Janice follows and she is wiping tears off her face. Jessika doesn't say anything she just hugs Sonya and then Janice.

"Call me if you need anything, ok?" Janice says as she kisses Jessika on the cheek.

"I will, Janice. Thanks for everything."

"Alright Jessika, if you need anything I will be at home but if anything happens call me immediately. If I

don't hear from you then I will see you in the morning."
Sonya says as she pats Jessika on the back.

"Be safe and I will see you in the morning." Jessika
says as she watches Sonya walk off. She then looks at the
door to Samuel's room.

"Come on Jessika, it is time." Jessika says as she
pushes the door and walks in. The first thing she notices is
the recliner with a couple of pillows and a comforter,
courtesy of Sonya. She takes a few steps, she sees the foot
of Samuel's bed, and she gets nervous. She was finally in his
room and now she was scared to even approach him. She
felt that at any moment he would sit up and say, 'Momma
look at what you did. It is because of you I am in a coma. All
you had to do was leave him.' She sees that a curtain
surrounds his bed so she walks to where his head would be,
slides her bag to the foot of the recliner, takes a deep
breath, and grabs the curtain and pulls it open. Immediately
tears form in her eyes and she starts to cry. She thought she
was going to be stronger than this. The first look was all it
took to bring out the flood of tears. She just stares at him.
She looks down at him with the bandage on his head where
he landed on the rock. He looked so peaceful, just lying
there motionless except for his chest going up down. She
leans over, kisses him on the forehead, and wipes off one of
her falling tears from his cheek. She grabs his hand and she
just stares at him some more. She always said he was the
most handsome kid she had ever seen and looking at him
now just reassures it. His brown skin that is so smooth, big
brown eyes, cute little lips, long eyelashes, mini afro and his
little frame. The way he is tucked in the bed makes him look
even smaller.

"Oh Sam. I don't even know where to begin. I do want to say I am so sorry. I am very, very sorry. Momma never meant for this to happen. I wish I had done things differently. I look at you now and I can't help but feel bad for what has happened to you. I love you so much and it hurts momma to see you like this. If you can hear me, please know that I would gladly change places with you. I would rather suffer than to see you suffer for a minute. You are all I have Sam. You are it. Nothing else compares to you and I hope you know that. I wish you could give me a sign that you can hear me." Jessika says as her shirt is being spotted with tears. She lowers her head and watches tear after tear fall to the blanket. She knew it would be hard but she couldn't imagine it being like this. It is hard to judge how you would handle a situation that you never been in before. Jessika knew that this was her worst nightmare and since she has to face it, she needs to find the strength.

"Sam I miss you so much. I miss you joking with me and our last conversation was perfect. As a matter of fact, our last meal together was so memorable. That will always be my favorite meal. I wish you could talk right now. I will do anything to hear your voice again. Just one more time is all I am asking. I would even let you call me a hood rat." Jessika says as she laughs for a second. Jessika knew she didn't have the right words to say but the pain in her heart is speaking loud and clear.

"Sam, I remember when I first held you and unlike most babies you were so quiet and peaceful. You just stared at me with those brown eyes and you followed my every movement. I felt at that moment, as I do now, that you were the best thing to ever happen to me. I had some good moments but nothing like holding you for the first time. You were so precious and I told myself then that my life would be dedicated to you." Jessika says as she wipes her face with her hands.

"Then when I put you in the car, you just laid there sleeping in your car seat. Even though it took me about fifteen minutes to finally put the seat in the car correctly, I did it. I sat in the back with you and I kept on peeking at you every time the car came to a stoplight. We stop, I would peek, we stop, and I would peek. I guess you can say that was our first game of peek-a-boo. I wanted Raymond to drive slowly because I didn't want anything to happen. You should have heard those vehicles blowing their horns at us. I didn't care because I wanted you to make it home safely and that was all that mattered to me. We finally made it to our house and the minute I walked in the front door with you, you started screaming your head off. I was so scared and I had no clue what to do. Was that a sign of things to come? Did you know something that you were too small to tell me? Anyway, I got you settled in and I laid in my bed as you slept in your bassinet. I just laid there thinking about how I was so blessed to have you. Even though I had no clue what to do, I felt I was ready for you to be in my life. I had a husband, house, and money. I thought my future was bright, but it didn't take long to find out that it was a mirage. I watched you grow too big for the bassinet and then I kept putting you between Raymond and me so you could sleep with us. I did that because I wanted to be by your side but I also did that so he wouldn't touch me. Then we got you a crib set up in your room and the first night I laid you in the crib, you were so peaceful, but I cried like a baby. I wanted you near me so bad. You quickly outgrew the crib because you would climb right out of it. I remember the first time I caught you doing that. I watched you swing one little leg after another over the side. You let go and fell on your feet and grabbed the crib just in time to keep yourself from falling. You turned around and saw me standing there. The look on your face was classic. You didn't know what to do so you started crying. I was proud of you but I was worried that you were going to hurt yourself. Then you just kept on growing until it was time to go to school. I cried that whole weekend before your first day. I was so scared for you but as usual, you were ready to go. I watched you get out of the car and close the door behind you without a moment of hesitation. I cried and I mean cried that whole day. You were ready to take on the world and I kept on picturing you as my baby. You just kept on growing and doing amazing things. I was so impressed with your accomplishments but your own father wasn't. It was as if he was jealous of the attention you received. I don't know but I am sad to say that he is your father and for that I am sorry. Oh Sam, I could sit here and reminisce all night. I know you have the strength to pull yourself through this and I just know it. Baby I will be right in that chair the whole night and every day until you get out of that coma and I will not leave your side, no matter what." Jessika says as she begins to think about what Samuel would say to that.

"Oh Sam, I know what you would say. You would have said, 'Momma you are so nasty, I knew you didn't take baths because every time you hugged me I could smell you.' Or how about this, 'Not even to change your diaper Momma?' Jessika says as she begins to laugh but the harder she laughed the more tears came out.

"Sam, this is so hard on me. I can't believe I let something happen to you. I can't."

Jessika just sat there looking at him. Not knowing what he is thinking or going through. This is by far the worst thing to ever happen to her. All the physical pain she has been through cannot compare to what she is feeling on the inside, right now. Jessika stands up and walks around the bed. She takes her bags and she places them on the chair as she gets the bag that has her things she will need to take a bath.

"Sam, I am going to take a bath. I will be right over there. I want to be fully refreshed and relaxed when I get in that chair to get some rest." Jessika says just to let him know that she was still here for him. She grabs the bag that had her nightgown, face wash, and things of that nature. She walks over to him and kisses him on the cheek, fights the urge to cry and walks to the bathroom. She turns on the light and sets her bag on the floor by the sink. She then turns around, walks to the bathtub and turns the water on. She walks back to the mirror and she looks at her reflection. She notices the knot on her head, which is much smaller than it was four days ago. She then looks at her bandage and decides that she is going to let the cut air out, so she starts to remove the bandage. As soon as she takes it off, the stitches stand out like a beacon in the night. She runs her finger down the scar, touching each stitch. She pulls her hand away and she looks at the side that has no scar and then to the side with the scar. Jessika knew they would never look the same again. This scar was going to be there forever. No matter if she had enough money to get it fixed or not. In a way, she wanted it there to remind her to do what is necessary next time. She then takes the facial cleanser and begins to wipe the side with no scar, then moves to the other side and gently goes around the scar.

She starts to cry and she has to repeat the process because of the tears. After the third time of repeating it, she just gets frustrated and puts the cleanser away.

"Be strong Jessika. You are still a beautiful woman. Look at your pretty brown skin and Egyptian like eyes. You are a Nubian queen and you're precious in God's eyes." Jessika says as she starts to undress, walk to the tub and steps in. She turns the water off and slowly descends into the hot water. Once she finally sits down, she relaxes as her knees sting slightly from the cuts on them, and once she lies back, her cuts on her back stretch and pull. She ignores the stinging pain and she settles down and just stares at the tiles directly above the tub. This was a moment she needed. She just wanted to relax so when she gets out she can sleep comfortably in the recliner chair. She was excited that she gets to sleep in the room with Samuel and she knew that only through the grace of God, she was able to get to do that. The hospital wanted her to stay under supervision for at least two more days but Sonya pulled some strings so she could be with Samuel. She was going to make sure she took advantage of this opportunity. So, Jessika begins her relaxation ritual. She takes a deep breath, blows it out, and focuses on the water dripping from the faucet. She lets that soothe her to a deep sleep.

Drip

Drip

Drip

Jessika takes another deep breath to relax her body.

Drip

Drip

The dream she has reminds her of the last time Raymond was nice to her, which was few years ago but seemed like a decade.

Drip

Drip

"Hey Momma. I am going fishing. I am going fishing." Samuel says as he jumps on Jessika's bed.

"Huh, what is going on?"

"Daddy is taking me fishing, with Kenny and his Dad." Samuel says as he starts jumping again.

"He is?"

"Yes."

"You want to go?" Jessika asks as she starts to wake up.

"Oh yeah. My best friend Kenny will be there so I will be ok."

"What time is it?"

"Momma it is 5:00 am."

"I need to get some sleep." Jessika says as she pulls the cover over her head.

"Momma get up. I want to eat some pancakes and only you can make them the way I like them. Please Momma, please." Samuel says as he tries to pull the cover from off her head.

"I just want to sleep." Jessika says as she lets go of the cover so Samuel can see her face.

"Jessika that would be nice if you could."

Jessika stopped what she was doing and she looks toward the direction the voice came from.

"What did you say?" Jessika asked.

"I said that would be nice if you could." Raymond says as he walks back towards the bed. Jessika was so surprised to hear him say something nice. Just last night he kicked her in the back and made her sleep on the floor until 3:00 am because she accidentally pulled the covers in her sleep. Now all of a sudden he is nice and that took her by surprise. Just the fact that he said that in a calm voice was enough to make her want to do it.

"Are you saying that so you can get some breakfast too?"

"I am not hungry. I just want Samuel to be well fed as we sit on this boat for the next five hours." Raymond says as he looks at Jessika and continues to be calm.

"Alright. Give me five minutes." Jessika says as she sits up in the bed.

"No, I am giving you 4 minutes and 59 seconds." Samuel says as he runs out of the room.

"I will be in the garage." Raymond says as he touches Jessika on the shoulder and walks out of the room. Jessika sat there and listened for when Raymond would walk into the garage. She then gets up and walks to the bathroom to brush her teeth.

"He is acting strange this morning, touching me and stuff." Jessika says as she grabs her toothbrush and puts toothpaste on it. She then looks at his toothbrush and a thought pops in her head. She looks at the toilet, then his toothbrush, toilet, and then his toothbrush.

"I can't be that mean. I wish I could do it because he deserves it for making me sleep on the floor."

 As soon as she is through brushing her teeth, she starts to wash her face, the telephone rings and she goes over to answer it.

"Hello."

"Good morning Jessika. This is Thomas."

"Oh, hey Thomas."

"Can you tell Raymond to bring his designs with him? I want to look at them."

"Ok I will."

"Did he tell you the good news?"

"No what good news?"

"I am thinking about making him a job offer. I told him that I would look at his work and if it is something I can work with, the job is his."

"Oh that would be great. I will definitely tell him."

"Ok I will talk to you later Jessika. Bye"

"Bye." Jessika says as she hangs the phone up. Now things were starting to make sense. Jessika knew there had to be a reason Raymond was nice to her. It boils down to him getting a new job. She should have known that money always make him act different. He sees this as an opportunity to make more money so he is trying to be in the right frame of mind. He was okay with more money as long as he was making it. Jessika had plenty of opportunities to make twice as much as what he was making but he wouldn't let her. He didn't want her to make more money than him because he used it as something else to degrade her about.

"Oh well." Jessika says as she finishes washing her face.

"Momma, your time is almost up."

"Can't a girl get a break?"

"Nope."

"That is not nice, Sam."

"Neither is looking at your face."

"Sam, I am going to get you." Jessika says as she chases after Samuel. This was the highlight of her life. Samuel always brought the best out of any situation. He always knew what to say to bring a smile to her face and she loved him more because of it.

"Momma you are too slow." Samuel says as he makes his way into the kitchen. Jessika comes in breathing hard.

"There she is folks, the loser." Samuel says as he points at Jessika.

"I let you win."

"I let you win." Samuel says mockingly.

"Sam."

"Sam."

"Stop it."

"Stop it."

"Stop saying everything I say."

"Stop saying everything I say."

"Sam, stop copying me."

"Sam, stop copying me."

"You know I don't like you copying me."

"Why?"

"Because it is not nice."

"Why?"

"It just isn't."

"Why?"

"Sam don't make me hurt you."

"Why?"

"Sam." Jessika says as she gives him a stern look.

"You are boring." Samuel says to show his disappointment.

"You knuckle head." Jessika says as she walks over to him and kisses him on the cheek.

"Yuck." Samuel says as he wipes off her kiss.

"I love you Sam."

"I can't blame you."

"You love me?"

"Maybe."

"What if I don't make these pancakes then?"

"Momma I love you so much. You know that." Samuel says as he runs up and gives Jessika a hug.

"I knew you would change your mind." Jessika says as she gets out the ingredients to make the pancakes. She then hears the door that opens up to the garage shutting and she listens closely to see if Raymond was coming towards the kitchen because she didn't know if he changed back to the regular Raymond and she didn't want to get caught by surprised if he does something to her.

"Sam you have fifteen minutes to eat." Raymond says as he sticks his head in the door.

"Hey Baby, Thomas called and he said for you to bring your designs with you."

"Cool. Thanks Jessika." Raymond says as he closes the door and walks away. Jessika and Samuel look at each other with a surprised look on their faces.

"What? That is it? No retard or stupid."

"Sam, stop it." Jessika says, as she knows she thought the same thing. Something about this job has gotten him acting nice. Jessika is hoping he gets the job because maybe it would make things better for her.

"You two didn't play kissy face last night, did you?"

"What!" Jessika says with an embarrassed look on her face.

"You know. Kissy face." Samuel says as puckers his lips up and pretends to kiss his hand.

"Sam, I can't believe you asked me that. Don't you forget I am your mother."

"Yeah, my kissy face mother." Samuel says as he stands up.

"Sam you better stop calling me that. That is not nice." Jessika says trying to hold in her smile.

"Baby, I just loves you so much." Samuel says in his best Jessika impression. "Well stupid, I love you too." He says in his best Raymond impression. Jessika just bursts out laughing as she flips the pancakes over. She knew Samuel had a way to always make her laugh.

"Is that what happened or what?"

"That definitely didn't happen last night and I can't even believe that I am answering this question. Why are you asking me that?"

"I am asking you that because he is acting nice. This movie I saw last week…"

"That is what I am talking about. Sam you are not supposed to be watching movies like that."

"What are you going to do? You can't erase my mind so let me finish."

"I am not through with you."

"Anyway, this man was real nice to this woman the next day because he was kissy face with her."

"What am I going to do with you?"

"Make me pancakes."

Jessika just smiles as she puts the pancakes on a plate and hands it to Samuel.

"I need some syrup, butter, honey, and jam. Waitress, I am not going to leave you a tip. This is the worst service, ever." Samuel says as he pretends to be an angry customer.

"I will get right to it."

Jessika loved how spontaneous Samuel was with his jokes and characters. He could make any situation better by pretending.

"Here is your syrup, honey, butter and jam, sir. Anything else?"

"How about some hush."

"Hush? What is that?"

"That is when you be quiet and let me eat." Samuel says as he bursts out laughing.

"Sam you are too much, but I love you."

"I can't blame you."

"You love me, right?"

"A little."

Jessika just smiled because she knew how much Samuel truly loved her.

"Sam, you better hurry up because you have five minutes." Jessika says as she makes her a cup of coffee with her Keurig.

"No I don't."

"Yes you do. You have five minutes."

"Why are you trying to blame stuff on me?"

"Sam, what are you talking about?" Jessika asks because she was confused by what he was saying.

"You accused me of having five minutes and I never took any five minutes. I don't even know where you keep five minutes so stop saying I have it." Samuel says as he laughs and spits food all over the table.

"Sam, you are unbelievable. You know I didn't mean you took and have it in your, whatever. I am not going to explain myself." Jessika says as she watches Samuel eat his pancakes. He loved her pancakes and she took pride in the fact that she finally got them right.

"Do you want some milk?"

"No but I will take some moo juice."

"You are too much." Jessika says as she pinches his cheeks. "You are cute though."

"Puppy dogs are cute. I'm a thug."

"Not in this house."

"How about a convict?"

"Wait until you get older before you start thinking about careers." Jessika says as she bursts out laughing.

"Ladies and gentleman. Jessika Cotta has said her first joke. Let's give her a big round of applause. NOT!"

Jessika gets a glass out of the cabinet and the milk out of the refrigerator.

"How much do you want?"

"I want to drink out of the milk jug."

"Do I ever let you drink out of the milk jug?"

"No, but I do anyway."

"Sam, you better be telling a story."

"No story here."

"I better not catch you putting your mouth on this jug of milk."

"Good as long as you don't catch me then you will never know."

"I am never drinking milk again." Jessika says as she hands him the glass of milk.

"I can't believe I finally get to go fishing." Samuel says as he eats his pancakes.

"You don't know the first thing about fishing."

"So, but I will catch the biggest fish."

"What if you don't?"

"I don't think like that. I will do it and you wait and see."

"I will be here to see."

"Good. Are you going to cook the ones I catch?"

"I don't know about that. It is according to the type you catch. You just be careful out there in that boat."

"I will. Kenny's dad has a big boat."

"How big?" Jessika asks as jealousy creeps up because she wished she could go with him.

"Not as big as your head, but it is big."

"Sam, I am going to get you back for saying that."

"You already have, these pancakes are torture."

"Whatever." Jessika says as she puts the milk back in the refrigerator.

"Ok Momma. I am done."

"Did you like them?"

"I did but I don't want to eat too many, I don't want to sink the boat with those anchors you made."

"Get out of this kitchen right now, you knucklehead."

"Yes ma'am." Samuel says as he stands up puts his dishes in the sink. Just then Raymond walks in holding a fishing pole and a worm.

"There are more pancakes if you want some." Jessika says as he stares at them.

"No thank you. Samuel come over here and let me show you how to put a worm on a hook. Since you have never been fishing before, I want to show you how to do it."

"Baby, not in the kitchen."

"We will only be a minute." Raymond says as he doesn't even look at Jessika but stares at Samuel.

"Ok I am ready." Samuel says as he walks up and stands next to Raymond. This precise moment was when Jessika wished she had a camera. She can't remember Raymond spending quality time with Samuel and here he is being nice to her and everything. Jessika quietly wished for more days like this.

"Alright, you take the worm like this and you just impale it on the hook like this and OUCH!" Raymond screams as he jerks his finger back from the hook. He stuck his finger in his mouth and looked at Samuel and then Jessika and started laughing. Jessika and Samuel didn't know what to do so they started laughing also. For the first time in a long time they were laughing together. Samuel looked at Jessika then to Raymond, then back to Jessika and he smirked.

"Mom, pray for me."

Drip

Drip

"Sam what did you say?" Jessika asks.

Drip

Drip

"Mom, pray for me."

Drip

Drip

Jessika all of a sudden felt cold and she then opens her eyes and realizes she was still in the bathtub and that the water has gone cold. She had fallen asleep and now she can't even enjoy the hot bath she had made. She pulls the plug out in the tub and waits until most of it was gone before turning on the shower and finishing cleaning herself up. Jessika then thinks back to her dream and she realizes that she can remember everything the way it happened except the end part. She doesn't remember Samuel asking her to pray for him.

"He didn't say that and I am positive of that." Jessika says as she begins to get scared.

"Maybe he is trying to tell me something."

Jessika turns off the shower and grabs a towel to dry off with. She takes a doo rag out of her bag and ties her hair up in it. She grabs her robe and she walks out the bathroom. She walks to Samuel's bed and she noticed that he was still lying there and nothing has changed except the time. She had been sleep an hour and a half. Jessika starts to get a weird chill down her back. She begins to wonder what that dream meant. Is there some significance to the dream?

"Sam are you asking me to do something?" Jessika asks Samuel as he just lays there in his coma. She didn't expect him to do anything but she wants to know what was meant by the dream.

"Ok, Jessika you are going crazy."

Jessika starts to pace the floor and she walks around the bed. She walks to the door and back to the window, to the door and back to the window. Then she decides to do what Samuel asked her to do.

"Ok Sam, I am going to pray for you." Jessika says as she grabs the two pillows and sets them down on the floor in front of her. She drops down to her knees and grabs Samuel's hand.

"God I come before you now asking for your grace and mercy. My son Samuel lays here in a coma and only you can bring him out of it. I pray that you bless him with a speedy recovery as well as a normal life. I pray that Samuel will forgive me for putting him in harm's way. That he will forgive me for not doing enough to help us. God if Samuel doesn't make it, can you let him know that I love him and I truly miss him. Please God extend you precious hand out and save us from all harm and in your loving son's Jesus name we pray, Amen."

Jessika says as she stands up and looks at Samuel. She then leans over and whispers in his ear.

"Sam I love you and if you can hear me, I am telling you that I miss you so much." Jessika says as she kisses him on the forehead and before she could stand up, his heart machine starts beeping. Jessika immediately gets scared and she momentarily lost her breath. She looks at the machine and she notices that line went from a heart beat pattern to a flat line. An alarm on the machine goes off and Jessika runs to the other side of his bed and pushes the nurse's button.

"Help. Something is wrong with my son. If you can hear me, I need help in room 356." Jessika says into the intercom.

"We are on our way ma'am."

"Please hurry." Jessika says as she runs back to Samuel's bed.

"No Sam. Don't do this to me." Jessika says as she starts to caress his face. "Please baby, hold on. Don't leave me, please don't leave me." Jessika says as she starts crying. She watches the machine still showing a flat line for his heart pattern so Jessika panics and runs to the door to Samuel's room and opens it up so she can scream for help. As soon as she opens the door she is almost knocked down by two nurses.

"Something is wrong with my son."

"We heard the alarm go off at our nurse's station."

"What is wrong? Is everything all right?" Jessika asks as she follows the nurses to Samuel's bed. She then stands at the foot of his bed as the nurses start to do their routine checks when things like this happen.

"Everything will be ok. We just need for you to stand outside of the room." One of the nurses says as she starts to tell the other one what to do.

"I am not going to step outside. That is my son and I am staying here."

"Ma'am you will only get in our way, so please step outside."

Jessika just stood there and watches as the nurses frantically try to revive Samuel. Suddenly Samuel's doctor walks in with one more nurse.

"Mrs. Cotta, I am going to have to ask you to step outside of the room."

"No way, I want to stay with Samuel."

"Mrs. Cotta we will do all we can for him, but we need you out of the room now." He says as one of the nurses walks up to her.

"Well will take care of him." She says as she grabs Jessika by the arm and gently pulls her towards the door.

"No. I want to stay with my son."

"Ma'am please. Help us help him, by leaving out the room." Jessika looks at them as they try to revive Samuel. She starts to cry and as the nurse walks her outside of the room. The second she steps out the room, Jessika breaks down. The nurse helps her sit down and walks back in the room. Jessika hears the door close behind her and she slowly puts her head down until it was almost in her lap. She cries uncontrollably as she pictures life without Samuel. Jessika begins to bang the back of her head against the wall.

"I hate myself. I hate myself. *I HATE MYSELF!*" Jessika yells as loud as she could. A nurse attending the nurse's station hears her and steps into the hallway.

"Are you alright ma'am? Is there something wrong?" The nurse says as she starts to walk towards Jessika. Jessika sees her coming, stands up, and walks into Samuel's room. She sees the doctor and the nurse's standing around looking dejected and some were writing down information

on a pad. They see her enter the room and their eyes meet
hers and not a word was said but the whole scene said it all.
Jessika then faints.

Jessika's

Dilemma

Chapter 4

"The Lost"

"Hello."

"Hey Jessika, its Sonya."

"Hey girl."

"How are you holding up?"

"I will make it. Even though I acted like a fool at the funeral in front of everyone. I feel so embarrassed."

"You were just reacting to what was taking place. It happens all the time."

"I know but I thought I would never be the one doing it. I do want to say how much I appreciate everything you did. There was no way I was going to be able to handle getting the wake and funeral done. I was so hurt and out of it. Thanks for all of your support. You are the greatest." Jessika says as she thinks about all that Sonya was able to pull off dealing with the home going services for her son, Samuel. She couldn't think, eat or sleep after he died. Jessika was a wreck and the guilt was beating her down. She knows that it is because of her inaction Samuel was lost and that hurts her so much. She hopes she will have the strength to get over what has taken place.

"Don't mention it, besides Jessika we are family. I am here for you."

"I am glad for that. I don't know what I would have done without you."

"Are you still going to come up to the hospital today?"

"Oh yeah. I plan on doing it in a few hours."

"So you are going to go through with it?"

"Sonya I can't see myself staying married to him. I have lost seventeen years of my life, I lost my only child, and to top it all, I could have been killed. Besides the detective told me they are looking to get him for manslaughter and that has a lot of years attached to it. I don't even love him anymore and I haven't loved him in a long time. I was foolish to put up with all that abuse. Look at where it got me. I have lost Sam." Jessika says as she wipes the tears off of her face. "I am sorry Sonya."

"I understand. Do you need me to be there with you? I am here at the hospital all day so just let me know."

"No, I got it Sonya. Over this past week, I have been praying for guidance and strength. The way I feel now, I am not worried about him at all. Now I can sadly say that I have nothing to lose."

"The police told the hospital that they are coming to pick him up at 3:00pm. That leaves you a little more than five hours. Don't wait too late ok?"

"I won't. As soon as I get off the phone with you, I am on my way. I am going to stop by and give you a hug, ok?"

"Of course. Be safe and I will see you soon."

"I will, bye."

"Bye."

Jessika hangs up the phone and she goes back to staring at Samuel's room. She has been doing it for the past hour. She just thinks about all that has taken place since he died. It took all her strength to stop her from going into Raymond's room and trying to kill him. She ended up having a nervous breakdown and she had to be readmitted to the hospital for two days. Sonya had to plan Samuel's wake and funeral for her. Jessika couldn't keep from crying at the wake. She cried so much that she began to have a migraine headache. At the funeral she acted a complete fool and she had to be held down as they lowered the casket into the ground for fear that she would jump in after it. She eventually had to be helped off of the funeral grounds because she just sat there long after everyone had already gone. She has been sleeping in a hotel the past couple of days because she couldn't bring herself to sleep in her house anymore. The house reminded her so much of Samuel and she needed a break from being around things that would make her grieve. She had a hard time sleeping because of the fact that Samuel is gone and she misses him dearly. She decided that today would be her first day back in the house.

"Samuel Jermaine Cotta. I do miss you baby. I can't even bring myself to touch your room yet alone go inside of it. There are so many memories, so many things in this room that you once touched, held, broke, or fixed. This room has a certain quality to it that makes it you. It is all I have left of you besides the pictures, awards, and plaques. I hate to box this up and put it away." Jessika says as tears run down her face. "What am I going to do without you, Sam? Who will make me laugh at the drop of a dime? Who will tell me their whole day in a way that it makes me want to be them at that moment? I wish you were here to say something smart to me. I want to hear one more put down or one thing to give me that feeling of happiness. I know you are looking down at me saying I better not touch anything but I have to baby. I have to eventually pack your things up because I am thinking about selling the house."

Ding Dong

Ding Dong

Jessika wipes her face with her hands and she goes to answer the door. She passes by her bedroom and a shiver went down her back. She had Janice bring her clothes to the hotel because she didn't want to even go in there. She glances in the bathroom and every other room until she made it to the front door.

"Hey Janice."

"Hey you Hollywood Actress."

"Ha-ha. That was classic."

"You bet it was. This was you right here." Janice says as she closes the door. "NOT MY SAM, OH NO, NOT MY SAM. LORD CAN YOU PLEASE CHANGE YOUR MIND. THERE ARE PEOPLE THAT DESERVE TO DIE BUT NOT SAM. OH NO, NOT MY SAM." Janice says as her and Jessika burst out laughing.

"Girl you are crazy."

"I can't do it like you but you definitely deserved an Emmy or something."

"I wish I were acting. I didn't know what to say. That is not true, I wanted to say take his father."

"Oh girl you are cold-blooded. I can't blame you though."

"I'm not going to trip like that though. That will only make it hard on me."

"That is true. So how are you doing?"

"I am good. I do want to thank you for cleaning up my house."

"Girl, it was bad too. I know you know what I mean."

"First hand."

"It took me two days but here you have it. It was the least I could do."

"What are you talking about? You were my getaway driver."

"I am glad for that too."

"Why, you could have been killed?"

"One, I would have done it because I care about you and two, I am driving a 2018 Maxima because of it."

"You go ahead with your bad self."

"Ok. No more Dodge Neon."

Jessika just smiles as she listens to Janice brag about her new car. Jessika was just glad that she had people like Janice in her life. Janice volunteered to clean up Jessika's house. The way Jessika remembered it; it was dirty with blood, and broken furniture. There was no way she would have been able to see the house the way it was and been able to clean it up. It is easier to be in here now because she only has a memory of what took place not a physical picture of it.

"I am going to need your help with one more thing."

"What is it?"

"Can you do Samuel's room for me? I can't even walk in there. I know I wouldn't be able to get very far in there because everything would bring back a memory of Samuel."

"No problem Jessika. Sonya and I planned on packing your house up for you."

"Oh no. There is too much for the two of you to do."

"Don't worry. Sonya is getting a group of people from her church to help. We should knock it out in no time at all. We have a contractor that said he would repair the walls and fix the cabinets in the kitchen for you as well."

"That would be blessing. I think I am going to cry."

"You big sensitive baby." Janice says as she gives Jessika a hug.

"I know I cry too easy. I can't help it."

"Are you going back to the hotel or do you want to go to lunch with me?"

"No, I have to go give Raymond the divorce papers. Maybe we could go to dinner."

"Girl just have the papers served to him. That way you don't have to even talk to him or anything."

"I know but I have to talk to him. There are some things I want to know."

"You be careful then. Call me once you leave and I will meet you somewhere."

"Ok and thanks for everything Janice."

"Sure. I will see you later."

"Bye." Jessika says as she closes the door. She turns around and just starts looking the room over. This was supposed to be a house that the family was going to outgrow, instead the house out grew the family. Jessika had big dreams for this house ever since the first day she walked through the front door and all you could smell was fresh paint. She saw herself furnishing the house just the way she envisioned it. The yard was supposed to be a work of art but she never had the time to do it. Every room was supposed to be the way she wanted it to but it never turned out that way. Still there were a few good things about the house but they were over shadowed by the bad. The bad memories are the main reason why the house is being sold. Jessika knew she could not live in the house because too many things would remind her of the bad times and she needed a fresh start.

"Well house, the next time I see you it will be to move out my things." Jessika says as she opens the front door and steps out of the house. She locks the door and walks towards her rental car. The day was bright and sunny. It was perfect day for a long drive.

"Janice you look like one of those car commercials. You are just staring at your car."

"I can't help it. Ever since I got it, I keep checking every so often to make sure it is still in the driveway. I am so use to driving in hoopties that I finally have something worth being seen in. Next thing you know, I will have me a man."

"Stop it. If you stop being so picky because good men start with a good foundation on the inside."

"Well I like the ones that have finally made it to the outside foundation."

"You are crazy. I will call you in a couple of hours." Jessika says as she gets into her rental car and starts the engine. Jessika knew that this was one of the last times she was going to be in this neighborhood. She was looking for an apartment on the other side of town. Somewhere near the graveyard where Samuel is. As she is driving towards the freeway entrance she looks down the dirt road where her life changed and without blinking she kept on driving and left her past behind her.

"Don't you cry Jessika. Don't you dare cry." Jessika says to give herself strength to fight the tears. They wanted to come but she wouldn't let them. She wouldn't give the past a chance to steal her tears like it stole her son. Jessika then enters on the freeway, heading to the hospital.

*   *   *

Jessika circles the hospital parking lot looking for a good spot. She finds one and pulls into the spot. She turns the car off and looks at herself in her driver side mirror above her head. She noticed the scar on her face and even after the stitches dissolving, she can still feel it when she laughs or sneezes. The skin still tries to stretch apart and when it does she immediately feels her face for any blood. The doctors did a great job of working on the cut but with such a clean cut as it was, it is hard for it to look as if her face was never cut at all. So she looks her scar over again and she unties her hair that she had in a ponytail and she pulled a piece over so it would lay on the side of her face that has the cut on it. Then Jessika changes her mind and puts her hair back in a ponytail. She wasn't going to run or hide from anyone or anything. From this point on she was going to face every obstacle with confidence and no more fear. She puts the mirror back up and she opens the door, closes it and begins walking towards the hospital. She makes it past one row of cars when she sees a lady getting out of her SUV. Jessika watches her walk to the back of the SUV and raises the door. She sees about four small, semi bulky boxes. The lady tries to pick up more than two at once but she couldn't so Jessika decides to go and help her. As she gets closer she reads the boxes and it says, "Oakley's Coffee House".

"Hey, excuse me ma'am. I will give you hand." Jessika says as the lady turns around to see who was talking to her. Jessika is taken back by how pretty the lady was. She had on a nice gray business suit and some shoes to die for. Her face looked very familiar like an actress or something. Jessika was trying to think of where she has seen the lady before. Then she sees her badge and notices that she was a doctor.

"Hi, well if it's not too much trouble. I would definitely appreciate that." The lady says as she welcomes Jessika's help.

"You must love coffee." Jessika says noticing that all the boxes have a different blend of coffee in them.

"Well, all of this is for my coworkers but I am totally addicted to coffee and to make matters worse, I am married to a coffee shop owner so my husband is my supplier."

"It is easier to get it that way when your husband supplies it." Jessika says as she wishes she had a husband she wanted to talk about.

"It has its privileges. Well, my name is Nyssa Oakley, what's yours?" Nyssa says as she extends her hand out.

"Jessika Cotta. Wait, are you the doctor from the news report a few months ago, the one that had HIV but is now healed?"

"Yes that is me."

"I was wondering why you looked so familiar when I walked up. I was so moved by your story." Jessika says as she remembers details from the piece they did on the news.

"Thank you. It was tough dealing with it but I promise you that if it wasn't for God, I would have thrown in the towel years ago and would not have waited on the blessing of being healed."

"I admire your courage and strength you have." Jessika says as she wishes she had half of Nyssa's courage. If she did, she would be known as a fighter and not known as a victim.

"Not to be funny but I know your story as well, from the news. You are the lady that lost her son due to your husband. I remember now because of the scar on your face."

"Unfortunately that is true." Jessika says as she fights back tears.

"I want to encourage you in your time of loss that God still loves you. It goes without saying that you will miss your son and the grief will be there but God will never leave you to grieve alone. I found that out when I was going through with my HIV. I felt like life was over and I was just waiting to die because of the pain and heartache I felt because of HIV but God gave me a new strength and a new purpose of life that I wouldn't understand if I hadn't gone through my trial. So be strong." Nyssa says as she sees Jessika tear up.

"Thank you. I needed that dose of encouragement. I realize that I will miss my son everyday but I don't have to act like that is the end all be all. He would want me to enjoy every day like he did."

"True, I acted like my life was over for years and I was so miserable. It wasn't until I fully gave my situation over to God that I was able to move on from that situation and old unresolved ones as well. I got over anger and learned forgiveness and that helped me see the light."

"I really need help with forgiveness. My situation right now is me trying to forgive my husband. So much pain and anger is all I feel when it comes to him. That is something that I must deal with because as I am talking to you, I am feeling like anger is creeping up on me and I have to deal with it because I am going to talk to him now."

"Ok, then let's talk as we bring these boxes inside the hospital." Nyssa say as she hands Jessika two boxes of coffee and grabs the other two boxes. She balances them with her leg as she closes the rear door of her SUV. She then begins to walk through the parking lot with Jessika.

"That forgiveness piece is tough to deal with. I was angry at God for my HIV, I was angry at my mom for running out on me as a kid so I had a plate full of forgiveness that I refused to eat from. Once I did forgive everyone else, I was able to see life for what it truly was." Nyssa says as they maneuver through cars in the parking lot. Jessika listened because she had to face a similar dilemma now and it was no easier than what Nyssa spoke of.

"Well I am about to be face to face with what forgiveness is in a few minutes. I am on my way to see my husband now before they take him to jail."

"Wow, well take your time and heal from it all before you make any quick decisions. Forgiveness is real when you have dealt with and understand your circumstances. It has to be more than lip service and it has to be final." Nyssa says as she made sure she had eye contact with Jessika when she said that last part.

"No doubt. I so needed to hear that because I have been flip flopping on forgiving him because the past won't let me forgive him." Jessika says as quickly flips through her memories in her mind.

"I understand that but the future will be brighter without that burden of the past."

"I will keep that in mind as I begin my future and work on the things I need to do to be normal again."

"Speaking of work, what do you do Jessika?" Nyssa asked as they continue maneuvering through the parking lot.

"I am a model, or I was one. Not sure what the future holds for me" Jessika says as she wonders about her career that she had enjoyed.

"That cut doesn't do anything to hamper your beauty. We are all flawed and just because some or more pronounced that others doesn't give it any more weight. You will be fine and I know work will come to you."

"Thank you Nyssa. I am worried about the scar and all because society puts pressure on models to be perfect." Jessika says as she remembers many training sessions where they spoke of trying to be perfect.

"Well it just so happens that I need a model for the photo shoot me and my husband are going to do for our coffee shop. We want to do a series of art and I think you will be perfect. Would you be interested in that?" Nyssa asked as they finally make it to the front of the hospital.

"I would love to do that. When is the photo shoot?" Jessika asked with pure excitement.

"Let's schedule something in a few months. You get settled in your life and I will talk to our photographer and we will work out the dates."

"Sounds great to me."

"Great, see Jessika I told you that scar will not have any hold on you." Nyssa says as she winks at Jessika.

"Thank you so much Nyssa, well Dr. Nyssa. Thank you for the chance with the photo shoot and I will definitely use your advice." Jessika says as they walk through the hospital lobby doors. The coolness of the lobby was refreshing since they walked from outside carrying these boxes.

"Well over here is fine. Thank you so much for helping me with the boxes. You saved me from making two trips." Nyssa says as they walk to the information desk and set the boxes on top of it.

"No problem. Thank you for the free session." Jessika says as she is reflecting on their conversation they just had.

"No problem. If ever you need to talk, give me a call. Here is my business card. We can meet over coffee and I promise I won't put you to work. We can meet as friends and not business so don't worry about that. I will get back to you if I don't hear from you so we can make this photo shoot happen."

"Thank you so much Dr. Nyssa." Jessika says as she takes the business card and reads over it.

"Just call me Nyssa. Well, Jessika be strong and I will talk to you soon." Nyssa says as she gives Jessika a hug. Jessika knew she needed a hug and it was so welcomed.

"I will. Bye Nyssa." Jessika says as she walks off towards the elevators. What a blessing it was for her to meet Nyssa and to be encouraged to do exactly what she should do. God is watching her now to see how she handles all that will come her way. She wants to please him but she knows that she must get her emotions in check because they will cause her to react in a negative way when she is trying to be on her best behavior. So as she rides the elevator, Jessika smiles at how God is always placing people in your life for a purpose. Some of those purposes are for life and some are for a few minutes but whatever the reason, it should be recognized as God working in your life. When the elevators door opened, Jessika walks straight to the nurse's station.

"Hi, I am looking for Nurse Sonya." Jessika says to the nurse working in Sonya's normal station.

"Let me page her for you." The nurse says as she turns around and walks to the paging system.

PAGING NURSE SONYA TO THE NURSE'S STATION

PAGING NURSE SONYA TO THE NURSE'S STATION

"Thank you."

"You are welcome."

Jessika knew she needed a quick prayer and words of strength to help her with her talk with Raymond. She wasn't anticipating an easy conversation because she is going to present him with divorce papers as well as inform him of her intentions of selling the house. Those two items were things she no longer wanted. Things that would only keep her from enjoying what life she has left. She needed a new start and this was just the beginning.

"Jessika."

"Hey Sonya." Jessika says as they hug.

"Girl you are still one pretty lady."

"Thank you. It's going to take me time to get used to this scar but for the most part I am ok."

"I think once you get use to the stares and questions, you will be fine. I can say that it doesn't take away from your beauty, not even one bit."

"Thanks, girl."

"So you are on your way to see him."

"Yeah."

"Don't worry, he is still at peace. He hasn't changed one bit since he came in here. I talked to him last night and we talked about the incident and the funeral. I don't want to say too much but I think you will be pleased with what God has done to him over the past two weeks."

"I am glad for what God has helped me with the past two weeks also. I have been through so much and God has basically been there for me and I can't forget you and Janice."

"All praises go to God. Janice and I were just put in place to help you see that."

"True."

"You better call me and come by here to visit me. Just because you won't have a reason to visit doesn't mean you shouldn't."

"You know I will. I could never forget you and what kind of friend would I be if I just left and never came back to visit you?"

"Not a good one, I can tell you. So, when are you going to go back to the agency?"

"They are letting me come back when I am ready but let me tell you how good the Lord is. Raymond had me turn down a contract about nine years ago. Well, the client had a major setback at the same time so she never did anything with her clothing line. Last month she was able to get back on her feet and she remembered me. She called my agency a couple of days ago and the agency explained to her what happened to me and she still wants to use me. You know I am not going to turn it down again. That was my dream contract and God tailor made it for me and I am going to make the most of it."

"Oh, bless you girl. That is so good."

"I know. I am so happy about that and I can't wait to start and get back into the swing of things. This scar will not take everything from me. I won't let it." Jessika says feeling better about dealing with her scar.

"That is what I am talking about. That scar doesn't take away from the blessing of being as beautiful as you are and I know you will be fine. I am proud of you."

"I didn't think I would have it in me to get past what has happened but I have."

"Thanks be to God. Well, I don't want to hold you up. Just be strong and do what you have to do. I do want to tell you this scripture that came to mind. It is about forgiving. It is Matthew 6: 14-15, it says; "For if you forgive men when they sin against you, your heavenly father will also forgive you. But if you do not forgive men their sins, your father will not forgive your sins."

"I understand Sonya, and I will take it to heart."

"That is all I am asking."

"Hey, can you say a quick prayer for me?"

"I would be glad to. Are you ready?"

"Yes."

"Oh, Heavenly Father we are standing here united through a battle that took resolve and faith. We are blessed that you choose us to be here and want to ask for your guidance of words and thoughts as Jessika talks with her husband. You know the story and you know the outcome. We are asking that you make it easy and rather pleasing conversation and that you watch over Jessika as she takes up her new life, with you as her guide. We say this prayer in Jesus name, Amen."

"Thank you so much Sonya. I just love you."

"I love you too but you have to leave now because you are about to make me cry." Sonya says as her eyes tear up.

"You know how I am; it doesn't take much at all. Bye now."

"Bye."

Jessika knew she had a true friend in Sonya. There hasn't been anything that Sonya wouldn't do for her. As Jessika gets back on the elevator, before the door closes she looks back at Sonya and smiles. Sonya looks at her and is wiping tears out of her eyes. Jessika shakes her head and smiles and fights off her own tears. Once the doors closed, Jessika's smiled turned to a stern look on her face. She knew she had to summon all her strength because she was about to face the one person that has made her life full of pain and strife. She has never stood up to him and this will be the first time where she totally feels like she has the upper hand. She knew that she has to take care of the divorce situation now and not wait because she doesn't want to feel sorry for him and change her mind. Once the elevator doors open she immediately takes a deep breath and starts to walk towards Raymond's room. As Jessika is walking, she pays no attention to the people taking second looks at her scar. She is trying to stay focused on the fact that she is about to do something she has never been able to do before. As she gets within fifteen feet of Raymond's room she notices that there is a police officer sitting outside of his room. The sight of that gave her an added boost of strength. As she gets closer to the police officer she takes more deep breaths.

"Hello, Officer. Can I go in and talk to Mr. Cotta."

"Who are you ma'am?"

"I am his wife." Jessika says as a sick feeling comes over her. She didn't like the way that sounded. Just the thought of still being married to Raymond just makes her feel sick to the stomach so she wanted these papers signed in the worst way. The police officer looks at Jessika and then he takes a second look at her scar on her face.

"I am sorry Mrs. Cotta. You may go in. If you need anything, I will be right here."

"Thank you Officer." Jessika says as she walks to the door.

Knock

Knock

"Who is it?"

Jessika heard him ask and for a moment she was scared to say something but she knew she needed to do this so her life without him can began.

"It's Jessika."

"Oh, come in."

Jessika closes her eyes and she takes her final deep breath and pushes the door open. Jessika knows that she has prepared herself for two scenarios. One, he hasn't changed and he is just trying to pull a fast one on everyone. Two, he has changed and he admits to what he has done. She sees Raymond sitting on the bed with his hospital gown on. He looks like he has lost at least fifteen pounds. He was definitely thinner than before he was shot. He has his clothes that he had on that night they got put in the hospital, in a folded pile next to him. His eyes met hers and just like she normally does, Jessika looks down avoiding his stare. Jessika clutches the divorce papers tighter as she walks in the room. She stops a few feet from the bed. Jessika then thinks about Samuel and how she needs to do this to move on with her life.

"Hi." Raymond says as he turns so he can face Jessika. The first thing Jessika notices is how calm he is. His demeanor has definitely changed over the past two weeks. He was exactly the way she met him over seventeen years ago.

"Hi." Jessika says, as she decides to look him in the eyes. She knows she has nothing to lose. For once she is not nervous and she realizes that it is not as hard as she thought it would be. This is the first time in a long time that she has seen him without a frown on his face. She is reminded how handsome he was.

"You look good." Raymond says as he looks to see what Jessika reaction would be. Jessika just looked at him. One, she couldn't believe he was giving her a compliment and two, he put this long scar on her face and if feels like an insult to comment on her looks, sincere or not.

Jessika wanted to say something mean but she needs to keep her composure and just focus on being free from all ties with him.

"Thank you."

"Man does this feel awkward."

"You are right about that."

"I have thought about this ever since I got in here."

"What?"

"This conversation we are about to have."

Jessika has been looking for a wavering in his voice or something to hint to her that he is trying to pretend but it isn't there. She is starting to believe what Sonya had told her all along.

"Will you please just listen to me? I know that after everything you really don't owe me that much. I just want to say this and I will shut up."

Jessika nods her head to show him that she was ok with it. Jessika starts to wonder what he had to say. She knows for a fact that if he begins to say that this is all her fault, she was going to throw the divorce papers at him and say, "Deal with it." She is willing to give him the benefit of the doubt and listen to what he wants to say.

"Ok. I want to first say I am sorry."

Jessika eyes got big and she is shocked to hear that. She could not believe that Raymond said those words to her. He has never taken responsibility for anything he has done. He has always blamed the other person in whatever the situation was. No matter how much the blame points to him, he would never admit it.

"I can understand your strange look. I deserve it."

Jessika nods her head.

"Have a seat because you are making me nervous." Raymond says as he points to a chair. Jessika could not believe this transformation that has taken place. A few weeks ago, he could care less if she stood up for days and it has only been a few minutes, and he feels like she has done too much standing.

"Thank you. Like I said before, I want to say that I am sorry. I am sorry for all the pain I have caused you over the past seventeen years. All the times I have hit you and humiliated you." Raymond says as he gets up and walks to the window. Jessika watches him closely as she listens to every word. These were words she has waited the whole marriage to hear so she wanted to make sure she heard them. Raymond sits on the ledge and Jessika spots a tear fall on his cheek.

"Jessika I have done some mean things and some things that I am not proud of." Raymond says as his voice cracks. "I am so ashamed of the way I have acted." As Raymond breaks down crying, Jessika just stares at him. She is in total shock at what she is seeing. Raymond is showing a side of him that she didn't even think was possible. He is crying and saying the words that he should have said years ago. Jessika did not know what to say. She didn't want to interrupt him from saying the things she deserved to hear. He owed her that and she wanted to at least make sure that he paid in full.

"The pain and guilt I feel because of my actions will haunt me for the rest of my life. Every day I will think back to the things I have done and it will truly tear me up. Can you hand me that box of tissues?" Raymond says as he points to the box on top of the bedpost. It takes Jessika a few seconds to register what he said because she was in deep thought.

"Thank you." Raymond says as he wipes the tears off of his face. The more he wiped the more they came back. "Jessika, I have killed Samuel." Raymond said as he breaks down and cries. Jessika just sat there watching him. She dare not walk over to him and console him. She was still skeptical about whether his intentions were honest or not. So she just sat back and watched him cry. It was actually soothing to see him finally show some emotions. Jessika remembers crying for days over the beatings he put on her. She felt that the tears he is crying now, would not be a drop in the bucket to the millions of tears she has cried because of him. All the times she cried without an arm to hold her, hug to soothe her, or even a reassurance that everything would be all right. It was only right that he knows, at least a little of what she felt like.

"I have taken the life of my son, our only child. I can't live with that. I can't live with that pain. Just like I had a hard time dealing with the fact that I was a terrible husband." Raymond says as he goes through tissue after tissue. He is definitely not faking. The way he is crying is showing true feelings. Jessika was amazed at how calm she was staying as he was crying. She would usually cry at the drop of a dime if someone else were crying.

"Jessika I am truly sorry for the way I have treated you. I am sorry for all the harsh things I have said about you over the years."

As Jessika is listening she starts to wonder about what he is saying. Now she wanted to know a few answers to questions that she had.

"I don't mean to cut you off but I do have a question for you. Why? Why all the years of abuse and neglect. You are sitting in here crying and I want to know why does things have to come to this before you do what is right?" Jessika says as she draws strength from the fact that he is pouring out his feelings for what he has done.

"I have went over that question in my mind the past two weeks. It all started when I was growing up. I remember very vividly my parent's marriage and what I saw on a daily basis. My mom ran that marriage and my father didn't have a say in anything. She told him what to do from the moment he got up until he went to bed. My father was basically voiceless in his own home. He did whatever she told him to. She wanted a newer car, he made it happen.

She wanted bigger house, he made it so. She told him he didn't make enough money, he got a second job. At home she talked to him like he was a child but in public, when she had an audience, she would belittle him even worse. My Mom would talk so bad about him and always compared him to other men she felt were manlier than him. We would go over for dinner with friends and all the women would make their husband's plate and there was my dad making my mom's plate. I remember the first time I came home and found my dad crying and I didn't know what to do. I was shocked that my dad was broken like that. To make matters worse it wasn't until one day he got fed up and they were arguing and she punched my dad in the face and I watched him cry like a kid and it was right then and there I told myself that would never be me. When your parents came to me and asked me to meet you, I felt that since you were so young that you wouldn't put up a fight and I didn't have anything to worry about. I saw a little glimpse of my mom in you when you were questioning your parents about introducing you to an older man and I panicked. I didn't want to seem weak so I agreed to be with you but I knew I didn't want to let your parents down."

"Why did you not tell my parents? Why let them put you and me through all of this? You could have backed out and all would be well."

"You have to understand Jessika. My own parents never thought of me the way your parents did. My dad felt I was a failure because I wasn't a manager or an owner of something. He felt that since I was in my 30's that I should be well established somewhere and making good money. He was that way at my age and he expected nothing less. Just the fact that I was only one level above entry level, he couldn't stand it. Then to top it all off, I wasn't married or anything. Nothing was good enough for him. He had courage to talk down to me but not my mom and I didn't care about him either way. So when he died, I didn't blink but now my mom took her control factor out on me. I was told what to do and how to do it every day until she died."

"So you took it out on me? I didn't deserve all the pain you gave me."

"I know Jessika and I am sorry for that. I can tell you this; you were the one thing I could control. I couldn't control my career; parents or the way people felt about me. I strongly felt like I could control you. You were my wife and I felt that being your husband gave me rights over you. At my job, I would lose a promotion to someone else. I had no control over anything. I was always being told what to do and how to do it. I couldn't use my creativity to show my worth. The same way with my parents because they have controlled my life for the longest, just the fact that I changed careers because of their comments made me realize that they had control over me. You were the one thing that I could control. You were young and you didn't know a lot about certain things. I abused that by asking you to adhere to things like the schedule and things of that nature. I saw that I could get away with it and I enjoyed the power it gave me. It made me feel good to be able to control someone. I am sure that was how my mom felt bossing my dad around. It was like a drug to have control like that and once that started to get old, and then I decided that I had to step it up. Just like what my mom did to my dad, she kept him at bay by degrading him, so that was my next step with you. I started to call you names and trying to make you feel less than me."

"Yeah but Raymond you were calling me a stupid, retarded and all kinds of personal things. That was the worst thing you could have done to me. It was so degrading to hear that from my own husband. It hurt so much to hear those words over and over again." Jessika says as tears start to form in her eyes. She is starting to get emotional because she has never even questioned why he did certain things to her. Just finding out why doesn't comfort her any more than not knowing.

"I know it hurts. I am sad to say that was the reason why I did it. I never should have treated you that way but I had nothing else I could use to bring you to the level that it did."

"I have cried so much over how you treated me. I hated you because I knew I didn't deserve to be treated like that."

"You are right. You didn't deserve to be treated like that. I wish I could take it all back but I can't. I wish I could start these seventeen years over but I can't." Raymond says as he shows a look of concern on his face. It was a look that Jessika was not use to seeing. It comforted her somewhat to see him showing this level of remorse. It was something she thought she would never see in her lifetime.

"So why did the abuse start? It wasn't enough to degrade me so you had to hit me." Jessika says as she grabs a tissue from the box out of Raymond's hand. It was the closes she has been to him in weeks and she felt no fear.

"I felt at times that I was losing control. If you questioned me or didn't want to do something, I felt things were getting out of hand. I couldn't stand to think that I couldn't keep control over you. It was scaring me to think that you could see through me. I was afraid of being treated like my father was."

"You were afraid of losing control but you wasn't afraid of losing me?"

"I felt you had nowhere to go."

Jessika listens to Raymond excuses for putting her through so much and it isn't helping her. She totally believes that there is no excuse that he can come up with that will be good enough.

"I look at you now and I see what I have missed out on. I have missed out on a world of love and happiness. All of that was taken for granted. I realize that now."

"Why the sudden change of heart? Did it take you almost losing your life to realize these things?" Jessika asks because she knows that there is an underlying reason on why he is the way he is right now.

"Yes. I am going to tell you right now what happened to me. It might seem strange to you but to me it was real as this conversation we are having right now. I can't deny what I saw and how I felt in the midst of what happened. All I know I have never been that scared before in my life. Here is what happened, as soon as the cop shot me, I fell back and for the first time in years, I felt helpless. I felt a total loss of control. I remember looking at the blood coming out of me and feeling the burning sensation in my chest and stomach. I was so shocked and frightened. I looked at you and for once I felt exactly the way I made you feel. I felt helpless, frightened, weak, and humiliated. I looked at Samuel." The tears start to roll down his face. "I see him just lying there, not moving. I want to just stand up, hold him, and tell him I am sorry. Tell him that I didn't mean to hurt him. I was only reacting to what he did. I know now he was only trying to protect you from me. Then I passed out and I only vaguely remember fading in and out on the way to the hospital. I do remember the guys in the ambulance talking bad about me. They had no clue I was listening but they made me feel low. They were telling each other what they thought of men that abused their wives and kids and it made me feel guilty. Then I finally went unconscious and I had a vision. I was in total darkness and it was quiet. I was so scared. I had no clue what to do. I couldn't see anything and that frightened me. Then all of a sudden, in the distance, I saw this bright light getting brighter and brighter. It started out the size of a baseball but it kept on getting larger and larger. I started to really get scared then. The closer it got the brighter it got until I could no longer look at it. I bowed my head to hide my face from the light. I then heard a loud booming voice say, *"ARE YOU DONE YET?"* I just kept my head down because I did not understand the question. The voice was so loud and stern that I was frozen in fear. I had never been that scared in my life. The voice came again, *"ARE YOU DONE YET?"* I am so scared from the sound of the voice that I could not even speak. I opened my mouth but nothing came out. The voice came again and it was louder this time, *"ARE YOU DONE YET?"* It was so loud that it had my eardrum pulsating and my heart was thumping hard. I knew I had to answer it or it would continue to ask me. I finally managed to say, "Done with what?" I said it so low that I barely heard it. The voice heard it none-the-less. The voice came again and it said, *"DO YOU NOT KNOW?"* I start to think and then I said, "No." I heard a loud, *"BOOM!"* Then the bright light got brighter and it consumed all the darkness. I had my eyes closed but the light was so bright that I could still see the light. I started seeing pictures of you and Samuel, over and over. The pictures were flashing before my eyes. I watched every one go by. I saw you beaten, bruised, and in pain. I saw Samuel crying time after time. Not once did I see a happy picture of you or Samuel. I really started to notice things I didn't pay any attention to. The reason why I never seen a happy picture of you and Samuel was simply because the two of you were never happy. Then the pictures started to flash faster and faster. They were flashing so fast that it was making me dizzy. I felt disoriented and as the pictures flashed by faster, my head and my heart would thump harder. I heard a loud, *"BOOM!"* This time it stayed and the sound did not fade; it just stayed at a loud pitch. Now my ears, head, and heart were at the point where they felt like they were going to explode. The pain was so unbearable that I started to cry. I fell to my knees and tears were falling off of my face. All of a sudden it got pitch black. I couldn't hear anything but my heart. I was so scared that the light would come back that I kept my eyes closed. I then heard a voice say, *"IT IS TIME."* Then I woke up. I notice my shirt is soaking wet and then I turned on the light and I grabbed the mirror sitting over there by the bed. I look at my face and I realize that I had been crying. I was so scared and I still remember that dream like it was yesterday. It still scares me to think about it. Anyway, I just lay there afraid to go back to sleep. I stayed up four hours waiting on the sun to shine. Morning did come and it was funny because I wanted to talk about what happened to me. I realized that I had no one to talk to. Then Sonya just so happened to come by to tell me how Samuel was doing. I asked her to stay because I needed to tell somebody because I needed to understand what happened. After talking to her for a couple of hours, I realized that God was letting me know that he was through with my foolishness and he was ready for me to accept him. Right then and there I gave my life to Christ because I dare not face that voice again. You talk about being scared straight. I had never been that fearful in my life. I realized that was God and he was telling me, enough. He showed me all the pain and suffering I gave you and Samuel, he put it in me, and I could not stand it. It was too much to take. I wanted to call you so bad and tell you I was sorry and that I gave my life to Christ. Sonya told me to wait and let God's plan work. I told her that I prayed that maybe someday, not necessarily today, but someday you could forgive me for what I have done." Raymond says as he lowers his head and Jessika watches him cry. Jessika felt sorry for him because he truly understands his errors. He has showed her in this conversation that a change has come over him. She doesn't know how soon she could forgive him, but she was willing to try.

"I am going to be honest with you. It will take me awhile to forgive you. Your actions over the past seventeen years have caused me all kinds of physical and mental pain. Some things I will never truly recover from. I have prayed to God for the necessary strength to eventually forgive you and move on with my life. You know that over the past ten years Samuel was all I had. He was my only strength, comfort, and love. I would allow myself to get up every morning because I knew that Samuel was there. I put all my love and feelings into him and I made sure he would know every day that I love him. Now he is gone and I am not only going to blame you, but me as well." Jessika says as she looks at him to see his reaction to what she just said.

Raymond just looked at her with sad puppy dog eyes and shook his head. Jessika could see the pain in his face because it was written with sorrow. His expressions said it all and now his loss of words also.

"I see you have papers in your hands. Are they for me?" Raymond asked.

"Yes. They are divorce papers."

Raymond mouth dropped and he just starts to smile.

"I figured that would happen eventually. After all I have put you through, I don't blame you for doing it. I just thought it would be later."

"I have thought and prayed about this and I feel that this is best."

"I understand. It hurts me but I do understand. I do want to say that I do love you. I know over the years that it may seem to be otherwise but it is true. I am not saying this to make you change your mind. I just want to say this because you never knew." Raymond says as he turns away so Jessika can't see him start to cry.

"I do appreciate you telling me that. You are right, I never knew. I just know that right now I don't love you and it would be totally hard for me to try."

"That is cool. I deserve that." Raymond says as he picks up used tissues to wipe his face.

Jessika watches him react to what she says and she realizes it was easier to do but it is harder to deal with. She always thought that once she got married that it would be for life. She felt that she could handle anything that came up in a marriage but now she knows that some things are just too much to take.

"Let me sign the papers." Raymond says as he stretches his hand out for the papers. "I am not going to fight for anything. You can have it all. I am going away for a while and I won't need it." Raymond says as he signs the papers without reading them.

"I might as well tell you that I am going to sell the house. I can't live there with all that went on in there."

"I understand. I really didn't expect you to."

"I will do this for you. I am going to give you the money from the house. That way when you get out, you will at least have something to start with."

"Thank you. What are you going to do?"

"I have the money from Sam's life insurance."

"Good. There is no way in the world I would accept any of that money, not after what I have done. I do want to thank you for not coming in here with the same anger and cold heartedness that I gave you over the years. Also for believing me when I tell you I am sorry for everything."

"It is not that hard when I see your true feelings. Over the years I didn't think you had it in you to be kind. Now I know different."

"I don't know who that person was then but I know now that I will continue to change for the better. I guess it is almost time for me to go." Raymond says as he points to the door. Jessika turns and looks at the door and through the window she sees a couple more policeman.

"Jessika you take care."

"I will and you do the same."

Jessika just looked at Raymond and the sad look on his face. It seems as if this is a totally different person. That this is someone paying for someone else's mistake. She feels sorry for him even though he put her through so much and his actions caused their son to die. She can't believe that she is feeling that way but her heart has been cleansed of all anger. Jessika hears the door open and she turns to see two detectives and two police officers.

"Excuse me folks, but Mr. Cotta it is time to go." One of the detectives says as he pulls out some handcuffs.

"Well, Jessika I guess this is goodbye." Raymond says as he hands her the divorce papers.

"Yes."

"Bye."

"Bye Raymond." Jessika says as she turns and walks out of the room. She glances back and she sees Raymond looking at her with tears in his eyes. One officer was handing him his clothes so he can put them on. Jessika steps out of the room and she is having a hard time containing her tears. She starts to walk fast as she passes the nurse's station and she heads towards the bathroom. Once inside of the bathroom she runs to the last stall, locks the door and just starts to cry. Jessika had no clue why this is so hard on her. She thought it would have been easy to get rid of the one person who hurt so much. Jessika figured it would have been easier if he were still the same. If he was still evil hearted and mean it would have been much easier but since he has changed, it is much harder to do. Jessika knows it was the right thing to do but a part of her still feels bad. Everyone would be so mad if she had changed her mind and decided to stay. After all he has done, it is only right that he suffers for his actions. Jessika begins to wonder if Samuel were still alive, would she be getting a divorce. She knows she wouldn't but since that is not the case, she is going to have to accept what she has done and be thankful.

"Pull yourself together Jessika." She says as she grabs some tissue and wipes her face. She unlocks the stall and walks to the mirror. She gets some paper towels and wets them to wipe her face. She takes a look at the scar on her face and walks out of the bathroom. As soon as she walks out she sees the policeman escorting Raymond to the elevators. Jessika just stands there watching them. She notices that Raymond is not walking like a proud man. He is walking like he is going to his execution. His head is hanging low and his whole body language says it all. He is a dejected man with not much to look forward to. Jessika clinches her fist to help her control her tears. She waits as they get on the elevator before she starts to walk that way. Jessika can only wonder what is going through his mind. His actions caused him to lose everything he has. He literally has nothing and about time he gets out of jail, he will not have anything left from his marriage except clothing and pictures. That has to be tough to think about. As soon as Jessika makes it to the elevator, the doors open and there are two ladies on it. One is covering up her face and the other one has a mad look on hers.

"Going down?" Jessika asks before she steps on the elevator.

"Yes." The mad woman responds.

As soon as the doors close the mad woman starts to whisper to the one covering up her face. She was attempting to talk low enough so Jessika couldn't hear her but Jessika could hear every word she said.

"This is the last time he will hit you. I am not going to let my daughter get beaten on. Do you hear me?"

"Yes ma'am."

"I am going to take care of this right now. He will pay for this."

"Ok."

"I can't believe you put up with this crap. I have taught you better than this. What is your problem letting him beat you?"

"I love him."

"Love doesn't hurt like that. No man should hit you especially if he loves you."

"I know."

"As soon as we get home, we are calling the cops and he is going to jail. That is regardless if you like it or not. Do you hear me?"

"Yes ma'am."

"Good." The angry woman says as the elevators reached the 1st floor. As the door opens, the angry woman grabs the other by her arm and pulls her off the elevator. Jessika steps off of the elevator and watches the woman pull the other one across the floor to the doors. Jessika wanted to say something but she couldn't. She knew exactly how that woman, that was being beaten felt. It was as if Jessika could actually feel her pain and it made her sad to see the woman like that because someone probably felt the same way when they saw Jessika like that. Jessika is glad that the woman has her mother to help her because she didn't have that luxury at all. Her parents feel bad for what they have done. It is not necessarily their fault because they had no clue that Raymond would be that way. No one truly did, not even Raymond. It just so happen that he was at a breaking point and Jessika was his release. As Jessika is walking across the lobby she looks around and she smiles because she knows that there will be no more visits from her. That makes her happy because for once she can say that and truly mean it. Once the doors open to let her out of the hospital, Jessika starts to pick up the pace. She has faced the one person she has avoided for years. She came out unharmed. She now can be truly be happy in knowing that she can start her life over again. It will be hard to be happy without Samuel but she knows that he is in heaven. He is having the time of his life and is not feeling pain but joy and happiness. That makes her smile to know that he waited until she prayed for him before he went to heaven. That she was able to tell him everything she wanted too. Just the fact that her last words to him expressed love and compassion for him is something that brings her joy.

"Sam, I love you baby." Jessika says as she skips through the hospital parking lot. She is overwhelmed with joy and she has a new lease on life.

Jessika's

Dilemma

Chapter 5

"The Start over"

"Unnnnnhhhhhggggg!" Jessika says as she tries to stretch off her night's worth of sleep. She picks up the phone's receiver and puts it back down to stop it from ringing. She knew it was only the wakeup call from the front desk and they were used to her not saying anything. After months of sleeping in the same hotel, everything became routine. She couldn't wait until she finally moves into her apartment. The apartment people told her it would be done and ready to move into in a few days. Still, it was her best night sleep in eight months. She took some sleeping pills and it did the job. She hasn't felt this rejuvenated in years. She sits up, yawns and she begins to smile. She knows that today might turn out to be a real good day. She was going to go to her house and have the garage sale. That money is what she is going to use to buy some furniture for her new apartment. Then she was going to finally put the house on the market so she can be through with her last loose end. She already opened up an account for Raymond so all she has to do is deposit the money and everything will be over. Jessika has already answered about every question she could from everyone asking her why she would leave him anything. It wasn't an easy decision but it was one that she could live with the most. A part of her knows that the past is the past. She doesn't even focus on the negative things, because her future will outweigh any bad she has gone through. The house or anything to do with the house is the last thing she wanted. She wanted to get rid of every piece she could and what she doesn't sell she will donate to a battered women's shelter. Sonya, Janice, and friends had finally finished with cleaning the house and packing Samuel's room. They have all the rooms ready to be seen and all furniture and items are marked to be sold. They have sent out flyers throughout the neighborhood and even the surrounding ones, too. They are expecting a big crowd. Jessika glances over to the alarm clock and it says,"8:35." She didn't have to be at the house until 10:00, which was only fifteen minutes away.

"Get up Jessika before you are late." She says to motivate herself. As she stands up she finally realizes that she no longer has any lingering pain left over from the last incident. The only reminder she has is the scar, on her face, and she is finally feeling somewhat comfortable with that. She is just happy that walking, bending, and even stretching no longer brings her any pain. The first weeks afterwards, she had some minor pain but now it is like it never happened. Jessika stretches one more time, and then she lowers her head and says a quick prayer. She then heads towards the bathroom so she can get her morning started.

Knock

Knock

"Who in the world is that?" Jessika says as she backtracks to get her robe and then she walks to the door to answer it.

"Who is it?"

"Room service."

"Room service? I didn't order any room service." Jessika says as she looks through the peephole and she sees it is the bellboy from the lobby's restaurant. She then opens the door.

"You must have made a mistake because I didn't order any breakfast." Jessika retorts.

The waiter looks at Jessika with a surprised look and then he looks down the hallway. Jessika immediately started to get scared because why would he give her that look and then look to the side as if someone is standing there. The bellboy looks back at Jessika and then smiles. Jessika began to get uncomfortable with the whole situation.

"Well, ma'am breakfast was ordered and you are going to have to pay for it."

"What? I am not going to pay for anything. You are going to take that food back right now." Jessika says to the bellboy to show her anger. He then starts to smile and that made her even angrier.

"Look here, you are going to take that food back."

"No he is not. You are no fun." Janice says as she comes from around the corner of the wall.

"Girl, don't you be playing like that. You almost got this man's feelings hurt."

"Thank you sir and this is for your troubles." Janice says as she hands him $10.

"Thank you ma'am and you too." He says jokingly to Jessika.

"Sorry but you were about to be told off." Jessika says as she smiles to play off her embarrassment.

"Come on and bring the food in because I am hungry." Janice says as she starts to pull the cart in. The bellboy places the food on the table and walks out.

"Girl you ordered this?"

"Yeah."

"Ok, was there no food at your house?"

"Oh be quiet. I came to eat breakfast with my sister. Is that ok with you?"

"That is cool." Jessika smiles as she sits at the table. She was happy that Janice came. She was getting very lonely sleeping in the hotel.

"I wasn't sure what you wanted for breakfast so I got us two buffets."

"That is fine. I don't know what I really have a taste for. I have eaten just about every dish down there."

"Well it all smells good so dig in." Janice says as she removes the lid from her plate and looked over the breakfast buffet. The plate had toast, biscuits, sausage, eggs and hash browns.

"Thanks for coming."

"No problem. I know you are tired of being in this hotel."

"Very much so. I can't wait until Thursday when I finally get my place."

"What are you going to do about furniture?"

"I am going to take the money from today's garage sale and buy some things. I don't want anything expensive, just something to get me started."

"That is how you should do it. Don't rush anything."

"Exactly." Jessika says as she begins to eat some of her food.

"I know it cost a lot of money to stay here." Janice says as she looks around the room. This particular hotel had rooms that had a bedroom, kitchen, dining area, and large bathrooms.

"Yeah but I had a big insurance policy on Samuel which I haven't even touched. I have paid for this with the insurance policy Raymond took out on Samuel with his job."

"Oh well at least something good has come of it all." Janice says not wanting to dwell on talking about it. "So have you gone back to the agency yet?"

"No I will be back on Tuesday. I have spoken to the client that I was telling you about and she is coming in town on next week. She is flying in a photographer from Las Vegas to do a big photo shoot so we will be official." Jessika says as she shows her excitement on her face.

"That is awesome. I have always been so jealous of you because your very first job was at a modeling agency. You get to dress up, take pictures and travel. Now that's the type of job I want. Now my first job was at Bo Bo's Pork and Goat Dive. I was only sixteen and man did I stink every night I left that place. Being a waitress wasn't that bad but I was too close to the food. I have seen pigs and goats entrails cooked in ways that would make you sick to the stomach."

"Just like you are doing me now?" Jessika say as she eats her sausage.

"Yeah kind of like that." Janice says as she starts to laugh. "You are lucky to have a job like you have."

"I know. My agency has taken care of me over the years even when I thought I was hiding my personal problems from them. I wish I had known that people would have helped me get away in the first place. I had no clue that everyone suspected something."

"Not everyone was blind to the fact. We all knew something was up no matter how much you tried to hide it. We were only waiting for you to say something."

"I was so dumb."

"Don't think about it like that. You didn't know what to do."

Jessika just shakes her head in agreement. She knew that all the time the abuse was taking place, she felt so helpless. She felt that no one cared. She let the embarrassment of being abused cloud her thinking. She would rather keep receiving beatings than ask someone to help her. Just the fact that her asking for help meant she was totally helpless, was a thought that Jessika didn't like.

"Well, it is over now."

"Thank God for that, Jessika. I was so proud of you when you got on that witness stand. I broke down in tears when you said some of the things that happened to you. Jessika I knew you were being beaten but not like that. I felt so bad that I never once helped but I did take pride in how you were finally ready to say enough was enough. It was just the fact that you were willing to tell your side of the story, and that said volumes about your character. It showed everyone how you have gotten stronger these past months. How you would no longer let him get away with what he had done to you and taken from you." Janice says as she continues to eat her food. Jessika sat there staring at her food. She can recall being on the witness stand and talking about some of the things that took place in the seventeen years that they were together. Some things she had forgotten or chose to never recall again. It seemed that the more she talked about one situation the more others kept popping up in her mind. Just her telling the story was more painful than actually going through it. She hadn't realized just how bad things were until she heard herself talking about them. She had downgraded the beatings so much until she believed that they weren't that bad. Watching the faces of the jurors and the people in the courthouse, as she told her story, told her otherwise. She realizes now that strength does start from within. Over the past couple of months she has told herself over and over that she would get past Samuel's death and start to forgive Raymond. Just the fact that she did that over and over, she realized her mind slowly accepted it and it became true.

"Did you see how Raymond was looking when I was telling my story?

"He looked like he should have. He should have felt bad and less than a man?

"He was looking so remorseful."

"What? Jessika you are tripping. I can't believe you said that. Have you forgotten the fact that Raymond has kicked your butt for seventeen years and he didn't show one bit of remorse then?"

"I haven't forgotten it is just that I know that he is not the same. He has definitely gave his life to Christ."

"Girl they all find God when they go to jail. The minute they are back out, they will eventually go back to their old ways. I have seen it too many times to know that is what happens." Janice says as she is trying her best to get Jessika to see things her way.

"We have been talking and he knows his mistakes and he is definitely sorry for what he has done."

"Jessika, I am not going to let you sit here and feel sorry for him. That man deserves everything the system is going to give him and then some. He is in a situation he can't control so he decides to be on his best behavior so they will be lenient on his sentence. I just want you to be careful. He could be trying to make you think he has changed and then when you let your guard down, he will take full advantage of you again." Janice says as she finishes the rest of her breakfast. Jessika just sat there, unable to eat any more. As much as Jessika feels she should be mad at Raymond and even hate him for that fact, she doesn't feel that way. She knows that she has seen him at his worst and she put up with it, so seeing him in a new light is easy to take.

"It is true. He did put a serious beating on me over the years. It was not his fault that I stayed and put up with it. I was the one that didn't leave and I kept Samuel in that environment. So the bulk of the blame lies on me too. I can't fault Raymond for that."

"I am just saying Jessika, you have to be firm Monday when you go in to say your part before the sentencing. What you say will play a big part on the sentence they give him. Don't forget what he has done to you and to Samuel."

"Ok." Jessika says so she can end the whole conversation. She was fed up with all the negative talk people have had towards her trying to forgive him. Her mind wants her to make sure he gets an eye for an eye, but her heart feels that he has suffered and anything more would simply be piling it on. She can live with the fact that deep down inside he never meant to kill Samuel. In seventeen years, he had never even given Samuel a spanking or anything. If Samuel did something wrong, he would take it out on her. That doesn't make it right but it tells Jessika that he loved Samuel more than anything. That most definitely included her and she understands that because she loved Samuel more than him also.

"While we are talking about men. Girl tell me about Mr. Leon Dixon." Janice says with a big grin on her face. Leon Dixon was a model that Jessika has known for over ten years. They always had a very cordial relationship and the few times they shared a runway together, they would spend times talking about life.

"You tell me about Johnathan Mathis."

"You first girl. You haven't even said one word about him since you guys talked about being more than friends. Stop hogging all the good stuff and tell me about the man."

"What is there to say? We have been great friends. Once my divorce was final, he sent me some flowers and he subtly asked me out. I was scared at first but I was like I have been imprisoned for seventeen years and I deserve to get out there besides he is a sweet person."

"Fine too."

"Girl. He is fine though, huh?"

"Indeed. I thought Johnathan was fine, well he is, but it is something about that tall, dark, and handsome man you got." Janice says as she starts to fan herself with her napkin.

"I can tell you this, that man is great. He is so kind and respectful and after a few dates he asked me if I would mind if he courted me and treated me the way I should be treated. I told him he better treat me like that and nothing less. I love little things he does that people take for granted like opening doors and things like that."

"I know what you mean. The first-time Johnathan did it for me, I was ready to be married to him." Janice jokingly says as they start laughing.

"It is different when you have someone that takes pride in the little things as well."

"I am learning that too, because I have always tried to find the man with the most money. Now, I have a man that isn't rich in money, but he is definitely rich in the spirit."

"Most definitely. I love the fact that Leon is a model too. He understands the business and he is open to me working, travelling and everything else that comes with it. He is more established than I am in the modeling world but he is so humble and kind. The industry hasn't rubbed off on him in the wrong way so he is more laid back than most."

"That is good to know. My Johnathan is what I have needed my whole life. I love our conversations and our dates have been so much fun. I can't remember having this much fun with anyone before."

"Our men are a blessing to us. We have talked to God about what we were looking for and he delivered us some good men which are so hard to find. So I know that Leon and I are going to take our time and enjoy ourselves."

"We are too. I am loving just spending time and not worrying about anything other than the moment." Janice says as she gives Jessika a high five. "We should do something together. Like a dinner or maybe even a movie."

"Let's wait until after Monday because I just want to focus on that."

"That is cool."

"It would be nice though."

"Oh yeah. Hey it is 9:00am and you need to get dressed. We are supposed to meet Sonya at the house at 9:45am."

"Oh man, I better hurry up then." Jessika says as she jumps up, grabs her clothes, and runs to the bathroom so she could take a shower. She was excited about finally getting rid of things that reminded her of all the abuse but there was a part of her that was feeling sad. After all, it was something that for all purposes started off as a good thing. It turned for the worse and it just picked up speed until it could no longer be stopped. Jessika steps into the shower and the hot water was so soothing that she just wanted to stand there and let it run down her body but she couldn't because she was already late. Once she was through, she steps out of the shower and lotions up. She then puts on her robe and opens the door so she can defog the mirror from all the steam.

"How much time do I have left Janice?"

"It is 9:25."

"Thank you." Jessika says as she starts to get dressed. She combs her hair back into a ponytail and looks at the scar which has healed nicely and shrugged her shoulders because she was not afraid to show it. She made it a routine to show it as much as possible because hiding it actually draws more attention to it because once someone finally notices they ask her about it. "Janice give me five minutes and then we are out of here."

"Ok."

*   *   *

As they are driving on the freeway towards the house they were just talking and carrying on. As soon as their exit came, they both simultaneously got quiet. They were driving over the spot where the last battle, as Janice calls it took place, and it got their full attention. They both just looked over the side and didn't say a word. It was still a reminder of what shouldn't have happened. It affected them the same and once they were past the spot, they continued with their conversation. Jessika knew she never wanted to speak on it. She wanted it to be gone and getting rid of the house meant she wouldn't have a reason to pass by here unless she is coming to visit Janice.

"You are going to be so surprised at how we hooked the house up. We have tables in every room displaying the small items. We cleaned, dusted, and just about everything else that needed to be done to the furniture. The house looks so good it could be a model home and that is no lie."

"We shall see."

"Girl look." Janice says as she points to the cars parked in front of the house. "People are lining up to buy things already."

"Yes. Let them come and buy it all."

"You might make some decent money. After all you are selling things for cheap."

"That is because I want to make sure that nothing is left over. If I could find a buyer for the house today, I would take someone's best offer."

"Who knows, someone might show up and do just that." Janice says as she pulls into her driveway next door to Jessika's house.

Jessika just wanted to get it over with. She wanted to move on and she knew that the house was the last major thing to get rid of.

"You ready to do this, Jessika."

"Yeah. I feel I am definitely ready."

"Let's go then." Janice says as she steps out of the car. Jessika gets out and they walk across the dividing yard between Janice's house and Jessika's. As they are walking towards the front door, Sonya walks out of the house.

"Good morning ladies."

"Hey Sonya." Jessika says as she gives Sonya a hug.

"What's up girl?" Janice says as she waits for her turn.

"I am blessed. Everything is working as planned. The house is ready, so Jessika if you are ready now we can get started. No need to wait fifteen minutes if people are here and we are ready, don't you think."

"That sounds good to me. The sooner we get started the sooner we get finished."

"Which room do you want to work Jessika?" Janice asks.

"I was thinking about the garage. I don't know if I would make it inside the house. If I am busy working in the garage then I won't see most items leave the house. That way I don't have to worry about changing my mind on selling anything."

"Alright, then Janice you work the bedrooms and bathrooms and I will work the living room, den, kitchen and dining area."

"Ok that sounds fine to me Sonya."

"Good then let's get started." Sonya says as she walks over to the cars that are lined up in front of the house. Janice holds up her hand so Jessika can give her a high five and she turns and walks into the house. Jessika walks towards the garage, unlocks the door, and pulls the door up. She sees that all the items are neatly stacked on the ground around a table that had a moneybox on top of it. Jessika hadn't been in the garage in a long time. Jessika looks around and she sees that all the toolboxes, fishing rods, and car parts are stacked up against the walls. She knows that most of the things will go fast so she might end up being in the house after all. So until she gets a customer, Jessika decides to look through some of Raymond's old things. She goes to the top toolbox and she opens it up and notices that most of the tools had never even been used. Some still had sale stickers on them. She closes it back and sits it on the ground. She opens the next one and she sees that it is more of the same. She closes it back and then she sits the first box back on top. She then goes to the stack of fishing tackle boxes. She opens up the first one and she sees that it has a lot of rubber bait and that was all that was in it. Jessika picks up a hand full of them and she digs around the bottom of the box. She doesn't know why she is so curious about his things but she is. She then closes the tackle box and just looks at all the things that were in the garage that he never used. He had all kinds of things that he never got around to using. Jessika thought that was strange but she had to realize that he was all about control. She figured it made him feel in control to be able to buy things regardless of whether he was going to use them or not. Whatever the reason, it was for naught because she was definitely going to make sure she sells all of it. Nothing is to be spared. She then sees that Raymond had five fishing poles and one small one. Jessika immediately knew that little one was for Samuel. She walks over to it and picks it up. She looks it up and down and then she starts to picture Samuel holding it.

Jessika begins to second-guess selling the fishing pole but she comes to her senses and realizes that she needs to let go.

"Hi Jessika."

Jessika turns to see who called her and she sees that it is Thomas, Samuel's friend's father.

"Hey Thomas." Jessika says as she puts the fishing pole down.

"How are you?"

"I am good. I am actually better off than I thought."

"Good. I know this is something you didn't know but I knew what he was doing to you a long time ago and that was why I didn't give him the job. I expressed my displeasure with it and he tried to lie his way out of it but my son told me that Samuel told him everything. I just want to tell you I am sorry for not doing more to help you. I should never take an abuser's word at face value. I should have followed up with you and protected you. So please forgive me."

"Oh thank you Thomas. That is sweet of you."

"Don't mention it. You have been through a lot so this may be too late to say but if you need anything, let me know."

"I will definitely let you know."

"Ok then."

"Would you like to take some of these tools and fishing things off my hand?"

"Oh yeah. That is the least I can do."

"Good. I will give you all the tools and the fishing rods for $100."

"I will take it." Thomas says as he takes out his wallet to pay for the items.

"Alright here you go Jessika." Thomas says as he hands Jessika the money.

"Thank you so much Thomas. I will call you if I need anything."

"No problem. You enjoy your weekend and good luck on selling everything. Bye."

"Bye." Jessika says as she watches Thomas put the fishing rods under his arm and grabs the toolboxes.

"Do you need some help?"

"I got it."

Jessika starts to smirk as she watches Thomas struggle with the toolboxes. She notices his arms are shaking and he was trying to hide the straining look on his face.

"OWW, OWW, OWW, OWW."

"Are you sure?" Jessika says as she tries to hide her laugh.

"I think I got it. Oh boy, somebody help me. Anybody help me." Thomas says as the toolbox slides out from under his arm and falls on his foot. He drops everything and starts to hop around on the other foot. He tries to put the foot down and realizes that is too painful for him, so he starts to hop again.

"Let me help you."

"No. I got it Jessika. It just slipped, that's all."

"Are you sure?"

"Um, yes." Thomas says as he picks up the toolboxes and fishing rods, and walks out of the garage. Jessika just shakes her head and laughs as he struggles all the way down the driveway and to his truck. Jessika watches Thomas load up his truck and drive off.

"That was funny."

Jessika then begins to look through some of the things that are stacked up in the garage. She gets bored with that so she sits down and waits on the next customer. It seems that most of the customers are women and they all bypass the garage and go straight into the house. Jessika even sees the lady from across the street walk to her house. She was such a classy lady that just showed so much pride in who she was. Many holidays, Jessika would look out her kitchen window at the woman's house and watch her and her family enjoy a good meal or have fun in her backyard. There were no good times like that for Jessika on any occasion. Every day was a day of walking on pins and needles to not upset Raymond so there are no memories of holidays past that Jessika wants to remember. It is funny how Jessika use to dream of having her life and now she wants a piece of Jessika's. All of a sudden she sees a familiar looking Jeep Cherokee. Her heart starts to pound hard. She squints to get a better look and she sees that it is Leon's jeep. Jessika got so excited and she loved this feeling. She had never experienced this feeling before. She starts to get nervous so she pretends like she doesn't see him parking his Jeep Cherokee. She grabs the money Thomas gave her for the toolboxes and fishing rods, and she begins to act like she is counting it. She grabs a sheet of paper and a pencil and quickly starts to right down numbers on the paper to make it seem like she had been doing it for some time. While her head is still down, she peeps up and she notices Leon getting out of his Jeep Cherokee. She watches him walk towards her and her heart skips a beat because of her excitement. She knew that she was starting to have feelings for him. She welcomed a new start on life and she wasn't going to let what she had been through hinder her from having a good time. She knew Leon was the type of person she could spend the rest of her life with, but she wanted to take her time and do things right this time. As Leon enters the garage, Jessika starts to count out loud to pretend like she didn't notice him.

"10, 20, 40, 60, 80, 100 dollars."

"Jessika."

"Oh, hey Leon." Jessika says in a supposed to be surprised way. "I didn't expect to see you today. I thought you were still in New York?"

"I know. I thought I would surprise you and see how you were doing."

"That is so sweet of you." Jessika says as her heart beats faster at hearing that.

"I missed talking to you because I was so busy with the runway work and you know how that is."

"Yes I do so how did that go?"

"It went ok. I worked with that one designer from Bosnia. That one eccentric older gentleman that has green hair."

"Oh yeah I know who you are talking about." Jessika says as she begins to smirk.

"I know why you are laughing because I laughed when I found out it was him."

"Did his clothes live up to its reputation?" Jessika asked as she no longer controls her laughter.

"He had some clothing I would never wear but that is the fashion world. The crazier the idea the better when it comes to modeling. It was like that time you had to wear that black leather dress with that bright orange straw hat, red sandals and knee high blue socks." Leon says he starts to laugh.

"Now that was a hot mess. There was nothing fashionable about that. I was embarrassed." Jessika says as she joins Leon in laughing.

"No I was embarrassed for you. You were such a trooper because you walked like you would truly wear that."

"See I probably made a believer out of someone that thought that outfit was cute."

"I doubt anyone thought that was cute. Nobody in their right mind would do that."

"You might be right about that."

"Jessika, I really missed you. I just couldn't wait to get back here so I could see you.

"That is sweet Leon. I am glad you are back because I feel the same." Jessika says as her hearts flutters. The sincere way that Leon makes his feelings known to Jessika has her wishing for more.

"Anyway, I know you are busy. I just wanted to see you and to let you know I am back in town."

"Ok, I will call you later on so we can talk."

"How about we get together later?"

"That sounds better I will call you as soon as we are done."

"Ok, that sounds good Jessika. I will talk to you later."

"Bye Leon." Jessika says as she wishes she could run up to him, give him a hug, and kiss. She knew she wanted to be under control. She wants to experience what real love looks like and she is excited to have her chance with Leon but she wants to be smart about moving too fast. They have only been courting, as Leon says, for a few weeks. The good thing about their situation is that they have ties to no one else so they can take their time and enjoy the process of getting to know one another on a deeper level.

"I know that wasn't that tall, fine man of yours." Janice says as she runs into the garage.

"He isn't my man."

"Yet."

"Yet."

"I saw him when he walked up. I was talking to this lady that kept on asking me questions about your bedroom set. I tried to hurry things up so I could come out here and see him."

"Girl, stick with your own man."

"I just wanted to see him. I am happy with my man."

"I never thought I would ever hear you say that." Jessika says as they start to laugh.

"You are right. I never thought so either. I have been with some creatures but now I have a real man."

"Amen."

All of a sudden the house door opens up and Sonya sticks her head out.

"Janice, come on back in here. There are too many people in here."

"Yes Momma." Janice says as she runs back into the house.

Jessika just sits down in her chair and she begins to think about Leon. She thought she would have a hard time adjusting to dating someone after all she has been through. She felt she could never trust someone again. Leon has been an angel since the first day they met. He has always been the type of man she has dreamt about. He is really what every man should be. Jessika can't help but to think about starting a life with him. She knows that anything will be better than what she has had. Jessika was willing to give it a try.

"Excuse me, are you Mrs. Cotta?"

"For now." Jessika says as she turns around to see her neighbor from across the street. This is the same lady that Jessika use to watch from inside her kitchen and wished they could change places.

"Hi, my name is Amy."

"Hi Amy. You can call me Jessika."

"You are so pretty. This is such a pleasure to finally meet you."

"Thank you."

"I came over just to see what you had and to tell you something." Amy says as she looks around the garage.

"What is it?" Jessika asks as she is curious to what Amy could possibly want to tell her.

"I want to say how proud I am of you."

"Proud of me? For what." Jessika asks as she is really confused.

"For not killing him." Amy says with a 'I'm so serious' look on her face.

Jessika was thrown for a loop at what Amy said. She couldn't believe that she said that. That thought had never crossed Jessika's mind. She had never thought to even lift a hand to Raymond. Now this lady is thanking her for not killing him.

"Why would you say that?"

"I know that is what I would do. If my husband even lifted a finger to me, I would beat him so bad. I would have given him the hot grease treatment and the whole nine yards. My husband knows better than that. I tell him that all the time so he won't even put the idea in his mind."

Jessika immediately wished she had this lady's courage. Maybe things would have been different if Jessika thought that way. Maybe Raymond would have backed off if she had stood up for herself. It seems to be that when he feels that someone else has control he gets passive. When he is in control he turns in to the aggressor.

"When I heard that you were being beaten, I felt so bad. I was telling everyone that I never knew. I never suspected a thing."

"It wasn't something to be proud of. I just tried my best to hide it. I didn't want anyone to know."

"You shouldn't do that. You should find yourself help as soon as it happens. That is the problem with most women that are abused. They feel embarrassed or they feel in their heart that they love their man. The first time it happens, a red flag should come up in your mind. You should know that if it happens once, it would happen again. No man can love you and beat you at the same time. Love is something that would make you do anything for someone, not anything to them. Under no circumstance should a woman subject herself to abuse. Not for her family, kids, love or sake of pride. There is nothing you could do that warrants being hit. You are a very beautiful person and you deserved better than that. I wish I would have known because I pack heat and I would have brought my .45 over and we would have put one right between his eyes." Amy says as she pretends she is pointing a gun and pulling the trigger. Jessika wanted to smile but on the inside, she felt like kicking herself. Once again she had someone that would have helped her get out of her situation. Jessika chose to hide it because that was easier than putting your business in the streets. She felt that as long as no one suspected anything then she could deal with it on her own. All that did was made her more fearful of being known as an abused wife. The fact that she would have felt worse if someone knew, made staying there that much easier. I guess when it comes to pain; we can handle physical more than mental.

"I wish I would have done a lot of things. I would still have my son here." Jessika says as she gets sad just thinking about it.

"He was a cute kid too."

"The best."

"I am going to let you be, but I wanted to tell you that." Amy says as she begins to walk out the garage.

"Thank you."

"Just know that there will not be a next time." Amy says as she holds up her fist.

"Most definitely not because I have learned my lesson." Jessika says as she rubs her scar.

"Well I have got to go. Take care."

"I will and you too." Jessika says as she watches Amy walk off. Jessika didn't quite know why she felt she had to tell her what she did. Maybe that is her way of reassuring herself that it won't happen to her. Whatever the reason, she did make sense. There were things that Jessika could have done but she didn't. There were signs that told her of things to come but Jessika refused to acknowledge them. Jessika knows now that was her first mistake. She should have left but it can't be undone so she must learn to cope with her non-actions. Jessika can't help but to think how life would be if she had left in the beginning. Her life would have turned out so different. Samuel would be here and she would be so happy. Now her life is full of memories. She has to start over and it begins tomorrow. Everything she has done up to now is leading up to the grand finale tomorrow. She must face the court and Raymond as she says her part before they sentence him. She knows that this is her final chance to say how she feels about him now and in the past. It is her last chance to make sure that she cleanses herself of the whole situation. So as the people are going into her house Jessika can't help but to feel sadden by the fact that all of her memories are leaving one by one. Everything she wanted, worked for, used or took pride in is about to be a figment of her imagination. Total strangers are taking pieces of her away and she will never see them again. It is so ironic how life is when you spend time acquiring things and with a twist of fate the same things you cherished you are giving them away as if they meant nothing. The only thing Jessika truly wanted was Samuel. She would give away everything and more to have him by her side. She prays that a family can make the most of the items that are purchased and that it will enhance a household that is full of love unlike the house it just left. Jessika does feel bad about having to sell Samuel's things because deep down inside she wants to keep it all and when she gets her new place she wants to get a two bedroom so she can setup Samuel's room as if he is still alive. That is what she truly wants to do but that wouldn't bring Samuel back and that would only make life harder for her. The best therapy for her now is to let the things go because she has plenty of pictures, plaques and a few sentimental items of Samuel that will get her past the tough times. So as the hours go by and item after item is making its way out the house, Jessika is getting more relieved as the bigger furniture is leaving and before long they will be done. She had sold just about everything out of the garage a long time ago. So know she was just waiting on confirmation on how the inside was looking.

"Ok, we are pretty much done." Sonya says as she walks out of the house with Janice.

"Great, as you can see, so am I."

"There are a few pieces of furniture left and a few items that wasn't sold but we can do like you said and donate it to a shelter." Janice says as she hands Jessika a list of things sold and not sold.

"Yes let's do that. I am not coming back to this house again so let's make that happen."

"I will set that up for tomorrow."

"Thank you so much Sonya. No thank you both because you have done far more than I could have ever asked."

"Don't mention it. We are sisters, family no doubt. We look after each other." Sonya says as she puts a hand on Jessika's shoulder.

"Yes and we love you and we wanted to do this for our little sister." Janice says as she hugs Jessika.

"I love you ladies too." Jessika says as she hugs them both and fights tears in her eyes.

"I am hungry. Jessika do you want to go and get something to eat?" Sonya asks.

"I was about to say the same thing." Janice chimes in.

"I would but I am going out with Leon. I am going to call him right now."

"Ok, I guess we will have to catch up with you later then." Sonya says as she winks at Janice.

"I am going with you Jessika because we are a package deal." Janice says as she grabs Jessika's arm.

"Not tonight." Jessika says as she tries to pull away.

"She deserves a night to herself with Leon. You can tag along some other time." Sonya says as she shakes her head at Janice.

"Whatever, I have my own man anyway." Janice says as she pretends to pout.

"Good call him then." Jessika says as they all start laughing.

*   *   *

"Hello."

"Hey, Jessika. I am just trying to make sure you made it to the hotel safely.

"I did. I want to thank you for a wonderful dinner. You made me feel so much better."

"It was the least I could do. I wanted to take you dancing at our spot but I know you have to get rest for your court appearance tomorrow."

"I would have loved that but you are right I need to unwind and get my mind right." Jessika says as she is disappointed that she didn't get a chance to go dancing because of her court date tomorrow.

"Are you ready?"

"Yes, I do believe so."

"Have you written down everything you want to say?"

"Just about."

"Can I tell you something?"

"Yes, you can Leon. I need some words of advice right about now."

"Good. I just want to say that I know you have been through a lot over the past years. There are a lot of bad feelings you have kept inside of you. You never had a way to release your true feelings and tomorrow, basically, you get your chance. There are two things you can do. You can go before the court tomorrow and tell them how much you want to see him suffer. How you want them to give him the same treatment you received. You can talk about him in every negative way you can think of and you would be telling the truth. That is how it happened so it is true. You can also go in there and tell them how he is now. Tell them that he has changed and not so much as learned his lesson but understands the wrong he has done. Tell them about his change of heart towards you and the remorse he feels. You can say that and you will also be telling the truth. Which truth is greater? The truth that speaks of the past or the truth that speaks of the present? We know that only God knows. I am by no means telling you not to say what is on your heart. I wouldn't do that because you have the right to say just that. What you have been through warrants you the right to say exactly what is on your heart. What I am asking you to do is say what is in your heart not on it. Here is what I mean by that. Think about how you truly feel not what you think you feel. Not even what you think you should feel. No matter what you say tomorrow, it won't change the past. No matter how it comes out. The past has been done. You have the right to make the future totally different from the past. You can show God your true character. If you are about payback and revenge, then that is what you will say. If you are about love, understanding, and forgiving then that is what you will say. A true test of your faith comes when you have to make a decision, one that will affect you and others as well. This is something you need to pray about because it is something that I feel is greater than you. It is greater than what you feel. All those years of abuse you suffered, God was there. He was working on you but he was working on Raymond also. It might not have seemed that way, but God had a plan for him all along. It took drastic measures for him to realize it but it happened and it was God's will. So what I am basically saying is, when you speak tomorrow let it be Jessika talking and no one else. No outside influences, just your heart ok?"

"Ok." Jessika says as she thinks about what Leon said. She knew that he was speaking from a Christian point of view. He gains nothing by asking her to speak one way or another. That meant a lot to her.

"Leon thanks for that. You have opened my eyes."

"I wasn't trying to do anything more than encourage you. Just pray on it and let God do his thing."

"I will."

"I am going to let you go because that was all I wanted to say well besides you are so beautiful and I am more than happy that we are getting to know each other more deeply."

"See you starting stuff, now I will be thinking about you as well."

"Ha-ha that is fine by me. Ok. Bye Jessika."

"Bye Leon." Jessika says as she holds on to the receiver. She waited until he hung up before she did the same. Jessika then looks at the paper where she was supposed to be writing down what she was going to say. She had been sitting there for two hours and had not even written one word. She didn't know what to say. There are so many mixed feelings that she can't even put them into words. She wants to say this but she needs to say that. She could say this but she can't say that. She will say this but she won't say that. Jessika gets a feeling of being overwhelmed so she pushes the pad off the table, gets up and walks to her bed. She just plops on it and begins to cry. She didn't imagine it being this hard. Jessika knows that there will be people, in the courtroom, who want her to say the worst things she can. They want to make sure that Raymond gets the longest sentence possible. Then there will be a few people who want her to let God handle it. Then there is Jessika who wants both things to happen. She feels bad that she isn't sure what she wants to do. She looks at her scar every day and she wants him to suffer because of it. She reads the bible and prays so she wants God to do his will. Then all of a sudden that one scripture pops up in her mind. The one that speaks about serving two masters and how you will love one and hate the other. She is at the crossroads now and both paths will bring her satisfaction. She knows that whichever one she chooses, it better be one that she can wake up every day and be cool with it. If not she will suffer just as Raymond will. Jessika then gets up under the covers, turns off the lamp and closes her eyes. She just wants to lie there and rest. Tomorrow is a day that will change her life.

"God all I am asking you for is the strength to do this. Right now, I can't." Jessika says as she wipes the tears off of her face. She knows that anybody else in this predicament would know what to do. Why does it have to be so hard on her? Why can't she have her mind made up and just stick to that? Jessika thinks back to other bad decisions she has made and how she doesn't want to repeat them. Tomorrow

is coming and Jessika knows that there is nothing she can
do about it.

Jessika's

Dilemma

Chapter 6

"The Dilemma"

"All rise. The Honorable Judge Bradley court is now in session." The bailiff says with a little extra on every syllable to show everyone that he loves his job a little too much.

"You may be seated." Judge Bradley says as he sits down. He lines up his folders and opens up two of them. He puts on his glasses and then he looks around the courtroom. He looks at the prosecutor, defense team, and the courtroom spectators. He takes a deep breath. Jessika knew that was his normal ritual. He did it every time she was here.

"Today is the penalty phase of the trial. Up to this point we have heard from the state and the defense team. All points have been measured and I have looked over all findings. Mr. Cotta you have chosen to not have a jury of your peers instead to have the verdict be delivered by the judge. In which case it is I. Now, it is the time to for you to speak and say what you must to help yourself. Defense team, does your client wish to speak on his behalf?" Judge Bradley asks as he directs the question towards Raymond's lawyers.

The two lawyers he has start to whisper to one another and then they begin to hold a conversation with Raymond.

"Yes sir, he does." One of the lawyers says as Raymond shakes his head in agreement. Jessika just looks at Raymond and he has the look of someone who hasn't slept in days. He is looking like a man who has been tormented. Jessika looks around the area where she is sitting. She has Sonya sitting by her side holding her hand. On the other side is Janice holding her other hand. Next to Janice is Samuel's teacher from school who took off just to be here for support. On the other side of Sonya are people from her church who helped set up her house to be sold. They are here for support. Behind them are people that read about the case in the paper and want to come and see the trial. So basically the room is full of people against Raymond. From strangers to people that once called him friend. They are all here to see what the verdict is. Jessika remembers when she first got here this morning. How all the women were telling her to be strong and say what you must say. They are there for support but to also make sure Jessika doesn't let Raymond off the hook. That is all that they have been saying to her since the trial began. Everyone is acting like what Jessika says will affect all abused women in the world. That whatever comes out of Jessika's mouth will actually make a difference in the lives of all other cases to follow.

"Mr. Cotta please stand." The judge says he motions with his hand. "You may address the court."

"Thank you sir. I will be brief. I want to say that I am sorry for my actions. I have done seventeen years of terrible things to the two people that I should have loved the most. I did everything imaginable to make their lives miserable. I want Jessika to know that over the years she has seen the worst of me. It doesn't get any worse than that. I wish I could change the things that took place but I can't. I have started to change my life for the better. Jail time, I do deserve and that is what I am willing to accept. I am not asking for leniency from anyone. I deserve the maximum penalty. I have killed my son and destroyed a home that was supposed to be full of love and affection. I turned it into a house full of pain and strife. I just want to say that I am sorry for what I have done. Thank you sir." Raymond says as he sits down and wipes the tears from his eyes.

"Is there anyone to speak on the behalf of the defendant?" The judge asks as he waits on a response. The courtroom got quiet and everyone started to look around. After a few more seconds, the judge says.

"Ok, now we will hear from the victim's family and friends."

Jessika listened as Samuel's teacher said her spill about how great he was. Next was Janice and she explained to the judge how much she thought of Samuel as her son. Then Sonya went up to say how she remembered Samuel and how she loved him so. Once they were through, Jessika knew that it was her turn. Jessika gathers her thoughts and she stands up and she walks towards the podium. Once she is standing at the podium, she looks back at all the people in the courtroom. It seemed like everyone was waiting to hear what she was going to say. Everyone just sat there staring at her as if she was about to give a historical speech. A speech that would change the course of her life and everyone that hears it. Sonya gives her a smile and Janice gives her the thumbs up. Jessika then looks at the prosecution and they just nod their heads at her. The judge looks at her showing no emotions at all. Then she faces the defense lawyers and they are looking straightforward. They are not even looking at her as if they know that Raymond will get the maximum sentence. Jessika then makes eye contact with Raymond. He has tears in his eyes as he sits there to listen to what she has to say. Jessika clinches her fist to fight back the tears but they ran down her face anyway. She takes a deep breath. She then looks at the judge.

"Whenever you are ready Ms. Cotta." The judge says with the same emotionless expression on his face.

"Ok." Jessika says as she thinks about what she is going to say.

"Please remember to speak loud, ok?" The judge says as he sits back assuming she was going to be a few minutes. Jessika nods her head and opens her mouth to speak, but then she closes it again.

"Be strong Sista." Jessika hears from one of the women in the back of the courtroom.

"You can do it." Jessika hears from the other side of the courtroom.

Jessika closes her eyes to gather strength.

"Ok. I want to start by saying that no matter what I say, nothing can change what happened. What has taken place over the past seventeen years is a done deal. I can't change anything or do anything different. I can't go back and stop anything from happening. I wish I could go back because if I could change one thing it would be the death of Samuel. I would willingly go back and suffer more abuse and have Samuel here, than to be living without him. That is how much he means to me. I wouldn't duck a punch, dodge a kick, or shield my face from anything. I would take the full punishment in order to have Samuel here. To see him smiling is second to nothing. To hold him is second to nothing. To kiss him is second to nothing. To touch him," Jessika says as the tears start rolling down her face," is second to nothing. My Sam meant the world to me. I loved him like I loved no one else. He was my heart and I miss him dearly. Not a day has gone by that I don't wish that he were here. His smile is on my mind constantly. His jokes are on my mind constantly. His poems that he wrote me are on my mind constantly. I loved him so much that I wish I had been the one to die. All the abuse that I went through was something I could live with. The abuse was targeted at me not Samuel. Samuel did not suffer physical abuse. Not once was a hand laid on him for anything. Samuel was my heart and soul and I realize something else too. That he was yours too." Jessika says as she points a Raymond.

"Over the years, you have given me the worst physical beatings I could imagine, but you never touched Samuel. I got put in the hospital, but Samuel was unharmed. I got humiliated and hurt beyond anything imaginable but Samuel wasn't touched. I realize that you loved Samuel so much that you would not even lift a finger to him. You would shower him with gifts but not hugs. You would do everything in your power to make sure he had everything he needed except a father. You wanted the best for him but you didn't want him to feel loved. You have shortcomings and they are numerous. How you chose to show your love through the years is questionable but just the fact that you never tried to give him any first hand pain is something I had to realize. Do I think you tried to kill him that night? Of course I don't. I know you would not have lifted a finger towards him. In seventeen years, you never even punished him. Did you kill him? Yes. Without a shadow of a doubt, you killed him. Are you totally at fault? No. I am part of the reason our son is dead. I had a right as a parent to protect him and I failed. Should you be punished for your actions? Yes. Just like I am going through my punishment phase of my actions, so should you. I do know that yours started the first time you admitted to me you killed him.

That was one thing you never did in seventeen years. You never admitted you were at fault for anything you have done in the past. You put it off on someone else. Just the fact that you told me and the court that this is your fault, tells me that you are suffering with what you have done. The man from a few years ago would have sat in this courtroom and acted a fool. That man would have changed the whole scenario to make it seem like it wasn't his fault. That man was not humble enough to admit to his mistakes. That man, I don't see here today. I want to say this and then I am through. I want to recite 1John 1:9 and it goes like this, "If we confess our sins, he is faithful and just to forgive us our sins, and to cleanse us from all unrighteousness." I also want to say this, that even though our lives are going in separate directions. I want you to know that I do forgive you for what you have done."

That statement was greeted with moans and "Oh come on", and every other retort the courtroom people could think of to say that they didn't agree with what she said.

"Wait, before you people even trip, you have to understand that he is on trial for killing our son Samuel, not for abusing me. I had to separate the two and you should also." Jessika says as she steps away from the podium and goes back to her seat next to Sonya and Janice.

"God bless you for having the courage to say exactly what you needed to no matter what others think of you. You did exactly what a Christian should do." Sonya says as she hands Jessika a tissue.

"I am proud of you. You have opened my eyes to what you feel and I understand. I know I was the main one telling you to talk bad about him but I know now that was wrong." Janice says as she starts to hold Jessika's hand.

"Ok, so now it is time for the sentencing. We have heard from the defendant and the victim's family and friends. I have taken into consideration your good behavior since you have been incarcerated. I want to say, that abuse has never sat well with me. I know of many other activities you could have done instead of hitting your wife. You could have chosen to act like a real man but you didn't. You took the road of a coward. Only a coward would treat his family worse than he would treat a stranger. I don't hear of you hitting folks you didn't know who threatened your control. You don't control 95% of the things that happen in your life but yet you didn't lash out at those circumstances. You choose the one thing you could control and you destroyed everything about it. You destroyed a marriage and family. You didn't even have enough decency to give them a good life. It was all about you. You didn't care how they felt; it was all about you. Everything had to evolve around you. Well, I am about to give you some "you time". You deserve the maximum sentence allowable. Your ex-wife might not feel you do but I do. Maybe you never physically harmed your son but just the fact that you beat his mother in front of him. That gave him years of mental pain. If your son had lived through this last incident, how do you think it would have affected him? I will give you credit for realizing you were at fault for what took place. That shows this court that you are on the road to recovery. Still there is the cost to pay for such actions. Therefore, I am sentencing you to fifteen years for manslaughter."

Raymond bowed his head and started to cry. The courtroom erupted into shouts of joy and happiness. Jessika just sat there. She knew in her heart she had done all she could. She tried to help him but the damage was already done. Jessika could barely hear her own thoughts because of the shouts of happiness. Jessika looks at Sonya and she has tears in her eyes and she turns and looks at Janice and she is just shaking her head up and down.

"Ok. Deputy he is now released back into your custody for the term I have stated. This court is adjourned." The Judge says as he stands up and walks out of the court. Everyone started to pat Jessika on her shoulders saying things like, "You won. He got what he deserved." Jessika couldn't help but wonder if that was true. She knows he deserves to do time for what he has done to her but yet in her heart, she is past it all. Just the fact that she is free from him makes it that much easier to forgive him. Jessika stands up and she watches as the police put handcuffs on Raymond. He just stands there with a blank look on his face. He turns and looks at Jessika. He gave a half-smile and mouths the words, "Thank you." Jessika shakes her head up and down and begins to cry. She knows the man she sees is nothing like the man she had lived with. This one is suffering the ultimate price for the old one's action. That made Jessika sad but it is out of her hands.

"Don't cry Sista. You are free." One of the ladies in the courtroom says to Jessika as she looks back to acknowledge who said it.

"I am." Jessika says as Sonya hands her another tissue.

"Thank you so much Sonya. I don't know what I would have done without you."

"You did it all yourself. You faced your fears as well as did what you knew was the right thing. Jesus is pleased with you. I am sure of that."

Jessika gives Sonya a big hug and just sobs on her shoulders.

"Jessika I am so proud of my baby sista. You did good up there." Janice says as she pats Jessika on the back.

"Thank you too. For everything." Jessika says as she gives Janice a hug.

"Let's go." Sonya says as she grabs Jessika's arm.

"It is done." Janice says as she looks back as they walk out of the courtroom.

Once they get into the hallway, there are people out there telling other people about what just took place. People are pointing at Jessika and saying who she was and things of that nature. Jessika just kept her eyes focused on the door that leads to the outside. All she knows is that once she steps out of the building, she will officially be on her own. No more trials, lawyers, or judges. Now she can get on with her new life.

"What are you going to do now?" Sonya asks as she pulls Jessika through the hallway.

"First, I plan on slowing down." Jessika says jokingly to Sonya to let her know that she was walking to fast.

"Oh I am sorry. I was just trying to get out of here."

Jessika just smiles as she grabs Janice with the other arm and they walk out arm in arm.

"I am hungry. Let's go get something to eat." Janice says as she starts to rub on her stomach.

"Let's go because I am hungry too." Jessika adds.

"Well let's go celebrate a new beginning for Jessika."

"Yeah. Let's go celebrate your freedom."

Jessika thinks about what they said and she should do that. She should celebrate her freedom even though it cost her everything. She knows that her freedom can't replace Samuel but she knows that he wouldn't want it any other way. She feels in her heart that Samuel is happy that his mother is no longer being abused and Jessika knows that she can live with that thought. There will be no more abuse. After all she has been through, Jessika knows in her heart that she won't put up with it. The victim role is no longer in her script of life and now she is the leading lady. No man will ever put his hands on her in a threatening way again. Jessika glances at Sonya and she sees the mother that she needed. Sonya was exactly how a mother should be. She was God fearing, she would never let anything happen to her kids, and that was how Jessika felt she was to Sonya. She was the mother figure Jessika always wanted in her life. Jessika then looks at Janice and she has the big sister that she always wanted. The kind of sister that would do whatever it took to make sure her little sister was well protected. Jessika smiles at the prospect of having a put together family that was there for her no matter what.

"Where do you want to go Jessika? It is your day, after all." Sonya asks, as they are a few feet from the doors.

"Let's go to Tight White's Soul Food Palace."

"Yeah, while we are there we can count the Jeri curls that we see. That place is full of the most out of date people." Janice says before she starts to laugh.

"I haven't been there but I heard the food is pretty good." Sonya adds.

Jessika just smiles as she walks out of the courthouse. The sunshine hits her in the face and she welcomed the warm feeling it gave her. This day is extra beautiful because she feels as if it is a new beginning for her. A day that will be remembered for the rest of her life and seeing that it is a good day adds to the special vibe she has. As they are making their way down the steps to get to the street, Jessika hears a car horn and she looks in the direction of the sound. She sees Leon's Jeep Cherokee parked in front of the courthouse.

"There goes your man." Janice says showing a big cheesy smile.

"Did you know he was coming?" Sonya asks as she starts to wave.

"I had no clue." Jessika says, as her smile gets as large as Janice's. Jessika was glad to see him. She waves at him and Leon motions for her to come to him. Jessika looks at Sonya and Janice.

"Go ahead and we will catch up to you later." Sonya says as she walks up to Jessika and gives her a big hug.

"I want to come?" Janice says pretending like a kid that was being left out of a field trip.

"I will call you ladies later." Jessika says as she hugs Janice and says her goodbyes. She turns and starts to walk toward the Jeep Cherokee. She notices that Leon is smiling and that made her heart jump. Jessika knows that she hasn't had that effect on a man in over seventeen years and she welcomed it. As she gets closer, a thought runs through her mind. It was a thought that she waited a long time for. She knows in her heart that she just left her dark past and now she is walking towards her bright future.

OMEGA

Bonus Story:

"Strength when weak"

The battle of a teenage boy dealing with life as it tears his family apart. Can he do all he can to keep it together and rely on God or will he take the easy route and give in to the same thing that is tearing his family to pieces?

Alpha

Journal entry: #657

Today was one of the hardest days of my entire life. I have crossed over into the realm of no return. I have done something I have avoided time and time again. Through this saga, I have kept my distance from it so I can feel as if I had some control over it. After my actions today, I can no longer say that is true. I chose to participate in the destruction of someone. I chose to be the source of strength to someone who wasn't fully capable of doing what I helped them do. I watched in sadness as my actions took a life further down the road of destruction. I was asked to help finish a task that was started but could not be physically finished. Because of this task being completed prior to this day, the person couldn't do it. The task, you see, involved a needle, drugs, and a belt. I watched as this person attempted to insert a needle into an arm that screamed for the life-taking poison that was inside the needle. The arm convulsed, shook, and pulsated to draw the needle closer.

The arm acted as if this was a mating ritual and it needed to entice the needle to it. It felt it needed to do something special to get the attention of the needle. All it needed to do was sit still. I watched as the person tried to fit the belt around an arm so they could stop the flow of blood. They needed the belt to act as a tourniquet. I watched the distorting strain on this person's face as they gritted yellow teeth. They gritted so hard you could hear them rubbing together. This person was using every ounce of energy they had in a drug-infested body, to get that belt tight enough. Tight enough to make a vein visible so they could poke a needle into it and inject poison. The person wasn't strong enough and the sight of that made me mad. If you are going to do something, at least have enough strength to do it. If you want to accomplish something, then get the satisfaction of doing it yourself and not depending on others. I was angry as I thought this and after two minutes of watching this person curse and yell at themselves because they couldn't muster the strength, I gave in. I jerked the belt from the person in a fit of rage. I grabbed the arm, which had no substance to it. All I felt was bone, incased in skin. I took the belt and I looped it around and then I pulled it through the buckle. I tugged real tight and I could see the person was feeling the tightness of the belt around their arm but all I got was a grin. The temporary pain, from the belt, was nothing compared to the feeling the person knew they were going to feel. The person was so close to finishing the task that was started. I took a step back as the person grabbed the needle, which was already filled with death, and readied it in the free arm. This arm didn't look any better than the other one. The only true difference is this one was the designated hitter. The main purpose of this arm was to supply the goods while the other one had marks from prior hits. I watched in disgust as my actions sped up a killing mission. The person took the needle and found the vein that was to be used. I watched, with a sick feeling as the needle broke the skin, and entered the vein. I watched the frail hand push the needle's head down so the poison could take the path to the bloodstream. In total disbelief, I watched the person undo the belt so easily. This was the same person that had all kinds of struggles with getting it on. Just to see how easily they had strength to take it off brought a feeling of stupidity over me. I watched the person throw the belt down and fall back into the chair that held up a body that seemed so lifeless. I watched as the person's eyes rolled back in a sunken head. I watched them fade off into a place that was void of all reason and cares. I took a step back as the person lost all sense of reality because the poison was now taking effect. As a tear rolled down my cheek, I watched the destruction of someone. Someone I care deeply for and at the same time, hate with a passion. Someone I protect and at the same time, leave unguarded at a moment's notice. Someone I think of constantly and then try to forget immediately. Someone who is supposed to put me first in their life but knows I am really last. This someone that brings me grief mentality, physically and spiritually is the focus of my life right now. Before I go and pray, I want to finally write the person's name in my journal for the first time. I have avoided this for so long because I love this person with my whole heart. I have refused to acknowledge who the person was as I tried to deal with the situation. After my actions today, I give up. Journal you have been my secondary outlet to God. I don't depend on you for anything but to be a tool to write down my thoughts. You have been there for me because you know nothing else. God on the other hand is there for me in my time of need. I must go spend time with God. This journal entry will forever be the defining moment in my struggle. As I finally include the person by name that is destroying, not only them, but me as well. Before they die, I will show them this. This is my journal but it has been their life. Everything, I wrote in the journal, I didn't tell them because they knew already. The person I helped kill is my mom.

End of entry.

KNOCK

KNOCK

"I will be right down." Mychal screams into the hallway as he runs into his room to grab his backpack. His lonely echo follows him. He knew that he was running late and now he had to hurry. As usual, he retraced his steps to make sure that he had everything he needed. A few years ago, screaming in the hallway early in the morning would have gotten him a playful scolding. Nowadays, it is greeted with silence. A few years ago, running through the house meant he would have to hear a cheerful reason to stop. Nowadays, running is greeted with silence. Mychal longed for the days when the house was filled with love but now it is filled with silence. Silence because drugs has taken all that was good away and left nothing. It has destroyed the one fabric that holds most families together. It took that love and it turned it into something only it could give. Drugs didn't try to replace the love with a temporary fix. Oh no, it left nothing to fill the void. It only left memories that grow faded by the day. Memories are ok, if you don't want the real thing. Mychal missed the real thing and no memory can conjure up the same feelings as actually being in that moment.

"Keys? Check. Backpack? Check." Mychal says as he touches his chest to make sure his key was under his shirt on his necklace and reaches behind him to make sure he had his backpack on.

"Oh boy, I almost made a fatal mistake." Mychal says as he closes his room door tight and locks it. The new situation calls for it to be no access into his room. There was too much to lose if he forgot and he knew that. He walks to the bathroom and clicks off the light switch. He then walks down the hallway and the silence that was filling the house was depressing. It was as if the house was completely empty. He could hear noises from outside his house but nothing on the inside. The only noise he could hear inside the house was his shoes as they landed on the hardwood floor. Since there was no carpet in his house, sounds that bounced off of the floors, sounded louder than normal. He then walks toward the kitchen and is immediately reminded of last night's event. The sight he sees brings up an image he was hoping he would forget. He is hit with a sick feeling because last night was truly a low point for him. Last night made him more than a victim, it made him a participant. He sees the frying pan with the burnt slices of bread in it. The bread was burned to a crisp. The kitchen still smelled of how burnt the bread was and the smoke still lightly lingered in the morning light shining through the kitchen window. He looks at the kitchen table. He sees the spoon that still had drug residue on it. He sees the lighter, a small piece of aluminum foil and the belt lying on the floor next to the table. He sees his mom lying with her head on the table, drooling. It hurts his heart more than anything to see her like this. She was only a shell of her former self. She was beginning to remind him of an elderly woman. Not only because she looks so frail, with the truth being told, she wasn't that big to begin with. Before the drugs took effect, she was petite by all standards. It looks as if the drugs have sucked all the life out of her. She looks well beyond her age. She is only thirty four but he feels as if she is beginning to look all of fifty. She was only average when it came to beauty but how she took care of herself made her look more appealing. He was a guy image of her. They had the same pointed nose, round face and dark brown skin. He didn't mind at first but now that she has gotten to this point, he hates to think about it. He looks at her brown hair, which was at its all-time worst. He can remember waiting in beauty salons for hours for her to get her hair done. He didn't mind the long wait because the finish product was always something to behold. Now, there are times when she doesn't care what it looks like. He looks at her eyes, which are moving at a high rate back and forth. If they were open they would be blood shot red. They would look as if she hadn't been asleep in weeks. As if the red veins were a road map to her empty soulless pupils. He sees her dry, crusty lips and he can recall the red lipstick she always wore. He used to love to give his mom a peck on the lips because they were so soft but now they were so unappealing that the thought of doing that brought a sick feeling to him. He sees her skin, which is no longer smooth looking. It now reminds him of alligator skin, with its rough looking texture. She was no longer someone he could walk up too and give a big hug to. He no longer could give her a kiss. He wouldn't dare touch his mom at this point in her life. It was sad to think that way because she was the only family he has. His dad left many years ago and after he walked out he never contacted them. His mom was adopted and she didn't care for her adopted parents so there was no one to call his grandparents. His mom never took the time to find her real parents so basically it's just the two of them. She was all he had and all he didn't want. With her growing up the way she did, Mychal felt she should have went out of her way to make his life different. He felt with her doing drugs and basically giving up, she failed him. He looks at her now, sleeping and she looks very peaceful, almost too peaceful. He walks over to her and he puts two fingers on her neck to check to see if she was still alive. Part of him wanted her to be dead and the other part felt compassion for her. He knew her situation was brought on by bad decisions and who can be faulted for something that we all do. We all have made choices that hurt us; some are just not to this magnitude. Still he knew that deep down inside, she was still his mother and he loved her for that fact. He knows that he continues to pray for her and that God will deliver her from this situation. He knows it, feels it, and believes it. So now he just stands over her, watching her sleep. He can't help but wonder if her soul cries for help. If the goodness in her is trying to find a way out but is having a hard time due to all the darkness that fills the downtrodden body. It can't find the light and it wanders around aimlessly looking for that one speckle of light to show it a way out. He just surveys her as he gets a thought about how she once was. He can remember coming down one morning to breakfast. He had smelled the turkey bacon frying in the skillet, the faint smell of blueberry pancakes, and the well-done scrambled eggs. He knew she would have a tall glass of chocolate milk waiting on him. It would have been sitting in the freezer so it could be so cold and thick, just the way he loved it. He walked into the kitchen and seen the table set just the way he liked it. His plate was stacked with the pancakes, bacon and eggs. Next to his plate was the sports page because he loved reading them every morning at breakfast. There would be a Ziploc bag next to his plate, full of green grapes and strawberries. She knew he loved to eat them as he walked the two blocks to school.

"Good morning Iris." Mychal says as he kisses his mom on the cheek.

"Good morning son." She says as she makes her lunch for the day. Mychal knew that calling his mom by her first name always got a smile out of her.

"These pancakes look and smell good. You sure hooked them up."

"Thank you."

Mychal knew his mother's short replies didn't mean that she didn't want to talk to him. He knew that she was in her work mode and that usually meant thinking of nothing else. It usually happened once she got dressed for work. It was not like she didn't have a lot to say, it was that her mind was always occupied with work. She worked long hours at her job and then she worked more long hours at home. She was always thinking about work and sometimes trying to have a conversation with her was useless. Mychal had grown accustomed to this situation so he never harped on it. He would always laugh when she would talk about something that he mentioned days before.

"Don't forget that I need you to sign that consent form so I can go to the museum with my class." Mychal says in between bites of pancakes.

"Yes son." Iris says as she puts her lunch in her briefcase. She snaps her fingers as if she forgot something.

"Your USB is still in the computer." Mychal says since she always leaves it in there.

"Thanks." Iris says as she walks toward the desktop computer on the end of the counter. She kept her computer that she did all her work on in the kitchen. To her, this was her sanctuary. The kitchen was where she felt she did all of her best work. From her delicious meals that Mychal cannot remember not liking any of them. This was also where she stayed up late working on proposal after proposal for her job, working long hours on the computer and getting little sleep. She poured more time and effort into her job proposals than she did Mychal. He never had any resentment towards her for that. At times, when she took a break, he would get a chance to get on the computer to play a few solitaire card games. Just like the game he was playing last night after she went to bed. He snuck on the computer to play because it was late and she didn't like him being up late on school nights. He finally accumulated enough points to where he could leave his name in the top ten of all times. So as she made her way towards the computer, Mychal just continued to indulge in breakfast. He was trying to get it down as fast as possible. He wanted to get finished because he knew that any minute, Kimyah would be knocking on the door so they could walk to school together.

"Iris, I haven't forgotten about the house we talked about getting. I can't wait to see it."

"Son, please tell me that you wasn't on the computer last night?"

Mychal stopped eating. The tone in his mom's voice said it all.

"Mychal! Please tell me you saved my information project before you closed out of the program I was in?"

Mychal just stared at her.

"Oh son. No, no, no. It took me all night to finalize my numbers and now I need to have the presentation done by noon. That is in five hours. That was a couple of weeks' worth of work. I was looking forward to this day."

Mychal sets his fork down.

"I have worked my tail off for years to get this promotion and now I don't have the most important reason why I should get it."

Mychal just stared at her.

"I can't do it anymore. I give up." Iris says as she returns to the table where Mychal was and sat down. He could see she was visibly shaken. Mychal never felt so bad before. He knew she had told him many times before what to do before he gets on the computer and he forgot. No longer does the breakfast appeal to him. Iris just looks up at him and gives him a smirk.

"You will be late for school" She says as she tries to smile. Tears where starting to form in her eyes as the sadness of what is the obvious sets in. Mychal would usually try to console his mom at a time like this but now he was speechless. He knew that he made a mistake that was so costly to his mom and he truly felt he didn't have the right words to make the situation better. He knows that she has harped on the difference maker this proposal was going to be. How their simple living was going to be transformed to very comfortable living. How her twelve years of working for her job was finally going to pay off. She started at the bottom and had made her way to management. This was the opportunity she had hoped for. This was her break and the chance they needed to make things easier for them.

"Ok." Mychal says as he grabs the Ziploc bag, his backpack and walks out of the kitchen. That was the beginning of the downfall. Mychal remembers it well because he played a major role in it. Just like what happened last night, he was part of it no matter if he wanted to or not. So looking at her now, in this state, makes him feel somewhat responsible. He knew he started a chain reaction that is now out of control. That fuels him to be here for her no matter what. He looks over the kitchen and he is shocked at how it has changed so drastically. He remembers how his mom would change the décor every three months because she always had a new style of colors she wanted to try. She took great pride in the kitchen and the sight he sees now shows nothing of it. The sight he sees now is of someone who just doesn't care anymore. Her drug infested body was a shell of herself and oh how he despises her. The sight of her hurts his heart as much as it hurts his stomach. If only she could be like she once was so they can be a family again but now the reality of it is that is the past and what he sees now is the future.

"See you later, Iris." Mychal says as he walks off because he knew no smile was coming. Not today and as a matter of fact, not in over a year. As he is making his way to the front door, he thought he could catch a small trace of turkey bacon, but he knew better.

"It is about time. I was about to leave." Kimyah says as Mychal walks out of his front door.

"Sorry. I went to bed late last night, so I accidentally woke up late." Mychal says as puts on his backpack and locks the door.

"Why?" Kimyah asks.

"Um, no reason."

"You are lying. If you hadn't said "um" I would have believed you."

Mychal just looked at her. He knew that she was asking him why because she was the only person that knew his situation with his mom. She was the only person in the world he trusted and the only one he has let in his personal business. It was only right that she would ask him why, not out of curiosity, but because she genuinely cared about his welfare.

"Not now K." Mychal says as he tries not to look at her. He knew one look into her eyes and he would spill his guts. Kimyah had that power over him with her long, straight, black hair that went down to the middle of her back. It was always shiny and just free flowing. Mychal always joked that her hair shined like a long Jeri-curl without the grease. Her small frame hadn't quite started developing yet but her body still showed potential of what's to come. Her half African-American, half Chinese mixture showed through her model-like features. One look at her eyes and you could tell the Asian features took hold of it. It was a captivating look that drew extra attention to them. She had the high cheekbones that accented her face when she smiled. Her lips were the perfect size and Mychal always wondered how soft they were. She was stunning and Mychal has had feelings for her since the day they met. That was why he was so eager to be her friend but it wasn't until he started telling her about his mom, that he found the one thing that attracted him the most; her caring heart. She had a heart so big and it showed when she made sure that when he hurt, she hurt. That was exactly how a Christian should act. That was scripture and Kimyah was an example of it. She went out of her way for him and he knew it. She was the one that invited him to go to church with her. They got baptized on the same day and they have become the best of friends. He knew she was exactly what he needed in this crucial stage in his life and that he always thanked God for.

"If you don't want to talk about it then that's ok." Kimyah says as she tries to hide her disappointment in him not telling her. Mychal knew she wanted to know as bad as he wanted to tell her, but he could not disclose what he did last night. It was always easy to tell her what his mom did because she acted alone. Last night is a totally different ballgame. Last night he helped her and how crazy would he sound if he told her what he did. After all the days and nights he explained how much he hated his mom doing drugs and that he would never help her get, buy, or take drugs. He made a promise to her and he broke that promise in the heat of the moment. He didn't have the heart to tell her.

"K, it's not that I don't want to tell you. It would just take longer than our walk to school and I want to be able to explain it to you with no interruptions." Mychal says as a peace offering.

"Ok." Kimyah says in a voice to show that she was going to drop the subject. Mychal didn't want to lie to her but he felt he had to. He wasn't ready to try to explain what took place last night because he knows it would crush her and he didn't want to do that.

"Guess what I got?" she says showing off that winning smile of hers.

"I don't know." Mychal says as he tries to get in the playing mood. This was the first morning in a long time that he wished he could walk to school alone. He has never felt this way since he met Kimyah but one other time.

"What is something we use to eat everyday as we walked to school?" Kimyah says as she starts to get excited.

"No way." Mychal says as he was starting to feel better at the thought of what she was talking about.

"That's right, My-My. I have grapes and strawberries." Kimyah says as she pulls out a large bag of them. Mychal took one long look at them. It just occurred to him that he hadn't eaten this morning and they were looking so delicious to him.

"Remember what we called them?" Mychal says as he grabs the bag.

"Oh yeah. Grips and Scrawberries." Kimyah says as she starts to laugh. "It has been a long time since we have had them."

"Too long. I know you remember the song."

"I know you don't expect me to sing that song again. We haven't sang that song since the 5th grade."

"K, you are only in the 8th grade. You are not too old. Now come on and sing it with me. You know the melody. The one from the Isley Brother's song, "Everything is going to be alright, he's coming back, just like he said he would."

"This is so embarrassing."

"K."

"My-My." Kimyah says as she finally shakes her head in agreement.

"On the count of three. One, two, and three." Mychal says as he fashions his hand like he is holding a microphone between them.

"Grips and scrawberries are s-o-o-o tight,

In a ziploc bag,

On the way to school,

Grips and scrawberries equal happiness,

On the way to school,

On the way to school."

They both say as they fall out laughing. It had been a long time since walking to school together was fun. The past year and a half has been a strain on all that was good. Usually they were talking about Mychal's situation and that normally meant either Mychal was venting or they were praying together. He needed to get the despair of the night before out of his system. Mychal truly felt that having someone doing drugs and you being a part of the situation, is just as bad as taking them. That was why it was so important for him to talk to Kimyah every morning so they could pray. He felt cleansed by it and it also started his day fresh and gave him a reason to strive. Mychal knew he wasn't strong enough to take on the task of helping his mom. Every day he prays for the ability to press on. There has been many times where he just wanted to give up. Mychal finally controlled his laughter, he looks at Kimyah, and wanted to just release all the feelings he had bottled up inside of him. He wanted to walk up to her, hug her, and cry. He wanted to let her know that he was losing it and the whole situation with his mom has turned for the worst. She smiled at him and it put a calming effect on him that subdued his last thought.

"That's what I am talking about My-My. Do you see what the grapes and strawberries did for us? God used the simplest thing to brighten up our morning. I bet you were down because of whatever happened last night. God reminded you of his grace and love by bringing happiness back in your day. I hope you see that." Kimyah says as she stops walking so she can grab a handful of grapes and two strawberries. Mychal watched her eat the grapes and he thought back to what he remembered in the kitchen a few minutes ago. He just thought about grapes and strawberries and now he was eating some. God knew he needed something to remind him of how the situation could be when God was in control.

"You better eat some before we get to school because you know once everyone sees them they are going to want some." Kimyah says as she pretends to throw a grape at his face.

"You are right." Mychal says as he grabs a hand full of grapes and stuffs them in his mouth.

"I am so impressed. I definitely want you as my future husband." Kimyah says sarcastically.

Little did she know that he was truly hungry. Last night he didn't eat at all after what he witnessed. He lost his appetite because of his actions. He had never seen his mom taking drugs. The worse her addiction became, the less she was hiding it. He would normally see the after effect of the drugs. She would either be wired up and bouncing off the walls, or she would be sitting still and no matter if Mychal called her name or even shook her, she ignored him as if she was no longer in her body. So last night, he only sat in his bed and cried. He cried for a good two hours. He prayed a little and felt sorry for himself but he wanted so desperately to call Kimyah but his mom sold his cellphone for drugs. Can you imagine the irony in that? Imagine getting a phone bill and you don't even have a phone to use. That was some of the things that happen when drugs are involved.

"These strawberries are extremely sweet, like me huh." Kimyah says as she nudges him out of his daze.

"You know it."

"Well, I have to go to my history class to talk about my extra credit so I won't be able to sit by the side of the building this morning. Are you going to behave without me little boy?" Kimyah says to get a laugh out of Mychal.

"Yes ma'am." Mychal says as he stuffs his mouth again.

"You are too much. Unless you feel like talking then I can do it after school. It is just that we have Youth Bible Group after school and I didn't want to make us late." Kimyah says in her third attempt to get what happened out of him.

"Go ahead. I will be fine." Mychal managed to get out between putting strawberries into his mouth.

"Ok, but let me say a quick prayer for you."

"I need that."

"Heavenly father, I just want to thank you for being you. All merciful and very compassionate. I am saying this prayer so you can touch Mychal and let him know that you are still in control and that you are taking care of his situation as we speak. Just keep your loving arms around him to protect him. I say this prayer in Jesus name, Amen."

"Thank you K."

"No problem. Well, ok. I will see you later. Just meet me at my locker after school, ok?" Kimyah says as she grabs a few more strawberries.

"Ok. What about these?"

"Eat them. Bye My-My." Kimyah says as she does her usual wink that accompanies her goodbyes.

"Bye and thanks." Mychal says as he watches her enter the school. He just stood there as she walked up the stairs. He was glad he had free time because he wanted to go to the front office to get some information packets on drug use/prevention. Mychal felt that the least he could do is research up on ways to help his mom. He saw the packets in there the last time he was in the front office. The idea came to mind last night when he was watching a show about addictions. The only thing he has done about his mom's situation is pray and unfortunately nothing has happened. His mom just seemed to get worst. It is not that he doesn't have faith in God; it's that maybe God wants him to put in more effort to obtain the end of the situation. Maybe God wants him to be more proactive and that's what he aims to do. Mychal takes a step into the school and he notices two boys staring at him. It wasn't a stare like they hadn't seen him in a long time or that they even recognized him. They had a look as if they were up to something. Mychal just continues to look at them as they tap each other and start to walk towards him. Mychal knew he didn't know the boys so the reason why they are even coming his way is obvious. So before the boys could even open their mouths, Mychal grabs a couple of strawberries and hands the bag to them.

"Thanks." The boys said as they ran off. It wasn't as if Mychal was afraid that they were going to do something to him because he was bigger than both of them, he just didn't want them to cause a scene begging.

Mychal then turns and he starts to walk towards the front office. He knew that the time is now to start to help his mom. What happened last night scared him and he doesn't want to be put in that situation again. He starts to look at all the lockers and classrooms as he passes by them. He sees some students engaging in conversations, some having trouble getting their lockers open, some just sitting down on the floor in front of the lockers. Mychal can't help but to wonder what their home life is like. He wonders how normal their lives are. Are they facing anything similar to what he is facing? Do they have to watch their parents waste away? Do they have to lock their bedroom door so their belongings won't get sold for money to buy drugs? Do they worry about coming home and finding their mom dead from an overdose? Do they have to live with the fact they are helping someone die? Probably not because the most they have to deal with is what will they wear to school or something simple like that. Mychal knew he was facing grown folk problems, which in most cases would fold the average thirteen-year-old. He knew he had God and that was the all the strength he needed. He also knew that God gave him Kimyah to further that notion. Mychal just hates that at times his situation gets him down and no matter how much he prays and talks to God, he doesn't necessarily feel better. He sometimes wondered if that was his lack of faith taking over or his lack of patience in God's plan. He wanted to just pray about it and be done with it. No more worrying or no more second-guessing the outcome. It just isn't that easy to do

when you see someone continuing to do what you pray they won't
do. How they seem to be getting worse more than they are getting
better. It's as if your prayers are not working and there really is no
relief in sight except death. That was something Mychal thought
about because it could happen at any moment when drugs are
involved. They almost go hand in hand. Without finding help they
are like Siamese twins, joined and inseparable. Mychal hoped it
would never get to that point. His mom's death was not an option to
him. Yeah it would make things a lot easier because he would no
longer have to put up with his mom being in the state that she was
in. He wouldn't have to worry about being around drugs at all. He
would go back to having a normal life, filled with normal problems.
He also knew that he had no clue where he would go. It's not like
there is anywhere for him to go. He knew he had to help her
because his well-being depended on it. In order for things to go
back to the way they once were, he needed to be equipped with
the ability to ease her pain. He felt that he could better provide help
if he knew the options he had. The pamphlets should provide him
with the information he needs or anything else, they would give him
hope that things could get better. Mychal makes it to the front office
and walks in. He had not been in here since his last meeting with
his counselor last year. He wasn't the type of student to get in
trouble so his visits were far and few. As he is standing in the open
door he is immediately greeted with stares. There are at least ten
kids seated in the waiting area, which was rather large. It took up
the majority of the room. It was twice as large as the space behind
the receptionist. Mychal just surveys the area. He sees two boys
whose clothes were all dirty and torn. It looks like they were in
there for fighting on the school bus because in between them was
a school bus driver with the extra loud orange shirt that said it. The
boys were still attempting to kick each other even though the bus
driver was between them. There was this other boy sitting down
next to someone who is probably his mother. She looked as if she
rolled straight out of bed, and came straight to the school. It seems
like she didn't put in any effort to comb her hair, brush her teeth,

wash her face, or iron her clothes. She was the worst looking person he has ever seen that was fully capable of correcting everything that is wrong. Her son was obviously embarrassed by the way she was looking because he was trying to distance himself from her. He was slowly inching his way to the chair next to him. She had no clue to what was going on because she was giving a stern, angry stare to the receptionist who was trying not to show that she was nervous because of it. Then there were three boys sitting next to each other. The one in the middle was sleep with his mouth wide open. The two boys that were on both sides of him were wadding up tiny pieces of paper and dropping it into the sleeping boy's mouth. They were trying their best to not laugh as they were dropping them in. They must have been at it for a while because tiny wads were piling up and it could be seen peeking out of the boy's mouth. Next to them were two girls who were just staring at Mychal. He couldn't tell if they were staring because they like what they see or because they were just rude to stare in the first place. If they liked what they saw, that was too bad for them. He only had eyes for Kimyah, even though Kimyah didn't know it. Still he wouldn't give them the time or day. Then there was a boy and a girl sitting next to each other. The boy had a disciplinary sheet that is given to someone who breaks one of the school's rules. The girl was signing the portion that was supposed to be signed by the parent. He then took the sheet and compared it to a signature on another sheet of paper. He studied them and then he gave her the thumbs up. Mychal then surveyed the rest of the waiting area for the pamphlets he needed. They were usually stored on a four-foot wooden shelf. It was normally in the far right corner once you walk in the office. It is definitely not there now because there was a tall fake plant there. He continues to look about the office when he notices the shelf on a wall next to his counselor's office. He knew he had to get one; Mychal just didn't want to see his counselor. He walks up to the counter and tries to get the receptionist's attention. She peeks up ever so slowly as if she doesn't want to give the impression that she realizes someone is standing at her desk. She finally looks up happy to not be in the angry mom's stare.

"Yes."

"I was wondering if I could get one of the pamphlets on that shelf back there."

"Oh sure." She says as she smiles.

"It's for an extra credit project." Mychal says as if he needed to explain his reasons for wanting the pamphlet.

"Ok." The receptionist says as if to say whatever.

Mychal walks around the counter and he strolls up to the shelf. It had a ton of pamphlets on it. There were pamphlets on alcohol, depression, diseases, drugs, health, and nutrition. There was a world of things to learn about. Mychal focuses on the drug pamphlets and he grabs one of each. Just as he was about to put them in his backpack, his counselor walks out of her office.

"Mychal Stone. How are you doing?" She asks with a puzzled look on her face.

"Hi Miss Weeks. I am doing well."

"What are you doing? Is there something you need?" She asks as she tries to look at what he was attempting to put in his backpack. Miss Weeks has been his counselor since he first got into middle school. She was a middle-aged woman with some very thick-rimmed glasses. She looked every day of her age. She was very overweight and Mychal felt bad whenever other students made fun of her. She was very nice and she genuinely cared about everyone. Mychal liked her but at this moment; she was the last person he wanted to see.

"I was bored so I thought I would just read these pamphlets." Mychal says as he immediately realizes that he just said the worst excuse in the history of excuses. There were a number of things he could have said like he was getting them for a friend, or doing an extra credit project like he told the receptionist. Anything was better than basically saying he was so bored that he couldn't find anything better to do that come to the office and grab some drug pamphlets.

"Ok, but if you need something, don't hesitate to come and see me."

"Yes ma'am." Mychal says as he backs up and walks out from behind the counter. He quickly exits the office and makes his way towards his first class.

*   *   *

"Good afternoon everyone. I am glad so many of you made it out this evening. After Brother Johnson prays for us we are going to pair up with our accountability partners and go over anything that the two of you need to address." Miss White says as she stands in front of the room. Mychal loved coming to Youth Bible Group. Youth Bible Group took place every Friday, from 4pm to 8pm. The group touched on many different things that effect youth in society. There was a time to pray together, a time to fellowship, and a time to brainstorm over ways that they could be more involved in things other than church without losing focus of being Christ-like. That was what was most important to Mychal was finding ways to incorporate Christ in his life at all times. He loved God and learning more about him and all the wonderful things he is about. This was his outlet from his home life. Most of the time here, he would pray for his mom. They had prayer rooms where you could go in at any time during the class and pray. On days when things are real bad, he would go in there and just sit. He would let God talk to him. He would try to release all his emotions in there. There were at least

244

twenty-nine other youth from the neighborhood and surrounding community. The youth here seemed so much different than the ones at school. They had more focus and desire than most youth. Mychal liked that a lot because he really didn't have any friends. Kimyah was his only true friend and he kept it that way. Here, he could talk to other youth about things that they struggle with and he would find ways to better his situation. Of course he never mentioned his mom to anyone except for Kimyah. Since she was his accountability partner he had no need to. If someone was going through the same thing he was, he had no way of knowing.

"Brother Johnson, lead us in prayer." Miss White says as she bows her head. Mychal was in deep thought the whole time that Brother Johnson was praying. One, he knew that Brother Johnson was long winded so prayer could last a good five minutes. Second, he was constantly thinking about his mom. Normally he would go home first and speak to her before he came here but lately Mychal has had no desire to do that. He did not want to see her because it would always ruin his mood. So Mychal tried to free his mind and focus on what Brother Johnson was praying about.

"Thank you Brother Johnson. Ok, break out with your partners."

Mychal looks at Kimyah and they immediately go to the farthest table in the room which is the one closes to the prayer rooms. Kimyah knew that Mychal would begin to talk about his mom and that sometimes he is overcome with emotions and would need to slip off into one of the rooms. So they sat at their favorite table. Mychal watched as Kimyah laid out her bible and her notepad. She always took notes about what they were talking about. She told him she wrote it down so she could pray about it when she got home. Her notepad was almost full and that was saying a lot because it had at least five hundred pages to it and they have only been going to Youth Bible Group for only three months. So she flipped through the notepad until she got to an empty page. She grabbed her favorite pen and instantly looked up at Mychal. They just stared at each other. Her eyes were saying, "Spill the beans." His eyes were saying, "I am trapped." He knew that there was no way he was going to get out of telling her what took place last night. He could lie but after his past attempts at that, he knew better.

"So you want to go straight to the main course?" Mychal asks even though he knew the answer.

"I am that hungry." Kimyah says without missing a beat to his reference of his story to food.

"Are you sure you don't want an appetizer first?"

"My-My, I have nothing to talk about. So let's get down to the real thing." Kimyah says displaying less patience with his avoiding tactics. "I didn't say anything about it the whole way here. I wanted to wait until now so come on."

"Ok." Mychal felt a nauseating feeling come over him. He was about to tell her something that he wished never took place. He knew he could have simply walked away and left his mom to fend for herself. If she was able to do it fine, if not then oh well. He knew that should have been his attitude but now the damage is done.

"Last night I was doing my homework when I heard the smoke detector buzzing. I immediately ran down the hall to see what was going on. The way my mom is now, all doped up all the time, I just knew there was a strong possibility that the house could have been on fire. She hasn't been too responsible and that definitely worried me. So I run to the kitchen and I see that she was attempting to make a grilled "something" sandwich. There was two pieces of bread stacked on top of each other on a skillet. The skillet was dry, no butter, and no cooking spray. She was basically trying to dry fry two pieces of bread. I immediately grabbed the frying pan and I moved it to an off burner. I turned the stove off and I immediately turn to find her. Lo and behold she was sitting at the kitchen table in her own world. She had a spoon in one hand and she was holding it over a lighter, which was in the other hand. She was trying to heat up the contents that were on the spoon. She was totally focused on what she was doing and didn't see me or even acknowledge the smoke detector going off. She was clueless to the smoke that filled the kitchen. I couldn't take the sound of the smoke detector any longer so I turned the fan on over the stove. I grabbed the nearest dishtowel and I start to fan in front of the smoke detector. If you have ever heard one of those things from close range, you will know how annoying those things are. So now I was a little mad. I was aggravated by her non-actions as well as her actions, if you know what I mean. Anyway, I turn to her because I was ready to fuss at her and she pretended like I wasn't even there. I walked up to her and stood directly over her. As if I was invisible, she continued on her mission to take the drugs. She had already transferred the drugs to the needle she had and now she was attempting to inject them into her body. She grabbed a belt she had sitting in her lap and I watched her try to put the belt around her arm so she could find a vein to inject the drug into. I watched her struggle and shake to get that belt on her arm. As I stood there, she cursed calling herself everything in the book. She got so agitated that as she cursed, spit was flying out of her mouth. It was a pathetic site, one that I couldn't stand to look at any longer." Mychal says as he pauses. He knew he was about to drop a bombshell on Kimyah. One that she had no idea it was even coming. Mychal took a deep breath as his mind screamed for him to finish. His heart was pounding as it was overflowing with nervousness at the thought of what he was about to say.

"Finish Mychal." Kimyah says as she readies her pen so she could continue to write their conversation down.

"Well, like I said I was already mad because of the smoke detector going off and her disregard for anyone's safety. Then she was cursing and carrying on as if the only thing important to her was taking that drug. I was sick of her at that point. Sick of her actions, I was sick of her cursing and most of all I was sick at the sight of her. So I grabbed the belt."

At that point Kimyah looked up at Mychal and he felt liked his breath had gotten sucked out of his chest.

"I grabbed the belt and I tightened it for her."

Kimyah dropped her pen.

"I tightened it for her because I was sick and tired of her."

Tears formed in Kimyah's eyes.

"I couldn't stand to see her like that so I helped her just so that moment would be over.

Kimyah stared at Mychal as her tears ran down her cheek. Mychal could see that she wasn't taking it very well. He cannot tell if those are tears of anger for what he done or tears of disappointment at his actions. Mychal wanted to get up and go to the prayer room and just hide. He did not want to be sitting before Kimyah right now. He could not stand to see her like this. Kimyah puts her head down and she starts to cry. Mychal just sat there watching. He was frozen and just like last night, he was unable to help. It felt as if he knew all of this was going to be the result of his actions; he knows he would have done things differently. He cared deeply for Kimyah and she is devastated by what he has done. She has cried before but never like this. This is as if he hurt her deeply and that is making him feel worst. To hurt Kimyah was basically to hurt all that was good in his life and Mychal couldn't accept that. He wanted to walk around the table and give her a big hug and tell her how much he was truly sorry but he knew that this wasn't the time or the place. Kimyah looks up at him as if she heard his last thought.

"K, I am so sorry." Mychal says as he extends a hand across the table towards Kimyah. She didn't move an inch, she just continued to stare and cry so he pulled his hand back. He knew that whatever the reason was for her to not hold his hand wasn't good.

"I am going to go and get you some tissue." Mychal says, as he doesn't expect a reply so he stands up and he walked to the front of the room to get some Kleenex's. He turns and he sees that Kimyah is still staring at his chair. She has not made any visible movements since he left as if she was in shock. So Mychal sits back down and hands the Kleenex's across the table. Kimyah takes one and she wipes her face and as soon as she stopped, tears started flowing again.

"My-My, I am so disappointed with you. I am hurt by what you said you did because I would have not thought in a million years that you would ever do something like that." Kimyah says as the tears just continued to flow. No matter how many times she wiped her face, it was still wet with tears.

"I know. I couldn't believe that I let myself get caught up in that situation. I wasn't thinking."

"You are right you weren't thinking. There is no excuse for what you have done. If anything you should have taken that needle and thrown it away or something. Anything was better than helping her."

"I know." Mychal says as he puts his head down.

"I can't even express the hurt I feel. You have let me down big time. My-My, that is your mother. That is the only family you know. Did you not think about the consequences of your actions? You helped her do drugs. You helped her habit and I would have felt better if you would have told me that you watched her struggle to take the drugs. I wouldn't have cared if you said that she struggled the whole night. At least she would know that under no circumstances would you help her. None, now she probably feels like anytime she needs you that you will be there to help her. You have definitely crossed the line."

"I am sorry for that. I felt I had no choice."

"What do you mean?"

"I mean, what else could I have done? She needed that stuff real bad. I wish you had seen that look on her face. I had never seen her look like that before. It was the scariest as well as the most disheartening look I have ever witnessed. I didn't know what to do."

"You could have thrown that mess away. You could have called the cops. You could have come and gotten me and we would have thought of something together. Anything was better than what took place."

"Kimyah that is my mom we are talking about. Not some stranger on the street. I love her. To see her wanting that stuff as bad as she wanted it was too much for me.

"If you truly loved her you would do something about her situation. Hold her accountable for her actions. Don't let her kill herself and possibly you. What if you had been sleep and the whole house would have burnt down? You would have died and you would have to blame yourself as much as you would your mom. I don't want to see anything happen to her and I definitely don't want anything to happen to you. So you must decide if you are going to spend the rest of your life taking care of her or are you going to do something about it." Kimyah says as the flood of tears has stopped considerably. Mychal just sat there soaking in what she had said. He cannot see this situation going on forever. There has to be an end to this. He wants more than anything to be able to live a normal life. Mychal knew that he wanted his mom back and that was most important to him.

"My-My, this is unreal. I cannot believe this. After all of our talks and you were saying how much you hated drugs. Do you remember our conversations?" Kimyah asks as she pushes the box of Kleenex aside.

"I do remember them."

"Do you recall telling me that you would never in any way help her take drugs? Do you remember that?"

"Yes I do."

"Do you remember what I said I would do for you if that happened?"

"Yes."

"Well."

"You said that you would not like what took place but you would be there for me regardless."

"That is exactly how I feel now. I am upset at you for what you have done but I am still here for you. I will be by your side no matter what. Just promise me you won't do that again. Can you make that promise to me?" Kimyah says as she extends her hands across the table. Mychal immediately grabs her hands as if his were being drawn to them like a magnet. He relished the thought of being able to caress her soft hands; hands that he always look forward to holding. He knew that she probably didn't realize how much he enjoyed this moment right here. It meant so much to him to hold her hand and he was going to make the most of it.

"I promise to do what is right next time. I will not help her in any way. I promise." Mychal says, as he is amazed at how easily that rolled off his tongue.

"Thank you for that My-My. I know you will do right next time." Kimyah says as she sports her pretty smile. Mychal needed that from her more than anything. She had a way of brightening up his day with her smile and this time was no different. He felt in his heart that Kimyah was the most precious thing in his life. The way she helped him in his time of need was always right on time. How she always knew what to say and what to do. That meant a lot to him. He knew that he constantly thanked God for her and he knows exactly what he needed to do now.

"K, let's pray."

"Most definitely. I feel that is needed." Kimyah says as she raises her hand to get Miss White's attention. Miss White notices her hand and starts to make her way towards them.

"Yes Kimyah." Miss White says as she finally makes it to the table.

"Mychal and I would like to pray together in the prayer room." Kimyah says as she looks to Mychal for support.

"Ok, that is fine. You know which room is designated for it." Miss White says as she walks away. Anytime two or more people wanted to pray in private but together, there was a special prayer room for it. It was larger than the rest of them but it had a glass door so people can see in. It was like that so everyone would be held accountable for going in the prayer room together. You would think that they wouldn't need something like this but you never know these days.

"Thank you Miss White." Mychal says as he pushes the chair back and stands up. Kimyah does the same and they walk over to the prayer room. Once inside, they shut the door and they get on both knees together. They face each other and Mychal nods to let Kimyah know that he was about to begin. He closes his eyes and before he could even say a word, all kinds of thoughts flow through his mind. He was thinking of a million things to pray about but he knew he needed to focus on what was at hand. All of a sudden he felt Kimyah hands grab his and that gave him the added courage to pray what was exactly on his mind.

"Heavenly Father, we just thank you for your grace and mercy. We thank you for your son dying on the cross for us. We come before you right now asking for your guiding hand, asking

All the time Mychal was praying he could feel Kimyah's grip getting tighter when he said things that he felt meant the most to her. He knew that when he spoke of her, that he wanted to say more but he didn't have the courage. He knew that this wasn't the time and he was just thankful that she was in here with him and that meant everything to him.

"That was a wonderful prayer, My-My. You didn't have to say what you said about me." Kimyah says as she lets go of his hands and stands up.

"It was the least I could do." Mychal says as he stands up and opens the door for Kimyah to go out.

"Ok everybody it's time to eat. So, everyone make your way to the next room." Brother Johnson says as he stands in the doorway of the room.

"I am about to go act a fool. I am so hungry." Mychal says as he makes his way to the door.

"I am too." Kimyah says as she follows.

Praying always gave Mychal a feeling that everything was going to be okay. He knew that it was a way of giving it to God and letting him take control of the situation. Mychal felt at ease for the first time all day.

*   *   *

"Ok you think you are so smart huh."

"K, you are just mad because I have gotten more questions right than you." Mychal says as he sticks his chest out.

This was another reason why he loved going to Youth Bible Group. Every time they walked home, they would quiz each other over things of the bible that are not necessarily known by the average bible reader. It was their way of staying knowledgeable about the bible and to have bragging rights if you got the most right.

"Ok, I have one for you. Who wrote the first five books of the bible?"

"K, I thought this was supposed to be hard. The answer is Moses."

"Your turn."

"Since you want to give, "who wrote what book questions," then I have one for you. Who wrote the book of Hebrews?"

"No one really knows who wrote Hebrews. You thought you had me."

"You got lucky."

"How many years after Malachi was there no prophecy?" Kimyah ask as she has a look like she thought of a tough one.

"Let's see, I think it would have to be four hundred years."
Mychal says shaking his head up and down.

"You make me sick."

"Ok, I have one for you. What book in the bible doesn't
make any reference to God?"

"Now you could have done better than that. It's my girl
Esther. Of course I would know that."

"Whatever." Mychal says as he shakes his head.

Mychal was enjoying this walk home. He was still feeling good after
praying with Kimyah. The prayer, in a way, helped him remember
to leave things in God's hands and then have the patience to see it
through. He sometimes feels as if God isn't working fast enough.
As if he needs to see some sign or just a little improvement in his
situation. He knows that is the wrong way to think because God
doesn't work on our time. He fixes every situation when he is
ready. Mychal just hopes he does everything necessary to prove
that he believes that.

"On what mountain did Moses see the burning bush?"

"Oh my. That is a tough one." Mychal says as he stops
walking so he can focus on trying to find the answer." I know it
starts with a letter in the alphabet."

"You are crazy." Kimyah says as she hits him on the arm

"I would have to say, Horeb. Am I right? Mychal asked.

"Yes you are."

"Ok K, I have one. From which book of the prophets did
Jesus read at the synagogue?"

"Isaiah." Kimyah answers as she raises her arms over her head like she just won a race. "My turn. Who fulfilled God's promise that Abraham's seed would bless the whole earth?

"The one and only Jesus Christ." Mychal says as he begins to strut.

"You better had gotten that right.

"What is the shortest book of the bible?"

"2John." Kimyah says as she nods her head. Mychal knew that Kimyah knew a lot about the bible. "Let's just call it a tie. Ok, My-My?"

"That is cool because I ran out of questions."

"Me too."

"It feels good out here tonight." Mychal says as he takes in a deep breath of cold air.

"40 degrees really isn't that bad. Not since I have my new hat." Kimyah says as she turns around so Mychal could see the back of it.

"That's a hat. I thought that was just a bad wig." Mychal says as he takes a step away from Kimyah because he knew she would probably retaliate.

"My-My! I can't believe you don't like my hat. My dad bought it for me."

"K, your dad is not famous for his style of dress. Do you remember those famous jeans? Do you remember those jeans that had about twelve pockets on them? There were pockets everywhere there wasn't supposed to be one."

"Don't you go there, My-My. I don't feel like laughing again."

"Oh no, we must go there. Those jeans were something to behold. I can't help but remember them. Just let me try to describe them to you so you can remember how unforgettable they truly were. Where can I begin? Let me start with the color of them. The color alone made them one of a kind. I have seen many colors in my day but the color of those jeans were out of this world. I have never in my life heard of mustard brown. Who would buy some mustard brown pants? Since when has mustard ever been brown? Then the texture of those pants was a cross between denim and velvet. The shine those pants had were second to nothing. Now let's get on those famous pockets. On the front side of the pants he had two pockets in the front, which is normal, but those pockets on both knees were different. What do you suppose someone would put in a pocket that is on your knee? Some chips? Some gum? What would truly be the purpose of that? Ok, so that is four pockets on the front side, and eight more to go. If that isn't some sort of fashion first then I guess I am not hip to fashion. Next, we go to the backside of his pants that had eight, let's count them, eight pockets on them. That must be the all-time record for pockets. On the seat part that normally has two pockets, he had a whopping three pockets. How is that even humanly possible? What would you need with an extra seat pocket? Then, not to be out done, he had one pocket on the back of the thigh part of his pants. What would that pocket be doing right there? Who would use such a pocket? Can you help a brother out Kimyah?"

All Kimyah could do was sit down on the sidewalk and try to hold in her laughter. She was giving him a wave that meant to leave her alone.

"Continuing on, next we go on down to the pockets that are on the back of both knees. Now I don't know about you but the pockets on the front of the knees should have been plenty. What would fit comfortably in the back of your knees? How is it even possible to get away with such a design? I have heard of the fashion police but where are they when you need them. Then to top it all off, he had enough nerves to have a pocket on the bottom of both pants legs. What is truly the purpose of having pockets on the bottom of both pants legs? Anything worth carrying two inches off the ground, on the back of your leg is not anything someone would want. Is there something I am missing? Have I not gotten the invitation to ride on the fashion wagon?" Mychal says as he stops so he can fall to his knees and release the laughter he had growing inside of him. Kimyah eyes were all watery as she was holding her side.

"Oh man my side is killing me." Kimyah says as she tries to catch her breath.

"No those pants are killing me." Mychal says as he tries to get his composure.

"I must admit that my dad was wrong for those pants. He also tried to be different. Sometimes it worked and sometimes it didn't." Kimyah says as she dusts herself off because she had been sitting on the ground.

"Very wrong." Mychal says as he starts walking again.

"I just saw something I have never seen before." Kimyah says to get Mychal's attention.

"What? Where?"

"Breathe out your mouth again." Kimyah asks, as she stands closer to Mychal.

"Like this?" Mychal asks as he blows out of his mouth.

"See, when I blow out of my mouth the air freezes and it comes out white. When you blow out of your mouth it comes out green. What's up with that?" Kimyah says as she starts to smile a big cheesy smile.

"I tell you what's wrong with that, you trying to be funny is what's wrong." Mychal replies.

"I had to say something since you were talking about my dad."

"Well, we are here." Mychal says to make reference to them finally making it home.

"Indeed we are."

"What are you doing tomorrow?" Mychal asked as he stops between their houses.

"Nothing I know of. I haven't talked to my parents so I really don't have a clue."

"Well, when you have a clue come by and see me, ok?"

"I will My-My." Kimyah says as she just looks at Mychal. Mychal noticed her looking and he tries to keep the stare but he nervously looks away. He wanted to at least get a hug from her but he didn't have the heart to make the first move.

"I will see you later." Mychal says as he starts to take a step back.

"My-My." Kimyah says as if she was going to say something.

"What's up?" Mychal asks, waiting on her to say what was really on his mind too.

"Nothing. Bye." Kimyah says as she winks and walks to her door. She unlocks the door, looks back at Mychal, waves, and goes into her house.

"Bye." Mychal says, as he is disappointed that she didn't say what he wanted her to say. What makes him more disappointed is that he didn't say what he should have said. He knew that he cared a lot for Kimyah but he wasn't good at expressing his feelings. He wanted so badly to say something but he ended up saying nothing. Now that he said nothing he had to go home feeling like his night wasn't truly complete. Walking up to his house he could feel his mood changing. The feeling of happiness and relief was fading and it was replaced with a feeling of depression and sadness, as he knew what he was about to see. Over the past year and a half, there haven't been many days that he would come home and not be reminded of what has taken place. It was as if the effect of drugs on his household was so strong that not only does it affect his mom but anything that she is around. The house was just as dead as the long-term effect that drugs has on the body.

"Please be sleep. Please be sleep." Mychal says as he takes a deep breath and sticks his key in the door. He could not hear any movement on the inside of his house so he was hoping his mom was asleep because he didn't want to deal with her. He wanted to enjoy the little bit of the feeling he had the past four hours. He knew one look at her and he would instantly lose it. So he turns the key and pushes the door open. He notices that almost every light is on from the front door all the way to the back of the house. He steps in and he shuts the door behind him and locks it. He takes one step forward and stops. He notices that it is extremely quiet and that scares him. He starts to walk down the hall and the first thing he notices is the hall closet is cracked open and the light was on. He walks towards the door and he slowly pulls it open. He sees that everything looked like it had been disturbed. The leather coats that once hung in there are long gone. They were the first casualties of the drugs. Now the only thing that was left was photo albums and boxes of paperwork from his mom's last job. All the boxes were busted open or turned over. Every box from the top shelf had been dumped on the ground and the contents were everywhere. There were photos all over the closet and the sight of them made Mychal angry. Here were precious photos that she had no regard for. She dumped them out as if she knew of no one in the pictures or wasn't part of any moment captured on them. Mychal saw his baby pictures, pictures of them on the only two vacations he can remember, her office party pictures, and all his school pictures. He slams the door shut. He starts to walk a little faster as he makes it to the living room. He sees the couch pillows were all thrown across the room as if someone was looking for something under them. The couch was pushed a good two feet from where it normally sat as if someone was searching for something under it. The television was still on its stand in the corner of the room. It hadn't been touched and there was good reason for it. His mom tried to take the television out of the house to sell it for drugs but it was too heavy. A 52-inch television was too heavy and bulky for a one hundred-pound drug addict. She ended up dropping it and it hasn't worked since. So now it sits in the corner, covered with dust, never to be used again. Now it was nothing more than a prop, sitting in the living room. The rug that occupied half the room was overturned and it showed the only clean spot on the floor. There wasn't anything left alone in the room. Everything else grew legs and found its way out of the house. The lamps, coffee table, and paintings all had lame excuses why they were no longer part of the house. At first some of the reasons were believable but after a while they became so made up that he stopped asking about things that went missing. It made him angry that his mom thought he was so dumb that he would fall for the excuses. The look on her face when she told the lies was one of someone who truly believed what they were saying. Mychal then walks pass the living room and he heads towards the kitchen. He can faintly hear light tapping. The closer he got the louder the tapping became. He rounds the corner and steps into the kitchen. The kitchen was still a mess from the night before. The same frying pan with the burnt bread was on the stove. The smell was still lingering. The kitchen hadn't been clean since the last time he did it. Just like all the chores in the house. He ended up doing them all. His mom was sitting at the kitchen table. She was looking just as bad as she did the night before. Her hair was all over the place and her eyes were the usual blood shot red. Her lips were still dry and crusty and her clothes were dirty. Come to think of it, those were the same clothes she had on for the past two days. She was tapping on a calculator as if she was adding up some figures. All around her was items from different parts of the house. She had her shoes, clocks, dishes, some pictures he drew in elementary, dictionary, calendars, and some mail. Mychal just stands in the entryway of the kitchen and shakes his head. When someone is under the influence of drugs, anything is possible in their mind. He was pretty sure that she had a perfectly good excuse for having all those things in the kitchen. He wanted to just walk on out and go to his room but something was nagging at him. The feeling wanted him to go and find out what she was up to. Find out why she went out of her way to destroy the front section of the house. Since he didn't make it pass the kitchen he was sure that she didn't miss a room. He looked back towards his room and saw that his room still looked as if it was locked. He quickly looked back at his mom, he looked over the area, and he didn't notice anything from inside his room in her piles. Still, he wanted to make sure she didn't touch his room. He started to make his way towards the room, he first comes to her room, and the light was on. He peeked inside and he notices the same thing he has noticed for a while. She had things all over the place but everything that was semi valuable was gone. If she could carry it, it was gone. He kept on walking and he stops to check out the bathroom. He steps inside and he notices that most of the medicine bottles are empty. The medicine for stomach aches, flu, sinuses, allergies, and cough was all empty. The bottles were empty as well as some of the bottles of cleaner. It was as if she was mixing some strange brew or something because there were remnants of everything in the sink. Mychal just walks back out and begins to make his way towards his door. He tries to open the door and notices that the door is still locked. He knew she hadn't gotten in. He looks a little harder at the lock and notices that it looks as if someone had been messing with it. He bends down to get a closer look and he sees scratches that are fresh because just this morning, they wasn't there. The thought of that made his pressure rise. He has told her time and time again to don't even attempt to open his door. That his room was totally off limits and under no circumstance must she enter or try to enter. For this very reason, he had a locksmith come out and install a heavy-duty lock on his door. He knew he had to do something because his mother was getting worst with her stealing. First it was things in her room, then she made her way around the house, and before she could get to his room, he took matters into his own hands. He caught her ordering things online with her credit cards, receiving the items, and then going out and trading the items for drugs. So one day he saw her credit card sitting on the counter and he made an appointment with a locksmith, who by chance loved the fact that the client wanted to pay before he came out to do the job and gave a generous tip. Mychal believes that was the last thing done on the computer because it magically disappeared or fell into the trash and was accidentally thrown away. That was the story told to him by his mother. That was hard to believe since the computer went missing after the trash can did. Never the less, he was glad that he had the lock installed. Now he had to go fuss at her because she broke one of the rules he laid down. It was funny how the roles have reversed and that was very strange thing to be a part of. Mychal was mad because he had so much to lose if she got inside his room and he had to show her he meant it when he said stay away. So as he was walking back towards the kitchen he tried to go over in his mind what he was going to say. He walks into the kitchen and just like before his mom was steady tapping on the calculator. She didn't even acknowledge that he was standing there. She just carried on as if he was invisible. Mychal cleared his throat to get her attention but she didn't pay it any mind. Now he was really getting angry.

"Iris! What in the world are you doing?"

"Not now because I am very busy." His mom says as she waves him off.

"Busy, huh? What are you doing with all this stuff in here?" Mychal asks, as he stands a little closer to her. He finally could smell her and he could definitely tell that she hadn't taken a bath in a few days. He became nauseated at the thought of that. At one point in time, she used to smell so good. Mychal used to love to guess the type of perfume she was wearing. He could always tell when she was home because her sweet aroma would precede her.

"What does it look like I am doing? I am getting things together for my garage sale." His mom replies matter-of-factly.

"Oh you are huh? How are you going to do that? You can't sell the stuff in the front yard because the neighborhood committee said that wasn't allowed. So how do you plan on doing it?"

"Whatever. I will do it over Stephon's house."

"Who is Stephon? Do you mean Stephon from your job? Wasn't he the one that eventually took your position?"

"No not that Stephon."

"Then what Stephon do you mean then? Stephon who?" Mychal says, as he knows that he is catching her in a lie.

"Stephon, umm, umm, Curry. Yeah Stephon Curry, that's who." His mom says as if she had convinced him as well as herself that, that was who it was.

"Oh that Stephon. I was sorry to doubt you." Mychal sarcastically says as he realizes that they would go back in forth with this unless he puts an end to it. He knew she made Stephon up or better yet, took him right off the Golden State Warriors. Arguing with her about it was pointless so he was ready to move on.

"So I guess you are trying to figure out how much you are going to get for these items?" Mychal says as he kicks over a pile of shoes.

"Hey, don't touch the merchandise. I can get a lot of money for these items." His mom snaps as she looks up at him with an angry look. Mychal could see into her eyes and he saw nothing but emptiness.

"Oh my bad. How much do you think you could get for all this stuff? $20 or $30?" Mychal asks as he once again takes a look at the items.

"Are you crazy? I am going to at least get a couple of thousand for these things." She says as she waves her bony arm over the items on the table. Mychal tried his best to hold his smirk in. Anybody in their right frame of mind would not try to sell these items because no one would buy them.

"A couple of thousand huh? Let's see how this is possible. I am going to start with these shoes right here." Mychal says as he grabs one ladies dress shoe and one tennis shoe. The reason why he did that was because he looked over the pile of shoes and none of them had a match. They were all singles. "Ok, how much for the jacked up ladies dress shoe and the Nike tennis shoe? Mychal tries to ask with a straight face. He knew it wasn't funny to mess with his mom while she was in this state but he couldn't help it. He wanted to get her back for messing with his lock.

"I have added them up and I will say $100 for the tennis shoe and $65 dollars for the pumps.

"What? No one is going to buy one shoe for that much money."

"Well, I am not going to sell both of them because those are my favorite shoes. As a matter of fact, all of these shoes are my favorites. I am not that crazy to give away both shoes. I wouldn't have anything to wear if I did." His mom says as she starts to pick up shoes and cradles them in her arms.

"Do you not hear me? No one is going to buy a used tennis shoe for $100."

"That one they will."

"What makes you so sure Iris?" Mychal asked

"Those are Air Jordan's." His mom says as she reaches for the tennis shoe. Mychal moved the tennis shoe out of her reach.

"These are not Air Jordan's." Mychal says as he looks more closely at the tennis shoe. He knew they weren't Air Jordan's. He still took a closer look at the tennis shoe and then he noticed there was some writing on them. It was written in black and it is visible if you look closer due to the shoes being all white with a red Nike swoosh.

"Air Gordan's." Mychal says out loud. Mychal could tell that someone had written or attempted to write Air Jordan on the tennis shoe. That someone was his mom and to make matters worse she misspelled Jordan by spelling it with a G instead of a J.

"Not Air Gordan's but Air Jordan's." His mom says as she continues to reach for the tennis shoe. Mychal just hands it to her because seeing how frail she was, was making him sick.

"See Air Jordan's." She says as she rubs her fingers across the word's she wrote. Mychal just stared at her. It was sad to see her like this. Mychal grabbed one of the clocks that were on the table. It was a small 8-inch by 6-inch clock that was very light. It felt as if it was hollow except for the small clock machinery and a battery. It was made of some very lightweight wood that was the cheapest type.

"How much for this clock?"

"Since that is a Swiss clock, I would say $200 or maybe $250." She says as she starts to tap on the calculator as if she is adding up some numbers.

"That is not a Swiss clock. What makes this a Swiss clock?" Mychal asks as he looks over the clock.

"I will tell you what." His mom says as she jerks the clock from out of his hand. "This right here says it."

She was pointing at some letters that was engraved on the clock. Mychal grabbed the clock back from her and he looked over what the engraving said.

"Oh, let me read it for you. It says, "Thank you for drinking Swiss Miss Hot Chocolate." He says as he hands her the clock.

"See I told you, all the way from the country of Swiss." She says as she takes the bottom of her dirty shirt and wipes the front of the clock off.

"Yeah, you sure know your countries." Mychal says as he looks for something else to grab. There was so much to choose from but he settled for a small box that had a small plastic tea set. It had a small teapot, four teacups, and four saucers.

"Oh man. I bet you could get at least a couple of hundred dollars for this."

"What are you talking about?" His mom says as Mychal lowers the box so she could look inside.

"You know it. It is very hard to find good China and I have the whole set. I wish I could sell that China cabinet with it. It would go together perfectly." She says as she shakes her head as if to show that she agreed with her idea.

"I thought China dishes were glass not plastic."

"You don't know fine China like I do. They make them in plastic now so they won't easily be broken."

"How do you know that this is China?"

"Fool, look at the writing on it. Can't you see Chinese writing when you see it?" She says as she tugs on the box until he lets it go. She sets it down on the other side of the table away from Mychal.

"Just because it has Asian writing on it doesn't necessarily make it Chinese."

"You don't have any clue what you are talking about." She snaps as she takes another short stare at the plastic tea set.

"You right." Mychal says as he grabs one of his drawings that he drew in elementary. They were stick figures of him, his mom, and his dad. They were in front of the house. He saw drawings of army men and all kinds of animals. Looking at them now he notices how terrible they were.

"Don't get your fingerprints on the front part. I am going to frame them. That is some fine paintings and drawings that I can get some major money for."

"What? These pictures right here?" Mychal says as he taps the drawings. "These are stick figures. There is a drawing of a man with big feet and hands and a stick body. This is not fine art."

"Give me those." She says as she touches Mychal's hand in an attempt to grab the drawings. Mychal felt a hard callous hand. It felt like someone who had to do hard labor with no gloves on and their hands received the bulk of the punishment. He gladly handed over the papers because he did not want to feel her hands on his skin. Mychal grabbed a stack of things he thought was magazines but they turned out to be calendars.

"Iris, no one wants an already used 2009 calendar." Mychal says as he looks over the calendar and drops it into her lap.

"Somebody would want to remember 2009. This would definitely help them." She says as she flips through the calendar.

"Oh yeah, somebody really wants to know that you were getting a root canal on June 6th. Better yet how about dads back waxing appointment? Wow, I can see someone remembering 2009 because of those things. Those were monumental dates in the history of mankind." Mychal says as he is getting real tired of this conversation he is having with his mom.

"What is this?" Mychal says as he grabs a stack of mail that was barely visible on the table because of the other items were on top of it.

"Oh. I was going to sell our address to one of those companies that send out junk mail. That way we could become rich and all we have to do is go to our mailbox to receive our check."

Mychal slams the mail down on the table.

"You are unbelievable. Do you not hear yourself talking? Do you hear how crazy and off the wall you are? You are pathetic and I am sick of it. I am going to bed. Good night." Mychal says as he turns to go to his room. He purposely kicks over the pile of shoes as he was stepping over them. Mychal shook his head at what just took place. He knew if this was a television show; folks would be rolling in their seats right now. He was trying to be funny but yet he didn't laugh because the reality is that his mom needs some serious help. She no longer thinks like a responsible adult with any common sense. She is thinking on a whole different level. It was sad to see a woman with a college degree talk as if she failed to make it out of middle school. Mychal finally made it to his room, and he grabs the gold necklace that held his keys from the inside of his shirt. He finds the key and sticks it into the door. He turns the lock and he pushes the door open, then he felt a hand on his shoulder. He turns around and it's his mom with one hand behind her back.

"Iris, what do you want?"

"I was wondering if I could come in your room so we could talk."

"No. We just got through talking, I am tired, and I want to go to sleep."

"Just for a second." She says as she tries to look past Mychal. Mychal knew she wanted to scope out the place or possibly snatch something while she was in there.

"No way. I told you many times before that you would never be allowed in here again. I meant it when I said it.

"But I am your mom and I said let me in." She says as she tries to push past Mychal. The thought of this made him angry. So he gives her a slight shove and she almost went flying to the wall parallel to the door. Mychal was shocked that she was that light and fragile. It felt like he was pushing a life-sized rag doll.

"Ok, ok. I see how you are." She says as she regains her balance.

"Good. Now you know how serious I am." Mychal says as he gives her a frown.

"I just want to help you clean up your room. That's all I want to do." She says, as her mood swings back to extra nice. One thing about her is that she could change from happy to angry to sad in less than a minute. It didn't take much and most of the time nothing was truly sincere, meaning she didn't really care one way or another.

"Clean up my room? You have got to be kidding me? Look at the house Iris. The house is always a mess. Every day it is a pigsty. I have to clean up behind you every day. You don't do anything but make huge messes. Look at what you did to the house today. You messed it up collecting your garage sale items." Mychal says through gritted teeth.

"No I didn't. That wasn't why I was looking through the house. I was looking in the closet, living room, and bathroom for money. I was hoping I could find some dollars or maybe some change lying around. I was trying to come up." She says as she tries to smile but her lips was so cracked and dry, that she could barely make a difference in her facial expression.

"You are impossible. Ok, I will see you tomorrow Iris. Go to bed. Get away from my door, go back to the kitchen, and count something." Mychal says as he begins to close the door. His mom sticks a skeleton like hand through the remaining gap between the door and frame.

"One more thing before you close the door. How much do you think I can get for this?" She says as she pulls a bottle of something from behind her back. It was a black, murky and very thick.

"What is that?" Mychal says even though he felt he already knew the answer.

"This stuff is better than Nyquil. It is my new cough, stomach ache, sinus, and flu remedy. Here take a whiff of this." She says as she tries to extend her arm further through the door. Mychal could already smell the bleach that was in it.

"I know that is not Clorox that I smell?"

"You know it. That is for people's sinuses. One whiff and their sinuses would be wide open."

Mychal just shuts the door. He didn't know what to do. His mom was way over the edge with this.

"So do you think $5 maybe $10 for it?" She yells through the door. Mychal ignored her, as he made sure the door was locked. He kept his light off because he felt moved by what he had just witnessed. He felt his eyes begin to fill with tears as he rested his head against the door and he listened at his mom's feeble attempt to turn the knob. She realized it was locked and walked away. Mychal tried to keep the tears in but he couldn't. He let them fall and there was more than he thought. He hadn't really cried that much since the whole situation took place. He had a few tears fall here or there but nothing to this magnitude. He felt them rolling down his face until they landed on his jacket. He quickly removed his jacket and dropped it by his feet. He felt the warmth of the tears and that made him feel like he has lost it all. He was truly in a saddened state, one that he felt he was strong enough to avoid. The tears that were flowing down his face were ones he had no control over. His body told him enough as it was no longer able to keep his feelings at bay. He knew he needed to release them but he didn't want to because he wanted to show no weakness. Mychal felt he was at the point of almost giving up. What was the true purpose of fighting what was taking place? He was being out smarted by a drug that doesn't even have a brain. A drug that isn't capable of thinking or doing anything and he was the weaker of the two combatants. The drugs were winning the battle and that made him cry even harder. So hard that he fell down to his knees and crawled up in the fetal position. The only thing left to do was to suck his thumb like a baby and show the final sign of surrendering. Just as his thumb was making his way towards his mouth, he heard a car horn outside. Mychal stands up and walks to his window. Looking through the burglar bars he sees a car pulling out from Kimyah's house. He hoped she wasn't in it. He looked across the seven feet of grass that divided his house from hers. He looked through her dining room window, which was adjacent from his bedroom. The light was off but he could see the hall light was on. He wanted so desperately for her to walk past the dining room so he could see her. He wiped his face quickly because he didn't want to miss anything.

"Please walk by. Please walk by." Mychal said over and over, somehow trying to will her to do so. He wanted nothing more at this moment than to see her long black hair. All of a sudden Kimyah walked by the dining room and stopped. She backed up until she was in the dining room door way. She stood there nodding her head up and down as if she was listening to someone. Then her mom walks up to her and gives her a hug. Her mom looked as if she was Kimyah's twin except she was full bloodied Chinese. She looked so young and pretty. Mychal watched in sadness as Kimyah kissed her mom and gave her a big hug. He was sad for two reasons. One, he wanted to be able to kiss and hug his mom in the same manner. He wanted nothing more than for her to be like she once was. Secondly, he wanted to be the receiver of Kimyah's hugs and kisses. He liked her so much and he hated the fact that he couldn't tell her how her really felt. If only he had the courage to do so. If only he was strong enough to help his mom with her addiction. It seemed that everything he wanted to do the most, he couldn't. He just didn't have the ability to summon the needed strength to tackle his problems and the thought of that opened the floodgate of tears. He watched as Kimyah walked out of the hallway, in front of the dining room, and probably off to her room. He slumped down in front of the window and cried. He cried and he thought about how helpless he was and that scared him. He was alone except for God and Kimyah. He was waiting on God to work his will. Mychal knew he wasn't acting like someone that gave their situation to God. He only hoped that this would pass and he would be able to wake up in the morning and be ready to face whatever came his way. He finally picks himself up off the ground and he walks to his bed and plops down on it. He rolled on his back and he said a quick prayer. Once he was finished, he pulled the cover over his body, and watched his mom's shadow under the door as she walked back and forth. He clutched his keys that were around his neck. He had all but forgotten that the keys were on a gold chain that Kimyah had brought him. She had saved up a couple of months' worth of allowance to buy it. It was his most prized possession. He had a television, radio and clock that were worth something but the necklace was worth more than all them combined. Mychal made sure he had it with him where ever he went. He was not going to let his mom sell it for drugs so he put his keys on it and kept it around his neck at all times. So now he was holding the necklace and he let the comfort of that soothe him to sleep.

274

Chapter Two – The Search

Honk

Honk

Mychal jumps up out of his sleep. He sits up and he looks around the room as he tries to focus his eyes. It was definitely morning because the sun was clearly shining in through his window. He looked at his clock and it said 10:30 am. That means he slept a good nine hours. That was a feat he hadn't accomplished in a while.

Honk

Honk

Mychal immediately jumps up and runs to the window. That was the second time he had heard a car's horn going off. He knew that his neighborhood was extremely quiet due to the large number of elderly people that lived there. They were quick to call the neighborhood committee when things got too loud. Since it was still morning, he knew something had to be going on. He looks towards the street and he sees something he can't believe.

"No way." Mychal yells at the window. Mychal felt a sickening feeling down in the pit of his stomach. It was so strong he had to hold back the urge to vomit. Looking out the window made him wish he had never got up. He saw his mom walking in the middle of the street, dragging a trash bag. She once again had on the same clothes from the past few days. Around her neck were about five pairs of mismatched tennis shoes connected by the shoe's strings. She was trying her best to walk in a pair of mismatched high heel shoes. She was holding up the early Saturday morning traffic by attempting to walk in those shoes. She would take a few steps and fall awkwardly to the side because the weight of the trash bag was weighing her down. She was struggling mightily and the people in the cars were running out of patience. Mychal just continued to stare in disbelief. He wouldn't dare run out there and help her. He was too embarrassed to do that. He really wanted to distance himself from her. So he watched her until she was no longer in view. He then goes to his room door and unlocks it and steps out into the hallway. He locks the door and turns to walk down the hallway when he accidentally kicks over the black, so called medicine that his mom made. The bottle sprayed the black gunk all over the wall as it flipped over.

"Great." Mychal says as he walks down the hall and turns to go towards the front door. He notices that it is wide open. He could feel the cold air rushing in and he immediately begins to shiver. He walks to the front door and he peeks out to see how far his mom has gotten. He is relieved to see that she has made it around the corner and in the distance, he could hear a car's horn blow. A thought popped in Mychal's head and he felt he needed to help her. He didn't want her to get hurt and in her state, she is vulnerable to anything. He hated her the way she was but she was his mom and a part of him still wanted to be there for her. He knew that he was all she truly had and that he shouldn't turn his back on her. So, he runs back to his room and he gets the jacket that he left on the floor and some shoes. He makes his way back to the front door when he sees his landlord walking up the sidewalk that lead to his front door. Immediately Mychal begins to worry. He knows that for the past year and a half the rent money has been drafted straight out of his mom's saving account. Even though she hadn't worked in a year, she still had plenty of money saved up. She did a good job of money management when she was employed and when they fired her, she got a two-year severance package which isn't due to end for another nine months. So why he was paying a visit was making him nervous.

"Good morning Mr. Keys. What brings you out here?"

"I was just coming to pay the property a visit. Your lease is up in three months and I was wondering if your mom was going to renew her lease. Is she home so I can confirm that?"

"No sir. She just stepped out. She said something about going to check out some garage sales before she went to the office for a very important meeting." Mychal says as tries to look Mr. Keys dead in the face so he wouldn't feel like he is telling a lie.

"Ok. Well I tried to call but the number wasn't working. Is there a new home number that you guys have?"

"Well sir, my mom is still looking for the best phone company for us. So she hasn't made a choice on which one we should use." Mychal says trying to sound convincing.

"That is strange. Why cancel one phone company before you get a new one lined up?" Mr. Keys says, as the tone went from concern to suspicion.

Mychal knew he had to get out of this conversation because he wasn't a good liar and it was showing.

"If you don't mind sir, I am late for meeting a friend. Just come by sometime on Monday morning. She is off that day and she will be able to explain everything then." Mychal says as he begins to close the door. From the peephole, Mychal watched Mr. Keys walk back to his car and drive off. After a few seconds of waiting, Mychal opens the door, locks it, and runs off in the direction that his mom went. The cold air hit his lungs like a ton of bricks. It definitely took a few seconds for him to catch his breath. He runs by Kimyah's house and straight to the corner that his mom turned on. He looks down the street as far as he could and she was nowhere in sight. He waited a few seconds longer for a car horn or anything that gave a clue to where she was. The air was flowing straight through his pajamas and he begins to shiver uncontrollably. He knew he was too late to stop her. She was on a mission to get some drugs and not even cold weather could prevent her plan. Mychal turns and he starts to head back towards his house. As he is walking on the sidewalk in front of Kimyah's house, her front door opens and it is Kimyah. It was as if the whole world stopped what it was doing. No longer did Mychal hear cars passing by. No longer did he think about his mom. No longer did he feel the cold air. One sight of her made his problems seem to not exist. He looks at her and she was beautiful as ever. She was smiling at Mychal and he couldn't help but smile back. He sees how her face just glowed with beauty. She has on a black turtleneck sweater and some faded blue jeans. Her hair was as long and shiny as always. She was motioning for him to come to her. Mychal starts to turn up the sidewalk to her house when he stops in his tracks. He forgot that he didn't brush his teeth, comb his hair, or wash his face. He could feel the morning crust in his eyes and he definitely didn't want Kimyah to see him like this.

"Come here My-My. Hurry up because it is cold." Kimyah says as she hugs herself in a way to show that she was cold.

"Huh, not now. I am busy."

"Busy doing what? Kimyah asked

"Huh, busy. It is cold." Mychal says sounding every bit of a lie.

"Ok. I was just wondering what you were doing outside."

"Nothing." Mychal says as he walks off.

"Hey, would you like some breakfast?" Kimyah yells at Mychal as he quickly walks down the sidewalk towards his house. Mychal was hungry and he knew that there wasn't much to eat in his house. He hadn't had time to go to the grocery store. That was just another chore that he had to do because his mom could no longer be trusted with the credit cards.

"Yes." Mychal says as he begins to run to his front door.

"I will bring it right over." Kimyah yells.

"No give me fifteen minutes." Mychal yells back.

"Ok." Kimyah yells in return.

Mychal closed his front door and stood there embarrassed by what just took place. He had to smile because that was classic. So he just smiles as he walks to the bathroom to do his morning ritual of getting freshened up. He quickly returns to his bedroom to find something to wear. He starts to get dressed and he is hit with a thought. He was thinking about how cool it was to have Kimyah bring him some breakfast. The thought of that made his heart race. The girl he cared so much about was about to take care of him. He couldn't help but smile at the thought. Then he remembers how pretty she looked in that turtleneck. How she looked like an angel calling him to her and the confused look on her face when he stopped and made up lame excuses on why he couldn't come any closer to her. Even that confusing look she had was cute to him.

"Can you bring me breakfast? Heck yeah." Mychal says pretending that he went back to that moment when she asked him. Mychal laughed at the thought of him being so bold. He knew that when she is around he couldn't even begin to think clearly when it comes to expressing his feelings for her. No matter what he thought, he couldn't seem to be able to put it to words. Not something that was understandable and made perfectly good sense. He didn't have the ability to do that. All of a sudden he hears a knock on the front door and he runs out of his room. He gets to the kitchen and he slows to a walk. He then takes a look around the house and he sees that the house is a mess. He had forgotten what terrible shape it was in. It was too late to clean up so he had to just tell her what happened. He knew that she would understand.

"Ok. Compose yourself." Mychal whispers as he takes a deep breath, trying to slow down his pounding heart. He grabs the doorknob and opens the door.

"I will have to say about time. You almost had a frozen breakfast." Kimyah says as she hands him the plate, which was still warm. He lets her walk through the door before he closes it.

"You have to excuse this nasty house. Hurricane Iris hit last night and I didn't feel like dealing with it."

"That is fine My-My." Kimyah says as she stands waiting on him to guide her to wherever they are going.

"We have to go to my room because that is the only clean place in the house."

"Lead the way."

Mychal turns to walk to his room and every room they passed by, he got more and more embarrassed at the sight of them. So he quickly made his way to his room.

"Nice room My-My."

"Thank you." Mychal says as he sits on his bed. Kimyah walked towards his desk and she pulls the chair out and sat down.

"We almost have the same type of desk. How neat is that?"

"Uh huh." Mychal says as he digs into the grits, eggs, and bacon.

"We had so much food. My dad cooks like there is an army at my house. Since we hadn't made our two week trip to the store, I thought you might need something to eat." Kimyah says as she watches Mychal eat.

"Thank you for that." Mychal says as the food warms his stomach and her kindness does the same to his heart. Mychal loved her for just that. It was so hard for him not to like her. She did everything the way you would want someone to. She never faltered from her true self.

"Look at you with all the Christian books. You have a few that I have. I would have never guessed you were a Christian." Kimyah says as she starts to laugh.

"Was it the cursing or the way I act?" Mychal asks so he can join in on the joke.

"I think both but it could easily be your foul mouth." Kimyah says as she covers her ears. "It didn't take you any time to finish down that food, I would have to say you were a little hungry there."

"Starving." Mychal says as he shakes his head up and down in agreement.

"Famished?" Kimyah asks to keep the game going.

"On empty." Mychal says as he sets the plate on the bed next to him.

"Where is your mom? Kimyah asks as she looks in the hallway.

"Oh you didn't hear her causing a major traffic jam this morning?"

"Uh, uh. I had the music up so loud in my house. You remember that the Saturday morning mix comes on. They play the best Christian songs. So I had the whole house off the chain. What did she do?"

"She only was walking in the middle of the street, pulling a trash bag of stuff from here."

"What? You didn't try to stop her?"

"Of course I did. Did you not see me in my pajamas outside your house?"

"Oh that was what you were doing. I thought you were just a little off." Kimyah says as she stands up and pushes the chair in. "So where do you think she was going? Wait, don't answer."

"K, I do believe that was exactly where she was going." Mychal says as he knows that Kimyah is talking about his mom going to buy drugs.

"I sure hate to hear that. Was that why the house is a mess because she tore it apart?"

"Basically."

"Oh, poor My-My." Kimyah says as she walks up to Mychal and sits next to him on his bed. She put one hand on his shoulder and she starts to pat him on his back. "I wish she wasn't like this." Kimyah says as she continues to pat him on the back in a reassuring type of way.

"Me too K. I wish every day. That is all I continue to pray for."

"Don't you worry? God will take care of this situation, you wait and see."

"I know K."

"In the meantime, I will be glad to help you clean up." Kimyah says as she stands up and stretches.

"K, you don't have to. This is my problem not yours."

"Do you want me to slap you? Your problem is my problem. Now get off your lazy butt and let's clean this place up."

"Yes ma'am." Mychal says as he jumps up and he gives Kimyah a right hand salute.

"That's right. You are in Kimyah's army." Kimyah says as they start to laugh. Mychal was happy that she wanted to help him. He knew the house was a total mess and he didn't want to spend the entire day cleaning up by himself.

"I will go and get some cleaning supplies."

"Hurry up before I change my mind." Kimyah says jokingly.

*   *   *

"I can't believe it took us three hours to clean up." Mychal says as he sits down on the couch in the living room. It was their last room to clean and it also happened to be the easiest. They cleaned and disinfected every room except his mom's room. They cleaned the hallways and closets. The house was now the cleanest it had been in a year.

"That was a serious job. It would have taken you all day to finish by yourself." Kimyah says as she plops down next to Mychal.

"You are so right. I thank you so much for helping."

"No problem, My-My. I would do anything for you."

"I do appreciate that."

Mychal truly was ecstatic at the sound of her saying that. He wanted nothing more than to hear her say that and mean it.

"I am getting hungry." Kimyah says as she looks over at Mychal.

"Me too. I think we worked off that breakfast."

"So let's say we go get something."

"Where?"

"How about our favorite spot, My-My?"

"Most definitely. Do you think your parents will take us?"

"Let's go ask them." Kimyah says as she jumps up and then turns and sticks her hand out. Mychal grabs her hand and she pulls him up.

"Let me go and get my coat." Mychal says as he runs out of the living room and heads towards his room. He could smell how clean the house was. It looked a thousand times better than last night. He grabbed his coat and made sure he locked his room door and met Kimyah at the front door.

"Let's go."

As they were walking back towards Kimyah's house Mychal could feel a few sprinkles hit his face.

"That is funny. The weatherman said that we had a chance of freezing rain today and tomorrow. He is hardly ever right." Kimyah says as she looks back at Mychal. Mychal just shook his head in agreement. He was thinking about his mom who left the house this morning with some jogging pants, t-shirt, and some mismatched high heel shoes. At a moment like this when he should be happy to be spending time with Kimyah, he has to be depressed worrying about his mother. He had to worry if she was ok or if she was putting herself in harm's way. So he felt like telling Kimyah no about going to get something to eat and he wanted to search the neighborhood for her. At least attempt to try and find her. That way he would feel better about that than going to eat and being happy while she was probably hurting herself one way or another. He was definitely torn between the two decisions. Should he choose happiness and have his heart jump for joy by spending time with Kimyah? Should he choose misery and go searching for his mom?

He knew whichever one he chose was a good one. There was good in both of them and that had him conflicted.

"Ok God. If you want me to go with Kimyah, have her parents say yes to taking us to get something to eat. If they say no, then I will go searching for my mother."

Mychal whispers to himself as they walk through Kimyah's front door. Once inside her house he notices how bright and lively her house was. The whole atmosphere was just so different. It wasn't as if she had better things than he did, but you could just feel the love in the air. It was as if houses have spirits and how you live inside of them is what type of spirit you have. Take for instance his house was full of sadness, misery and depression. Kimyah's house was so full of love, care, and life. It warmed him up spiritually just being there.

"Pops, Mom, where are you?" Kimyah yells.

"We are in the kitchen." They yell in unison.

Kimyah grabs Mychal by the arm and pulls him down the hallway to the kitchen.

"Hey Kimmie. Hey Mychal. What a pleasant surprise. How are you doing son?" Kimyah's father says as they walk in the kitchen. Kimyah let's go of his arm and walks to her parents and gave them each a kiss. Mychal took a few seconds to look the kitchen over. He was slightly saddened by it because their kitchen reminds him of how beautiful his mom used to decorate her kitchen.

"I am doing fine sir. How about you?"

"Well son, I am blessed." Kimyah's father says as Mychal notices the shirt he had on. It was an odd looking brown color. There was a row of buttons all the way around the collar, from one side of the collar, around the back, and all the way to the other end.

There was the usual buttons down the front of the shirt but there were buttons down the back of his shirt as well. It was another one of Kimyah's dad fashion statements.

"That sure is a fine shirt you have on sir. What color is that? Mychal asks as Kimyah's gives him a surprised look.

"Why thank you. I think the color is rusted gold."

"Wow. It looks good on you."

"Thank you son." Kimyah father says as he walks out of the kitchen.

"I could kill you, My-My." Kimyah says as she raises her fist at Mychal.

"What?" Mychal says innocently.

"Mom we need a favor." Kimyah says as she puts her arm around her mother who was reading the bible at the kitchen table. Mychal wished his mom would do things like that. He wished his mom went to church. Even before she became addicted to drugs, she never went to church. No matter how many times he asked her, she never once went but she made sure he went. Mychal couldn't figure out why she harped on him going but she made no effort to go. It was as if she knew right but didn't want any part in it.

"What is it Kimmie?" Kimyah's mom says as she looks up. She was normally quiet. She talked when she felt it was necessary but other than that, she could be in a room with you and you wouldn't even know it.

"My-My and I were wondering if you could take us to get something to eat."

"Where?"

"The Land of Milk and Honey."

"That is so far, Kimmie."

"I know mom but we are real hungry. Besides we haven't been in a while."

"I don't know. After the way Mychal talked about your Dad's shirt, we should make him walk." Kimyah's mom says as she smiles at Mychal.

"So you are going to take us?"

"Yes I am but I am only going to drop you off. I guess I could go to the Christian bookstore and pick up some items. Get your coat so we can go."

"Great. Wait here My-My. I will be right back." Kimyah says as she runs by Mychal and out the kitchen. Mychal just continued to stand where he was and when he looked at Kimyah's mom; he noticed that she was staring at him.

"Mychal I sense something is troubling you. How is your mom? Is everything all right at home?"

"Yes ma'am. Everything is fine." Mychal says as he starts to feel uncomfortable talking about his home life. He wasn't good at letting people into his home life. Part of the reason why he didn't was simply because he was embarrassed by what was taking place. Secondly, he just didn't feel comfortable expressing his feelings. He knows that Kimyah's mom means well, he just wasn't going to tell her much.

"If you ever need anything then let me know. I was kind of worried when Kimyah asked to take a plate of food over to you this morning. She reassured me that everything was ok and that she just didn't want to waste her Dad's breakfast." Kimyah's mom says as she closes the bible she was reading.

"By the way, thank you for that breakfast because it was good."

"I am glad you liked it. You are always welcome to come and get some, ok?"

"Yes ma'am."

That was music to Mychal's ears. The last thing he needed was a reason to come over to Kimyah's house.

"You never said how your mom was doing." Kimyah's mom says curiously. It was as if she knew something and she was just waiting on Mychal to say or confirm what she knew.

"She is ok. Just busy as usual."

"That woman sure is. I haven't seen her in months. Tell her she is also welcome to come over."

"Yes ma'am." Mychal says, as he is glad the conversation was over. He was definitely not going to tell his mom anything. He can only imagine his mom coming over here with her items to sell or possibly stealing things out Kimyah's house. How embarrassing would both of those situations be for Mychal? He is amazed at how she hasn't seen his mom at all. His mom was rarely at home and he knew she had to walk to get to wherever she was going. She gave up the car a long time ago. So she mainly walked and she always chose to walk in front of Kimyah's house, just like this morning. Mychal was just glad that Kimyah's mom wasn't one of the lucky people to have seen his mom.

"Alright, I am ready to go." Kimyah says as she sticks her head in the kitchen.

"Did you ask your father if he was going to go with us?" Kimyah mom asks as she grabs the car keys off the counter.

"He said he was just going to stay in and watch the Kung Fu theater marathon." Kimyah says as she motions for Mychal to start moving.

"Ok, let's go then." Kimyah's mom says as she follows them to the door.

Mychal hoped that once they got in the car and started to drive out of the neighborhood that they wouldn't run into his mom. He imagined how embarrassing that would be to see his mom walking down the street. Probably still pulling that garbage bag, trying to find someone to buy that junk she had.

"Here Kimmie warm up the car for me, I need to get some things to return back to the store. I will be right out." Kimyah's mom says as she hands her the car keys. She walks back into the house and Mychal and Kimyah walk to the car. Once inside Kimyah starts the engine and immediately turns the heat on.

"It is going to take a few minutes to warm up. It is so cold out here." Kimyah says as she looks back at Mychal. Mychal just shook his head in agreement.

"What's wrong My-My? Why are you so quiet?" Kimyah asks with a concerned look on her face.

"I am worried about my mom. She left out this morning with no jacket on and now the weather is getting worst since it is starting to drizzle. You want to know what else is bothering me?"

"Of course." Kimyah says as she starts to have a serious tone."

"I wish I didn't have to worry about her. Why can't I just live a normal life? Why do I have to spend all my time focusing on her?" Mychal says as he fights tears. He wished he didn't care about her. He wanted nothing more than to let her follow her own course and not be affected by it at all. He wanted every day to be about him and not about her.

"I know this is hard on you. I can see it in your eyes and in your voice. I have always noticed it but I just didn't want to harp on it all the time. I have always been here for you if you wanted to talk about it, but I tried my best to not force you to do it. I can only imagine how I would feel if that was my mom. I would be devastated by it. I know I wouldn't be able to function. Just the fact that you have made it this far and have shown unbelievable strength through it all is very impressive to me. I can't even begin to tell you how I admire you for trying to be there for your mom. How even when things are up and down, you have never given up on your relationship with God. Anyone can keep a good relationship with God when things are going well for him or her. Most folks would give up when things continually stay bad. You have stayed true to your belief that God is in control. I have watched you give 100% at Youth Bible Group and at church. In front of me, you have not said one discouraging word about God. I admire you for that. It is hard to constantly give you advice on what you should do when I know I wouldn't be able to do it if the roles were reversed. I give advice to you so that if anything comes my way, you would in turn be able to help me, regardless if the advice was something you couldn't do." Kimyah says as she gives a little smile to Mychal hoping he would return it. Mychal sat there thinking about what she had said about him being strong and faithful. Yet he can remember crying his butt off last night, ready to throw in the towel because he was cracking under the pressure. He can also think back to all the times that he has questioned God. He wondered if Kimyah knew those things, would she still feel the way she does now.

"So, what do you want to do now, My-My?"

"I don't know. I want to go get something to eat but at the same time, I can't help but to worry about my mom."

"I understand. If we don't go and get something to eat, what could we do? Do you have something in mind?"

"I feel guilty like I should be out there looking for her."

"She is your mom and that is the right thing to do. If you want, I can tell my mom that we changed our minds."

"Wouldn't she question why we did that, since we came over your house to ask her to take us?"

"She will but we don't have a choice if we are to look for your mom."

"What do you mean, we? You are going to help me?" Mychal asks as he tries to hold in his smile.

"You thought I wasn't." Kimyah says surprisingly.

"Well, it's cold and rainy out so I didn't think you wanted to take a chance on getting sick."

"I don't and neither do you but that is not going to stop you from going."

Mychal shakes his head in agreement. It meant a lot to him to have Kimyah go with him. He wanted her to go but he would have never asked her with weather conditions the way they are today. He wouldn't put her in a situation like that because he cared for her too much.

"Well, here comes my mom so I will tell her." Kimyah says as she rolls down her window, letting in cold, freezing air and rain. Her mom runs to the window.

"Mom." Kimyah says as her mom puts up her hand signaling for her to wait to finish.

"Hey Kimmie, I just got a call from someone that needs prayer as well as uplifting. I won't be able to take you after all."

"We understand." Kimyah says as she reaches back and turns the car off. "Come on My-My."

"Sorry Mychal." Kimyah's mom says as he steps out of the car.

"No problem ma'am." Mychal says relieved that they didn't have to lie to get out of going.

"You guys can come inside and I can make you something to eat."

"Well mom, I think that me and My-My are going to go over his house and order a pizza."

"Well why can't you order one over here?" Kimyah's mom asks with a puzzled look on her face. Mychal just looked at Kimyah and he knew it was hard to pull one over on her mom. Mychal was speechless because he had no clue that Kimyah would lie to her mom.

"Mom, what about Dad? You know he can't have junk food and we don't want you to have any reason to fuss at him about his health. I would rather not even tempt him like that. Besides, we would have to be totally quiet if we were over here." Kimyah says as she lays all of her reasons out for her mom, hoping to overwhelm her with points to make her say yes.

"Well, ok. Let me get you some money so you can pay for it." Kimyah's mom says as she pulls out some money." Is $50 enough?"

"Plenty thank you mom."

"Thank you Ms. Spencer." Mychal says as he starts to back up. Kimyah gives him a small nudge and they start walking back towards his house.

"We need to go all the way inside your house so my mom won't become suspicious. "

"Ok, Mychal says as leads her to his house and they go inside. Once inside they just stand there looking around as if they were in a haunted house and they just heard some strange noises. The warm, loving feeling he felt in Kimyah's house, doesn't greet him in his. It was dark, gloomy and very quiet.

"So how long do we need to stay here?" Mychal asked.

"Not long. Just long enough for her to go inside the house."

All of a sudden the rain starts to pour down even harder. It was sounding like small pellets were hitting the roof. Mychal walks to the living room window that was facing the street and he pulls back the drapes. He notices that the rain was falling heavy. Kimyah stands next to him.

"Wow." She says as the rain pelts the window.

"Wow is right." Mychal says as he wonders what they were going to do now. There was no way he wanted to go out there with the rain falling that bad. Visibility wasn't that great and they also had a greater chance of getting sick.

"What do you suggest we do now?" Mychal asks Kimyah as he closes the drapes.

"We could pray."

"That is true." Mychal says as he walks to the wall and clicks on the light switch.

"That is the same as going to look for her. Both ideas are a way to make sure she is safe and protected. There is great power in prayer."

"Let's do it. We can do it right in here." Mychal says as he walks to the couch and sits down.

"Let's get on our knees and go before God, just like in the prayer room."

"Ok." Mychal says as he joins her in the middle of the living room. He falls to his knees and grabs her hands.

"Wait let's get comfortable." Kimyah says as they remove their jackets. "Ok, let's get down to business."

They took turns going back and forth. They prayed openly and truthfully. They believed with every prayer request they made, that God was hearing them and preparing an end to the situation.

"I feel much better K."

"Me too." Kimyah says as she gets up and sits down on the couch. Mychal gets up and follows her. "Prayer helps because it helps you release feelings and desires that are on your heart."

As soon as she mentioned that, Mychal thought about his journal. That was the one thing Kimyah knew nothing about. She had no clue about it because Mychal never mentioned it to anyone.

"K, there is something that I need to show you."

"What is it, My-My?"

"Follow me and I will show you." Mychal says as he gets up and walks to his room. Once inside he goes to his bed and picks up the mattress. He grabs his journal from under the bed and he hands it to Kimyah.

"What is this?" Kimyah says as she flips through the pages. "You have been keeping a journal. How long have you been doing this?"

"Awhile." Mychal says as he stands there and watches Kimyah flip through the journal. She stops to read some of the things he wrote.

"I don't know what to say, My-My. Some of the things you wrote in here I knew of and some things I didn't."

"You are not mad at me are you?"

"No, My-My. Never that. I was just saying." Kimyah says as she reaches the end of the journal. "This whole thing is about your mom?"

"Yeah, every single page." Mychal says as he puts the journal back between the mattresses. "That has been my release for the pain and agony she has caused me. I knew I could write it down and feel a little better. I wouldn't show my feelings but I could write them down. I wanted to release my anger in other ways but my journal was the easiest way to do it.

"If that makes your situation better, by all means do it. Don't keep those feelings bottled up. That is not healthy when you do that." Kimyah says, as she looks Mychal right in his face. He felt she was trying to get her point across. "Believe me, I have a diary and I write just about everything down. I have all kinds of stuff from my family, friends, school, and church. I even have stuff on you in there." Kimyah says as she starts to pretend like she was shy. Mychal was glad to hear that but the whole conversation was making him nervous.

"Hey, I am still hungry so what are we going to do?" Mychal asks so he can change the subject.

"I don't know since you don't have a phone we can't truly call for a pizza and I left my phone at home."

"By the way, I do thank you for lying to your mom. Wait that doesn't really sound like something I should be thanking you for, right?"

"It doesn't but it is true. I didn't want to have to explain your mom's condition with her. That is for you to do if you want too."

Mychal thought that was cool that Kimyah would do something like that for him. He knows that lying to your parents is wrong and he isn't so much thankful about her doing that. It's the fact that she would go to great links to cover for him, is what impresses him. She isn't covering for him because he did something wrong but to not draw too much attention to his situation. It is already a touchy situation and having more people involved in it could make it worse.

"Let's go and brave the elements to get something to eat." Mychal says as he waits on Kimyah's reply.

"I thought that was the reason why we didn't go look for your mom."

"It was but I am not going to ruin my whole day waiting on her to show up. We have prayed about it and I want to leave it at that. Let's go do something that doesn't involve her." Mychal says to make his point.

"Ok, what do you want to do?"

"Let go to Micky D's."

"That's what I am talking about."

"Let's go and get our coats." Mychal says as he walks out of his room and makes his way to the living room. As soon as they got there, Mychal heard a key in his front door. Kimyah stopped and looked at Mychal. They both stood there and watched as the lock turned and the door opened. Mychal's mom stood in the doorway, soaking wet. She had on no shoes and her clothes were stuck to her skin. She was shaking uncontrollably and the look on her face was like a zombie. She stepped into the doorway and dropped to the floor. Mychal immediately ran to her as Kimyah closed the front door. Mychal cradled under her and picked her up. He was reminded at how light she was. She was definitely underweight. Mychal carried her to the couch and placed her down. She was shivering so hard that Mychal was afraid she might have hypothermia.

"Kimyah, could you run to the closet closes to the bathroom and get a comforter, please."

"Sure." Kimyah says as she runs out of the room and down the hall. Mychal just stares at his mom and he realizes that moments like this are the times when he feels sorry for her. Here she lies in his arms, shivering.

"Mom, why would you do this to yourself? Why destroy yourself like this? Don't you care about yourself? Don't you care about me?" Mychal whispers in her ear as she continues to shake. Kimyah runs in with the comforter and they wrap her in it.

"What else do you think we should do?" Kimyah asks.

"She needs a good hot bath. I know this is too much to ask but could you help her. You know, with her being a lady and all. She might not have the strength to do it."

"No problem. I do it for my grandmother all the time. She isn't capable either so it shouldn't be a problem."

"Thank you K. You are the best." Mychal says as Kimyah winks at him as she walks out the room. Mychal could still feel his mom shivering and he knew that until she got out of those wet clothes, she was going to continue to shake. Mychal picks her up and carries her to the bathroom.

"Kimyah, there is some bubble bath stuff under the cabinet."

Kimyah nods her head as she checks the water with her hand. She reaches over to the cabinet and grabs the bubble bath.

"Pour the whole thing in if you know what I mean." Mychal says as Kimyah tilts the bottle over so the ¼ of bubble bath that was left could enter the water.

"I got it from here. Do you have any soup or tea?" Kimyah asks as she stands up.

"I think so. Let me go check." Mychal says as he sits his mom down on the closed toilet seat. He braces her next to the sink and walks out. He walks to the kitchen and goes to the only places that had food related items in them. He looked over the things and notices that they had a can of chicken noodle soup. He gets the can out as well as the can opener out of the drawer. A few months ago he could have used the electric can opener but those days are gone. All electrical items have been gone for a while. His mom made sure they didn't stay around long. He grabs a medium pot out of the cabinet and he turns the oven on. He began to prepare the soup.

"Kimyah, is everything all right?" Mychal yells out from the kitchen.

Kimyah opens the bathroom door and sticks her head out.

"Everything's cool."

"I found some chicken noodle soup and I am heating it up right now."

"Ok. Do you have some of those green pads you clean pots out with?"

"I do. Is it that bad?"

"Oh yeah."

"K, I owe you big time and I mean it."

"I don't mind and I mean it." Kimyah says as she sticks her head back in the bathroom and closes the door. Mychal knew this reminded him of all the times that he daydreamed that he was married to Kimyah. How they would just do things together. How life would be so good and he would be so happy. This moment had that same kind of feel to it. He continues to stir the soup as it is boiling. He looks in the cabinet for an empty bowl. All he could find was a big Tupperware bowl. It was larger than the pot he was cooking the soup in. He knew he didn't have any choice so he grabbed the bowl and he realized something was in it. He looked inside the bowl and he saw a 10 pack of needles and two aluminum foil balls. They had been rolled up as if something was inside of them. The sight of them made Mychal mad. He knew this was her stash of drugs and that he needed to do something with it. He felt he had to hide it from her so she wouldn't find it. He quickly grabs the items and runs to his room. He puts them inside his trashcan that is under his desk. He locks his door and goes back to the kitchen. He continues to cook the soup until it was ready. He pours it in the bowl and sets it at the table. He fixed his mom a tall glass of water. He then sits at the table and waits for Kimyah to get done cleaning her up.

"My-My. Could you get your mom something to wear?"

"Yeah." Mychal says as he goes to her room and digs through her dresser to find something for her to wear. He finds a cotton-jogging suit set and some panties; he grabs it and takes it to Kimyah.

"This should keep her warm." Kimyah says as she grabs the jogging suit.

"Is she awake?"

"Yeah."

"What has she said?"

"Not much. She has answered a few simple questions of mine. She knows what's going on if that's what you have in mind." Kimyah says as she closes the bathroom door. Mychal went back to the kitchen and sat at the table. He didn't know what to expect from his mom when she came out. Since she has been on drugs, she has had drastic mood swings. One moment she is happy and the next second she is mad. She would switch so easily as if she had no control over her emotions. I know drugs affect a lot of things but Mychal feels it is safe to say that it affects everything. Nothing was immune from drugs. Everything the body is capable of doing can be affected by drugs because Mychal has seen it in his mom. He has watched her do things that she wouldn't normally do. He has watched her not be able to do things that were once second nature to her. She went from the smartest woman he had ever known, to the dumbest. He has watched her say things that someone of a mature, sound mind would never say. He has watched her not be able to do things that a normal child could. He watched her neglect her need to take care of herself. She no longer showered on a regular basis. Brushing her teeth and combing her hair was out of the question. That was why Mychal felt what Kimyah was doing, was definitely special. Not everyone would be up for the task and she is doing it without hesitation. That spoke volumes about the type of person she truly was. After a few moments, the bathroom door opened and Kimyah and Mychal's mom came out of the bathroom. Kimyah's sweater was visibly wet from the task of trying to get Mychal's mom clean. She had a look on her face of someone that is worn out. It was just a while ago she was helping him clean up the house. Even though she was smiling, Mychal knew she had done something she didn't want to do. Mychal looked at his mom and he could see that she was smaller than Kimyah. Kimyah is every bit of thirteen and very petite but his mom was even smaller than she was. The jogging suit that once fit her was now hanging off her body. It was as if she had borrowed the jogging suit from someone larger than she was. Her hair was slick back and it had a shine to it that Mychal hadn't seen in a while. It looked very clean and no longer did it look dry and brittle. Kimyah walked in the kitchen and she sat down next to Mychal. Mychal's mom walked slower as if she was embarrassed to be in the condition she was in. The closer she got the less Mychal believed that. She looked like someone who just didn't have the strength to do anything. She had the appearance of someone that was on their deathbed, awaiting their final breath. Mychal pushes the chair out with his leg so she could sit down. Without any acknowledgement to what he just did, she sat down. Mychal looked at his mom in the state she was in and he was ready to cry. He wanted to cry because his mom, the woman that carried him for nine months was looking as if she had given up on life. She had a look on her face as to say, "I can't fight this anymore". She was beginning to not even look like his mom any more. She no longer looked like anyone he had ever known just a person that was basically bones wrapped in some brown skin. He could remember hugging her for extended periods of time and squeezing as tight as he could. He knew if he did that now, he would break her in two. Mychal looked over at Kimyah, and the look on her face said the same as what he was thinking. Everyone just sat there without saying a word. The silence was very weird because it felt as if everyone was afraid to speak as if they were hiding from someone. Mychal looked at his mom's face, which seemed to have aged since talking to her last night. She looked like someone who had been through a war and came out defeated. She was clean and you could smell the sweet fragrance of the soap that was used. Her skin looked much better since it was cleaned and that Kimyah helped her put some lotion on. Her skin was no longer ashy and flaky. How long all of this freshness was going to last, Mychal knew he couldn't answer that. He was just happy that she was clean and he hoped she was sober.

"How do you feel Ms. Stone?" Kimyah says breaking the silence.

"I feel ok." Mychal's mom replies in a low whisper as she barely moved her mouth.

"You look and smell good." Mychal says trying to be kind.

His mom just sat there staring at the food. She didn't even give him a reply to what he said. That kind of got to him. He felt she should have said something because that is the least she could do for him since he puts up with her.

"She was pretty dirty. We had to scrub most of the dirt off of her." Kimyah says in a low tone. Mychal thought about what she said and he couldn't help but wonder how someone could let their body go like that. How is it that drugs take away the desire to do everything but the drug? Why is it that simple things like taking a bath or brushing your teeth is too time consuming? Drugs make you feel like nothing else is important. Mychal was looking at the firsthand effect of someone under drug's control.

"We made the soup for you so go ahead and eat." Kimyah says as she tries to encourage Mychal's mom to eat. She just stared at the bowl as if she had never seen soup before.

"Where did you get this bowl from?" Mychal's mom asks without even looking up. Her eyes were fixed on the bowl. Mychal knew what she meant when she asked about the bowl. She was talking about the drugs that were in it. The thought of that made him mad. Here she was worried about the drugs and she hadn't felt it was necessary to do anything else. That made him mad because they have spent the last thirty minutes catering to her needs as if she is the most important thing in their lives. Here she sits worried about the contents from the bowl that she no longer sees.

"It doesn't matter where we got the bowl from, Iris. Just eat ok?" Mychal snaps. Kimyah looked at Mychal with a surprised look on her face. She had never heard Mychal talk to his mom like this and she was taken aback by his tone. Mychal really didn't want to say it in front of Kimyah but his anger got the best of him.

"My-My!" Kimyah says as to say that she can't believe him for saying that. "It is hard to believe that you said that."

"I am sorry." Mychal says, as he feels sorry for saying that in front of Kimyah. He wasn't sorry to his mom but just to Kimyah. He knew Kimyah did not know what she meant by it and he didn't want to clue her in. He didn't know why he didn't want to tell her, he just chose not to. If he had told her about the drugs that were in the bowl then maybe she would understand his mentality right now.

"Iris, eat. We have gone through a lot of trouble for you and the least you could do is eat." Mychal says in the kindest tone he could muster. He sat there and watched his mom stare at the bowl but not move a muscle.

"Please Ms. Stone. You need to eat. Your body is very weak and you need to put some nutrients back into it. I know you don't want to pass out like you did earlier." Kimyah says as she walks around the table and stands next to Mychal's mom. Kimyah was showing patience that Mychal once had. That part of him was long gone. Too many times he did the same thing only to be burned time and time again. Mychal watched Kimyah walk over to her and that made him even angrier. Here she was taking Kimyah from him and possibly having her on her side. The thought of that really made him not want to have any patience with his mom. He watched as Kimyah picked up the spoon and tried to feed his mom some soup. He watched as his mom opened up her mouth and took the spoon in.

"See Ms. Stone, chicken soup is very delicious. You can't tell me you are not hungry." Kimyah says as she puts the spoon back in the soup and readies another spoon.

"It is good." Mychal's mom says as she takes the spoon from Kimyah. She put the spoon in her mouth and quickly sets it down in the soup so she could get more. Mychal just watched as she begins to eat faster and faster until all the soup was gone. It was as if she hadn't eaten in days. The soup was still hot and it didn't even faze her as she ate it. She then drank all the water that was in the glass. She sets the glass down and wipes her mouth.

"Don't you feel better?" Kimyah asks as she sits down next to Mychal.

"A little. Where did you get this bowl from?"

At the sound of that, Mychal got so angry. He was more sick and tired of the desire she had for the drug than her lack of appreciation for what they have done for her. He can deal with her not saying thank you but he could not deal with the fact that the drugs had a hold on her that kindness could not break. Nothing short of him giving her the drugs would make her happy.

"Look here Iris. You are not getting what was in that bowl. I hid it and you will never find it. Do you hear me Iris?" Mychal yells at his mom. Kimyah sat there with her mouth wide open.

"Why are you doing this? Why are you so mean?" Kimyah asks as she grabs Mychal arm so he could look at her. Mychal knew Kimyah could not feel the same way he does. His anger is not a spur of the moment thing; it was a gradual process that has taken place for over a year. It has just steam rolled to this point right now.

"K, she needs to not worry about that. She needs to be thanking you for helping her get cleaned up. Thanking me for fixing her the soup. The last thing on her mind should be where I got the bowl from. How about that Iris?" Mychal says as he stares at his mom who just sat there.

"Do you think being mean to her is going to help? How is that going to make this situation better?" Kimyah asks Mychal as she watches him stare his mother in the face. Mychal's mom breaks down and starts crying and the sight of that made Mychal even angrier.

"Why are you crying?" Mychal asked his mom as she starts to cry louder. Mychal didn't feel sorry for her. He was tired of her and he was at the end of his rope.

"Mychal. What is your problem?" Kimyah asks as she walks to the counter and grabs a couple of paper towels and hands them to Mychal's mom. Mychal knew Kimyah was mad at him because she only called him by his name if she was.

"He is always mean to me." Mychal's mom says between choked up sobs. Mychal grew angrier at every tear that fell off her face. Kimyah looked at Mychal as if to say, "I know he isn't" Mychal just looked away. He knew that his mom was putting on an act and that Kimyah was falling for it.

"He is always yelling and screaming at me. Telling me how sorry I was." Mychal's mom says as she grabs Kimyah by the waist and begins to hug her. The sight of that really made Mychal angry so he stood up and kicked the chair Kimyah was sitting in over.

"See what I mean?" Mychal's mom says as she continues to hug Kimyah. Kimyah just looked at Mychal with a look of disbelief.

"Mychal I am so shocked at you right now. Why are you acting like this? What is your problem?"

"She is my problem. I am so sick and tired of her."

"So you think this is making it better by kicking over chairs and being mean?" I think we all need to sit down and talk about this." Kimyah says as she continues to pat Mychal's mom on the back. His mom just sat there acting like a little kid up under their parent. Mychal paced a few more times before he went and picked up the chair that Kimyah was sitting in before he kicked it over. He sat back in his chair and waited on Kimyah to sit down.

"I am going to sit down Ms. Stone and we are going to talk about what's going on." Kimyah says as she gives her one last pat. She walks over to the chair next to Mychal and she slides it away from him and sits down. Kimyah, by doing that hurt Mychal and he wanted to get up and go into his room. He wanted to go in there and cry. At this point Kimyah was all he cared about. To see her mad at him and not even want to be sitting next to him, hurt him deeply. He looked at his mom and watched as she tried to contain the sobbing that she started. Mychal felt she was faking and just trying to gain an edge with Kimyah over him. The thought of that kept the anger he had for her at the top.

"Ms. Stone, I am going to be honest with you and I expect you to be the same. I care for you and I don't want to see you like this. There is obviously something wrong with you. If there is something we can do for you to help then by all means let us know." Kimyah says as she tries to get Mychal's mom to look at her. Mychal's mom tried her best to not look up but she must have felt the pressure from Kimyah, looking at her, so she looked up. Mychal noticed how bloodshot her eyes still were. He hasn't seen them white in a while.

"I don't have a problem and there is nothing wrong with me." Mychal's mom says as she tries to sit still. She was moving like she was totally uncomfortable. Mychal wanted to burst out and say how much of a junkie she was but he knew he was already in the doghouse with Kimyah, so he kept it to himself.

"Ms. Stone. I saw how malnutrition you are. I can see every one of your ribs. You are deathly underweight."

"Girl, what are you talking about? I am on a diet. That is why I am so skinny." Mychal mom says as she raises up the jogging suit top to show her belly. Mychal had to look away because she was so skinny that her whole rib cage was protruding out through her skin.

"Come on Ms. Stone. You are not on any diet. I told you that we need to be honest with each other. You are way smaller than me and I don't see any need for you to be on a diet. Are you sure there isn't another reason why you are so small?"

"I am sure. I have been trying to lose a few pounds that's all."

"Ok. I will take your word for it. Just for the sake of arguing, if you were doing something that caused you to lose weight and possibly put your life in jeopardy, would you tell me?" Kimyah asked as Mychal got the feeling that she was trying to get the answer out one way or another.

"No I wouldn't."

"Why not, Ms. Stone?"

"I don't know you that well, nosy girl." Mychal's mom snapped as Kimyah's jaw dropped open. "I am getting tired of answering your stupid questions. I told you there is nothing wrong with me."

Mychal could tell Kimyah's questions were agitating his mom. He wasn't about to let her talk to Kimyah any kind of way so he felt that this was a good time to start asking the questions. He was okay with letting Kimyah do all the asking but he can tell that his mom was about to act ugly.

"There is something wrong with you. Do you want to know what it is?" Mychal asks as he is waiting on his mom to snap at him the same way she snapped at Kimyah. She just sat there looking down. "What's wrong with you is the fact that you don't care. The reason you don't care is because you are addicted to drugs."

"I am not addicted to drugs. Why do you always say that?" Mychal's mom says as she begins to cry again. Mychal immediately looked at Kimyah as if to say, "don't even think about it." Mychal knew she was only crying so Kimyah could bail her out again.

"I say that because you are addicted to drugs and you don't care. Have you thought about how the bills were being paid around here? No you haven't thought about it because you don't care. You could care less if we have lights or a place to live. You ever wondered how we always managed to have food in the refrigerator or in the cabinets? Of course you didn't because you don't care. Do you even have a clue to what size I wear in my clothes? Of course you don't because you don't care. You don't care to clean the house. You don't care about taking care of yourself and you don't care about anything but the drugs." Mychal says as he was waiting on her to say that it was true. He wanted her to admit that she didn't care about anything. He needed her to fess up to her mistakes so that they can begin to help her. She just sat there crying and she looked up every few seconds to see if Kimyah was coming to her rescue. When she notices she wasn't she continued to cry harder.

"You see Ms. Stone. We know that something is wrong with you. We can tell that you are no longer the same person you once were. We want to help you. Do you hear me, Ms. Stone?" Kimyah asks as she tries to look her in the face.

"I hear you." Mychal's mom mumbles under her breath.

"Good. Let's start right now by praying. We need to take this problem to the Lord. I need to ask you a question. Do you have a personal relationship with Jesus Christ?"

"I do."

Kimyah looked up at Mychal to get a second opinion on her answer. Mychal shrugged his shoulders because his mom never went to church even though she made sure he knew who Jesus Christ was and how to have a relationship with him.

"Well. I am going to pray for you Ms. Stone and we are mainly going to pray for deliverance from things that we have no control over. Is that ok with you?" Kimyah asked.

Mychal's mom shook her head yes.

"Ok, let's bow our heads. *Dear heavenly father. You are most powerful, all knowing and all doing. We come before you right now asking that you deliver us from our ways. We are facing an adversary that has a hold on us that we haven't been able to shake. We need your strength and guidance to see us through. Ms. Stone is fighting an addiction that is keeping her from doing the things necessary in her life. We ask that you touch her heart and loose her from the bonds of the addiction. We pray that you watch over her and guide her to all the necessary help she needs and we say this prayer in Jesus name, Amen."* Kimyah says as she lifts her head and opens her eyes. Mychal does the same and he looks at the spot where his mom was once sitting. He wanted to see the look on her face since she hasn't prayed in a while. He wanted to see if there was a change in her eyes. If the prayer moved her liked it moved him. He looks across the table but she was no longer sitting there. Mychal immediately starts to look around the kitchen and he sees his mom digging in the cabinet where the bowl that had the drugs in it was, before he used it for the soup. Mychal looks at Kimyah who was shaking her head. Mychal hoped that Kimyah could see why he was frustrated at his mom so he wouldn't feel so bad at treating her the way he sometimes treated her.

"I don't believe it." Kimyah says as she just has a confused look on her face.

"Believe it." Mychal says as he stands up and walks towards his mom. She sees him coming and she starts to dig around in the cabinet faster. Mychal wanted to grab her and shake her so hard. He knew he wouldn't do it in front of Kimyah.

"Iris, we were supposed to be praying together. As a matter of fact, we were supposed to be praying for you and you are over here. Why are you over here and not over there?" Mychal asks as he points to the table.

"I wanted to get something."

"It couldn't wait? You just had to have it at this moment? I told you already that I hid it so it is no longer up there." Mychal says as he tries to show restraint because he wanted to grab her and sit her down in the chair at the table. Mychal's mom looks at him and then she takes one more look in the cabinet. She closes the cabinet door and walks to the table and sits down. Kimyah stares at Mychal as he sits down. She had a look in her eyes as to say, "I am sorry I doubted you." Mychal was glad he could see that because it made him feel better.

"Ms. Stone. God doesn't appreciate what you just did. We were asking God to help you and you walk away from us. That is not right." Kimyah says as she resumes her role as peacemaker.

"I don't care. I am tired now and I want to be left alone." Mychal's mom says as she starts to frown up at Kimyah.

"Guess what, Iris. We are not going to leave you alone." Mychal snaps.

"I don't feel good. I just want to lie down and get some rest."

"How about this, when you wake up we will resume our talk, okay Ms. Stone?"

"Yeah, yeah." Mychal's mom says as she quickly blows off Kimyah. She stands up and so does Mychal.

"Where do you think you are going?" Mychal says as he blocks her path.

"I am going to lie down. I told you I didn't feel good."

"Let her go, My-My." Kimyah says as she notices that Mychal wasn't going to move. Mychal really didn't want her to. He wanted her to stay in the hot seat and answer some more questions. Even though he knew she wouldn't answer them truthfully, he wanted to do it just to aggravate her. It kind of made him feel good to watch her squirm every time they asked her a question.

"I had no clue she was over here acting like that."

"That is nothing. You should see her when she is really making no sense at all."

"I am sorry for snapping at you when I thought you were being mean for no reason."

"No problem. I know you are not here every day so you had no way of knowing. I just didn't want you mad at me for long."

"I don't think I could be. I was trying to stay mad before she went left on me but I couldn't."

"Good." Mychal says as he looks down the hallway as his mom finally makes it to her room. She slams the door.

"I guess she is mad." Kimyah says with a smirk on her face.

"Oh well. Hey let's go and get us something to eat."

"Ok, because I am starving."

*   *   *

"Welcome to McDonald's. How may I help you?

"I will have a number three with no onions and what about you Kimyah?"

"I want the grilled chicken salad."

"What kind of drink would you like?"

" I will have a coke and she wants a water."

"Very good My-My. You finally know something I like."

"Will this be together or separate?"

"I don't want no grill chicken salad on my burger." Mychal says as he starts laughing. Kimyah and the girl at the register just looked at him.

"Anyway, is it going to be together or separate?" the girl asks Kimyah this time instead of Mychal. Mychal just stood there embarrassed. He knew his weak attempt to be funny didn't work.

"Together." Kimyah replies as she hands the girl the money.

"Hmm. He is not funny and he is broke." The girl says as she gives Kimyah change and walks to get their food. Mychal notices her telling some of the other workers what he said because they were all looking at him, shaking their head. Mychal wanted to go hide.

"Well comedian. That joke went over well." Kimyah says as she smiles at Mychal.

"Just how I planned it."

"How about you plan us some napkins, ketchup and some straws." Kimyah says as she points to the condiment island and not a moment too soon. The girl came back with their food and Mychal made sure he did not make eye contact with her. He grabbed the things and he followed Kimyah to an empty table around the corner from the counter.

"I know how bad you wanted to sit in view of your fan club but this one is a little cozier." Kimyah says as she sits down and separates the food. Mychal just shook his head. McDonald's wasn't as packed as they normally are on a Saturday night. Mychal thought it probably had everything to do with the weather. He had to fight the freezing drizzle the whole two blocks. It had slowed down from earlier but the rain still stung when it hit your face. He couldn't even talk to Kimyah on the way. They both just covered their faces as they walked.

"I am so hungry, I could eat two salads." Kimyah says as she drowns her salad in Thousand Island dressing.

"I know. Watching Iris eat had me craving some food." Mychal says as he takes a large bite of food.

"You impress me every time I watch you eat." Kimyah says in reference to Mychal stuffing his mouth.

"Oh yeah, I thought it was my jokes." Mychal says to remind her of what just took place at the counter.

"That too, most definitely." Kimyah says as she shakes her head. Mychal loved when Kimyah joked because she showed off her smile. Mychal could not help but stare at her. She was the most beautiful person in the whole world to him. He admired her beauty, charm and her heart. He was so taken by her that he could only hope and pray that she would always be a part of his life.

"Hey there is Maria." Kimyah says as she points to the McDonald's worker that was mopping the floors. She had just come out of the bathroom. "She is just so sweet."

"She is." Mychal agrees.

"Hey Maria, can you come here?" Kimyah asks as she motions for her to come to their table. Maria shakes her head and then holds up one finger as to say wait a minute.

"She didn't smile at all. That is a first." Kimyah says as she looks at Mychal. He knew exactly what she was talking about. Maria was missing one of her front teeth but it never stopped her from smiling. She would smile every time they came in here because Kimyah and Mychal went out of their way to speak to her every time they came in to eat. Maria normally restocked the condiment island but tonight she was mopping. Another McDonald's worker by the name of Sam normally had the mopping duties. Mychal watched as she finished mop spotting in the area. She laid her mop down in the corner and walked over to their table.

"Hey Miss Maria. How are you doing tonight? Kimyah asks as she puts her fork down and scoots over so Maria can sit in the booth next to her.

"Yeah and where is Sam?" Mychal adds.

"I am not okay. I haven't been for a while." Maria says in a voice that sounded as if she was down on her luck.

"What's wrong Maria?" Kimyah asked.

"My husband Sam is very sick."

"Oh, Sam is your husband. What's wrong with him?" Mychal says as he tries to picture the two of them together.

"He is very sick."

"What does he have?" Kimyah asked with a concern look on her face. A look that Mychal had grown accustomed to seeing.

"He is addicted to drugs. He had the problem for a while and I didn't know. He would come in to work and steal money and one day, last week he got caught. They fired him and I had to kick him out of the house. He lives with his brother and he isn't doing well. He is trying to quit but it is so hard."

Mychal and Kimyah just looked at each other. They were both thinking what a small world we live in that the same problem is everywhere and effects people you know.

"What is his family doing to help him?"

"They are doing everything they can Kimyah. I had given up on him. I asked him why would he do drugs and ruin our marriage. Why break up a happy home that has children there? I asked him why he would do that to me?"

"What did he say?" Mychal asked

"He couldn't answer me. It hurt him too much to tell me to my face that everything I mentioned was the cause for him doing drugs. He didn't tell me because he didn't want me to know that the pressure was getting to him. He was ashamed that he wasn't making enough money to do more for the children and me. The pressure from him feeling that way was too much for him to handle. He chose the drugs as an outlet to that pressure. Now the drugs has him doing things he wouldn't normally do. His family tells me that the best thing we can do to help is not beat him down because he is doing drugs. That will only give them another reason to do drugs. You want to always give them encouragement for not doing drugs for even an hour. Something that simple will start them on the road to recovery. Yes Sam has relapsed but he has a desire to do better. I really am glad because the children want him back home. I just want to wait until he is clean."

"We sure hate to hear that. We will pray for you. Keep us posted on how things are, okay?" Kimyah says as she pats Maria on the back. If Mychal knew anything about Kimyah's pats, they do work.

"My child, you are so sweet. The both of you are just precious. I will let you know and thanks for listening to me. Now I have to get back to work." Maria says as she stands up and shakes Mychal and Kimyah's hand. They both watched as Maria grabbed her mop and rolling bucket and continued her job.

"Isn't that something?"

"You are right K."

"Drugs are something else. It affects all walks of life. It doesn't care about anything or anyone. It just does what it does." Kimyah says as she finishes her salad.

Mychal figured Kimyah was finishing her food the same reason that he was. They were just real hungry because normally when it came down to feeling sorry for someone, they would lose their appetites. What she said was the truth. Drugs don't pick their victims. They don't look for weakness in certain people. They don't only target certain people that are easier to weaken than others. No they attack each person the same. For some, their tolerance is high and it takes longer to bring them down. For some though, it can take a single use to get them hooked. Once they are hooked, it seems that the drug takes over every command of the body. It gives it one single command and that is to do drugs. Not only do it but also do it as often as you can. Do whatever it takes to get the drugs. Hurt whomever you need to hurt and it expects you to spare no prisoners. Degrade yourself at all costs and make sure that you don't care. Make sure that you only have feelings for the drug. No family member or friend loves you as much as the drug. No one can make you feel the way the drug makes you feel. Everything you do other than take drugs is a waste of time. Why go to work when you can do drugs. Why spend time with your family when you could be doing drugs. Why eat when the money could be spent doing drugs. Why live when you can kill yourself doing drugs. It is amazing how drugs can make you feel as if it is the life providing force that guides you. Mychal felt that his mom was no different than Sam. Yes it was totally different situations and different reasons for doing drugs. Still the effect was the same; total destruction of their life. Both of them showed some of the same signs. The most important sign of them all was the fact that neither one thought about the effect their drug use would do to their family. Neither one weighed the costs or feared what would happen if they couldn't stop. Mychal did not want to believe that someone would do drugs and think that they could do it for the rest of their life. They have to believe that it would be a short-term thing. The reality of it all is that they have no clue and no say in how long they do drugs. For the lucky ones that can do it for a short time, they need to thank God for that. For those that use drugs until the end and never had a chance to realize the error in their ways, then God bless their soul. Mychal could not picture his mom doing drugs for the rest of her life. He wanted more than anything to get her off of them. He prayed that death is not the only way his mom will stop doing drugs. Talking to Maria made him feel that he could try the approach she is taking with Sam. It was worth a try because obviously the stern approach was only running his mom further away from him.

"My-My, I think it is time to go. My mom will come looking for me soon. I have been gone about two hours. We definitely don't want her going over to your house."

"You are so right. Let's go. I am done anyway." Mychal says as he stacks their trash on the tray and puts it into the trash receptacle. He grabs his coat and waits for Kimyah to bundle up for their walk home. He was ready to go home and try to use what Maria said on his mom. He knew that he needed to try something because his way wasn't working.

"Well, here we go." Kimyah says as she pushes Mychal out the door. Instead of following behind him as she did before to shield herself from the rain, she grabs his arm and wraps her arm around it. Mychal didn't know what to do. He was so happy to be walking with her arm in arm. He knew that it looked as if they were a couple and that made him so happy. He had always wished for the day when things would change for them.

"You don't mind doing this do you?" Kimyah asked.

"No." Mychal says just loud enough for her to hear. In all actuality he wanted to yell at the top of his lungs, "about time." This only made his night continually turn for the better. He finally felt that he had turned the corner with trying to help his mom. He wanted to go home and ask her to come out of her room. He wanted to sit down with her and tell her that he was so sorry for treating her so bad. That he was willing to be more patient with her. That he wouldn't expect more from her than what she was capable of giving. He would take any effort to start in the right direction. He wanted very much to tell her how much he missed the old her and how he was willing to help her at all costs. He wanted to be able to hug her again. He wanted to do that more than anything else. He hasn't hugged someone he loved in a few years and he missed that. He got hugs at church but it is not the same. He wanted it to be from someone he cared deeply for because he wanted to squeeze so tight and not let go. That was what he longed for and that was what was motivating his need to change the way he treated his mom. He can still remember better days than what he has seen lately. He knew deep down inside that his mom was nothing like the person she is displaying now. He sometimes forgets that she wasn't always like this. Sometimes, people only focus on the bad things and not good. Mychal must remember that his mom wouldn't act like this if she weren't on drugs so his anger should be at the drug and not his mom. Just like Maria, he needs to have patience and be willing to wait on the end. He shouldn't expect his mom to change overnight. Mychal felt that he should be open to it taking a year or more. He has to realize that she has been using drugs for a year and a half, so he shouldn't expect her to stop all of a sudden. He wished he had the same courage that Maria has. She understands what is going on and she tries to manage by whatever means necessary. She hasn't given up and by talking to her; she doesn't feel like it should be long. She believes that he will come around and get well and Mychal felt that he should do the same. Especially since he has been praying for this to happen and he is supposed to have faith in God.

"Well My-My, I am going to check in with my mom. I am going to ask her if I can go back over your house."

"K, as much as I want you to, I want to talk to my mom alone. I have been moved by Maria's testimony and I want to attempt to try to be more understanding."

"I understand. If you need anything, please come and get me, ok?"

"You know I will." Mychal says as he finishes walking her to her front door. Kimyah removes her arm from Mychal's arm and waves goodbye. Mychal returned the wave, but he can't help but wonder if not including her hurt her feelings. He knew he meant well by trying to talk to his mom on his own, but he felt that Kimyah truly wanted to help him. He watched Kimyah walk into her house and close the door without giving him a second thought. Mychal turns and walks towards his house. He hoped that he thought too much into what just took place between him and Kimyah. He knew that he would need her before this is all said and done. So Mychal quickly runs to his house because the freezing rain was something terrible and he so desperately wanted to get out of. He opened his door and quickly shut it to keep out the rain. Mychal notices that his coat is soaking wet. He feels that he needs to let his coat dry off in the hall closet because it was soaked. He definitely didn't want to put in his room closet with his clothes. So he thought why not just hang it with a bunch of boxes of paper. He opens the closet and he can't believe his eyes. The closet was a mess all over again. It looked as if it had never been cleaned up. It was actually in worst shape than before. Mychal turns and walks to the living room and notices that the furniture was all over the place. It was as if someone was rummaging around the place and didn't care who saw that they did. Mychal runs to the kitchen and sees all the cabinets was open as well as the refrigerator and freezer. Their doors were wide open and all the contents were on the floor. Dishes were all over the place. Clean ones and dirty ones were stacked together. Some dishes were broken and some looked as if they were thrown. Mychal immediately turns to go to his mother's room and looks down the hall and he sees that there was stuff smeared all over the walls. He turns the hall light on and he see that its lotion, shampoo, conditioner, Vaseline and some cleaning products. He notices that his door was not touched by the stuff so he runs to check to see if it was locked. It was still locked and it looked like it hadn't been messed with. He then turns and walks to his mother's room. He was mad at the fact that it took him and Kimyah about three hours to clean up the house and she messed it all up again. She did it with no disregard for anyone else. Mychal wanted to be nice and walk in the room and tell her that he understands but his anger wouldn't let him. He wanted so badly to walk in there and make her clean up the mess she had caused. He wanted to stand there and watch her, even if it took all night. He was not going to let her get off that easy. It made no since to Mychal that she would tear up the whole house looking for the drugs he hid in his room. Then Mychal felt his heart drop. He realized that he hid her drugs and that is why she was looking for them. Mychal didn't feel guilty for what he did but he realized that he was partly at fault for what took place. He told her he hid the drugs and in her addicted state, she was willing to look for them. Mychal knew the desire to find the hidden drugs fueled her to continue to look for them. The end goal was greater than the effort to get to it. Mychal knew he needed to show some compassion for her so he waited a few seconds before he walked in the room. He knew if he walked in there fussing and carrying on, they wouldn't get anything accomplished tonight. Mychal wanted to begin anew. He wanted to begin the new process of recovery for his mom and now would be a perfect example of it. What better way to show his mom that he will be behind her no matter what than by excusing her actions tonight? She would see that he is serious about helping her and hopefully she will understand. He pushed open the door and he noticed that the light was off but he could hear movement. He clicked the light on and took a step in the room and he was immediately met with the putrid smell of vomit and urine. He walks around her bed and he sees her sitting on the floor with her head propped up against the wall. Her face was covered with vomit and her jogging suit had a big wet spot where the crotch was. Her eyes were blood shot red and she was coughing and gagging. Spit was hanging from her mouth and she was in no condition to move. She was in the worst shape that he has ever seen her in. He had seen her bad but this was scary to him. He didn't know what to do. She was constantly coughing and spitting up whatever she had left from vomiting. Mychal walked up to her and he stood on the side of her, out of the way of the vomit and her coughing fit. Mychal didn't know where to touch her because she no longer smelled as good as she once did. Now she smelled like a rest stop bathroom that hadn't been cleaned in weeks. She was reeking with a foul stench and that made it that much harder to deal with.

"Iris. Iris are you ok?" Mychal asks as he gives her a small nudge. She looked up at him and then she started to cough again. This time it sounded worse than before. It was much drier than before and it sounded like it hurt her more to do it. Mychal felt sorry for her because he had no way to help her. They had no phone and he would have to run to Kimyah's house to call 911. That also meant telling her parents about his mom and then dealing with that problem. Mychal knew that if his mom didn't get help then she could die and he still would have to answer the questions. So he decides to go over to Kimyah's house to call 911.

"Iris, I am going next door to call 911. I will be right back." Mychal says as he attempts to stand up. His mom had reached out for his arm and gave it a little tug. She looked up at him.

"What Iris? What? Mychal says as he tries to figure out what she was trying to say.

"I n-need the stuff." She gets out before another coughing attack took over her body. Mychal covers his face to shield himself from her spit.

"What stuff are you talking about?" Mychal asks as soon as the coughing subsided.

"The stuff from out of the kitchen."

"Oh no. You are going to get some help. I am not giving you that stuff." Mychal says as he figures out what she wanted.

"You don't understand, I need that stuff to get well."

"No, that is why you are sick."

Mychal's mom starts to shake and she begins to start to cough again. This time she was gagging and trying to vomit but she had nothing left. It was nothing but dry heaves but unlike the times before she kept on doing it. Every time Mychal felt she was over the coughing fit it would start up again and be worse than before. She was in terrible shape and Mychal was scared. He had never been in a situation like this before. Here he stands watching his mom at the lowest point of her life. She hasn't been able to move because her room is only a few feet from the bathroom and she could have easily walked over there if that was possible. She couldn't and now she sits her in her urine and covered with vomit, coughing up her guts. Mychal knew that she sounded so bad that it was as if every time she coughed she lost a part of her life. She was now coughing and with one last cough she fell face first in her vomit. Mychal immediately grabbed her and set her back up. He grabs a shirt that was previously thrown on the floor and he wipes the vomit off of her face. The look on her face told it all. She looked as if the life had been sucked right out of her. Her eyes were barely opened and it looked as if she was losing conscious. Mychal made sure she was propped up against the wall.

"Please, Mychal." Mychal's mom says as he catches a whiff of vomit on her breath. His initial reaction was to turn his head and gag. It was only natural that the body reacts to what was taking place. Mychal so desperately wanted to get up and try to help her from a distance.

"Mychal, please I need it."

Mychal just looked at her. A part of him wanted to go and get the drug and a part of him didn't.

"I hurt on the inside. The pain is so bad." Mychal's mom says as she pleads her case. She was gripping her sides and she starts to cough again. Mychal immediately jumped back as his mom covers her mouth to catch whatever was coming out of her mouth. She peeks inside her hands and then she looks up at Mychal with sad eyes.

"Blood."

Mychal was so nervous and scared. His mom just informed him that she had coughed up blood. He didn't know what to do. He really had no way of knowing. He had never thought about a situation like this so he never prepared himself. The only thing he knew that would help her right now is what she was asking for. That was the right thing to do at this moment and this moment was all Mychal could think of. He was in shock and totally confused but he knew he had to do something quickly, so he got up and ran to his room. He went inside and went directly to his trashcan. He grabbed the drugs, the needles, and he ran out of the room. He ran into his mom's room and directly to her. He knelt next to her and he noticed her eyes light up when she seen the drugs. Mychal knew he was clueless what to do next. So he just stared as his mom and she looked up at him as to say, "What is taking you so long."

"Lighter." Mychal's mom managed to get out as she pointed to her pillow. Mychal stood up and walked to the bed. He picked up her pillow and he saw the lighter and a spoon. He grabbed both of them and walked back to his mom. She was already trying to open up the aluminum foil balls. She grabbed the drug and she put it on the spoon that she grabbed out of Mychal's hand. She tried to steady the spoon but she was shaking too much. Mychal took the spoon from her and took the lighter and he put the flame under the spoon, as he had seen her do the other day. He watched the drug cook and he didn't like what he was doing. He knew he was wrong.

"Now?" Mychal asked as his mom looked on. She shook her head yes as she grabbed one of the needles. She begins to input the drug into her needle. She looked up at Mychal and then at her arm as if to say, "you know what to do." Mychal takes off his belt.

"Promise me that you will get help." Mychal asks as he tries to gain some good out of what he was about to do. His mom shakes her head as she continues to stare at the needle.

"I am serious, this is the last time you are taking this drug." Mychal says as he looks his mom in the eyes and she once again, shakes her head. He pushed up the sleeve on her shirt and he wrapped the belt tightly around her arm. He watched as she readies the needle and begins to move towards her other arm. She was shaking so badly that she couldn't steady herself. She began to start coughing again and there were tears forming in her eyes. Mychal saw the expression she had on her face and he knew what he was going to have to do. He saw how she looked and he felt that it was the drug that was taking control of her. Making her weak, not able to do anything but want more drugs. So Mychal grabbed the needle and he sees the swollen vein in his mother's arm. He slowly lowers the needle until it poked through her skin. He looked her in the face and she nodded to let him know to finish it. Mychal pushes down the needles head so the drug could enter her vein. He quickly removed his belt and he stood up. He stood up because she smelled so bad. He watched her eyes roll into the back of her head and she begins to smile. She starts to move her head back and forth and she begins to laugh. Mychal just looks at her stunned. She starts to pick herself up. She stands up and she starts to laugh louder. She points at Mychal and she claps her hands. She pretends like she is going to stick her finger in her mouth. Then she fakes like she is coughing all the while she is laughing. Mychal doesn't figure out what she is doing at first until he starts to put two and two together. She was showing him that she was only faking. She kept on doing it, over and over. Mychal stunned look turns to anger by the fact that she would trick him into doing what she did. She flops on her back on her bed and laughs.

"Thank you, son. Thank you son." She says as she just lays back.

Mychal was so mad at her for rubbing it in his face by thanking him that he turned and punched his mom's door on his way to his room. He slams his door and locks it.

Chapter Three – Defeat and Overcome

Mychal opens his eyes. He felt so tired. He stared up at the ceiling not wanting to move. He listened to the rain that was tapping his window. He knew it was morning but he didn't know what time it was. Normally he could have just looked at the clock that was on his desk. The red numbers would have been so easy to read if he hadn't destroyed the clock. In a fit of rage last night, he smashed the clock into a bunch of pieces. He wished that was the only thing he destroyed but it wasn't. Let's talk about the radio, whose antenna was the first to go. It was so bent out of shape that it was ridiculous. The radio itself was just as unlucky because, like the clock, it is in pieces. Not to be out done, he smashed his globe of the world also. No longer does it have the arrows he placed on there to show the places that he planned on traveling with his mom. All it has is knuckle indentions on it. Mychal unplugged the television because he didn't want to smash that. So he just readied it. He knew that he was tired and he no longer wanted to fight. The fight was taken out of him last night. He has been facing an adversary that was too smart for him. The adversary was too strong and relentless. He was outmatched and outgunned. He was a defeated fighter and he never thought he would get to this point because he always stayed one step ahead. He felt he was always ready to do battle when it came time to but last night showed him he wasn't ready to do serious battle. Small fights here and there, he might have won but when it came to big ones, he wasn't equipped. He brought the wrong weapon to the fight or maybe he did bring the right one. He just didn't use it properly and it was used against him. He knows for a fact that he was out smarted last night. His mom took the one thing he thought he had over her and slapped him in the face with it. He thought that since she was acting the way she had been acting that he was somewhat smarter than she was. Granted she had made some questionable comments and done some things that showed no intelligence at all but that shouldn't been grounds to think that she wasn't smart. She had to have still had her smarts. What she did last night took plenty of them. She outsmarted him last night into thinking she was dying or just so sick that only the drug could cure her. She played the role well and knew that she had to do something to get the drugs that he hid. She knew he wouldn't just give them back so she hatched a plan and it worked perfectly. Not only did she get what she wanted but she also took the fight out of Mychal because he no longer wanted to stand in her way. He was going to give up and let this thing play out for better or for worse. She had won and he gives her credit for that. As he tried to sleep last night, he heard her giggles from outside his bedroom door and her giggles brought more shame to him every time he heard one. She was laughing at him because the tables had been turned. Just the night before he was laughing at her for her garage sale items and maybe his mom wanted it that way. Just maybe she was setting him up and if she was, it worked. He was fooled and now he really felt like a fool. Not only did she fool him; she actually had him go and get the drugs. Not only get the drugs but also administer them to her. She got him good and Mychal could taste the bitter defeat in his mouth. He was defeated and he felt that he was without purpose. His purpose was to get her off of drugs but now he doesn't care if it happens or not. His only purpose now is to just sit in this room forever because he couldn't face himself. He knew he couldn't face his mom after last night because he was too embarrassed to do that. He definitely didn't want to face Kimyah. Oh how she would be mad at him, probably so mad that she would never speak to him again. Mychal knows that he promised her he would never do it again. He lied. She said no matter what, she would be there for him but after last night she would change her mind. There is no excuse great enough that he could tell her to make her see it his way. She wouldn't have done it. She would have called 911 and let them take care of it. Kimyah wouldn't have given her mom drugs. She wouldn't have stuck the needle in her mom's arm so she could, so called, "get better". Who would fall for such a foolish reason to take drugs? Mychal would. Who in their right mind would think that taking drugs would save your life? Mychal would. Who would believe that the one thing that is destroying you would reverse its effect and stop killing you?" Mychal would. He proved it last night. In the thick of things, he did not think. He needed to think but he wasn't able to do it. His mind froze and he didn't listen to reason. He tuned reason out and he listened to convenience. Convenience told him that it's better to do something right now than to wait to find the appropriate method. Since he didn't listen to reason, he had a headache. Not to be out done, his heart was aching too. There was another pain he was feeling and that one had nothing to do with anything. He needed to go to the restroom. Well actually he had needed to go for the past hour. He had been up that long but he just kept on closing his eyes hoping that he would fall back asleep but it didn't work. So now he laid here in pain, needing to go the restroom and he wouldn't dare get up. He didn't want to face his mom and possibly see a smirk on her face as soon as she sees him. He couldn't give her that satisfaction so he was willing to wait it out. He was going to wait until she left the house before he went to the restroom. If she didn't leave the house then he was in trouble so he hoped that she would leave soon. She had been up walking for a while now and he knew she didn't stay in the house long after she woke up. She would immediately go out and try to get more drugs. So in the meantime, Mychal sat up because his bladder was killing him. He looks at the pile of junk that was once his clock and radio. He depended on both the items for so much and now they were useless to him. The globe was his favorite thing of them all and it is now crushed. Mychal looked at his desk and he forgot that he pulled his books out and slammed them down on the desk. The books were still sprawled out on the desk. Every book was closed except for one. Mychal found that to be strange since he purposely slammed the books down and what is the chance of every book closing except for one. Not only was it opened but also it was sitting on top of all the other books as if someone was reading it. Mychal thought for a second and then he made his way towards his desk. He had to step over the destroyed items. He looked at the book, and even though there was light shining in the window, he turned on his nightlight. He had recognized the book. It was called, "The Pocket Scripture Book." It contained scriptures on different things and it saved you the trouble of looking through the bible when you were dealing with certain things. You could look up scriptures dealing with faith by looking through this book, instead of fumbling through the whole bible. It doesn't take away from the bible but it just shortened your search for certain things. The book was opened up to the section dealing with strength. Mychal looked at all the scriptures on the page until his eyes came to one that held his attention. It was *2Corinthians 12: 8-10*. It read:

"For this thing I besought the Lord thrice, that it might depart from me. And he said unto me, My grace is sufficient for thee: for my strength is made perfect in weakness. Most gladly therefore will I rather glory in my infirmities, that the power of Christ may rest upon me. Therefore I take pleasure in infirmities, in reproaches, in necessities, in persecutions, in distresses for Christ's sake: for when I am weak, then am I strong."

Mychal read it a couple of times and every time he finished he felt better. He immediately grabbed his bible from under the pile of books. He quickly turned to 2Corinthians and he studies up on the verses to see if they were closely related to his situation. In the verses preceding the ones he read, Paul was talking about having a thorn in his flesh to torment him to keep him from being proud. Paul had seen some things that he couldn't speak of because he didn't want to be thought of highly because of it. So in order to humble himself he showed himself weak and in doing so he was strengthen by God through Jesus Christ. That was what Mychal got out of it. If that is what the verse was saying then good, if it wasn't then that was good also. God reveals things in scripture to those who are seeking things from it. Everyone can interpret scripture different and in this case what Mychal is gaining from it others might not see it. Mychal closed the bible and took a deep breath. He no longer felt defeated. He had regained a new purpose and he knew what he had to do. He had strength in his time of weakness through Jesus Christ. He has no reason to wallow in his past mistakes because he knew he still had some fight left in him. The things that happened up to this point took place because he needed to learn something. He needed to learn that even though he had felt he didn't have the strength to endure to the end that he in fact does. He had it all along; he just didn't know how to tap into it. He feels now that he is finally at the point to where he can make a difference in his situation. He knew how important that was. All of a sudden he heard the front door slam shut. He immediately opens his door and he walks out into the hallway. He heads to the front door and he opens it to see if his mom had left. She was indeed gone but he couldn't see where she had gone. He closes the door and he goes to the bathroom and finally relieves himself. He quickly washes up for the morning and he gets dressed. He knew he was going to go to church but he didn't know what time it was. He wasn't going to go at first but now he feels he should and his feeling is correct. The church is there so he could fellowship with other believers and to get a shot of the word so he can take on a new day. Since he destroyed his clock he had no way of knowing what time it was. It didn't seem too late but he couldn't really tell. There wasn't another thing in the house that told time. He then remembers that he had a thermostat outside his window that told time as well. Mychal walks to his window and he peeps at the thermostat and it says, "10:50." He knew the next service started at 11:00 am. He knew it was a 15-minute walk if he walked quickly. If he walked like he does with Kimyah, it would take almost an hour. He knew that wasn't the option. He needed to get there as quickly as possible due to the fact that church fills up fast. So, Mychal knew he didn't have much time to play around so he quickly got getting dressed in his Sunday attire and then grabs his bible and walks out of his room. He locks his door and leaves out of the house and he was immediately hit with cold, freezing rain. Mychal knew it wasn't going to stop him, so he does something he never thought he would do. He runs back in the house and gets a large trash bag. He makes a hole at the bottom of it for his head and two holes on the each side for his arms. He puts it on and it did resemble a poncho in a way. He was going to make sure he said it was one if asked. So he grabs his hat and he returns back out to the freezing rain. He knew the walk was going to be tough because of the freezing rain but he wasn't worried. He had a new sense of urgency. He wanted so badly to get to church because he had to finish feeding his spirit and also get off his chest what took place last night. He wanted to tell Kimyah what happened and how he plans on making it right. He wanted to say he was sorry for not using her help when he knew he would need it. He no longer was going to keep his mom drug's abuse a secret. He was going to sit down with Kimyah's parents so they could work out his options. He knew that he was serious this time because he had made nothing but bad choices and he got hurt twice. Each time he went a step further. First he just helped her find a vein. The next time he injected her with the needle. The only thing he could do to follow up that is to actually take the drug himself. He knew that wasn't even an option that he could live with. Under no circumstance does he want to be put in that situation. He hasn't fared well so far in doing the right thing when the pressure was hard. He folded both times so he knew better. He wanted to handle the situation correctly and he felt this was a step in the right direction. He knew he had a tough task ahead of him with the weather. Even though he had a hat on, he still kept his head down because the rain was way too cold on his face. The garbage bag/poncho wasn't helping much either. So he knew what he had to do so he dug deep and started to run.

*   *   *

"Do you want me to take that for you?" The usher says as she is referring to the garbage bag Mychal had rolled up in his hand. She watched him take it off when he walked in the door of the sanctuary.

"No ma'am, I am probably going to need it later."

"How about I get you a fresh one. My son does the same thing."

"Thank you."

"Just come and see me when church is out."

"Yes ma'am." Mychal says, as he looks past the other usher to see how crowded the service was. It was pretty crowded.

"Well, we have seats in the very front row or you can go up to the balcony."

"Balcony is fine." Mychal replies. He knew if he sat in the balcony, he could see the whole church. He wanted to find Kimyah. Normally he would either ride with them but this morning was weird. He thought he could hear knocking this morning but he dare not come out of his room. He can only remember two other times that he didn't ride with them and both times came after his mom started doing drugs. He told Kimyah that if he didn't answer the door it had something to do with his mom and that she should just go on. So he was pretty sure Kimyah thought that this morning as she knocked with no answer. So Mychal made his way to the balcony and it wasn't crowded at all. There were families sitting sporadically on the balcony level so there were plenty of seats left. Mychal walked towards the middle so he could span the whole lower level. He found a good seat almost dead center. He sat down and he immediately began scanning the floor level for Kimyah.

After a few minutes he gave up. So he was disappointed but he knew there was more to coming to church than seeing Kimyah. He sat back and he began to focus on the message from the pulpit.

"Oh yes there will be trials and tribulations. Don't you think for a second that you will get off easy because you are saved? Yes, you are saved from eternal death, but you are not saved from problems and situations that test your faith. Let's not forget about Brother Job in the Old Testament. God showed favor to him by blessing him with wealth, children and anything else he could ask for. Job was an outstanding believer because he did no wrong. He was so good at doing what was right God bragged on this brother to Satan. God allowed Satan to test Job, not because he did wrong but simply because God knew Job's faith was unshakeable. Job was confused at first as to why things were happening to him, but God put it into perspective for him. God told that Brother that just because you are a believer walking the straight path, don't think for a second that you won't be tested. Use that same faith that makes you a believer and use it for strength as you fight the daily fight against Satan." The Pastor says as he wipes his forehead with a cloth. You could hear the congregation voicing their approval to points that he was making. *"You know that you have strength in you to handle every situation you face. Remember God is not going to give you more than you can handle. You have the necessary strength to get you through. Even when you fail you still have the necessary tools to accomplish your goals. You see, strength comes from failing and then getting back up. When you fail with what you were doing at first, it makes you realize that you need to try harder and come stronger. So, you do and then you start tapping into the strength that is in you. That strength is Jesus Christ because your whole life you attempted to handle things on your own. Then you start to lose control, start to fail, start to lose the fight, you then turn to Christ and he sees you through. That is your strength in your time of need."*

Mychal knew this sermon was for him. That was the same thing that was bothering him. He kept on praying to God and then he would try to fix his problem. When he failed at fixing it, he kept on giving up and feeling like he couldn't do it. Mychal knew that he had to change it up. No longer was he going to fight a battle he really shouldn't been fighting in the first place.

"Thank you, Jesus." Mychal says as he looks up. He quickly looks around to see who had seen him. He was new to praising in public like he just did, so he was still nervous. He looks to both sides of him. He notices a student from his Youth Bible Group, sitting a few rows behind him. Mychal sees that it is just the student and his mom. He, in turn notices Mychal and gives him the, "what's up," nod. Mychal returns the nod as he faces forward. He knew the guy pretty well because they had partnered up for a few activities together in the group. Mychal was definitely jealous of him. He can remember the numerous talks that he had with him and how everything always seemed so perfect. He would always talk about how great his mom was. How she was always there for him. How she went out of her way to make sure that he was taken care of. Anything he wanted, within reason, he pretty much got. Mychal use to sit back and listen to the boy tell his stories and Mychal would just daydream that his home life was the same way. Mychal wished he could tell everyone how great his mom is. He knew in his heart that he would scream it as loud as he could if it were true. It always saddened Mychal to know that he has missed out on so much over the past year and a half that he won't be able to get it back. That time is forever lost. Lost because his mom wasn't there for him. She no longer was able to even think of him. All she knew was drugs. She forgot she had a son. She forgot she even had a life. Everything became secondary to her problems. Unlike that boy from his group, Mychal forgot what it felt like to have his mom there for him. He forgot the things she once did. Those things have been replaced with the things that have taken place recently.

"Church before I close, I want to have altar call. I want to give everyone a chance to cleanse his or her heart and mind right now. I want the saints to be able to lay their burdens down. These problems you came in with but don't leave with them. Come down and lay them on the altar. God is waiting so if you feel moved this morning then come on down."

As soon as Mychal heard it, he was standing up. It was as if he didn't have any control over what was happening to him. He started making his way down the stairs leading to the lower level and he could still hear the Pastor through the speakers mounted on the wall.

"Is there one troubled soul here today that wants to make it right with God. Maybe it's family problems, or job issues, or even church problems. The altar doesn't discriminate so bring it down. Don't wait too late because you might not get another chance."

Mychal knew that he was going to take advantage of this chance because he needed this more than anything. He finally makes it down to the lower level and he turns down the aisle so he could walk down to where the Pastor was standing. People were getting out of their rows so they could make their way down to the altar. Mychal tuned out everyone as he made his way to the altar. There was room on the very end and Mychal quickly grabbed it. He knelt down and closed his eyes. As the Pastor was praying for everyone, Mychal soaked in the words that were being said. He felt at ease and he knew he was ready to do what was necessary to fight his mom's addiction. As soon as the Pastor was done praying, he walked to the podium.

"Saints, let's close this deal. I want the praise team to come on down and join these folks down here and let's give them hugs and let's extend God's love to them."

Mychal turns, and he is immediately grabbed and turned every which way. He was receiving hugs from everyone and he felt good after every one of them, because it had been a while since he received a meaningful hug. Mychal was so gracious for everyone. He knew God heard his prayers about the hugs and how he wishes to receive them. Mychal squeezed everyone real tight just how he wanted to be hugged. He had hugged so many people that he stopped looking at their faces because the people just kept coming. Stopping to look them in the face only slowed things down.

"There you go saints, shower them with love and affection. That is what is needed at a time like this." The Pastor says as he watches what is taking place. Mychal thought to himself that he was in hug heaven. He knew he was there when through the crowd, and next in line to hug him was Kimyah. Mychal looked at her and he saw the tears in her eyes. He started to get teary eyed himself at seeing her. He knew he didn't want to cry in front of all these people so he tried to be strong. Kimyah walks up to him with her arms open wide. The first thing that went through Mychal's mind was, "about time." He had waited so long for this moment that he was overcome with joy. In all the years of knowing Kimyah, he had never hugged her. He had chances to but he never did. He doesn't count the half hugs that you give someone when you are walking side to side. Those are not as personal as a face-to-face hug. He knew he was going to take advantage of this opportunity. Mychal steps up to her to give her a hug when someone jumps in front of her and starts to hug Mychal. This had to be the only hug, which Mychal received, that he didn't want. Of all the times to give him a hug they waited until Kimyah was right in front of him, waiting to enclose her arms around him. The man that hugged Mychal was rather large, so Mychal couldn't see past him because he wanted to see Kimyah. The man kept on hugging him tighter and tighter. The tighter the hug got the more Mychal didn't want it. He wanted to be in Kimyah's embrace right now. The man pulls away from Mychal and starts to talk to him.

"Lil brother, I am so proud of you. It takes a big man to come to the altar." The man says as he continues to grip Mychal's shoulders real tightly. Mychal just shook his head in agreement.

"God Bless you." The man says as he hugs Mychal again and then walks away. The Pastor got back on the microphone.

"Ok, everyone take your seat so we can say the closing prayer."

"Mychal immediately looked for Kimyah and he saw her going back to her row that she was sitting on. Mychal was so disappointed in the missed opportunity. He wanted nothing more to have hugged her but that chance is gone. So as he was making his way up the aisle he didn't even look in Kimyah's direction. He couldn't stand to look at her now so he just kept on looking straight. All of a sudden he felt a hand grab him. He looked in the direction it came from and he saw the man that hugged him. The man gave him a thumbs up and all Mychal could do was give it back. Mychal was mad at the man for no other reason than one the man doesn't understand. Mychal was acting as if the man purposely tried to stop him and Kimyah from hugging. That man has no clue how Mychal feels about Kimyah. As a matter of fact, not even Kimyah has a clue. So if that being the case then Mychal shouldn't be feeling the way he does. Mychal just continued to stroll up the aisle. In his heart, he knew the most important thing was that he went down to the altar. Instead of going back up to the balcony, Mychal went out to the foyer to wait on Kimyah. He stood there and waited until the service was finally over. Once the people started to leave out of the service, Mychal found him a spot where he could see everyone because he didn't want to miss Kimyah. As the people were leaving out, Mychal watched the families leaving out together. He watched the mothers especially. Watched their every movement. He noticed everything about them. He watched them interact with their sons or daughters. Watched the smiles that were on their faces. He couldn't remember those days with his mom. That saddened him because he wanted so badly to have his mom behave the way these other mom's did. Mychal just wanted to grab a mother's hand and go home with them. He wanted to be a part of a normal home life. A home life that is just the way he wants it to be. One that is full of hugs and kisses. One that is perfect in every way. Mychal doesn't have a normal home life because before the drugs took over his mom's life, she was too busy for him. Even before the drugs she always had something to occupy her time. She had everything before him. He was second or maybe even third in her life. That was something he didn't realize until now. He was never the one thing she would hold and keep near her. No, it was her job and now it is drugs. That really hit him hard because he felt he hadn't done anything to deserve being treated like that. Now he so desperately wanted a change in her. As Mychal watched the last of the families leave out he realized he must have missed Kimyah and her family. He quickly looked around the foyer and they were nowhere to be found. All of a sudden, the usher he first talked to when he made it to church walked up to him.

"There you are. I knew you wouldn't leave without this." She says as she hands Mychal a trash bag.

"Thank you, ma'am." Mychal says as he starts to fix the bag the way he did the last one.

"You welcome." She says as she walks off.

"Oh well. It is time for me to go home." Mychal says as he puts the bag over him and walks toward the door. He noticed it was still raining. Mychal pushed the door open and he was slapped with cold freezing rain. It felt like the temperature had dropped. Mychal quickly made his way down the sidewalk and in between cars as they were trying to leave out of the parking lot. To Mychal's surprise, there were still a large number of people walking home too. It is not as large as normal but a good group. So he didn't feel as embarrassed as he would have if he were the only one walking. He knew that no one would recognize him walking with that hat and the trash bag on. He also wanted to make sure that as the vehicles passed by, that they didn't spray him with water. Suddenly, a car drives by and then it backs up until it is next to him. Mychal just kept on looking straight ahead.

"My-My."

Mychal heard that familiar voice and he was happy.

"My-My, get in. We will take you home." Kimyah says as she tries to stick her head out the window. Mychal sees her and he felt a little embarrassed as well as happy. So he walks over to the car as Kimyah slides over so he could sit down. Mychal opened the door and quickly removed the trash bag and rolled it up in a ball. He plops down in the car and puts the trash bag on the floor. He put his feet on top of it and closes the door.

"Thank you, Mr. and Mrs. Spencer." Mychal says as he starts to feel the warm air circulating through the car. It felt so good especially on his hands, which were hurting from being exposed to the cold rain.

"That is no problem son. I wouldn't let you walk home in this kind of weather." Kimyah's dad says as he starts to drive the car again.

"You poor thing, you must have been freezing out there?" Kimyah's mom says as she looks back from the passenger seat. Mychal is reminded how pretty she was.

"It was pretty cold out there."

"I can imagine." Kimyah's mom replied.

"I was so proud of you My-My." Kimyah says as she grabs his arm.

"Proud of what?" Mychal asked hoping that would prolong her touching him.

"For going down to the altar."

"Oh yeah."

"I came down there to give you a hug, but this man jumped in front of me and by time he got through, it was time to sit down again.

"That's right." Mychal says as the thought of that made him wished he had moved towards her faster than what he had originally done.

"That was great, son. It takes a lot to go down there in front of the whole church, but you did it with no hesitation."

"He sure did." Kimyah says proudly.

"What is it that you are going through? It had to be something big, maybe we can pray for you." Kimyah's mom asks as she looks at Mychal. Mychal looked at Kimyah as if to say, "a little help here."

"Well." Mychal says as he looks down at his feet.

"I think we should have went down there. We should have been putting Granny's problems on the altar." Kimyah says as she looks at Mychal. Mychal felt she did that to advert the attention away from him.

"You are so right Kimmie. What were we thinking?" Kimyah's dad says as he continues to look forward.

"That is true." Kimyah's mom says as she turns around and faces forward. Mychal was just glad to be off the hot seat. He knew he was going to tell them about his mom but he felt this wasn't a good time.

"That is where we are going right now. We are going to spend some time with my Granny." Kimyah says as she finally removes her hand from Mychal's arm

"How long are you going to be gone?" Mychal asked.

"Probably all day, right Dad?"

"Yes Kimmie."

That was something Mychal didn't want to hear. He thought they would at least be able to talk today. He wanted to let her know his plans on telling her parents about his mom. Now he knows he can pretty much scratch that plan.

"My Granny is getting worst. She hasn't been feeling any better so we are going to spend the day with her."

"Oh, ok." Mychal says as he tries to hide his disappointment.

"Do you want to come too?" Kimyah asks as she looks at her mom who turned around quickly when she said it.

"Wait, Kimmie. He hasn't even asked his mom. You can't expect him to be able to make a decision like that."

Mychal knew he didn't need his mom's permission. He could go and she wouldn't even know or care for that matter.

"Let's ask your mom first. When we get to your house, ask her to come out and I will ask her." Kimyah's mom says as she looks at Mychal. Mychal tried to conceal the look of nervousness on his face. He knew he had to back out of this now.

"That is ok. I am just going to stay home. I don't want to be in the way." Mychal says as he tries to sound convincing.

"That's right. You said that you had that extra credit project to do. I forgot that you didn't start on it yesterday." Kimyah says to help him cover up.

"Yeah that's right." Mychal says as he takes a deep breath.

Kimyah's mom turns back around to face forward. Mychal looks at Kimyah and he shakes his head. He knew that was a close one. Mychal didn't like the quietness that was taking place. He looked out the window, hoping they make it to his house soon. Mychal saw a familiar house that he sees when they would enter is neighborhood. He reaches down and he begins pick up the garbage bag that he was using to cover his clothes with.

"I know something. You better not ever talk about my dad's clothes again." Kimyah says as she begins to giggle.

"Why not." Mychal asks.

"Here you are walking down the street wearing a trash bag. That is worse than those pants my dad wears." Kimyah say as she starts to laugh. Her mom joined in as her dad starts to look back at Mychal.

"Son, you don't talk about my clothes, do you?"

"Not in a bad way, Mr. Spencer." Mychal says as he is put on the spot.

"Yeah right." Kimyah says as she looks at Mychal smiling.

"Kimmie. Don't treat Mychal like that." Kimyah's mom says as she tries to hold in her smile.

"I thought you appreciated my style?" Kimyah's father asks as he stops in front of Mychal's house.

"I do sir." Mychal says as he gathers his things. "Well, thank you for the ride home."

"No problem son." Kimyah's dad says as he turns around and shakes Mychal's hand.

"Tell your mom we said hello." Kimyah's mom says as she just sat there smiling.

"I will."

"Bye My-My." Kimyah says as she waves goodbye.

"Bye K." Mychal said as he stepped out of the car and into the rain. He closed the door and walked around the back of the car. He started to walk up the sidewalk to his front door when he waved goodbye so Kimyah's parents would drive off. He looks at Kimyah and he just shakes his head. Kimyah waved and just watched him as her car begin to drive off. Mychal so desperately wanted to go with them. He wanted to spend more time with Kimyah instead he must face this lingering problem. He walks in his house, and as always, he is greeted with silence. The feeling he had before he left is gone. He knows the reality of it is that he must face his mom. He must let her know that he is not standing for this any longer and will not be a part of what is taking place. He is going to give her a choice to quit drugs on her own or do it his way. His way involved Kimyah's parents. They would do whatever it takes to get him and her some help. In his heart, Mychal knew he had no choice. He didn't want to put his business in the street but that was the only way to go. He needed help because he has run out of options. God is telling him to get some help. He knows that is the right choice to make. No longer will just sitting back and hoping that is Mom will realize what is taking place do. She is not going to wake up one morning feeling like she doesn't want to do drugs anymore. That is what Mychal was expecting. That was what he felt saying his prayers were for. He was giving his problems to God so that one day he would wake up and his Mom would be back to normal. He just expected it to be that way. He finally realizes that that is not how it works. What would he gain if it were that easy? How would he know he had any strength when he was weak, if he was never tested? He needed to be faced against something that will break him down so much that he had to dig deep in order to make it through. That is exactly what he was attempting to do now. He had been broken down and now he can give up or he can dig deep and try until he beats it. Digging deep was what he chose and that was what he planned on doing. Mychal knew it started today and right now. So he finally begins to walk through the house. He had come in and just stood there as if he was waiting to be greeted or something. Mychal turns into the living room. He begins to start to straighten things back to the way they were supposed to be. First, he fixed the couch. He remembers one evening him and his mom were sitting in here talking about life. It was a few days before his mom hit rock bottom.

"Mychal, do you like this neighborhood?"

"Yes ma'am. I do."

"I know of better ones." Mychal's mom says as she is waiting on him to say something. "Do you want to know where?"

"Yeah."

"These houses are much bigger than this one. This one is a small two bedroom one. The one that I have looked at is a four-bedroom house. It has stairs, three bathrooms, large kitchen, living room, dining room and a den. Not to mention a garage and a backyard."

Mychal knew his face lit up like a birthday cake because his mom had a surprised look on her face. She had expected something out of him but probably not to this magnitude.

"Are you for real?" Mychal asked.

"Oh yeah. If I get this promotion, the bonus check I will receive is a lot more than what I am making a year now. The regular pay is almost double what I make now. We will no longer have to settle for hotdogs all the time. It will be going out to eat at least twice a week. We will be going to the movies a lot because I hate telling you that we can't go this week. We will be able to take trips to other cities and things like that. We will have the financial means to do just about whatever we want. How does that sound?"

"Iris, that sounds good." Mychal says as thoughts of the house go zooming through his head. It was just like he always wanted. He would have a backyard to play in. No more playing in the street or the little patch of grass that is in his front yard right now. He would have room to roam around and just hang out in privacy. He really liked the idea of the house.

"I love it when you call me Iris." Mychal's mom says as she reaches over and gives him a kiss on the cheek.

"Can we have a dog?"

"As long as you take care of it. Walking it, training it, spending time with it. If you agree to do all of that then I will strongly consider it."

"I will."

"Ok, then let me get back to work. I only wanted to spend a few minutes with you before I get caught up in this project."

"I am going to think about the places I want to visit."

" You go do that."

That was the last time he spent any significant time with his mom. He had just realized that was the last time his mom kissed him. He missed her soft pecks on his cheeks. He had all but forgotten the talks about the house. He found that to be funny how he was so happy about it but yet he so easily put it aside. I guess the fact was he had never had the chance to see it. After his mom didn't get the promotion, there was no need to talk about it. He would have felt bad mentioning it. The house was very much her big dream as it was his. Mychal can still remember before he left the living room, after talking to his mom. He went to the living room window and he looked out at the front yard. He saw the two big potholes that were in there. The potholes made it so hard to play in the yard because if you tried you would eventually trip in one. He looked at them and he couldn't wait for the day when he would no longer have to think about them. He was thinking back to what his mom just said about having a backyard. He wanted it so bad because he was tired of what he sees now. He wanted a backyard badly. So now, Mychal stands up and he walks to the living room window. The day he remembers, it was sunny out and he could clearly see the potholes. Now it is raining and all he could really see was that they were full of freezing rain. The holes were three feet by two feet so they were big. So he knew that there was a lot of rain inside of them. He just watched them overflowing with rain and how he wished they would have gotten the house. He wouldn't be here now living through a nightmare wondering when he was going to wake up. Hoping that he would wake up and see that everything had been normal. That day he wished would happen now. He knew that wasn't going to happen because he looks around and everything is too real. Mychal turns to go clean up the kitchen. He knew he had a large job to do in there. He wanted so badly to be able to clean the kitchen up and have it just the way it was before drugs came and took away the significance of the kitchen. He knew that the kitchen was the center of everything that happened in their house. He hoped that if he could just return it to its old ways it would spark a change in his mom when she sees it again. So he walks in the kitchen and he grabs the trash can on the side of the counter. He begins to pick up the dishes that were broken on the floor. He had to get the broken dishes from under the table. There was some in corners, on the cabinets and in the middle of the floor. His mom didn't really leave any dishes unbroken except for a few. One just happened to be the plate that she always used to put his pancakes on. It was the only oval shaped plate in the house. Mychal liked it so much because it gave him room to separate his pancakes into sections. It was big enough to hold everything she made which was normally three to four items. He picks up the plate and he holds it to his chest. It was just odd that she didn't break the plate. It felt as if she knew how important the plate was so she spared it. Even though it was wishful thinking, Mychal felt that there was a possibility that it was possible. If that was the case then there is hope that his mom can be helped. If she showed any sign of her old ways then it gave his hope light. Mychal set it on top of the refrigerator as he finished picking up the dishes. Once that was done, he picked up the food that was everywhere. He had to basically throw everything out. The refrigerator had been opened all night. Mychal had planned on saving some of this food but what took place last night, took that idea right out of his head. He now had to throw away the only thing he had left to eat. That wasn't good seeing that he had to have something to eat. He looked through the food but he didn't find anything he was willing to eat. He finished cleaning out the refrigerator and then he begins to sweep the floor. As he was sweeping under the cabinet, he came across a needle that was under there. He quickly sweeps it into the dustpan and shoves it into the trashcan. He tried to push it all the way to the bottom because he wanted no sight of it. It has caused him so much torment. Mychal finished sweeping and then he went to the sink and started to pull out the cleaning products from under there. He grabbed a bucket and he begins to mix the cleaning products together. He added some hot water and he was ready to disinfect the whole kitchen. He grabbed an old rag that was under the sink. He cleaned every inch of the kitchen. He hit every cabinet, counter top, handle, floor tile and anything that could be reached. He hoped to touch every inch of the kitchen. It was as if it was a deep cleansing that would turn the kitchen back to the way it once was. He was proud of the job he did on the kitchen. It seemed to shine and he could smell the collection of cleaning products he used. Mychal then proceeded to clean the hallway that was smeared with all kinds of bathroom products. He made quick work of that job and then he did the same to the bathroom. Mychal knew he had one more room to tackle and that was his mom's room. He walked to his mom's room and he stands in the doorway. He remembered what took place last night and he could smell it. He clicked the light on and he walked into the room, as the smell got stronger. He walked past the bed and he could smell the vomit and urine and it made him cringe. The whole thought of that put a visual picture back in his mind that he wanted to forget. He grabbed the sheets from off of his mom's bed and he threw them on top of the vomit. He scooped the sheets up, trapping the vomit in them and he ran to the kitchen. He grabbed a trash bag and he tied it up and put it by the front door. He went back to his mom's room and he poured some of his cleaning mixture on the spot where the vomit was. He mopped the floor and he collected clothes that were thrown around the room. He tried to put things away where they belonged. He walked out into the hallway and he just walks through the house. He was admiring the job he had just completed. It took a few hours to do. Cleaning wasn't his strong suit but he did a good job. He put away the things he used to clean with and he washed his hands. He went to his room and he plopped down on his bed. He laid back and as soon as he laid his head down, sleep fell upon him.

     *   *   *

Boom

Boom

Boom

Mychal jumps up at the loud thunderous noise. It takes him a few seconds before he realizes that the noise was coming from the other side of his door.

Boom

Boom

Boom

Mychal stands up and he begins to walk towards the door. He knew that it was his mom and he was agitated. He was that way because she woke him up and two, knocking so loudly on his door. It was a very loud and unnecessary knock. All she had to do was wait until he woke up and came out of his room. If she needed him, she could have knocked softly because she knows he is a light sleeper. Mychal felt that what she is doing now is unnecessary. He had planned on waking up and if she was home, sit down and talk to her about getting her some help. He should have known that as long as you are dealing with drugs, nothing happens the way you want it to. That plan was shot because he was now feeling anger instead of compassion. He wanted to open the door and fuss at her. Once he gets it out of his system, he would then talk to her. Mychal walks to the door and he opens the door. He jumps at what he sees. There was a man standing there. He was about six feet tall and weighed close to 250lbs. He was much larger than Mychal who was all of five feet tall and weighed 120lbs. He was sporting braids and a mustache and he had a scowl to his face. He was staring at Mychal with some dark, piercing eyes. His fists were clenched and Mychal noticed the man had some very big, muscular arms. Mychal noticed his mom standing behind the man as if she was scared to be seen. Mychal was confused at why the man was here but he felt that it wasn't good.

"Hey, little man. I am here to collect." The man says in a deep, overpowering voice. His voice alone made Mychal's hair stand up on his body. He was very afraid but he managed to answer the man's question.

"To collect what?" Mychal asked as he waited on the man's reply. Mychal's mouth became dry and parched. He was so nervous and scared.

"The television, little man." The man says as he pushes the door open so he could look around the room. Mychal knew he couldn't stop the man from getting the television. Physically it wouldn't even be a wise thing to do.

"That television?" Mychal asked as he pointed to his television.

"I guess so." The man replied.

"There is a bigger one in the living room." Mychal says so he could possibly keep his television and give away the broken one.

"That crap doesn't work. Don't try to play me. I don't like being played." The man says as he looks at Mychal.

Mychal tried to swallow but he had no saliva to do it. The man walked up to Mychal and Mychal stepped aside because he could tell the man was going to get the television. He watched helplessly as the man walks to the television and looks it over.

"This television sure is small. I was expecting something bigger." The man says as he looks back towards Mychal's mom. She was still standing outside the room. Mychal had told her numerous times to never come in his room and she listened. It was just weird to see her standing at the door, looking around as if she had never seen the room before. She heard the man question her about the television and all she could do was shrug her shoulders.

"Since it is so small, I want the XBOX360 you said he had." The man says as he looks at Mychal and his mom. Mychal's mom looked at Mychal. She wasn't about to ask Mychal for the XBOX360 because she knows he doesn't have one. She looked at Mychal and he couldn't tell if she was more scared of the man or him.

"I don't have a XBOX360." Mychal said as he stared back at his mom because she knows he never had one. She was supposed to get him one for Christmas but that was scrapped once she got hooked on drugs. The man set the television back down and he walked up to Mychal. Mychal's mom took a step back.

"Little man, I just told you I don't like to be played. Your momma told me you had a XBOX360 so I would advise you to give it up. Your mom owes me some money and if you want her to not get hurt then I would expect you to give me the XBOX360." The man says a he looks down at Mychal. Mychal wanted to take a step back but he was next to his tall dresser and he had no room to move. Mychal looked up at the man and he tried not to show the fear he was feeling.

"Where is the XBOX360, son." Mychal's mom asks as she looks at the man as if to say, "I am trying to help." Mychal looked at his mom and he immediately became angry at her. He felt betrayed by his mom.

"I don't have a XBOX360." Mychal says as he looks at the man as he reaches into his pocket. He pulls out a switchblade and he flips it open. He reaches out and he grabs Mychal by the throat. Mychal had no room to move so he was trapped. The man's grip was tight around Mychal's neck. Mychal was really scared now. He was totally helpless. This man was so much larger and stronger than him. Mychal began to cry as he tries to catch his breath. The man's grip was just loose enough so Mychal could breathe.

"I have told you twice already little man. I will cut you good, unless you tell me where the radio is. I am not playing with you. I will cut you and your mom because I need to get my money and I will at all cost." The man says as he presses the knife under Mychal's chin. Mychal could feel the steel, pointed blade on his skin. He had never been this frightened before. He knew his life was in danger. This was obvious someone that supplied his mom drugs. If he was willing to come up in their house and threaten them then he was willing to hurt them. Mychal managed to take a quick peek at his mom who was looking at what was taking place but she showed no emotions on her face. He looked back at the man because Mychal felt his grip getting tighter. The tighter the man's grip got the more tears came out of Mychal's eyes.

"So where is the XBOX360?"

"It's in the trash can by the desk." Mychal says as he tries to nod towards the trashcan. The man continues to hold Mychal by the neck as he walks towards the trashcan. Mychal had no choice but to follow the man. Mychal's mom tried to see what was in the trashcan from where she was standing. Mychal felt that his mom was worried because she knew there was no XBOX360 in the trashcan.

"There is no XBOX360 in there." The man says as he stares at the trashcan. Mychal's mom stared at Mychal with her eyes wide open.

"It didn't work so I broke it." Mychal says as he hopes the man will loosen his grip. The man's grip doesn't loosen. Instead it got tighter.

"Now I am pissed off. I gave you that last hit because you told me your son had some stuff that was worth some money. I don't see anything else in this room that is worth any money." The man says as he looks around the room. He continues to do that for a few seconds and then he begins to walk towards Mychal's closet, dragging Mychal with him. The man opens the door and he starts looking around the closet. He flips through Mychal's clothes that are on hangers and he kicks around Mychal's shoes. The man didn't see anything he liked so he backs up and he walks towards Mychal's desk. He starts to knock over books and look through the drawers. He finds nothing so he moves towards the dresser where Mychal was standing before they started the treasure hunt. The man pulls out drawers and drops them on the floor. He didn't find anything he liked. Mychal felt the man's grip getting tighter and tighter. The man just stared at Mychal. There was not an ounce of compassion in the man's eyes.

"I am going to get you good." The man says as he points at Mychal's mom. She just dropped her head. "I told you no one gets over on me. I am about to break you off." The man says as he momentarily sets the switchblade down on the dresser. He then punches Mychal in the stomach. Mychal doubled over in pain and dropped to his knees. He couldn't breathe at all. The pain was unbearable. It seemed that time was standing still as he was finally able to breathe. Mychal quickly took in a deep breath. He instantly felt the pain from the punch to his stomach. Mychal noticed that the man was still standing over him. Mychal looks up to see why and he notices the man smiling. Mychal felt the fear returning to his body. The man bends down and he grabs Mychal by the front of his shirt. Mychal couldn't stop the tears from falling again. They seemed to be a natural reaction to him feeling helpless.

"What's this?" The man says as he reaches around Mychal's neck. Mychal was waiting on the man's hand to grip his neck again. Instead of grabbing his neck, he reached inside Mychal's shirt and he grabs Mychal's gold chain. He rips it right off of Mychal's neck as the keys that were on the gold chain fell to the floor. "I should cut you for not telling me about the gold chain. Since this is about your momma and not you, I am going to let you make it." The man says as he pushes Mychal to the floor. He turns and he grabs the television and walks out of Mychal's room. Mychal's mom follows the man like a little puppy follows its master. Mychal sat on the floor crying. He was still shaking from the whole ordeal. He knew that he could have been killed. The man took the television and that was really no big deal to Mychal. He didn't watch it that much. The one thing Mychal cared the most about was the gold chain that Kimyah gave him. That chain meant the world to him. It was his most prized possession and it was gone. He knew he would never see that gold chain again. That made him angry at the thought of that. Just because he was mad it didn't stop him from crying. Mychal begins to pick up the keys that fell off of the gold chain. He puts them in his pockets. He stands up and he could feel his anger coming back. He picks up one of the drawers that were pulled out and he slams it on top of the other three. Mychal felt that his anger was to the boiling point. He had been mad before but not like this. He wanted so badly to punch holes in his walls of his room. He just wanted to destroy whatever was around him. He needed to release the anger he felt. As he looks around the room for something else to destroy, he hears his mom whistling loudly. That makes Mychal seethe with more anger. She was the reason for what just took place and she had the nerves to be whistling instead of checking on Mychal. She didn't care what affect this whole ordeal had on him. The thought of that made Mychal want to take action. So he storms out of his room and he heads towards the sound of whistling. He walks down the hall and he passes the bathroom and his mother's room. The sound seemed to be coming from the kitchen. He starts to walk faster as his anger rises. He walks in the kitchen and he sees her sitting at the table. She was about to eat a McDonalds burger that she had gotten some time that day. Mychal couldn't smell the burger so he knew it wasn't something that she recently purchased. She continued to whistle as Mychal walks up to her. She takes a bite of her burger and swallows it. She then looks up at Mychal.

"That was close huh?" Mychal's mom says as she smiles. Mychal just stared at her frowning. He could not believe that was the only thing she could think of to say. No, "I'm sorry." Or, "Are you okay?" Mychal didn't get those questions. What he did receive was someone who felt they had gotten off easy for something they did. The only thing wrong with that was Mychal didn't do anything to deserve being put in that situation. He was put in harm's way by his mom's actions and only he could see that. She couldn't comprehend what just took place. It didn't move her in the least bit to see her son at the point of being killed. She felt no sorrow in her heart. She had no compassion in her. The thought of that moved Mychal to action.

"Get up." Mychal says as he grabs his mom by the front of her sweater. He jerks her up so hard that she dropped her burger.

She was so light that even Mychal was surprised at how easy it
was to pick her up. He felt her bony, callous hands grip his arms.
He stood her up so they could be face to face. He got a whiff of her
burger breath and he looked into her eyes. He didn't see any
emotions at all. He could see one thing though. She was high on
some type of drug.

"What's wrong son?" Mychal's mom asks as she stares
back at Mychal.

"WHAT'S WRONG? YOU KNOW WHAT'S WRONG."
Mychal yells as he wipes his mouth. He was yelling so hard that
spit flew right out of his mouth.

"THIS IS WHERE IT ENDS IRIS. TODAY IS WHERE IT
ENDS." Mychal says as he starts to drag her out of the kitchen. His
mom was trying to loosen his grip on her sweater. As she was
doing that she slipped and fell so now Mychal was dragging her.

"YEAH, YOU WANT TO DESTROY YOUR LIFE AND
MINE. NO MORE. YOU WANT ME TO SUFFER WHILE YOU KILL
YOURSELF. NO MORE. YOU WANT TO TRICK ME INTO GIVING
YOU DRUGS. NO MORE. YOU WANT TO PUT MY LIFE IN
DANGER. NO MORE." Mychal yells as he drags his mom down the
hallway towards the front door. She was kicking and flailing. She
had an idea of what was going to take place.

"I WILL NO LONGER LET YOU BRING DEATH INTO THIS
HOUSE. I REFUSE TO LET YOU DO IT AGAIN." Mychal says as
he removes one hand from his mom's shirt so he could unlock the
door. He then pulls the door open and he was pelted with freezing
rain. It was so cold that Mychal could only take a few drops of it.
The cold air rushed past him and the shirt he had on gave him no
protection from it.

"No son, please." Mychal's mom says as she tries to hang
on to the open door.

"OH, NOW YOU WANT ME TO STOP. YOU DIDN'T WANT ME TO STOP GIVING YOU DRUGS. YOU DIDN'T WANT ME TO HELP GET YOU OFF DRUGS. YOU DIDN'T WANT TO STOP THAT MAN FROM ALMOST KILLING ME." Mychal says as he kicks her arm off the door. She let out a scream as Mychal took a step out into the freezing rain. Mychal felt the freezing rain soaking his shirt. Every inch of his body was shaking. It was extremely cold out here. Every step he took on the sidewalk had landed in at least two inches of water. Mychal smiled at the thought of that but the sidewalk wasn't his destination. He was headed towards the one thing he hated the most, the potholes in the yard. Mychal looked back at his mom as she continued to try to free herself as she screamed. Mychal paid her screams no mind as he takes his first step on the soaked grass. He was only a few feet from the potholes in the yard. He had his head down because of the rain but he could peek up and see that the potholes were approaching. He felt his mom fight less and less as he got closer to the potholes. Once he made it to the pothole he looked down at it and he saw all the freezing rain that had accumulated in it. Mychal liked the sight of that. He picks his mom up so she is standing face to face with him. She looked like a beaten and battered fighter. Mychal fought off his thought of compassion for her.

"IRIS, THIS IS WHERE IT ENDS. YOU ARE NO LONGER ALLOWED BACK IN THE HOUSE. DO YOU HEAR ME? IF YOU ARE DOING DRUGS, YOU CAN'T COME BACK IN. YOU NEED TO FIND THE STRENGTH TO HELP YOURSELF BECAUSE I AM WEAK. I WON'T SUPPORT YOU ANY LONGER. SINCE YOU ARE WILLING TO DESTROY ME AS WELL AS YOU, YOU LEAVE ME NO OPTION. YOU WOULD LET ME DIE FOR YOU TO HAVE THE DRUGS AND I WON'T LET THAT HAPPEN. I AM SICK AND TIRED OF THIS. YOU ARE MY MOTHER AND, YET I FEEL NO LOVE FROM YOU. YOU ARE SUPPOSED TO LOVE AND TAKE CARE OF ME. YOU ARE SUPPOSED TO PROTECT ME FROM DANGER BUT INSTEAD YOU ARE THE DANGER. IF YOU ARE ON DRUGS, YOU ARE NO LONGER MY MOM. I

DISOWN YOU. DO YOU HEAR ME, IRIS?" Mychal yells as he looks at his mom. She gave no reply she just stared at him. Mychal waited a few seconds more

"SO, YOU BETTER DECIDE RIGHT NOW. IS IT GOING TO BE ME OR THE DRUGS?"

Mychal's mom looked at him and she looked like she was about to say something. Mychal leaned closer so he could hear what she was going to say. The rain had him shaking and he was very cold.

"Don't make me choose." Mychal's mom replies as she shakes also. Mychal was so hurt by what he had just heard. How could she even have to decide on that? His hurt is easily comforted by his anger as he slams her down in the pothole. Freezing rain covered her whole midsection as his Mychal's mom let out a scream. She immediately tried to get up but Mychal put his foot on her chest and kept her down.

"WHERE ARE YOU GOING TO GO? YOU CAN'T GO IN THERE." Mychal says as he points to his house. *"YOU BELONG RIGHT HERE WITH YOUR DRUGS."*

Mychal gave her a push, so she would sit back down. This time she didn't move. She looked up with a shocked look on her face. Mychal just stared at her to prove that he wasn't playing. He looked at her and he saw the shocked look on her face got replaced by sadness. She lowered her head and started crying. Mychal just looked at her, sitting in the hole, soaking wet. He truly wanted to console her. He wanted to reach down and caress her head and tell her everything was going to be ok. He wanted to but he didn't. He knew he had to be firm and he knew he had to stick to what he said. So Mychal begins to back up and the whole time he was watching his mom. She just sat there crying. Mychal turned and walked to the front door. He waited to see if she would get up but she never did. He walked in the house and closed the door. He walked to the living room and he sat down on the sofa. He was looking through the window and he had a perfect view of his mom. She just sat there crying. Mychal felt his stomach getting nauseated. Here he sat watching his mom suffering and he didn't care. He was so mad at her that he didn't care if she sat out there all night long. He was still shaking because of what took place and what scares him the most is he was all alone. His mom would have let that man kill Mychal. She wouldn't have lifted a finger to help him. The thought of that is very scary. So now he wanted her to realize the error in her ways. Mychal figured his mom would get up and walk away. She would go wherever she gets drugs from and he would never see her again. Mychal watched in disgust as his mom tries to stand up. Her arms were wobbly as she braces herself to stand up. Her legs were in no better condition when it was their turn to be used. He noticed how her clothes were sticking to her body and you could see her bones protruding. She was nothing but skin and bones in every sense of that phrase. She was scary to behold because she was dying and she couldn't even see it. She was slowly killing herself and she was the only one oblivious to that fact. Mychal watched as she finally balanced herself and now he was expecting her to turn and head for the street so she can make her way to her next fix. Instead she started slowly walking towards the front door. Mychal wanted so badly to jump up and meet her by the door. He wanted to stand there and embrace her. If she was indeed choosing him over the drugs he knew that his prayers were finally being answered. That was a day that he was waiting for. The day when he had his mom back was a day to celebrate. As his mom is slowly moving out of the view of the window, Mychal stood up. He was nervous and excited at the same time. He didn't move though, he just stood there and listened to the rain as it fell. He couldn't stop his heart from racing. He listened closely as he could faintly hear tapping on the front door. His mind said run but Mychal fought it. He wanted to make sure that was her tapping and not the rain. He heard it again and he begins to walk toward the door. He grabs the knob and prepares himself for his mother. He opens the door and there she stands. Looking as sick and close to death as humanly possible. Mychal looks into her eyes and he saw something he hadn't seen in a long time; life.

Journal entry #658

I know I haven't written in my journal in a while. I have a lot I need to say but I don't have a lot of time. Let me begin three days after my last entry. Which seems like an eternity seeing that was over a month ago. Anyway, I left my mom soaking in freezing rain. Why might you ask journal? I was tired of her doing drugs, that's why. I had grabbed her out of the house and I threw her in the front yard and I told her she had to make a choice. She had to choose between me, and the drugs. She didn't want to choose, so I locked her out of the house. She was left sitting in a pothole in my front yard. The pothole was filled with freezing rain and she didn't care. She just sat there. I waited a few seconds hoping she would come to her senses, but nothing happened. I went into the house and she sat there shivering and crying. I went to the living room and I sat and waited. I left the light off, so I could see out the front window and no one could see in. I saw her crying with her head down. If she had her head bent any lower, she would have been face first in the puddle. I watched as she cried. I fought back my own tears because she was still my mom. The drugs couldn't erase that fact. I still loved her. Even though she didn't realize she loved me, I felt that she did. I gave her the benefit of the doubt. I watched her slowly climb out of the hole, drenched with freezing rain and shaking uncontrollably. I watched her try to stand on two bony, wobbly legs. I wanted to run out to her and help her. I wanted to take one of her arms and put it on my shoulder as I carry her inside the house, but I knew better. That would defeat the purpose of leaving her out there. I wanted her to get up on her own accord and decide for herself what would better her. So, I watched curiously as she stumbled to the front door. She knocked ever so quietly as if she knew I was waiting on her. That wasn't a bad thought because that meant that she knew, I knew, she would make the correct choice. I had to catch myself because I wanted to run to her like a child being told he can have any candy he wants in a candy store. I walked to the door and paused. No need to hurry, no need to make her feel she was that important to me. I have tried that in the past and it didn't work. So, I opened the door and there she stood. Soaking wet and shaking. It was as if it was déjà vu. It did happen just a few days before and just like then, she was a mess. Her eyes told it all. Before I had pulled her outside she was visibly high. Now her eyes showed something they hadn't in a while. They showed a life. Her eyes could finally be read, and they were saying that they were back. Ready to be normal again. I looked her up and down and I could not recognize my mom. She looked at me and she tried to talk but she was shaking too badly. I wanted to back up and let her in. I wanted to run and gather up a blanket for her. I wanted to, but I didn't. I would not move a muscle until she told me her choice. So, I just looked at her as she tried to speak. I even moved closer, so I could hear her better. Finally, she spoke up so I could hear her and what she said made me so happy. She didn't say she was choosing me over drugs. Nope, what she said was better. She didn't say an answer I was expecting. Nope, what she said was better. She simply said she was sorry. She said that plus the look in her eyes was all it took. To some people they might think that she didn't choose me over the drugs. I know my mom admitting she was sorry was the same thing. She had never said she was sorry for anything that she had done in the past year and a half. She merely ignored it and moved on. Now she finally understood the error of her ways and to top it off; she reached into her pocket and she handed me the drugs she had. She handed it to me and she fell to the ground and she cried her eyes out. It wasn't that fake cry she had done in the past. This cry was real. She repeated to me that she was sorry. I just soaked in what she had said. To make a long story short, that was the beginning of my mom's change in life. Kimyah's parents helped me get my mom help. In the meantime, Kimyah and I became even closer and you can say that we are dating. Let's just say we are more than friends now and I couldn't be happier. She has helped me cope with seeing my mom going through withdrawal symptoms and things of that nature. I can take great joy in saying she gave me a peck on the lips. Yes! Anyway, back to my mom, I can say with all honesty that she has been off drugs for almost six months now. All my prayers came true and I am so happy now. She has her good and bad days, but I will take them over the other choice. I must go now because we have very important meeting with Child Protection Services.

End of entry.

Mychal puts the book on his desk and he turns to leave out of his room. He knew the journal wasn't complete until he finished writing what had taken place. The journal was thick and it will be something that he will never forget. Every entry was hard and up until the end, he felt he needed to document what went on. Since things have changed, Mychal wondered if he even needed the journal any more. It was used as an outlet of his feelings when times were bad and now things are getting better. Mychal didn't want to think about that right now. He walked down the hall and he noticed how much life was back in his house. The house smelt so good. It was almost back to normal. He walks towards the kitchen and he could smell cookies being baked. He walks in and he sees Kimyah and his mom, sitting at the table talking. They were laughing at the exact moment Mychal walked in. That gave him a feeling of quiet joy that was unspeakable. To see the two most important women in his life, enjoying themselves, meant the world to him. He walks up to his mom and he gave her a big kiss on the cheek. He then walks to Kimyah and gives her a kiss on the cheek also. He then takes his seat between them. His mom looks at Kimyah and Mychal with a surprised look on her face.

"What?" Mychal asks, trying to keep from smiling.

"Did I miss something?" His mom asked.

Kimyah looked at Mychal and just smiled.

Omega

Other books by Cederick Stewart:

"Love is Majestic"

Love is Majestic is a story of a Christian woman looking for love after years of disappointments in dating. After a chance reunion with her first love, she realizes that love is more than a feeling, and that to grow that love; she must put God first in her life

"Enemy Inside of me"

Nyssa loved being a doctor, but she loved pleasing God more. It showed in her lifestyle as she is passionate about helping her clients overcome their disease. One day she is saddled with the same disease she has been fighting but now her love for God has been replaced with anger. Will she have the ability to use her faith to get her through or will she give in to the enemy inside of her

These books can be purchased at Amazon, Barnes & Noble and all online stores.

For a signed copy or book club entries and other inquires: cederickstewart@yahoo.com

www.ingramcontent.com/pod-product-compliance
Lightning Source LLC
Chambersburg PA
CBHW070743190726
48292CB00002B/390